4/21

D0210916

# THE HALF-ORPHAN'S HANDBOOK

## JOAN F. SMITH

NEW YORK

## [Imprint]
MAKE YOUR MARK

A part of Macmillan Publishing Group, LLC

120 Broadway, New York, NY 10271

THE HALF-ORPHAN'S HANDBOOK. Copyright © 2021 by Joan F. Smith. All rights reserved. Printed in the United States of America.

Library of Congress Cataloging-in-Publication Data is available.

ISBN 978-1-250-62468-0 (hardcover) / ISBN 978-1-250-62469-7 (ebook)

Our books may be purchased in bulk for promotional, educational, or business use. Please contact your local bookseller or the Macmillan Corporate and Premium Sales Department at (800) 221-7945 ext. 5442 or by email at MacmillanSpecialMarkets@macmillan.com.

Book design by Carolyn Bull
Jacket Illustration by Dion MBD

Imprint logo designed by Amanda Spielman

First edition, 2021

1   3   5   7   9   10   8   6   4   2

fiercereads.com

In times full of toil, or those full of strife,
stories of triumph are good for the soul.
Come by this book honest, or be left with life
that feels something far less than whole.

*For Kevin, for everything*

# Chapter One

My sixteenth birthday came and went on June first, when the air was hot and green-smelling, the sun was strong, and my father had been dead exactly three months.

On June second, my mother put aside her concerns regarding the way we'd been quietly ping-ponging through our daily lives, searching for ways to "fill time." She expressed zero worry about Sammy, who had been using Dad's favorite pocket square as a washcloth. She did not acknowledge the way her jeans gaped in the back from all the weight she had lost.

Instead she fixated on a new solution, one she was sure would prevent me from being forever scarred by my forgotten birthday: a copy of the three-page stapled printout I'd cast into the recycling bin in the school cafeteria. She held it aloft now, here in our sunny kitchen. The kitchen that smelled the same as it always had: grapefruit cleaner and dish soap. It felt unchanged too; the pale yellow walls, deep gray soapstone countertops, and off-white cabinets hummed with life, warmer than the rest of the house, always, thanks to the late-afternoon greenhouse effect.

But it did not hold two people who were still the same.

I dumped my backpack on the counter. "I'm not going," I said, working to keep my voice at its normal pitch. Walking faster than I'd meant to, I opened the pantry cabinet and scanned the shelves. There. Two rows up, snug in its reassuring spot behind a bag of chia seeds. Dad's last sleeve of chocolate chip cookies. Precious, precious cargo, given that he'd decided to check out of Hotel Life on a permanent and unexpected basis. I shut my eyes and drew in a breath to steel myself, then closed the cabinet.

The hope on her face fizzled. "Call-Me-Connie says it's amazing, Lila."

My mouth twitched at our family nickname for my school adjustment counselor, Dr. Barbash, who'd talked up the virtues of Camp Bonaventure since maybe mid-April. I'd very intentionally not mentioned the "fantastic opportunity" to spend "eight weeks away with other kids who have lost a family member" to my mother, but apparently my counselor had had other plans.

And now, at the sight of Mom's dejected expression, my familiar friend Panic stomped into my chest and settled her curvaceous hips into my sternum. My bones opened wide, sending a pang through my lungs.

She was actually considering this. Now? When I'd finally skated into June, finally gotten close enough to the point where I didn't have to fight every day to keep up an illusion of my old self. When I could finally breathe. Grieve. I blinked three times fast and squared my shoulders. "She also says Madonna is talentless. Plus, Call-Me-Connie is a close talker." My mother would consider the Madonna statement blasphemy, and close talkers skeeved her out.

"Your counselor's lack of musical taste and social violation of personal space hardly affect her ability to judge what might help you."

"This won't."

She sucked her lower lip between her teeth, released it. "Sweetheart."

"Mother."

"I missed your birthday."

She hadn't technically missed it. I'd spent it with her and my younger brother, Sammy, doing the same thing we'd done the previous ninety-two nights. (But who's counting?) Together

2

we made a show of consuming a family meal: a defrosted dinner from well-meaning neighbors (lots of casseroles), our friends' moms (lots of carby Italian), or Aunt Shelly (sometimes vegan, sometimes paleo, always bland and über-healthy). Aimless, quiet conversation, punctuated by scraping forks and remember-whens, at the four-seater table with one new vacancy. Then a movie—usually a comedy, so we could pretend to laugh—followed by an early retreat into our respective bedrooms.

But I didn't say any of that. Instead I said: "You've had a lot going on, Mom. Besides, I didn't feel like celebrating."

"Oh, Lila," she said, leaning against the counter. She rolled up the camp application and unfurled it.

Her voice was so foggy with sadness I had to turn away to hide the tears that came to my eyes. *Get it together, Cunningham.*

"You love your birthday."

I shrugged. I *had loved* it. Past-perfect tense for an imperfect past. Every year I looked forward to the double-chocolate cake that would sit right behind where Mom stood now, melty and spongy beneath a Tupperware tower. Easy-to-cut-with-just-a-fork cake. Unbaked this year.

"Honey?"

"Yeah?"

"Are you as okay as you can be?"

It was what we said now, because after a family's father/husband went behind their collective backs, lying to his wife and children for their entire lives and then electing to die, no one could truthfully answer that they were plain-old okay. What I wanted to say was, for the seventy thousandth time, *Can you please just explain why Dad's gone?*

Anger flared in my throat, surging through me like I'd touched a live wire. It zipped along, charging into my head and shoulders, until it evaporated. I fought as hard as I could to tamp down the quaver that threatened my voice. "I'm fine. I'll start dinner."

"Great. There's stuff in the freezer." She rolled up the application one more time. "I'll be in my office for a bit. Shout if you need anything."

I nodded, swallowing hard. I never used to cry. But these days, I cried myself to sleep. I cried in the shower every day until the hot water ran out. And I cried each time I opened his office, which still smelled like him: Barbasol shaving cream, coffee, and a tiny tinge of something metallic, like sweat.

Thirty-five minutes and four hundred degrees later, I pulled a casserole from the oven. Outside, our neighbors had fired up their grills, peppering the air with that early-summer barbecue scent. Mom emerged from her office, grinning.

"Guess what?" Her tone was high and warm.

I didn't enjoy the sound of it. "I don't like guessing."

She clapped her hands together. "Fine. It's meant to be."

I narrowed my eyes. "What is?"

"Camp."

"Why?"

"The owner waived the late-registration fee."

Sammy wandered into the kitchen, rolling a basketball under the table and kicking his sneakers into a corner. Unlike Mom and me, my brother still flopped and crashed and flailed, carried by the momentum of his twelve-year-old movement.

I peeled back the foil from the steaming dish and sniffed.

Salmon-quinoa mash: an Aunt Shelly specialty. I handed Sammy a plate. "One sob story and one waived fee doesn't exactly scream *fate*, Mom."

She shook her head. "It's not like that."

"Like how you upgraded Dad's coffin to walnut for free?" Sammy scooped the mash onto the plate and sat down at the table.

"Not quite." Mom ladled dinner onto two more plates. She handed one to me and whispered, "I chose the upgrade over the BOGO deal."

Buy one get one . . . for coffins? I met her eyes. "The funeral director tried giving you a BOGO deal?"

Mom wore a wry smile. "Affirmative."

"Is that a joke?"

"Nope. The pamphlet marketed it with words like *eternity* and *everlasting love* displayed in flowery script."

I choked back a laugh. "Anything for a dollar," I said, but the image of Dad's placeholder headstone—stuck in the freshly turned soil, too new for grass regrowth—flitted into my mind. Daily life without Dad was one thing, but the science and ceremony behind his actual death were another. Every time I thought about it, my heartbeat would slow down, my blood pressure tanking until my vision blurred. I felt as empty as Mom's unpurchased BOGO to-be-used-upon-her-death plot beside Dad's.

Sammy looked up. "What's a BOGO deal?"

"Never mind," Mom said.

"Did you get one for camp?"

Mom reached over the table and ruffled his hair. "I wish, buddy. You'll love camp. It'll be a good thing for all of us. A healing thing."

"A healing thing," Sammy repeated, doubt masking his face. "Like Aunt Shelly and her yoga?"

Mom sat down. "No. A healing thing like you get to hang out with a bunch of other kids who have gone through something like what you and your sister experienced. A healing thing like you get to play basketball and talk to people who make you feel better."

"Done," Sammy said. "You had me at basketball." He held up his fork to write his John Hancock in the air. "Sign me up."

I swallowed. "But we can't afford—"

Mom shook her head. "Stop right there. Not your concern."

*No, no, no.* I switched tactics. "I don't get how sending me to Dead Parent Camp for eight weeks is a good thing. Or why you'd even want to get rid of us for the summer. Or . . ." I paused, trying to keep my voice neutral. "Or, more than anything, why Dad did what he did."

Mom put down her fork and rubbed the bridge of her nose with her thumb and forefinger. I glanced at the empty wooden chair across from her, thinking about her prized paper calendar, where she penciled in writing assignments in her tiny handwriting, categorized each task with a different color, marked each day's passing with an infinitesimal green check mark. Yet this year, she hadn't taken enough care to flip it to June in time, thus missing my birthday and racking up enough mother guilt to bring up this camp in the first place.

"Listen. I know things haven't been easy. I'm working with my therapist on the right way to talk to you two about everything," she said, her voice soft. "And I don't want to 'get rid of' you. You're—*we're*—all we've got left. I want us to move forward in a way that's as healthy as we can, and I think this camp is the right place for you to learn how to do that."

"But that leaves you here. Alone." I pushed the mash around

my plate. "Yeah, no. I'm still not going. But Sammy can go if he wants."

"C'mon. Basketball? Camp babes? New buddies? I'm not the sharpest spoon in the drawer"—Sammy paused to put another bite into his mouth—"but I think Call-Me-Connie is onto something."

Before, Dad would have pretended to cut his food with the side of a spoon, doing a *hardy-har-har* impersonation of Sammy's line. Before, Dad would have laughed his trademark nearly silent laugh at the patriarchally dated yet lasting family joke we'd had since toddler Sammy first pointed at a baby bird and said, *Dad, that chick is such a babe.*

But this was not our before. We sat there for a long time, our table's attendance rate holding steady at 75 percent. This was my family now. After.

# Chapter Two

Grief. Sadness. Anger. On one level, I understood that the mix of emotions my family went through was a textbook case of mourning, especially given the cause of death. Suicide.

If I'd had to guess, I'd have said it was that extra element of betrayal that lit my insides on fire. My body rebelled against its loss: Food tasted pale; my eyes were puffy and irritated; my nerve endings sputtered and crackled in protest against everyday stimuli. Dads like mine did not die by suicide, and yet my dad had.

We had been divided, and Mom was determined we would not be conquered. The one thing she couldn't quite get was that Sammy and I had been left flailing in the dark because we had no idea why the guy we'd always thought we'd known—one of two people we were lucky enough to go to, no matter what, for trust and safety and all the things all kids should have but many don't—no longer wanted us. We'd been lucky, so lucky, and then our luck had run out. And if she would just tell us, then maybe we could understand. Maybe that could heal us.

Since Dad's death, most of my teachers had become caricatures of empathy. Whenever I walked into a room, either their eyes squinted in sympathy or their mouths twisted with pity. A couple of them even excused me from homework for the rest of the year. The exception: Mr. Balboni.

He was the sort of teacher who would leap up onto his desk, throw chalk across the room, and draw garish, exaggerated diagrams on the board to illustrate his bio lessons. The school stuck him in the worst classroom in the old wing: stuffy and wood-paneled, the windows crusted shut with one hundred fifteen years of dust. He'd come to my dad's wake, but since then, he hadn't treated me any differently. I tried to pay more attention in his class as a quiet thank-you.

The week after Mom detonated the grief-camp bomb, Mr. Balboni passed out old corrected work, so I kept my backpack open at my feet and shoved papers in as they landed on my desk. I was pretty sure the tail end of my junior year would be a skeleton in my academic closet, given the fact that my note-taking now trended toward doodling in the margins of my previous life.

My thumb brushed the pebbled black cover of the Moleskine notebook I'd swiped from Dad's office. It had been left there, the plastic open but the binding seemingly uncracked, beside the water bill and a confirmation of cable cancellation. It was the same kind of notebook he always bought. After I found it, I paced the floor, mussing the vacuum lines in the carpet, my mouth dry and my hands trembling.

Dad's phone was password protected. His computer had been confiscated by the university. I wanted so desperately for there to be some kind of explanation that was more than Mom's refrain, illustrated with an underscore-mark mouth: *He struggled with demons.*

In the notebook, I wanted to find something tangible that could offer me a warped sense of comforting reassurance, like the cookies in the cupboard.

It was blank.

I had stared at the pages for a few moments, pain shooting through my temples and sinking into my jaw. I was so tired of feeling sad. Maybe even more tired of fearing I'd never feel happy again.

In a burst of inspiration, I'd rifled through my desk drawer until I found a pot of (almost) dried-out ink and the pens from when I took (nerd alert) calligraphy lessons. Since the black leather cover wouldn't hold ink, I flipped to the stiff first page. I dipped the pen in the jar, willed my shaking hand to still, and etched in the words:

## The Half-Orphan's Handbook

Satisfied, I had sat back. Not bad lettering for being so out of practice. After that, the first rules had come easily.

> 1. The only people who can truly hurt you are the ones you love. Therefore, love no one.*
> 2. Stay away from liars. Liars are the worst.**
>
> *Free passes: Mom, Sammy, Aunt Shelly, ~~Dad~~
>
> **Example: Dad

It might sound ridiculous, but in a way, that little notebook was just like Dad's pantry cookies. It was a small, solid reminder of him, and inside were things I wish I'd known since the beginning of my life. My new rules. The ones I had to write because before, I hadn't known that hearts were like flowers, and that life could change them, peel away their layers like fallen petals. If I could guard myself enough, maybe I could control whether or not I'd be destroyed again.

Now, here in the overheated classroom, my best friend, Josie, twisted in her seat. She offered me a glass container. "Bell pepper?"

I almost shook my head, before I remembered that Josie's mom soaked the pepper slices in ice water so they stayed crisp and cold. We had lunch in the last block today, and my stomach was sour with emptiness. "Sure," I said, biting into one. Perfect. Sweet, juicy, and ice-cold, reminiscent of a hundred afternoons at Josie's house.

Even though our town prided itself on its diversity— *nurturing our diverse student body* was even in the school's mission statement—Josie was one of two Black girls in our classroom, and one of a handful in a grade of mostly cisgender white kids. Tall and willowy, she had 100 percent of the talent of a Broadway actress, but about 4 percent of the stage confidence to be one.

"Are you for real?"

I swallowed my mouthful of pepper. "Sorry. Spaced out. What's up?"

She exhaled. "I asked if you were for real. I told you I went out with Joey Quinn last night, and you didn't even react."

I almost smiled. That phrase—*Are you for real?*—was Josie's verbal go-to. I'd heard her say it a thousand times, about good things and bad: when I was scouted for the track team, when a guy I'd semi-dated last summer left for college and never called me again, and even when I called her after my dad died.

"That's great, Jos."

"Well. It wasn't a *date* date. Rose was there, and so were two of Joey's friends."

I pasted a smile on my face. Rose started tagging along with us—mostly, with Josie, and thus also me by default—in middle school, and it hadn't been lost on me how much closer the two of them had grown since Dad died. "Oh."

Josie's face was just too expressive. It fell. "Oh, Lila. Are you ready to go out again? I didn't think you'd want to."

Admittedly, Josie was right. I hadn't wanted to go out. At all. I couldn't imagine getting dressed to go out for a night or laughing with my friends in the back seat of Rose's car. I preferred alternating between torture (by going through family photos) and comfort (via reading old books alone in bed). My fingertips reached up and touched the hollow of my throat, where my tiny gold daffodil charm used to rest. Until I lost it. The necklace had been a gift from Aunt Shelly to Mom, who'd passed it down to me, and I promptly developed a habit of zipping the charm along the chain. Whenever I reached for the empty space, I still felt a jolt of loss.

My mouth twisted. "You're the one who said you needed a break from me," I reminded her. "Don't want the sad girl pulling down the mood."

"That is *not* what I said," Josie began. "I said a break—"

"Here, Cunningham. Last but not least," Mr. Balboni said, tapping a sheet he'd placed on my desk. He strode to the front of the room. "Now, the fun part. No more homework for the last three days of school. Consider it a gift. The final assignment I passed out is from the archives, people—midterm portfolios. On your simplified pedigree chart, you'll find a sticky note with a reminder of your grade. I didn't want to write directly on them and mess up the work of all you da Vincis in the room."

On my desk was a paper showing a few spare symbols and lines, and a sticky note with a large *A* scrawled in green ink. We'd been asked to chart our family tree for direct grandparents, parents, aunts, uncles, and cousins. Some of my neighbors' pedigree charts looked like geometry books, but mine was pretty plain. Sammy and I had no first cousins, so our holidays were spent with Mom's.

# Lila's Pedigree Chart

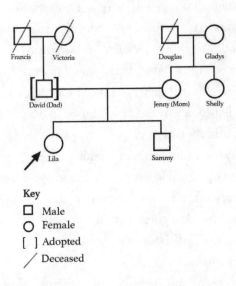

**Key**

☐ Male
○ Female
[ ] Adopted
╱ Deceased

I traced the open square marked with my father's name. When I turned this in, Dad was alive. Tears blurred my eyes, and my heart, leaden and heavy, sank to my toes.

This project had taken me about ten minutes to complete. I'd sat at the kitchen table with Dad. It was snowing outside, and we were playing the happy roles of Pleasant Snow Day Family. We split a toasted bagel and cream cheese, and he kept one earbud in to listen to a conference call while I doodled a rough draft. All status quo, all our family's relative normalcy.

But not now. The open square said *male*. It said *alive*. It lied.

The thing was, I hadn't just lost my dad—I'd lost my entire identity. It was radical enough to lose him so suddenly, but along with that came the fallout: I'd quit being a good friend. I'd quit enjoying things like spring crocuses and frozen yogurt. And after bagging out on half of my practices this spring, I'd even quit hurdling the Friday before Memorial Day.

I was certain that the only way to get back to a semblance of what I'd had was to understand *why*. Maybe, just maybe, if I knew his rationale, I would be able to pick my life back up.

Grief clawed at my throat, and I willed my tear ducts to dry up. No matter where I went or what I did, I couldn't escape my father being dead. All it took was one open square to remind me.

Dad had this collection of pocket squares for fancy occasions. Cobalt blue and beige for summer weddings, birds in muted autumn shades for Thanksgiving. He wore a cheery yellow-and-green one each spring to celebrate his "homecoming day," the day of his adoption. After Mom was hired to ghostwrite the content for a wedding website, I'd joked with Dad about making him wear a pink-and-gold one at my wedding someday.

Not anymore. My life had suddenly become full of open squares and empty dinner-table chairs. Now there would be no Dad at Sunday dinner. Christmas. Fourth of July. No Dad to make us grilled cheese with his signature secret: extra butter for a crispy exterior. No Dad to freeze washcloths when Sammy had a fever. Now Dad wore his yellow-and-green pocket square in his coffin, a small token to honor his own dead parents. I lifted my gaze from the pedigree chart. "This is a terrible assignment."

Mr. Balboni turned around. "Lila?"

Good old Lila Cunningham. Rule follower. Polite kid. Since kindergarten, my report cards had all said the same thing: *A pleasure to have in class.* I folded my hands together and placed them on my desk. "What's the point of this assignment, anyway?"

"Well, people use them to trace genetic lineage. It's why doctors will ask for your family medical history." Mr. Balboni's expression was mild, a bit cautious.

14

"What if you're adopted?" I asked.

"Then your family tree is still your family tree. You just eliminate the genetic component, unless it's a family adoption."

"Aren't there genetic tests for the medical stuff?"

"Sure. But they can get expensive."

I shrugged. "But accurate. This seems pretty useless."

My classmates stilled, waiting for Mr. Balboni to react. I leaned back and crossed my arms, feeling both triumphant and like an asshole.

Was what Dad had catching? I did a quick assessment. Sad? Yes. Depressed? Maybe. Suicidal? Not a chance. (Relief.)

Angry? Yep. The open square in front of me, Josie's *crunch-crunch-crunch* of the peppers, her going out with someone and not even telling me. My brain felt dizzy and left behind, somehow. Even though it seemed like the clock should stop when something life-shattering happens, it kept marching on. Time unspooled in front of me like an escaped bobbin of thread, or the comments section of a YouTube video.

Maybe that should be my third rule: *No matter what, life goes on.* I ran my tongue over my teeth, wondering how many people I knew who'd come to the same realization.

Mr. Balboni made his way to my desk. He bent down, his voice gentle. "Lila? You want to go see Dr. Barbash?"

*Yeah, so Call-Me-Connie can write up my list of camp supplies?*

I uncapped a marker and drew a slash right through Dad's square, then slid the paper to my teacher. "Here," I said, meeting the quietness of his tone so my classmates couldn't hear me. "I fixed it. Now it doesn't say my dad's alive." Without another word, I stood up, slung my backpack over my shoulder, and left.

# Chapter Three

After the last day of school, I lost eleven games of H-O-R-S-E in a row against Sammy. "I was going to say we should play a full dozen," he said when I gave up. "But this is pathetic. I'm not even sweating."

In contrast, I was breathing harder than I ever would have in the past. I hadn't figured that just over two weeks of zero training would have much of an impact. I didn't look any different, after all, but go figure. Sweat dampened my back and forehead, and my veins throbbed with pounding exertion.

I gave him a high five. "I tried, Sam-O."

He grimaced. "I know. That's the sad part."

"You want to come inside?"

He held up the basketball. "Naw, I'm gonna work on my jump shot till it's dark."

I trudged up the front steps. The days had just begun staying up past their spring bedtimes, the sun seeming to set much later today than it had all year. Tomorrow's forecast was for high humidity, and traces of its heavy dampness trickled into the night air.

At the front door, I turned around to ask Sammy if he wanted some water. I expected to see him in some stage of what he called "the loop"—dribble, aim, shoot—but instead he was standing where I'd left him. He rolled the ball between his palms, staring at the ground and making the face he made when he was trying not to cry.

I was a poor substitute for Dad. How could he not think of all the other early-summer nights like this one, when they'd shoot hoops and come inside covered in sweat and mosquito bites?

I cleared my throat. "Sammy? Do you want some water?"

He glanced up, his face clearing of its clouds. "I'm good," he called. Dribble, aim, shoot.

In my room, I changed into one of Dad's old T-shirts and a pair of pajama pants patterned with ice cream cones. I slid into bed with a tattered copy of my favorite classic: *A Tree Grows in Brooklyn*. Grandma Gladys had given it to me in fourth grade.

Mom ducked her head in my room. "Hey, Ladybug. If you need your workout clothes, they're clean."

I didn't look up. "Thanks, but you can donate them. I won't be training this summer. I quit."

Mom came in, setting the laundry basket down beside my desk. "I know. I heard."

"You heard?" I flipped the book over.

"Coach went right to Call-Me-Connie afterward."

"He's panicked about the Tigers losing a hurdler," I muttered.

"His *top* hurdler," Mom said, shaking her head. "He's worried about you."

Cue the crushing guilt that had plagued me since I'd left Coach's office. Two years ago, he'd begged me to join the team after he'd seen Josie and me goofing off on an obstacle course in freshman gym. I'd taken dance as a kid, and although I had the natural grace of a water buffalo, I had a talent for jumps. I was also a pretty good sprinter, but only for laughably small distances. Anything more than halfway around the track turned my legs into rush-hour traffic. I could barely eke out our required warm-up, which was just one mile—I had no idea how to pace myself for distance.

Hurdling was different. Thirteen meters to the first hurdle, then eight and a half between each one after that—ten jumps in total. The hundred finishes out with ten and a half more meters. I had it down to a science.

Dad was a huge runner. Despite my sloth-timed miles, he'd gotten me to agree to run the Falmouth Road Race with him this August. We'd started running (okay, a combination of thirty-second intervals, split between molasses-level jogging and walking) a couple of miles together on weekends, and we'd officially signed up for the race just two weeks before he died. Thinking about Dad making plans he didn't plan to keep always tied my head in knots, and I'd analyzed this timeline over and over again, because why bother asking if you're not going to do it?

I hugged my arms to my chest. "The team will survive."

Before I'd finished my sentence, though, my stomach had clenched in disappointment. When I could help it, I never let people down. Especially my team. I was loyal with a capital *L*. In middle school, after a bout with a fever, I'd stayed up past midnight typing up the school newsletter. Last year, when I'd traveled with my journalism class to Washington, DC, I'd baked everyone energy cookies for the bus ride. And freshman year, when a senior girl harassed Josie after she won a theater essay contest, I'd led my best friend down to Call-Me-Connie's office and held her hand the entire time she recounted her story. I took care of people.

I used to, anyway.

The corners of Mom's eyes crinkled in concern. "Want to talk about it?"

I breathed in the clean, comforting scent of her lotion. "Not really."

Mom sat on the edge of my bed, and I tucked my toes under her butt. She leveled her gaze on mine. "Your track clothes aren't even clean, by the way. That laundry basket is a prop I used as an excuse to come in and talk to you."

I smiled. "Nice play."

She rubbed my shins through the blanket. "Camp could be a beautiful place for you to train, you know. Fresh scenery."

I clenched my jaw. "I don't train anymore." I'd been at practice the afternoon of the day Dad died, and no matter what I did differently—new gear, new routes, new hairstyle—it was all I could think about when I was there. If I had come home sooner . . . "And you forget I'm not going to camp."

"You forget I'm your mother."

"You *forgot* my birthday."

"I remembered your birthday. I was just a little behind on the calendar." She reclined on the bed, propping herself up on her elbows. "Forgive me?"

Forgive her? The other bad part about all this was that my mom and brother were reeling, too. That was mostly why I hadn't been that angry about my birthday in the first place. Our family needed a break when we could get it. I wiggled my toes beneath her. "I told you. It's okay."

She beamed. "Great. Then you'll go to camp?"

I groaned. "Mom. The great outdoors? So not my thing. Neither is meeting new people. Or therapy." I drew the quilt up to my chin. Before Dad died, I might've jumped at the chance to go to summer camp. But now . . .

Every time I thought of Dad, my chest physically ached. It was a confusing kind of pain, like being homesick for a person instead of a place. A person who'd committed the ultimate permanent peace-out betrayal. A person I couldn't eat a sandwich with or watch a movie with or even make fun of for wearing high socks while running ever again.

It was as if, before, my whole life had been on a track, with hurdles that seemed monumental but were easy to overcome. A bad grade on something I thought I'd understood, a fight with Josie, a stomach bug, a twisted ankle. Run, two, three, leap.

Losing Dad had changed the game. It had gouged a hole in the track, sent a dragon chasing my heels, and put up ten-foot-high hurdles at unexpected intervals. Run, two, three, smash.

Camp was yet another thing out of my control. Another unwanted hurdle. I didn't want to be a person who:

1. required therapy
2. was a candidate for grief camp
3. left her mother home alone for a summer to deal with Dad's leftovers: white sneakers by the door, a crinkly sleeve of cookies in the cabinet, a Red Sox hat in the hall closet.

*How did I get here?* I sighed.

Mom reached over and picked up my book. Her face softened when she saw the title. She put it back down, smoothing her hand over the cover. "Not so fast, honey. If you don't go to camp, you're still going to therapy."

I picked at a thread on my quilt. "I don't want to."

"I didn't either. A lot of people don't want to before they try it. But trust me. It helps."

"If therapy helps so much, then why didn't Dad go?"

Silence. Beat. "He did."

My saliva turned to vinegar. "What?" I rocked backward on my bed, my stomach taking on a curdled-milk feeling. For the last couple of months, I'd been certain things might have been different if Dad had had some kind of formal diagnosis. Or even an informal one. My life today might be more understandable if my dad had acted the way he must have felt: willing to follow a path through the darkest of forests to something so unspeakable and harmful and permanent that even the thought of it felt like slivers of glass crunching into the sponge of my brain.

I pressed my fingertips to my buzzing temples. It was impossible to reconcile two versions of the same man. On the outside, he hadn't been moody, down, or depressed. If someone had asked me to predict the sort of person who would do what he did, I would've described the antithesis of my father. He was the first person up in the house every day, brewing my mother a cup of strong, dark coffee he'd bring to her in bed. I couldn't count the number of early mornings I'd wander into my parents' room, the hardwood floor cold beneath my feet. My mother, buried in sheets and laughing sleepily, on one side of her a hot glass mug on the brass nightstand, on the other my dad, cross-legged and grinning, his glasses pushed up on his forehead.

I have been condemned to remember my dad wearing a headset and discussing equations or variables with his research partners at the university while at the same time making silly faces at me. Dad racing us from the car to the front door. Taking Sammy and me bowling and out for spicy waffle fries. Shimmying and dancing in the kitchen while Mom sliced vegetables for dinner, pretending he wasn't funny, yet unable to clear the smile from her face.

But what did I know? I was no therapist. I was no writer, either; I couldn't use my words the same way Mom did, her fingers flying over her keyboard with passion. Sometimes I was an okay artist: I was good with color and shading, and my art teacher always said I had "an eye for scale."

But I didn't have one thing I so desperately needed: understanding. I lacked the logic to match the man who was supposed to hold my hand through life until I knew how to forge it on my own with the one who had made a choice of death with irreversible finality.

"It's complicated."

"You always say that."

A shadow of the *you'll understand when you're older* expression crossed her face, like a bird flitting through a backyard. She lifted her chin a fraction. "That's because it is. I saw the insurance paperwork in his office. He only went to the therapist twice. Two times, total. Even though he'd left the house for his 'standing appointment' weekly for over three years."

I was quiet. Here I was, 106 days since my father wasn't. Whatever "demons" he'd struggled with hadn't come with red eyes, antiseptic breath, or weeks lying in bed, so they had been easy to hide. Whatever war he was in was invisible. That was why, on an unseasonably warm day in February, he could roll our charcoal grill out from the shed, hose off the pollen, and make a big show of cooking shrimp skewers approximately twenty hours before never seeing us again. "Mom," I whispered, my eyes hot with unshed tears. "Can you please, please, please just explain why he did it?"

For a moment, I thought this was It. The time she'd finally

crack open the mystery behind the man I thought I knew more than anyone else in the world and the choice he made. I held my breath and made my body as still as I possibly could, waiting. Hoping.

"I don't know all the parts of his story, Lila. And there's a chance I never will." She sighed. "I do know that he was frustrated that his background was a question mark. His parents were there for him in the life basics—they fed him, clothed him, made a home for him—but they were pretty emotionally disconnected. He made a comment one time that in order to feel wanted, he tried as hard as he could to be good. That broke my heart." When she paused, my lungs deflated with a familiar sensation: disappointment. A secret locked behind a firewall.

"Mom, please—"

"What I do know is this: He didn't act with the intention of hurting us. At the point where the world lost him, he was in a place where his emotional pain took over. And I give you my word that I'll tell you more when I can. For now, Lila, until I'm able to—until I find enough to fill in those blanks, or until I know more about how to explain his addiction to you—*please*. I'm begging you. Please give me the grace to tell you when I can."

I stared at my lilac walls. This was more than she'd dropped so far. I turned the information over in my mind. The tears in my eyes vanished. "He was addicted to something?"

Mom didn't answer right away. She slumped forward, bracing her elbows on her knees and resting her head in her hands for a moment, her breathing loud. When she straightened up and looked in my eyes, I saw a myriad of conflicting emotions.

I'd always thought of my parents as two parts of one pair, a matching set—a pillow and a blanket, a car and its key. Now she was . . . dry cereal. A petal-free flower. When her answer came, it was quiet. "Yes."

"What did he . . ." I struggled to find the word. "Use? Abuse?"

She nudged the edge of the laundry basket with her foot. "All in time, Lila. This is part of that. I don't want to lie to you."

Mom's plea for time had been so passionate; I fought to do the mature thing and crush my rising frustration at her lack of answers. Instead I ingested the kernel of information, mulled it over. *Okay. Reframe.* "Is this something that Sammy and I need to worry about?"

"You mean, are you at risk of dealing with addiction someday?"

I nodded.

She ran a hand through her hair. "Well, everyone is, but addiction can have a genetic link. We don't know enough about your father's biological parents to know for sure, but yes, you and Sammy should be extra cautious." Mom sniffled. "Really wish he'd done that take-home genetics test I bought him last Christmas so we'd have that info for the future."

I thought about the diagonal slashes above Dad's square on my pedigree chart. His parents, my grandparents, who had died about a year apart when I was pretty little. When I had asked about it, he'd said his adoption was closed, he didn't even know his biological parents' names, and that was okay because his parents were his parents, and that was it.

But he must have wondered, right? Mom had told me once that when Sammy's hair brightened to blond, Dad stared at it for days before he finally admitted that he was curious about where it came from.

I'd never experienced an incredible compulsion in the way I thought people addicted to drugs or alcohol or anything else must. "But—" I cut myself off, because another thought occurred to me. "Mom, did you know he was going to—"

"*No.*" She sat up, her voice vehement. "Never. He said he was doing better."

"Okay, so let me get this straight. He tried therapy and it didn't work. So what you're saying is you want *me* to go to therapy when a therapist couldn't even make Dad feel good enough to not kill himself?"

She steeled herself. "Two visits is barely trying it, honey. It takes a lot of work, and a good match with the right therapist, which is tough for most people in this country to access and afford in the first place. And my assumption is that your father wasn't truthful with the therapist, either." Her tone was as measured as a recipe. She cleared her throat and continued. "Can you imagine the energy it must have taken to maintain the façade of therapy appointments for three years? When he could have been going? Maybe if he'd put in the work to get better, he would have. But I don't know. The only person who will ever know the full story is your father." Her face smoothed out. "We're left with a lot of broken pieces, honey. But one thing I can tell you with the utmost confidence is that he loved us. And we should treasure that. Just because his brain was sick doesn't muddy that love."

"I know." And I did know. At least, my mind knew. But that knowledge stung every nerve ending in my body, burning and aching and leaving smoking ashes where my muscles were supposed to be.

"Look. What if you just gave camp a try?"

I narrowed my eyes. "What do you mean?"

She shrugged. "Make a commitment to go for, let's say, one week."

I folded myself into the smallest Lila possible. "I don't know, Mom."

"You've had paper cuts that have lasted longer than a week. What do you have to lose?" She pursed her lips. "This probably goes against every parenting book ever written, but . . . if you don't want to stay after a week, you can quit. I'll drive up and get you. No questions asked."

I stared at her. "You swear? You'll come?"

She held up her hand as if making a vow. "Promise. One week in, it'll be the Fourth of July. We can catch some fireworks on the ride home."

"But I don't want to leave you alone."

Mom smiled her sad-truth smile. "Aw, Ladybug. Not your worry. I have my whole life to figure that out." She wrinkled her nose. "Besides, there's some kind of yoga retreat your aunt Shelly's been begging me to go on. I keep turning her down. But I'll make a deal with you—if you go to camp, I'll go to yoga. That way, we'll both do things we don't want to do. And afterward we can come home and eat ice cream and practice only one pose: Savasana." She flopped backward on the bed, mimicking it. "Your choice, kiddo."

The corners of my mouth twitched. "Mom, you're right."

"Of course I am. About what?"

"No part of this deal appears in a parenting book."

# Chapter Four

Thirteen days later, I found myself wedged into the front seat of Mom's car, my feet propped up on a duffel bag full of toilet paper (listed under RECOMMENDED SUPPLIES in the FAQ of the Camp Bonaventure website), riding northeast at precisely the speed limit.

Sammy kicked my seat. "You excited?"

"Thrilled. Overjoyed."

"Lila," Mom warned.

Sammy kicked the back of my seat again. "I can't wait."

"Ow. Stop, Sammy."

"I really have to pee."

"Gotta hold it till the next exit, buddy," Mom said. "There's one coming up."

Another thump against my kidney. *"Sammy!"*

"Sorry, Lyon."

I bristled. "Don't call me that." My voice came out sharper than I'd intended. The name Lila had been my mom's choice. My dad, clearly not one for good choices, had wanted to name me Lyon, one of the cities in France they went to after they had tried having kids for some long and strenuous (gag) period of time. They spent all their savings on a big trip, skipping from Paris to Lyon to Nice, and came home pregnant. And so the story goes: Mom craved soft unpasteurized cheeses she couldn't eat, while Dad painted a mural on the nursery wall to look like the French Riviera and tried to name me Lyon. My mom told him it was cruel and unusual punishment and/or only permissible for celebrities to name their kids after places of conception or near-homonyms for animals (since Lyon is more *lee*-on than *lion*), so they compromised on Lila. My dad still got away with calling me Lyon, though.

At the state-border rest stop, Mom paced in front of the entrance to the men's room. "I don't like it when he goes in alone."

"Dad didn't go in with him," I pointed out. "Sammy's twelve. He's not going to drown."

Mom picked up WELCOME TO MAINE and WELCOME TO MASSACHUSETTS brochures. She flipped each one over and then slid them both back into their plastic slots. "I'm not worried," she said, but she didn't brighten again until Sammy reappeared.

I pushed open the door to go back outside. The air smelled different up here—thinner, almost.

Mom put her arm around Sammy's shoulders while we walked out. "So, who are you going to miss the most while you're gone? Besides your mother, of course."

"Freddy," Sammy said. "He's pissed at me for leaving."

"Don't say *pissed*."

"Angry. He's angry."

"Freddy wouldn't be angry about that." Mom opened the car door for him and waited while he buckled up, like she used to do when he was six and in a booster. I pulled my phone out of my bag and saw a text from Josie.

Is your camp thing this week or next?

"Freddy *would so* be angry at that," Sammy said from the back seat, interrupting my train of thought. "Now the Dynamic Duo isn't together for basketball camp. He said he's going to partner with Colton Ford instead."

I rolled my eyes. "Colton Ford is a twerp. Freddy will get over it. The second you come home, things'll be the same."

28

"Oh, I know," Sammy said. "Freddy knows I'm the ticket to the ladies."

I grinned, laughter hitching in my chest.

The flash of Mom's smile was sad. Wistful. She turned the key in the ignition. "At least your ego is intact, Sam-O," she said. "Lila, what about you?"

"What about me?"

"Who will you miss?"

*Dad. My old self. Every person in my life prior to the first of March.* "No one."

"Why?" She tucked a strand of hair behind her ear. "What about your friends? Josie's called the house three times this week. I'd forgotten we even had a landline."

Did parents get an internal memo advising them to trap their kids into having unwanted conversations while they were held hostage in the car?

I picked up my phone. "I'm talking to her right now." Then, to make that true, I wrote back. *On our way there.* The three little dots that answered told me she'd gotten the message right away.

"Well?" Mom prompted. "What's Josie saying?"

"Mom. MYOP." I was smug about that one: flipping the *B* in *business* for the *P* in *phone*. She'd written a whole article with that very title about respecting the privacy of teenagers.

Sure enough, she scowled. "Your phone *is* my business. It's not like I'm snooping. Just making conversation."

Josie: Damn.

Josie: Joey Quinn asked me to the movies tonight. Wanted to see if you wanted to make it a double.

29

Josie: I'm too nervous

Me: Ha.

Me: Sorry.

Me: I'm just picturing myself dating right now, and hahahahaha.

Me: I have enough rejection in my home life.

Me: And the patheticness of that reality tells me I'm too crabby to be around

Josie: Even hermit crabs shed their shells at some point.

Josie: I miss you

I missed her, too. Our relationship had always been easy. But this text exchange was the most natural thing Josie and I had had in months, which said a lot about the state of my friendship affairs. It just confirmed the rightness of the first rule in my handbook, because aside from life-or-death matters, nothing sucked more than sourness between people who loved each other. Instead of writing back *I miss you, too*, a combination of stubbornness and too-little-too-late-ness made me pause. I imagined shoving everything I loved about Josie into a compact ball and tucking it deep inside myself someplace next to our memories and my father's blueberry muffin recipe, and then I flipped over my phone. "If you must know, Josie's not saying anything important."

"I'm sure you'll meet a bunch of people to connect with at camp over the summer."

"I am not going to camp for the summer."

"You agreed to a week. And . . ." She broke off when she merged the car back onto the highway, the tip of her tongue poking out between her lips in concentration. "I put some extra clothes in your bag. Just in case."

My throat hardened. It was difficult to swallow.

Mom relaxed back into her seat. "Plus, it's great practice for college, sweetie."

"I don't care about college."

"With your grades? You *better* start caring about college." She launched into a speech extolling the virtues of what Call-Me-Connie said about state schools versus reach schools and how much my teachers bragged about my science midterms and yada yada yada, finally winding down with ". . . planning for scholarships, especially now."

Her last two words rang in the car. "Mom, this camp is so expensive. I really don't see why we should be spending money on it. *Especially now.*"

"Well, child of mine, I'll give you two very good reasons. One, the life-insurance money came through. And two, you can't put a price on healing."

I scowled. "Really? Not according to Camp Bonaventure's website: 'Tuition cost by inquiry only.' "

Mom's eyes narrowed. "Let me adult, honey."

After a while, the radio lost its signal. Mom switched the station every time the static overtook a song, but she soon flicked it off. As we drove north, the exits got farther and farther apart. Sammy slept in the back seat, his mouth opened into a round O.

31

We clattered over a bridge that looked as if it were made out of iron Legos. On the other side, the trees grew so close together their branches intermingled, like a group of tall, friendly people with their arms linked to play Red Rover. Another car clunked past us, covered in faded bumper stickers about *coexisting* and making love instead of war and the sad truth about aluminum in deodorant. Whatever *that* meant.

"Daddy was so strange about bumper stickers," Mom murmured, breaking the silence. "He refused to put them on his car except for the time you were student of the month."

A small burst of pain settled in my chest. It was the first time she'd called him *Daddy* instead of *your father* since he died. It was as if he'd been relegated to his biological contribution to the Cunningham kids' makeup—one step above *your genetic donor. Your father's clothes are going to Goodwill today* or *Your father made a bad choice* or *Your father would have loved to have seen that hit, Sam-O.* The word *Daddy* banged into the quietness of the car, like the sudden clattering of a radiator in the darkest part of night.

*Well played, Mom.* I was afraid that if I spoke, I would cry, so I said nothing.

I pressed both my fists against my eyes until I saw stars, but I felt myself losing the battle. Instead I turned my face to the window.

Right now, I knew Mom and I were both thinking the same thing: that New Hampshire had it wrong with the LIVE FREE OR DIE state slogan.

That dying isn't supposed to be a choice.

That it's not fair to the people you leave behind if you make it one.

# Chapter Five

Before long, the passing landscape slid into wide spurts of gently sloping hills and marshes, punctuated by stretches of wintry-green forest. All the green was mesmerizing. So when Mom braked a little too hard, I was jostled against the window.

"Sorry," she said. "Almost missed the turn."

A wooden sign reading WELCOME TO CAMP BONAVENTURE swung on a silver chain, marking a dusty dirt road. Beneath our tires, rocks and gravel crackled; as Mom inched the car forward, towering oaks and pines enveloped us. Sammy rolled down the window. The summery, homey scent of burning leaves sent a fluttery feeling of existential dread through my pores.

After at least a full minute, the road curved sharply. I hadn't noticed how much the trees shaded the road until they gave way to an unmarred view of my unwanted birthday present.

Beside us was an open-air wooden structure, with a fleet of colorful bikes propped inside. Beyond it stood a building with an already familiar-looking wooden sign that read BONARTVENTURE. Clever. I didn't need the supporting cast of easels out front to figure it was the art room.

"Whoa," Sammy said, prompting me to turn from the bikes and easels. "Check out the lake."

I followed his gaze out the windshield to a low, barnlike building and two trios of colorful cabins separated by a giant glass gazebo. In the distance, a body of water shimmered in the late morning sun, boats and kayaks lazing on its surface. Actual, honest-to-God cotton-blossom clouds drifted in the wide expanse of blue sky, which was only a shade lighter than the water below.

I took in a small pull of air and shivered in my seat. Large bodies of water and I did not quite mesh. My anxiety grew wings, morphing into a horde of moths ricocheting inside my gut.

Mom joined the line of cars pulling up on top of a grassy field in front of a white clapboard house (identified by yet another wooden sign as THE LODGE). Campers didn't have to wear anything special, I had learned during my frantic late-night website research. No one wanted to *stifle our creativity*. But the camp counselors wore baby blue T-shirts on "important days," such as— you guessed it—move-in. A half dozen of the blue shirts dashed about, helping people with bags and pointing toward buildings. Car doors hung open like beetle wings, with some kids buzzing around and pulling out luggage or backpacks while others stood still and gaped.

"Lila! Did you see the basketball courts?" Sammy asked, opening the door before Mom could come to a full stop.

*"Samuel,"* Mom said. She only used his full name when she was nervous. "Don't open the door before I put the car in park. What's gotten into you?"

He unbuckled his seat belt and jumped out. "Sorry!" he called, shutting the door. He ran to the back and hit the trunk, like an impatient New York bellhop. *All set! Chop-chop!*

Mom leaned over and pulled the lever to release the trunk. Beside us, a little boy wearing thick glasses on his worried face scuffed his feet beside an older woman with gray, close-cropped hair. Then, perhaps the tallest person I had seen in real life—a fellow camper, I figured, noting the lack of a baby blue shirt— strolled over and pounded fists with him. A smile burst over the small kid's face.

Beyond them, two girls embraced, wearing twin expressions of happiness. A ring of alarm vibrated in my belly. Their hug was not a greeting of strangers. It hadn't occurred to me that on top of the whole wishing-I-weren't-a-grief-camp-candidate thing, I'd also be the new kid. "Mom?"

She reached over and grazed my arm. "Yeah?"

"It looks like these people are . . . friends already? I think they all know each other." My voice cracked.

"Oh. Well. The camp director did say most of them come back every year." She smiled a smile she probably thought was encouraging. It wasn't. "He sounded very proud of the return rate."

I bounced my leg up and down, knocking my knee against the cup holder. "I think I changed my mind about this one-week thing." Maybe I'd text Josie and tell her I was calling this whole camp thing off after all. I slid my phone from the pocket of my duffel bag.

Mom sucked in a breath. "Lila."

I unlocked the phone, and the Instagram app popped open. I dragged my thumb down the screen, but nothing happened. Why hadn't it refreshed? It stayed stuck on the same picture Josie had posted: a Snapchat screenshot of her and Rose, both of them clad in oversized sunglasses beside Rose's pool. I'd spent 80 percent of my summer there last year, though the closest I got to the water was dipping my feet into the shallow end.

I closed out of the app and opened my text thread with Josie, typing a shamefully belated response: *I miss you, too.*

Within a fraction of a second, a red exclamation point appeared next to the message. I stared in horror at the top of the screen. "Mom," I said, hearing the uptick in my voice. "Mom. There's no service here."

"Why do you need it? You said you didn't care about leaving your friends."

I gritted my teeth. "It's not about them. It's about what they're doing. And, you know, the world. What *it's* doing."

Mom closed her eyes. The sunlight beamed into our car, splashing across her face. She knit her eyebrows. Deep wrinkles formed between them, but something about the sun and the light made her seem younger. We didn't look too much alike. Both of us white and freckled, but my eyes were a dull brown, less interesting than her blue ones. I had light-brown curly hair, while hers was darker and straight. Before Dad died, I'd spent hours straightening my hair, but I'd refocused all my effort in the past almost four months toward the minor task of getting out of bed in the morning and making it through the day.

With her eyes closed and the sun lighting her up like that, Mom seemed so vulnerable. Some part of her looked . . . like me. My hard, deadened heart softened. Mom opened her eyes.

"Look," I said. "This incredibly shitty thing happened to us both. Sammy, too. But at least you can *choose* what you want to do! I can't. That's not fair."

"It's not." Mom ran a hand through her hair. "But, sweetheart, neither is life."

I said nothing and toed the duffel bag at my feet.

Mom took in a deep breath and exhaled. "Every second of every hour of every day since your father—since *Dad* died, I've spent living for you and Sammy. And that's . . ." She clenched her jaw, and seemed to wrestle with something before speaking again. "And that's how it should be. I'm the mom. I miss your dad. And I'm very torn up, thinking about the way he must have felt inside. But, honey? I'm hurting too. And you have no idea how many things needed to fall into place for camp to happen—for you to have the option to come here, to find a place that Call-Me-Connie, someone we trust, someone we have a good relationship with, could recommend." Her face was so sad that I couldn't look at it any longer.

I wondered if she could hear my heart cracking in half.

I parted my lips to respond, though I wasn't sure what I was going to say. A tap on the window saved me. Outside, Sammy gave a cheerful wave from beside a woman in one of those baby-blue counselor shirts.

I opened the door. "Hi?"

"Hi," the woman said. "I'm Mari. Lead counselor." She had a medium-brown complexion and pale green eyes. I'd never seen legs so long in my life. They stuck out of a pair of cutoff jean shorts. Her smile revealed a row of crooked bottom teeth.

I forced a smile back. "I'm just dropping off my brother."

"Really?" Mari hugged a clipboard to her chest and adjusted a beaded bracelet on her wrist. I started to pull the door closed but stopped when she spoke. "That's not what Sammy says."

*Traitor.* I narrowed my eyes at Sammy, who beamed. I swallowed. "Uh. Right. I—"

Mari gestured toward the clipboard she held. "I can give you a sec."

I glanced at Mom, and her expression was so goddamn hopeful that I almost relented. She unbuckled her seat belt and used her knee to nudge open her door. "You can heal here, Lila."

The tips of my ears burned. *Heal?* Like how counseling healed Dad?

"Honey . . . your dad would want this."

*Would he, now? Oh, well, in* that *case.* I couldn't stand any part of this. I couldn't fathom the ride home with her, or entering our ridiculous house without our ridiculous father. I glanced out the window, where Sammy waited, and finished pulling the door closed with a sharp click. I didn't want him to hear some bogus explanation about what our father would want. I steeled myself. "Jesus Christ, Mom. I'm not some knee scrape you can put Neosporin on—"

"Honey—"

"I don't need to be *healed*."

"We all do, sweetie. We do—"

"Stop it. Please. Just stop."

"You don't need to be scared."

"God, Mom, do you ever stop? No wonder he left us." The second the words left my mouth, I couldn't believe I'd said them. I wanted to snatch them from the air between us. "Mom. I'm so sorry. I didn't mean it."

Her mouth rolled into itself, and she gripped the steering wheel so hard her arms shook. I watched her knuckles drain of color. "I know you didn't mean that. But that . . . you . . . Not cool, Lila. Not cool."

"I don't even know why I said it. I'm sorry." Guilt rained over me, soaking my hair and settling into my toes.

"I forgive you," she said, her tone making it very clear that she more than likely did not. At least not yet.

I steeled myself, got out of the car, and turned around. "Okay. One week. I will see you in one week."

Fatigue sat on her shoulders. "Fine," she said. "I love you."

"And we love you, Mom," Sammy said, flashing her his most charming grin.

I slammed the door a bit harder than necessary, while Mom got out of the car and wrapped Sammy in a hug. She strode over to me, caught me in a brief squeeze.

"Be good, you two," she called, folding herself back into the car. She gripped the steering wheel and lowered her head.

*Good work, Lila. Insult your sad mom, and stew about it at grief prison.* Part of me wanted to call after her, until I remembered her pleading for one simple thing: grace. A breeze rustled the tops of the trees in the Maine sky, bringing with it an all-encompassing wave of something made of resignation, fear, and the thrill of the unknown.

I shouldered one of my duffel bags and Mari took the other. "I guess you could show me around," I said. "I'm staying for a week."

A smile broke out over her face. "Camp's eight weeks long."

"Not for me."

Sammy jerked his thumb toward me. "She's hormonal," he said to Mari.

"Sammy," I hissed.

I could almost see Mari racking her brain to try to figure out how to respond. "Oh . . . okay, then. I'll take you to the bungalows, Lila."

"Which way do I go?" Sammy asked.

She pointed to another of the blue T-shirts. Even from this far away, I could see he had a million freckles, and the light graying of his temples told me he was the most adult person here. "That's Jeff, our camp director. He can take you. Your bungalow is on the other side of the lake."

A thread of fear needled my brain. "Are you gonna be okay?" I asked Sammy. My fingers searched for my daffodil necklace, coming up empty. Old habits.

He gave me his overconfident Sammy grin. "Are *you*?" Without a backward glance, he sauntered toward Jeff.

Mari and I set off. I walked beside her along the worn-in path, trying to inconspicuously roll out my shoulders and stretch. Mari waved to a group of girls across the lawn, and they waved back.

My insides twisted with each step. I inhaled, filling my lungs until they could not take in any more air, then exhaled slowly—an old trick of Call-Me-Connie's. Home wasn't the same as it used to be, but I wasn't accustomed to staying so far away from our small brick house on Whittier without my parents—*parent*—either.

"You didn't get a welcome packet, right? They went out two or so months ago, so I wasn't sure, since a spot opened so late."

"A spot opened?"

It was Mari's turn to glance away from me. "Well, yeah. You know this camp fills up fast, right?" She put her hand on my arm. "Lots of kids in your position."

I held back a scoff. "My position?"

"Yes. Lots of kids who have shared similar experiences."

"You mean there are lots of kids with exclusive membership to the Dead Parent Club."

"You could look at it that way. But Bonaventure is technically a grief camp, so loss isn't limited to losing parents. Though it's certainly more common."

I swallowed. I'd forgotten the exact qualification for the camp: loss of an immediate family member. My amateur internet research had told me this was the plight of one in seven kids in the country. The concept of losing Sammy was too painful to even consider, so I changed the subject. "My mom said something about waiving a late fee. If there were no late people registering, then there would be no late fee."

"Touché. We had three late additions this year."

"Then how am I an exception? Whose spot did I take?"

"You didn't take anyone's spot."

I stopped walking. "I don't understand."

"The girl who had yours is . . . no longer with us."

"*No longer with us* as in what? Took up field hockey instead? Or no longer a member of Planet Earth?"

"The latter," Mari said. She kept walking.

I halted. "Hold up. *What?* Someone *died?*"

"Yes," she called over her shoulder. "I'm sorry to say."

I hustled to catch up. "And I'm in her spot?"

"Sort of." She hesitated. "Our camp is not the right choice for those who are at risk of serious personal harm. And I can't really talk about other campers."

"But—"

"*But*, hey, the bungalows are this way." She tilted her head to the left. "And as you can see, in front of us is the lake, and beyond that are the intramural fields. We've got swimming, archery, soccer, sailing . . ." The path we'd been on wound around the lake, connecting the buildings to one another.

Pinpricks of sweat rose up the small of my back, and I swiped my hand over my upper lip. *Breathe, Lila.* "Swimming? Is that a regularly scheduled activity?"

Mari laughed. "Don't worry. Even though it's Maine, we know how hot it gets here. Swimming's built in a few times a week." She chattered on, but I barely listened to her, mulling over the tiny fact that I did not know how to swim.

I tried to keep pace with Mari's gazelle-sized steps. But as we circled the lake, the uneven ground made my unworked legs burn. I adjusted the strap of my duffel bag and sucked in air, unused to feeling out of shape. I imagined Coach back at home, shaking his head in disappointment.

*Stop, Lila. You quit the team, so it doesn't matter what he thinks, remember?*

41

We came to a stop in front of the BLUE BUNGALOW, according to the sign out front.

"Up we go," Mari said. "The bungalows are all painted this bright because Jeff has a thing for Dutch canal homes."

I nodded. *Fine.* Weird as that was, I was too out of breath to say anything.

She took the steps two at a time, and opened the door to my new home "for the next fifty-six days" (try seven, Mari). I took in the wide, knotty pine floor, which had one throw rug in the middle. The rug was made of a bunch of different-colored fabrics looped together, and I knew without asking that it was an art project made by the campers. It was like a giant-sized version of one of those pot holders you'd make on a loom when you were a little kid.

Lining the room—which looked like a hybrid log cabin and seventies basement—were six beds, each one lofted just enough that a small chest of drawers fit underneath. It was neat, and it was clean, and it was so stereotypically *camp* I felt like screaming. The weight of my duffel bag pulled my shoulders down, and my fingers ached from carrying my tote.

"Let's see," Mari said, consulting with her clipboard. "Wainwright, Madison, Heather, Emilia, and Lila." She tapped the bunk closest to the door. "This one's yours."

"What about you?" I asked, swinging the duffel bag on top of the bed and releasing the tote to the floor. When it landed, I heard the soft crunch of cellophane from Dad's cookies. I'd run back inside and shoved them into the bottom of the bag, just below Dad's notebook, while Mom idled in the driveway.

Mari waved her hand to the opposite side of the room. "That one's mine, but you guys are old enough to not need me so much. I don't usually sleep in here unless it's raining." Before I could come up with an appropriate conversational response, she signed the paper in front of her with a flourish, tossed the clipboard on the bed, and checked her watch. "You ready?"

"For what?"

"Orientation."

"Okay, but . . ." I surveyed the room. "First, where's the bathroom?"

Mari brightened. "Come with me."

Outside, we followed a narrow gravel path that wrapped around the bungalow and led to another building: the GIRLS' COMMON ROOM. "The Com," Mari announced.

Instead of what I thought of as a common room—something you might see in a movie about college, with square, squat chairs facing a television, and maybe a kitchenette—the Com was a community outhouse of sorts, with showers, a row of sinks, and bathroom stalls. The lemon smell of antiseptic soap overpowered my nose.

"We have to go outside to pee in the middle of the night?" I asked. *Geez. Happy belated birthday, Lila.*

Mari grinned. "It's not scary. I sleep outside almost every night. You get used to it."

I didn't say it, but I wouldn't have to. I'd only be here a week.

# Chapter Six

Orientation was held on the grassy lawn behind the Lodge. Mari joined a bunch of other blue T-shirts up front, and I sat on the edge of a basketball court. Kids sprawled on the lawn in front of me. Some on blankets, some not. Almost all in groups of two or three.

I patted my back pocket for my phone, but checking it was futile. There really was no cell phone service up here. I hugged my knees and rested my chin on them, feeling sorry for myself. A pair of Converse sneakers entered my vision.

"You must be Lila," the owner of the sneakers said. She had a wide-open face, light brown skin, and mounds and mounds of curly, almost umber-colored hair. Next to her was one of the most striking people I'd ever seen. Tall, blonde, white skinned with ice-blue eyes—maybe Nordic in background—and exaggerated doll-like features that made her look like a cartoon princess.

"I'm Wainwright Flores," the first girl said. She shook the cloud of hair out of her face. One purple streak peeked out from underneath. "But everyone calls me Winnie." She pointed at the blonde. "And this is Madison Blumenthal. You're the new girl, right?"

"Right. Uh, hey."

Madison barely glanced at me. "Hey." She practically sang out the word—her voice was musical, the Southern twang unmistakable.

I forced a smile. "Where are you two coming from?"

"Lincoln, Nebraska," Winnie said. "You?"

"Massachusetts."

"I'm from Georgia." Madison sighed. "Winnie, are you almost done here?"

*Whoa.* My brain struggled to make peace between her jarring answer and her melodic tone.

Winnie plopped down next to me. "Don't mind her," she said. "Madison's dad threatened to cut off her college fund if she didn't come back to camp."

*College fund.* The contents of my bank account ($236.15), nearly two years' worth of barista tips from Sunday mornings at the Mug, made up my own college fund. After Dad died, Mom met with some financial planner who helped her figure out how to budget so we wouldn't lose the house. She'd chewed a hole in her cheek during the meeting—literally—and had to get a special mouthwash from our dentist. Even with the life insurance, I had no idea how she'd afforded this place of trust funders and rustic bungalows, but Mom would have said money was a *her* problem, not a *me* problem. I poked my finger into the grass until it met soil, and then I pushed some more.

Madison sighed and lowered herself down beside Winnie, taking great pains to avoid touching the bare skin of her stereotypically perfect legs to the grass. "This stuff makes me so *itchy*. I hate it."

I didn't care for the sensation of grass on my legs either—part of the reason I'd sat on the edge of the basketball court. "That makes two of us."

Madison flicked an imaginary speck off of her shoulder. "Mm-hmm."

"Madison makes a terrible first impression," Winnie said.

"I'm right here," Madison said.

"I know." Winnie shot her a pointed look. "So, Lila. Ah—we're sorry for your loss. Which died?"

"Which?"

Madison's nostrils flared and she peered at me with a touch of interest. "Which *parent*?"

Winnie's face fell. "Or, no. Not a sibling?"

I shook my head and used my thumbnail to sever a strand of grass from the earth. I split it in half lengthwise, watching it curl like cheap grocery store wrapping ribbon. "No. My dad."

"Mine too. Dad deaths are sucky," Winnie said. She smiled with just the side of her mouth. It wasn't the same kind of smile my friends at home gave me—the ones that were a little too bright or a little too sad.

Madison's shoulders tensed. "Again, Winnie? Do you have to start with this? Mom deaths suck too."

Winnie rolled her eyes. "*Maditude*. Of course they do." She leaned over and poked her friend.

All the blue T-shirts rustled to their feet then. A couple of them clapped their hands at a group of younger kids, Sammy among them. As if he felt me staring, he pivoted and scanned the crowd. I gave him a little wave, and he grinned.

Sammy. Couldn't stay angry with him for long.

"Jeff will talk about the history of the camp, and then he'll cry," Winnie whispered. She scooted backward onto the basketball court and reclined on the warm tar. "I've heard this six times already."

That was exactly what happened. He talked about how Camp Bonaventure was founded after 9/11, when a bunch of kids lost one (or, worse, both) of their parents and no one could relate to them. Some rich guy started the camp, making it his patriotic duty to give those kids something back—a symbolic fight against the terrorists who steered the giant silver-winged planes into the Twin Towers, the Pentagon, and that field in Pennsylvania. Jeff's dad had been on Flight 93.

Jeff had started as one of the oldest campers, and then he'd worked here through college "until all the kids aged out," he finished. "That's where I came in." He cleared his throat, rocking back and forth on the balls of his feet. "Camp saved me as a kid. And when I was an adult, opening it back up saved me again."

Winnie sat up. "Here's the sad part," she said.

Jeff pressed his lips together and seemed to consider something before continuing. He pulled out a tissue and wiped his eyes, then produced an index card from his pocket and read from it. "Here at Camp Bonaventure, you'll meet people who can understand you the way most of the other people in your life can't."

I did a mental calculation of all the people I knew who'd had a parent die by suicide, and came up with precisely two. Sammy and me. I tilted my head. Maybe Jeff had something there.

"The people you meet here will change you," Jeff went on. "You're at camp because you've lost someone really dear to you. That's universal in here, and unique out there." A rustle went through the crowd. "But I also want to remind you that if you ever feel like something's worse than just that terrible fact, if you're more than sad, we do have a sister camp for more intensive help, and you can come talk to me about that at any time. Door's always open."

Madison and Winnie exchanged a glance. Winnie frowned. "He skipped it," she said.

"Skipped what?" I asked.

"The sad part. The story about his own wife and kid."

I waited, trying to puzzle together how that was related to 9/11. "He was a teen dad . . . ?"

She shook her head. "Nope. This was after. He used to have a wife and kid. Now he doesn't."

I picked at the frayed hem of my shorts. I'd always had this theory that people were only allowed to endure one really awful

47

thing in their lives, but it was beginning to look like the people at this camp could certainly prove otherwise.

I made a mental note to add to my handbook when I got back to the bungalow. *Rule number four: Remember that grief lightning can strike twice.*

It shouldn't, though.

Jeff clapped his hands together. "Okay, kids," he said, his voice taking on a tone of cheerfulness impossible to fake. "Time for our icebreaker! This year we're doing speed-meet. Form two concentric circles, everyone. Equal number of people in each. Inside circle face out, outside circle face in." Campers got to their feet, shuffling into formation. "Here are the rules. Introduce yourself, and then say something you're good at. Every thirty seconds, Mari will call, 'Switch.' Inner circle, you stay grounded. Get the metaphor?" He laughed and looked around. "No? Okay. Outer circle, take a step to your right when you hear Mari."

I tilted my head back and let out a sigh. *Fantastic.*

"This is better than last year's," Winnie said from my left. She tugged her hair back and wound an elastic around it.

"What was last year's?"

"Favorite food."

I started thinking about what I'd have said for that. Pepperoni pizza? Double chocolate cake? If I'd wanted to come off as someone I wasn't—and if I'd felt comfortable bending the truth—I might've said avocado smoothies.

Mari clapped her hands twice. "Ready? Go!"

Round one. The girl across from me was about my height, with inky black hair, warm brown skin, and bangs.

"Hi, I'm Lila," I said. "I'm good at . . ." Sarcasm? Art? "Hurdling."

She beamed. "I'm Heather-Emilia Laghari. I'm good at

sensing emotions within the molecular interconnectedness of the natural world."

Cue my immediate, intense bewilderment. "Um, what?"

"You know, like how trees feel when they provide a service by shading the grass, or being the home of a bird? I'm sensitive to energetic movement." She leaned forward. "You like hurdling?"

"I—"

"Switch!"

"Nice to meet you," I said, stepping to the right. I shifted my attention to the next person. Fringy black bangs. About my height. I glanced back to Heather-Emilia, and then to the new person. "Oh, you must be sisters."

"Identical twins," the girl in front of me said.

"I'm Lila."

She huffed the bangs from her eyes. "Emilia-Heather."

"You have inverse names?"

"Yep." She flicked her gaze away from me.

And personalities, apparently. I thought I heard a snort coming from the other side of Winnie, where Madison stood. "Are you always this smart, new girl?" Madison called.

"It's Lila," I said through gritted teeth.

Winnie looked at Madison. "What on earth has gotten *into* you?"

"Switch!"

And so it continued. The young boy from drop-off, CP, rattled off his stats: He was from New York, lived with his grandparents, and was half white and half Korean.

*Switch.* Sammy. I smiled. "Doing okay, buddy?"

He grinned, his cheeks flushed. "Yeah. The dude beside me has *killer* would-you-rathers."

Dad's favorite kind of conversation starter. (*Eat a single hot dog once a day for the rest of your life, or have to wash your hands once a day with hot-dog-scented soap?* he might ask my mother, hooking his chin over her shoulder while she wrote. *Neither,* she'd say, wrinkling her nose but smiling.)

"Oh, really?" I asked, cutting my eyes to Sammy's would-you-rather pal.

He was tall. Way taller than me. Dark hair splayed over his forehead, with these bold, even darker eyebrows below. Light eyes against white skin. Ruddy cheeks. "I've got some decent ones," he said. "Any interest?"

I gestured to the boy on my right, a tall, immensely muscular Black kid who, once I really looked at him, I immediately recognized. He was a member of a track team my town competed against, confirmed by his blue school baseball cap. I made a conscious effort to stand up straighter, wondering if he'd know who I was. "Wouldn't want to intrude on your speed-meet."

"Deese and I are bunkmates. We've been hanging out all day. You don't mind, do you, Deese?"

"Not a bit," Deese said, squeezing the brim of his hat.

"You sure you're up for a would-you-rather question?" Eyebrows asked.

I found myself smiling. "Try me."

He reached down and picked up a small rock, then tossed it to Deese. Just like that, they started a wordless game of catch, the rock landing in their palms with muted thwacks. "One day. One superpower. Flight or invisibility?"

Forget either of those. Wasn't there one where I could manipulate time? I'd go back to the first of March, try to change history, and suffer the consequences in a real-life butterfly-effect drama.

But if I had to choose between his two options, I'd pick the one where no one would pity me for a day. "Invisibility," I said finally.

He lifted his arms. "Me too. You're the only other person who's said that."

"How could you *not* fly?" Deese asked. He chucked the rock behind him.

"She already flies," Sammy informed them. "Or she did, before she quit the track team."

Deese looked at me. "Track team?"

"Switch!"

Deese and I shifted over a slot, matching me up with Eyebrows. He tipped his head in greeting. "You run?"

I shook my head. "I'm a hurdler."

"Are you good?"

I kept my face passive. "Yes."

He raised those brows. "And she has a confident swagger! I like it. So many people are too humble. Let's see . . ." He shifted his feet. "Would you rather never use Google again, or ditch social media forever?"

Hmm. I'd pretty much become a social-media lurker since Dad died. I'd had to squash the urge to check my phone about fifty times already today. But. I also had a pretty insatiable appetite for information, so I practiced the regular habit of googling everything in the world.

"Well, social media sucks," I said.

"It does." His fingers tapped the edge of his thigh in a metered rhythm, as if he were playing the piano. "Especially after a tragedy. Right?"

My stomach flipped, thinking about Jeff's words. *People who can understand you the way most of the other people in your life can't.* "Right."

51

"I'm sensing a *but*."

"But I would cut Google with the logic that there are other search engines in the world that can tell me the same stuff."

A breeze stirred the tall Maine pines, ruffling his hair. He stopped his tapping, and a smile spread across his face. "You found a loophole," he said, a note of satisfaction in his words.

Air whooshed from my lungs. *Whoa.* I ducked my head. I'd worn an old pair of Reefs, and my toenails were painted Cajun Shrimp pink. One or two—okay, five—had chipped. And then I was conscious of the escaped locks of hair—my "wings," Dad always called them—standing at attention around my forehead. I ran my nails through my hairline and tried to smooth them back. They rose again. Almost immediately, I heard Grandma Gladys's favorite quip in my head. *Risin' like Jesus on Easter.*

I dropped my hand. Why did I even bother? It wasn't his business that my hair looked like it had been plugged into an electrical socket.

"Time!" Mari shouted. The circle formations dissolved, campers grouping back together. Winnie appeared by my side.

"I don't know what's up with Madison," Winnie said, leading me toward a table set up with boxed dinners, where the blue T-shirts passed out turkey, roast beef, and vegan options. "She's not usually like that."

I turned to Deese and his bunkmate, lifting my hand in farewell.

It wasn't until we got back that it occurred to me that I hadn't gotten his name.

# Chapter Seven

Lying awake in the middle of the night is a special kind of hell. Your body is tired; your mind is electrified. You will it to quiet down, at least until dawn, but it runs and runs and runs. Unlike my track career.

I used to be an excellent sleeper. I'd be freshly showered and lotioned up, reading in bed from nine thirty to ten. When the lights went out, so did my consciousness. I was up at six after a clean eight hours of shut-eye.

But ever since Dad died, I'd had all kinds of sleeping problems. My first night at camp was no exception. I'd almost fallen asleep when an owl made an *actual* hooting sound, which robbed me of any chance of slumber. I was a suburban kid, but this place was in the middle of nowhere. It was darker than it was at home too.

Call-Me-Connie had gone through the sleep-issues checklist with me, and I'd ticked off every line. Problems falling asleep. Problems staying asleep. Daytime fogginess. Recurring nightmares. Inability to concentrate. Night sweats.

Self-diagnosis: hopeless. Because this was another thing my dad had taken from me: the ability to sleep without worry. The second I closed my eyes, my brain took me hostage, participating in the sort of self-flagellation normally reserved for thirteenth-century religious martyrs. But instead of crudely made whips, my mind latched on to my happy memories, like when I used to lie in my bed and fall asleep hearing my parents still up and about—my mom on her computer, writing to meet a deadline, my dad munching on a bag of chips (when he could get away with it) and watching old movies. I'd half wake up if they went into the bathroom, and I'd fall back into slumber hearing them splash water on their faces or brush their teeth.

All night, I couldn't stop thinking about one evening last winter, during the week between Christmas and New Year's, when a storm kept the power out and us in for three days. Even though it was more staycay than vacay, it was the last time we spent any real stretch of time together, uninterrupted. We were glued to the TV until the storm hit. Newscasters flipped back and forth between lighthearted holiday stories—like the local family that had been struggling financially, only to wake up Christmas morning to an anonymous truckload of gifts ("Whoa," Sammy whispered, awestruck)—and breaking news about a girl who'd been murdered not too far from the Cape Cod town where we stayed every summer for one perfectly measured and budgeted week. I still remembered the victim's name: Dakota Frothingham. Dakota like the states, Frothingham like the park Sammy and I had adored when we were little. Punctuating that wild juxtaposition was the nor'easter climbing its way up the coast, the weather people painting its destruction in swirling aqua and dark blue Doppler radar whorls.

The day the storm hit, we spent the whole afternoon shoveling until we were somehow both cold and sweating. With motherly foresight, Mom had charged all the laptops in the house before the power went out, and the second night we connected one to a disc drive and sat around binge-watching old DVDs like *Titanic* and *Now and Then*. All four of us crowded onto the brown leather couch, covered in quilts and blankets, empty hot chocolate mugs resting between our legs and a fire roaring in the brick fireplace beside us.

"How are you not a hot mess right now?" Mom blew her

nose. She raised her palm toward the screen, which featured an innocent man walking toward his death in *The Green Mile*.

I shrugged. "It's just a movie."

"With a façade like that, you're destined to break hearts, Little Lyon," Dad joked. In the fireplace, a log fell with a whoosh; embers flew, and the air filled with the kind of crackle I now wished I'd been able to bottle.

"Oh please. Stop."

"Seriously," he said, peering at me. "This movie melts the resolve of ice queens and kings everywhere. What's up with you?"

"I'm just realistic. And you're all wusses."

He adopted some off-base Shakespearean accent. "Coldhearted! Thy blood runs blue through thy veins."

"All our blood runs blue," I said. "It only turns red when it's exposed to air."

"Blood isn't blue," Sammy said. "You're dense."

Dad nudged Sammy with his knee. "Don't call your sister dense."

"Watch out," I said. "'For he today who sheds his blood with me shall be my brother.'"

Dad laid his hand over his chest. "*Henry the Fifth*! Be still, my heart." He turned to Mom. "Smart, too, just like her mother. How did I get so lucky?" He nuzzled her hair, and she laughed.

By dawn I'd had enough of the mental torture. Resigned, I got out of bed, dug out my shower supplies, and tiptoed my way through the sleeping bungalow.

In the Com, three rows of plumbing sprawled in front of me: showers to the left, sinks in the middle, stalls to the right. With the exception of one tiny square mirror on the back wall, the entire interior was tiled in a grayish beige porcelain.

If I knew my HGTV (which I did, considering the amount it had been on our low-volume television this spring), I knew that Benjamin Moore would call this *greige*. Or maybe something more nature-sounding—*Rural Greige*. I could still smell a lemon antiseptic scent, but rather than scouring my nostrils like it had yesterday, it had faded into something soft. Almost pleasant.

Even though I was alone in the bathroom, I moved fast. I wiggled my toes out of my Reefs and into the shower sandals Mom had packed for me, pulled the heavy plastic curtain across the opening, and—once I was safely covered—undressed. I hung my towel on a metal peg outside the shower, and dropped my clothes onto the bench below it. I was used to changing in the locker room with my team, but I trusted them. I didn't need any of these new strangers to see how casual my body's approach to giving me breasts was. Let's just say that where some girls had mountains or molehills, I had hives. Barely.

The spigot creaked out a warm but weak spray. I stood beneath the showerhead for probably an entire minute before my hair was fully wet. While I waited, I splashed my face and rubbed my eyes, hoping the water would erase the dark baggage the night had so kindly left behind.

I rushed through my shampoo-condition-shave routine, and I was just finger-combing my curls when a bang interrupted my detangling. The plastic curtain rippled.

"Hello?" I cleared my throat. "Anyone there?"

Silence.

I turned off the faucet and reached around the curtain for

my towel, but my palm knocked against bare wood. I walked my fingers upward to find an empty hook.

Closing my eyes, I stifled my panic. I peered under the curtain to see if the towel had fallen to the floor, but no such luck. "Hello?" I called again.

Diagnosis: Hopeless strikes again.

I peered around the thick shower curtain, which reeked of what I could only imagine was BPA-full plastic. Hanging on a hook across from me was a thin, nubby piece of purple fabric. The bench where my pajamas had been was empty. I darted my eyes both ways, lunged, and used my pinkie finger to pull it off.

Back inside my stall, the fabric unfurled into a long-sleeved leotard the color of grape bubble gum. If I'd had to put a Crayola color name to it, it would be Purple Mountains' Majesty. Or Wisteria. Goose bumps erupted across my skin, and I shivered.

*Who the hell stole my frigging stuff?*

With no other options, I balled the leotard and used it to squeegee water off my skin. I surveyed the fabric and tried about six different ways to wrap it around my body, but only succeeded in tying myself up like a bondage queen. Sighing, I shook it out and then stepped into the garment, which had probably lost its elasticity during the era owner-director Jeff was a camper. By the time I succeeded in hiking the leotard over my waist and pulling it onto my shoulders—like trying to wriggle into a soaked one-piece bathing suit, except with long sleeves—I was sweating.

I threw my shower stuff back into the pink caddy my mom had so hopefully purchased and stomped out of the Com. The leotard clung to my skin, except where it sagged in the butt area. Apparently, its owner was more blessed in the buns department than one Lila Cunningham.

I made it halfway back to the Blue Bungalow, my shower sandals squeaking beneath my toes. *One week*, a voice in my head chanted. *One week. But wait!* I brightened. Actually, now it was just six days. *Six days! Six days. Six—*

"Late for early morning Jazzercise, Nineties Workout Barbie?"

I yelped, stumbling mid-step and barely catching myself. Desperate, I fumbled for the contents of my shower caddy. I managed to snag the body wash, but with such a firm grip that it exploded all over the front of my Purple Mountains' Majesty leotard.

Tears pricked my eyes. And of course, when I looked up, there he was: Eyebrows. Holding a white paper rectangle and grinning. "That's certainly not an outfit you see every day."

I squatted to collect the shampoo and conditioner. My razor had flown across the lawn, near Eyebrows himself. I stood, all too aware of my flappy leotard butt and the patchy wet spots that covered this cruel, cruel garment. "Trust me. It wasn't my choice."

Fleetingly, I wondered why he was at camp. Who he'd lost. In a move nearly feline in nature, he swooped low and palmed my razor. His whole body spoke of years of athletic prowess on one sports field or another. If he'd been a panther, I'd have been a three-toed sloth.

Which said a lot, since I'd broken two school records for hurdling.

He dangled the razor toward me. "This yours?" His smile was tangy and wide, like a thick eighth of an orange slice. A fuzzy sensation of warmth spread through me. I swallowed, trying to buy myself some time. Something about his smile made me feel both shy and yet drawn to him.

I recovered. "Gee. What gave that away?"

He shrugged. "I'm very well educated."

"Modest, too."

"So is this your uniform or something?"

"Ha," I deadpanned. "I wish. Someone stole my clothes."

His fingers drummed another tune on his leg. He seemed to be in a constant state of movement. "Are your shower curtains see-through?"

I wrinkled my nose. *There* it was. The epitome of straight-guy dreams: the girls' showers. At least he wasn't mind-numbingly hot *and* a perfect gentleman. Otherwise, especially if I were here all summer, he might have been a candidate for risking rule one of my handbook.

*The only people who can truly hurt you are the ones you love. Therefore, love no one.*

"I don't mean like that," he said at my expression. "Get your mind out of the drain. What I meant was if they aren't see-through, then you could have used one of them to . . ." He mimed wrapping something around himself.

Hot, not pervy, and brilliant. *Damn it.*

"I didn't think of that option," I said. Awkwardly.

His laugh was slow and languid, but something about it made me snap to attention. Even though I knew next to nothing about this would-you-rather boy, his smile was golden. "To be fair, I suppose seeing inside a girls' locker room might be on the goal list of many teenagers in America."

"It's not a locker room." I hugged my shower supplies closer to my chest. "Anyway, I would have had to tear the curtain down. The rings are too high up."

He eyed me. "You are pretty short." He reached out and touched the top of my arm with his fingertip, as if to illustrate. My skin welcomed the warm pressure of his touch. "Does that work for you with your competitive gymnastics career?"

"I'm not short. I'm average." My cheeks flamed. "And this leotard is *not* mine. Don't go there."

Undeterred, he pointed at himself. "I don't think I caught your name. I'm Noah."

"Lila."

"Oh!" he said, his face lighting up. "Then this must be for you." He held up what he'd been clutching: an envelope with my name emblazoned across the front. "It's your schedule. I had to go get mine from Jeff this morning, and he asked me to run this over to Mari, who was supposed to give it to you."

"Thanks. I'm only staying a week. By the time I get used to it, it'll be time to go." I took the envelope from him, accidentally brushing his fingers with my own. At the touch, I lifted my eyes to his. An ocean of warring urges ran through me: a pleasurable shiver and a jolt of light-headedness, held together by an undercurrent of unwanted desire. His skin was pleasantly warm. Mine was slick with the attractive blend of body lotion and nervous sweat.

"Jeff said the schedule changes all the time, anyway, so no one will get used to it." He pursed his lips. "You're only here a week?"

"Yup. Made a promise to my mother."

"That's too bad." His lips parted, and a dusky blush colored his cheeks.

The leotard stuck to my lower back. I shifted my hips, trying to casually unstick someone else's garment from my skin.

"I guess I'll see you around?"

"Thanks," I said. I waved the envelope. "For this." I backed up toward the blue bungalow. "Uh. See you around."

"You're pretty hard to miss," he said, raising those big bold eyebrows of his.

I was going to kill whoever had stolen my clothes.

# Chapter Eight

Inside the bungalow, I found my pajamas and towel neatly folded on the foot of my bed. I dug shorts and a tank top from my still-packed duffel bag and turned to the mirror.

I groaned. Clad in this long-sleeved leotard, I looked like a rejected Olympics gymnast from a different decade. To make matters worse, the wet patches clung to my armpits and chest, insinuating that I had a sweating problem worth addressing. I hooked my hand inside the neck of the offending piece and tugged.

"Oh, good! You're here. I was just—"

I whirled around. Mari stood at the bungalow door. She eyed my ensemble and frowned. I folded my arms across my chest.

"I thought that thing was gone," she muttered.

I narrowed my eyes. "Care to explain?"

She gestured around the room. "The blue bungalow," she explained. "It's tradition."

I stared at her.

"It's from the first year of camp," she said. "One of the girls brought it. It was her mom's old gymnastics leotard."

"It was her mom's, as in her mom who died?"

Mari hesitated. "I don't know that part. I think it was a prop they used in a play." She paused. "If it makes you feel better, they do it to everyone."

I blinked. "It is seriously messed up that a hazing tradition exists at a camp for kids whose parents are dead. And that said tradition is dependent upon the Lycra shroud of a potentially dead woman."

Mari sighed. "You're right. And they will be getting dish duty for this."

Mari somehow coaxed me over to the mess hall—creatively named MESS HALL—for breakfast. I scored a slightly bruised apple and a bowl of dry Cheerios. The milk came from a giant udder-looking thing at the bottom of a large silver tank, so I skipped it.

Most kids had cleared out of Mess Hall already. Unlike the utilitarian rows of rectangular fold-up tables at my high school in Massachusetts, this cafeteria had a bunch of small, circular tables, and the back wall was lined with booths. In a corner sat a few low-slung coffee tables and armchairs, reminiscent of a Starbucks. The walls continued the log-cabin theme from the bungalows, as if the cafeteria had been plunked down inside a giant replica of Lincoln's log cabin. (I knew what I was talking about, too, because a life-sized version of Lincoln's cabin sat on the grounds of my hometown museum.)

The room smelled like Mom's cooking—garlic and onions, but not in an offensive way. More cozy and pleasant. I'd once read a book where the main character, a teenager scared of living alone for the summer in New York City, cooked garlic and onions in her apartment every night to make herself feel like she had some company. A sour pang clattered in my jaw when I thought about Mom standing next to the sink and slicing onions. Alone.

I shook my head. I didn't want to be here, but I sure didn't want to be home, either. New York City, maybe.

I settled in a back booth and dug into my Cheerios, eyeing

the envelope Noah had given me. As soon as the cold metal spoon touched my lips, my stomach growled with appreciation. I'd barely touched the boxed dinner from the night before. A side effect of grief: Your stomach will eat itself before your brain reminds you that food is, you know, necessary for survival.

I leaned forward and tore open the envelope. The paper was thick and creamy white, and it held my summer itinerary: a rotating schedule of standard camp stuff like swimming (ugh), art, archery, and rec sports, along with the delicate task of group therapy. Three days a week. I bit down on my spoon.

A paper insert gave the details for an end-of-the-week WELLcome dance, and another one promoted the FareWELL Dance at the end of the summer. I chomped my cereal, wishing I had some sugar to sprinkle on top the way Mom used to do.

"Surprise," a cheerful voice said.

Standing at the edge of my booth were Winnie and Madison, wearing the respective faces of sheepishness and smugness associated with clothing-and-towel thievery.

"Very funny," I said.

"Mind if we sit?" Winnie asked.

"Sure."

Winnie beamed and slid into the booth. "Awesome."

"No, I meant 'sure' as in *yes, I mind*."

Madison rolled her eyes. "It's just a joke. Happens to everyone."

I stirred my cereal. "I'm only staying for a week. You could've skipped the initiation."

"You should've seen what happened at mine," Winnie said. "I couldn't get the leotard all the way on, because whoever's mom that was must've had the body type of a ten-year-old boy."

I scowled, but reminded myself she hadn't seen my baggy

butt. Winnie was built like one of those gorgeous nineteenth-century paintings of naked women with ringlet curls covered in fruit. "Yeah? I got it on. Just in time to run into that guy Noah."

For the first time since I'd met her, Madison perked up. "He saw *you* in *that?*" she asked. Her emphasis on *you* and *that* made it clear that she took great pleasure in the concept of a cute boy with great eyebrows seeing my Lycra-clad frame bumble outdoors.

Winnie stared at Madison. "Is there some kind of reason you're being this way?"

Madison set her jaw and said nothing. Winnie let the silence roll over the table. I shifted in my seat and let it happen. I was positive I hadn't done a thing to this girl, and if she wanted to be the epitome of a mean-girl trope, then she could have at it. Girls didn't need to be against girls this way.

"Whatever," Winnie muttered. She pulled my schedule across the table. "Sweet. We both have art next. Walk over with me?"

*Walk over with me* was something friends did. And someone who was supposed to follow one particular rule in her handbook didn't make friends. I tapped my tongue against the roof of my mouth.

*It's only a week.*

"Sure," I said. Not like I had much more to lose.

The art room—the first building I'd seen on the grounds of Camp Bonaventure—stood over by a vegetable garden and the wooden structure that housed the bikes.

"Jeff is out there every day at dawn," Winnie said, pointing to the garden. "He takes the director-as-part-of-the-community thing pretty seriously. Wears this big floppy hat and everything."

*Not interesting.* "Oh."

She nodded. "And rumor has it that Mari sleeps out there every night and helps water it or pluck the dead leaves or whatever."

*More interesting.* "Mari really sleeps outside every night?"

Winnie's eyes were friendly. "Yes. And she has a thing for Jeff."

I pictured his freckled face, and her overeager clapping and shouting. "I can . . . somehow see that."

Winnie held the door for me. "What's the summer project? Have you heard yet?"

"Summer project?" We slid into seats at a two-person desk scarred with deep grooves and paint flecks. I traced the indents with my finger.

"Yeah, the old 9/11 camp had some kind of agreement with the Guggenheim Museum in New York. Our art counselor, Madame D., picks out the standouts of the summer, and the Guggenheim features them during the fall."

I raised my eyebrows, impressed. We had gone to the Guggenheim on a trip to New York at the end of last summer. Our last trip as a family of four. Sammy had nearly fainted with excitement when he saw a sculpture made from cars suspended from the ceiling. To my dismay, I'd nearly fainted of dehydration. The filthy city blocks, reeking of baked garbage, radiated heat like a diner griddle.

Dad had stopped to buy a five-dollar bottle of water from a pretzel vendor. "Still want to move here someday, Lyon?" he'd asked, uncapping the water and handing it to me.

"You can visit me on weekends," I'd said. I tilted my head back and finished the entire thing in several gulps, scanning the angles and lines of the buildings above as they sliced through the thin blue sky. I loved New York: dehydration, baked garbage, and all.

I shook my head free of the memory, watching Winnie rake her fingers through her thick hair and tie it up on her head in a more voluminous version of the topknot I wore. "It's hot today, huh? So, yeah, the museum keeps sponsoring it, even though we're not technically 9/11-related anymore."

"Hard to take yet another thing away from the half orphans," I said.

Winnie grinned. "Your sarcasm is showing."

"It seems like you know everything about this place."

She glanced away from me. "I've been here every summer since I was twelve."

I chewed the inside of my cheek. Winnie seemed so . . . adjusted. Like the fact that her dad was dead was just a tiny part of her—the bigger parts were that she was sarcastic, liked to joke, and was friendly when she didn't have to be. The biggest part of me right now—the cloud that hung over my head, like one of those miserable cartoons in a cold-and-flu commercial—was the appalling reality that Dad Was Dead. How had she gotten to the place where a dead dad was somewhere around number seven on the list?

"Sorry," I said finally.

Winnie shrugged. "You get used to it."

I didn't know if I ever wanted to be used to it.

"The first year is the hardest," she added, ducking her head for a moment. She reached up and tightened the elastic in her hair.

The imaginary tangle of threads in my chest unwound a bit. "Of camp? Or the whole year?"

Winnie smiled. "Both. Camp is a break from the outside world. When you go back, there will be the big things—the first Thanksgiving, the first Christmas. There's no getting around it. They suck." She leaned forward and dropped the volume of her voice. "But people expect that. Our family went wild trying to distract me and my mom during the holidays that first year. What no one really knows about are the little day-to-day things. *Those* . . ." She trailed off, then recovered. "Those are hardest. After school. Sunday mornings. Buying cheese from his favorite employee at the deli counter." Winnie wrinkled her nose. "Then it's another Thanksgiving, and another Christmas. And this place. I know it doesn't seem like it to you right now, but it's my favorite place in the world."

I sat back and examined the room. Aged hardwood floors— the thick kind, like you'd find in an old barn—supported yawning rows of double desks. A long table flanked one wall, covered in spattered paints, rolls of paper towels, and cups half filled with water. On the other wall, a blank corkboard held tacks for finished projects, and clothespins hung upside down from a rope strung across the room, waiting to hold wet paintings. Beyond the door, I could make out the collection of colorful vintage bikes I'd spotted when we'd arrived just twenty-four hours ago. The whole room smelled like crayons and acrylic paint.

I cleared my throat. "Thanks," I said. "That . . . helps."

The art counselor swept in the door then, and Winnie groaned. "I always forget about Ms. D.," she said. "*Madame* D."

"Forget about her?"

"As much as you can forget about someone whose Francophilia is a deliberate departure from reality. Very *faux*."

Madame D. had a black cloud of frizzed-out hair, lips the hue of latte foam, and alabaster white-lady skin. I'd never seen someone so pale during the summer. She wore a long, baby-blue skirt with hundreds of tiny pleats in it.

"Students," she said, her voice surprisingly deep. *"Bonjour, campeurs."*

*"Bonjour, Madame D.,"* said the room.

"I know you're all waiting to hear about the project, but I'd like to say hello to all your familiar countenances."

Winnie rolled her eyes. "She's not even French," she whispered. I grinned.

Madame D.'s eyes flew across the row of desks. "Harry, good to see you, love . . . Oh, hello. Alicia, is it? Nothing? Silence? Aha . . . Wainwright, you devil, you, I've missed you, *oui*." Her gaze landed on me. "And you, my dear?"

"I'm Lila," I said. "Just visiting for the week."

"Hello, Lila-Just-Visiting," she said. She squinted at me. "My goodness, you have rich curls. They're every color of the cocoa-to-mahogany rainbow, aren't they? So *vivant*."

I patted the escaped wings framing my face. "Uh. I think they're brown?"

While Madame D. continued her theatrical examination of her *artistes'* faces, Winnie leaned over. "Screw this whole 'week' thing. You really should stay longer," she whispered. "It gets fun. Makes it all bearable."

*Bearable?* Bearable sounded . . . well, it sounded better than I could imagine. I yearned for bearable. I wavered for a fraction of a second, and then a rapid-fire series of pictures ran through my head. Mom alone. My bed. The police at our door. "Not my thing."

Winnie cocked her head, examining me. "You hesitated. You're thinking about staying," she whispered.

I shook my head. I wasn't thinking about staying; I was thinking about how much I enjoyed Winnie's company, which was a problem when it came to my life's new philosophy. The handbook. I tried to thread one of the wings back into my bun, but it sprang free. "Group therapy, group showers, group dinners, and singing 'Kumbaya' around a campfire won't change things for me."

My mood clouded over when I said the words, remembering Mom's insistence that therapy could help. Her firm faith in the idea had taken root somewhere in my mind. I wasn't ready to agree with her, but apparently she'd said enough to introduce an iota of doubt. My words tasted like little lies in my mouth, metallic and sweet. The whole point of the handbook was to stay away from people who could be liars, not to become one myself. You were either a liar or you weren't, and in life there was nothing worse than a liar. I clenched my teeth, then made a conscious effort to relax.

"Oh, and going home will?" Winnie asked. I opened my mouth to respond, but she cut me off, tilting her head toward Madame D. "Shh. The summer project."

I frowned. "Weren't you the one talking to me?"

Madame D. clapped her hands. "And now. This summer, the theme of our project is 'If I Were an Animal.'" She went on to explain the plan: First we'd—*they'd* sketch their selected animal, then sculpt it using any kind of creative material they could get their hands on. Like Winnie had mentioned, the summer would end with a showing, and the best projects would be chosen for the Guggenheim.

This kind of project scratched all my creative itches. It was right in my wheelhouse. I imagined the campers scouring the camp for supplies, ripping up old blankets to weave into life-sized teddy bears or stealing deflated inner tubes from the sailing house to construct into a walrus.

I shook my head. No need to soak in wistfulness or jealousy or whatever else I was feeling right now. Maybe I could do the project at home, while I kept Mom company, saving her however much this luxury sadness camp cost, and avoided my friends.

What kind of animal was I? Right now, probably a porcupine. Constructed of rusty skewers.

Winnie raised her hand. "Does our project have to be an animal?"

Madame D.'s expression was stumped. "Beg pardon, Wainwright?"

"For God's sake, you're from Pittsburgh," Winnie mumbled. She cleared her throat and spoke louder. "Can it be a *thing*? Or does it have to be an animal?"

Madame D. considered this. "It should be something alive, yes. You may choose to create something mythically alive, though. A unicorn, a dragon, or a centaur, perhaps. A chimera."

"Great," Winnie said. "My soul lives within Ariana Grande's ponytail. That's the most mythically alive thing I know."

I snorted, then clapped my hand over my mouth. "Well done," I whispered.

Madame D. flushed. "You may not make a project out of a pop star's ponytail."

"Why not?" Winnie asked, affronted. "You just said I can do something alive. I am guilty of idolatry for Ariana Grande's epic, living, breathing ponytail."

"You forget, Wainwright." Madame D. raised one finger. "Hair is dead."

Winnie crossed her arms. "I'll need to research this," she said.

# Chapter Nine

By the time I walked to the Healing Center for group therapy later that afternoon, I was grouchy. The hours I'd spent staring at the ceiling all night had caught up with me, and the idea of group therapy left me feeling twitchy. My sessions with Call-Me-Connie were one thing—everyone had to visit her for some reason or another, like for SATs, schedule planning, or college admissions. But this idea—a group of veritable strangers, waxing on about our various serious life tragedies in a "safe and supportive setting"—left my insides slick. Uncertain. I took my hair down and put it up again at least seventeen times on my walk over, yanking until my wings were mollified.

Inside, I lowered myself onto one of the many beanbags set in a circle, working to calm my flushed cheeks. All campers were assigned to small groups for a "more intimate experience," so the gods of irony must have given themselves a round of fist bumps when Noah showed up with Deese.

When Noah saw me, he grinned. "No leotard? Where's your uniform, Aly Raisman?"

So much for quelling my blush. "How long did it take you to think of that?"

"Oh, I'm quick."

I ignored his lightning grin, distracted by the magnificence of the setting. Despite my exhaustion, I had to admit that the Healing Center was an unexpected spot for therapy. In the movies, these types of meetings were always in a church basement and involved a folding table with a coffee urn, presumably stale cookies, and gray-brown lighting. And unlike Call-Me-Connie's cinder-block corner office, the Healing Center resembled a giant, oversized gazebo, except it was enclosed in shining walls of glass and had a small annex on its back. It had a panoramic view of the lake, where out on the glittering water, a group of campers dove off the docks. I shivered. One lone sailboat wobbled in the distance.

Inside the center, pillars of white fabric spilled from the ceiling, dangling from gleaming metal tracks. I didn't understand their purpose until Jeff came in and drew one of those gauzy pieces of fabric around the beanbag circle as if he were a doctor at the ER. I appreciated the gesture, but I had to imagine the fabric could only dull, but not mute, conversation.

"Hey, there," Jeff said. "You're the only one I haven't met yet. You must be Lila." Up close, I could see I was right: Jeff had so many freckles, he looked like the product of a Seurat painting, where a bunch of multicolored paint dots come together to make an image. I could even see the freckles on his lips. He was a little younger than I'd thought, maybe late thirties, and the gray glint in his red hair was probably premature. He held out his hand and smiled. "Two of my therapy groups are for new campers this year." He lowered his voice. "I've put you in this session with Deese, Noah, Alicia, and sometimes, Carlton Pete—he goes by CP. His grandmother wants him to be around older kids, so he'll float between both."

I pressed my lips together and reached up to shake his hand.

Jeff sat in a padded leather chair at the other end of the beanbag circle. "Okay, guys. First things first. I'll make the tour as brief as possible. Promise." He waved his hand toward the white fabric. "Over by the annex is the Quiet Area. Anytime you need a break, you can hang out there. Twenty-four seven. There's crafty stuff there, like knitting and beading, and doodle pads. Keeping your hands busy is a great way to declutter the brain. Plus, we have therapists on staff if you need a professional ear and I'm not around." Jeff cleared his throat and rubbed the back of his neck again. He had this air about him that said *I'm one of you, but more of a grown-up version.* It was depressing, so I decided to like him.

Jeff continued. "The Tsunami Room is the annex in the back. Don't be alarmed by the padded walls inside. The door doesn't lock—we're not gonna lock you up and throw away the key." He glanced around, seemingly hoping we all got the joke. "Anyway. There are Nerf balls, punching bags, and a bunch of bongo drums inside, for when you feel the urge to kick the crap out of something."

I shifted on the beanbag, filling the room with a sound like jostling Styrofoam peanuts. Throwing some punches and drumming my heart out? *That* was an activity I could get behind.

"On that note . . ." Jeff leaned forward. "Let's start. The way this works is that we pick a topic and talk it out. Helps us strategize the release of our emotions. Problem solve."

"I've never done therapy before," Deese said. "So we're just . . . talking?"

Jeff nodded. "Speaking our truths."

*Truths.* A huff of air left my nose, creating an unexpected snorty sound. I clapped my hand over my face.

"Lila?" Jeff's smile was concerned. "You okay?"

I coughed. "Um. Good. Just happy we're talking truths here, because"—I shrugged—"I don't deal well with liars."

"I hear you," Jeff said. "This kind of therapy helps us learn about ourselves in such a deep, broad way, and the better we know ourselves, the better we figure out how to feel in a variety of situations. But if for some reason—any reason—you're not ready to talk about those truths, or if you're feeling compelled to tell an untruth, I have a camp rule." He held up his hand, mimed tapping a phone. "You say 'snooze button.' And we all agree to respect the snooze. Give the person some time, and they'll likely come around to telling what it is they want to say, on their own terms." He looked around. "Sound okay?"

We all nodded.

Jeff beamed. "Great! I like to open with a guiding question. So, for my new campers: Whose idea was it for you to be here today?"

Silence. Obviously. The room filled with the crunch, crunch, crunch of the beanbags.

"I'm CP Byun, and my nana sent me here," said the small boy, finally breaking the tacit agreement of silence. He used one knuckle to push the bridge of his glasses higher on his nose, and I suddenly remembered that when I'd first seen him in the parking area yesterday, he'd been holding hands with an older woman before he was welcomed by a super-tall kid. "I live with her. 'Cause my mom and my dad both died."

My breath hitched in my throat. CP was by far the youngest person in the room—probably only seven or eight years old. A strange urge to hug him went through me, but I shook it off.

"That's really hard, CP," Jeff said. Then, gentler: "You must really miss them."

CP's face crumpled. He swiped at his nose with the back of his hand, and Jeff offered a series of what he probably thought were comforting phrases while he handed him a tissue. The camp had boxes of these luxuriously thick and velvety tissues everywhere—in the corner of the mess hall, on the desk in the Lodge. Extra-strength. *Three times as absorbent as other leading brands*, I thought, desperate to get out of that room.

The other girl in our group hefted an enormous sigh, and I worried I'd spoken out loud. After a moment, I recognized her from art class. She wasn't in my bungalow, so she must have been a few years younger than me, maybe thirteen or so.

"Alicia? Would you like to go next?"

"Fat frigging chance," she said. She had long, stringy dark brown hair, brown skin, trendy purple glasses, and a wide nose.

Jeff frowned but kept his tone light. "Did your sisters finally convince you to give it a try?"

Alicia shrugged. "Dad's traveling for work. Nowhere else for me to go."

"It doesn't hurt to give camp a chance, you know. You might like it."

Her body was wiry with anger. "Says you."

Jeff met her eyes. "Yeah. Says me."

The only sound in the silence that followed came from more beanbag shifting. Even though her surly attitude mirrored my own, I found myself desperate for some distance from her palpable fury.

Finally, Alicia broke the stalemate. She sighed. "Eat dirt."

"Can't," Jeff said. "Still full from my breakfast of mud." He grinned at her, and then at us to let us in on the joke. "Lila? Deese? Noah?"

I wasn't about to say a word. My eyes strayed to Noah, and to my great surprise, he was staring at me. When our eyes met, he smiled. "My mom sent me here for the fine dining," he said. "I stayed for the firm mattress and the free intramurals."

"Oh?" Jeff asked. His tone was pleasant, but his forehead wrinkled. The picture of concern.

Noah shook his head. "No. Actually, I wanted to come. Can't pass up a good vacation."

Jeff rubbed his chin. "No one should hide behind a mask, Noah."

"No hiding here. What you see is what you get. No animals were harmed in the making of Noah Kitteridge."

Jeff opened his mouth to reply, but Deese raised a hand. His shoulders were so broad he could only reach it up so far, his tree-trunk bicep landing in line with his ear. "I wanted to come here too. I actually found this place myself. Online. Because of my dad. Uh . . ." He faltered, shook his head, and spoke a little faster. "I used to look up to him. He was the athletic director in my town. His teams *won*. Dad was this really funny, kind guy, but he also struggled with alcoholism. He only got treatment once, and left right away, saying he didn't need help to stay sober. He had 'too much to live for,'" Deese said, making air quotes. "He drove the wrong way on the highway after celebrating the basketball team's victory this winter." Deese's shoulders dropped. He surveyed the group for our reactions. "And in his car was the softball coach. Which, by itself, isn't such a big deal, right? School employees celebrating a school win. She was in a coma for two weeks after the accident. When she woke up, she told everyone—friends, family, the news, you name it—that she was having my dad's baby. Right away, we launched from massive grief to being the scandal du jour."

Our group made a collective wince, and even Jeff paused in his response. Light filtered into the room, and dust particles swirled. I broke the stillness by wiggling in my beanbag chair again.

"That's really, really difficult," Jeff said. "Claiming he didn't need treatment is common substance-abuser mindset."

Noah spoke up. "It's not your fault, Deese." His face was serious. He leaned over and clapped his friend on the shoulder, and my heartbeat picked up speed at the gesture.

"I know it's not," Deese said. "But there's just lots of shame involved. My ma blames herself. Wonders why she didn't make him quit driving, just in case." He shook his head. "And just like that, life changed. There I was, a pretty easygoing guy. Lots of friends. Track team. A smokin'-hot girlfriend. Then I spent two weeks acclimating to living life without my idol, learning how to be fatherless, only to wake up one day to discover that not only was my dad dead, but also, surprise! He committed a massive betrayal. And the thought that I'm suddenly no longer an only child, that there's this tiny person who has the same father as me, or had . . ." He trailed off. "After? I lost all but one of my friends. My girlfriend dumped me. And the softball coach harasses my mom all the time. Not just for child support. We've had to call the police a bunch, because she comes to our house and throws lawn tantrums."

"Heavy," Jeff said. He shook his head and leaned forward. "Not fair."

Deese adjusted the brim of his blue hat. "Thanks, but . . . but the past is still there. I've only got another year of high school, so maybe it'll get better soon."

"No one here would judge you for your dad," Alicia said.

Jeff's freckled face split open with pleasure. "Alicia!" he said. "Well put."

Alicia scowled.

He turned to me. "Lila? You're up."

I shook my head and waited out the uncomfortable, naked feeling of an entire room's eyes sliding over me. *Sorry, Call-Me-Connie.* Deese was a lot braver than me.

"Okay," Jeff said. "Next time. Noah? Last chance."

Noah reclined in the beanbag. "Like I said, boss," he drawled. "Color wars, bug juice, and Bonaventure French toast sticks."

Outside, Noah and Deese walked ahead of me toward the boys' bungalows. Before I could lose my nerve, I jogged up and tapped Deese's rock-hard arm.

I kept my focus directly on his kind eyes. "I just wanted to say that you were gutsy in there. I get it. The part about the stigma."

Deese squinted at me. A small smile touched his lips. "Oh yeah? Your dad's a philandering drunk driver too?"

Noah crossed his arms and raised his eyebrows. The picture of skepticism.

"No," I said, pulling my shoulders back and lifting my chin. "But I get what you're saying about everyone judging you for something you didn't even do."

Deese raised his fist. I rapped his knuckles with my own, and he exploded his fingers. "People like us have to explode the pound," he said.

A breeze blew off the lake, whirling my hair around me. I spread my fingers apart, a small starfish birthing between us.

# Chapter Ten

Tuesday: I skipped swimming, went hiking, and did a series of pathetic sprints for "track and field." Almost threw up. Good thing I no longer had any plans to run the Falmouth. Five more days until departure day.

Wednesday: Art, followed by another silent therapy sesh. Very emo. Four more days.

On Thursday (three to go), Sammy wandered over to Winnie and me at breakfast. "Hi, Wainwright," he said. Sammy was the sort of kid who made it obvious he'd be popular in high school. He'd inherited some recessive California-good-looks traits I'd missed out on: skin that tanned instead of freckled or burned in the summer, square white teeth, and shockingly white-blond hair. Sammy was great at sports, and had the confidence of a Hollywood game-show host. For his sixth birthday, he'd asked my parents for a puka-shell necklace.

Winnie gave him an exaggerated nod. "Samuel Cunningham."

"Lila, Mom said I had to come have breakfast with you." Sammy half-hopped onto the bench and took the bagel off of my plate. "Gross. Why do you get the vegetable cream cheese?"

"You talked to Mom? And I like vegetable cream cheese."

He nodded. "Jeff let me call her. I need more underwear." He picked a speck off the bagel and wiped it on a napkin. "There are *chunks*."

"Tasty ones."

"Manufactured cream cheese is not changing the subject of our conversation," Winnie said. "You have to come to the dance tomorrow night, Lila."

"I'm leaving Sunday," I said. "No point."

Sammy wrinkled his nose. "Why do you want to leave so bad?"

"Badly," I corrected. But I paused. The truth was that other than the comforts of my bedroom, which I could picture so clearly in my mind—lilac walls, white down comforter, a canvas splatter painting of Aunt Shelly's in the corner—I didn't have much of a reason to go home. No summer plans with friends. No boyfriend. No Dad.

What I really wanted was for everything to just *stop*. I wanted to stop missing Dad. Stop lying awake and thinking about his last moments on earth. Roll backward into the Lila who generally liked her life and the people in it. The cycle I was in was exhausting: Not sleeping. Thinking of Dad, or being reminded of him in a thousand different ways a million times a day when I was trying *not* to think of him, being pulled under the weight of grief each and every time.

I never knew how much caring could cut me below the skin. Caring seemed like such a good thing, right? But it wasn't. Caring was the gargantuan weeping-willow tree in our backyard that Sammy and I had played beneath as kids. We'd made forts below the branches and stretched out in its shade in the heat of summer. From a distance, it looked like someone had poured melted wax all over it. For a few weeks each fall, it lit itself on sunshine fire, turning a marigold so rich it nearly hurt to look at.

That was *our* tree. It was perfect. Until it tried to kill our house one spring morning. A ton of water flooded the basement, eating away at Christmas decorations that eventually left sprouting mold in our storage boxes. My parents had to get this vacuum that sucked up sludgy water. Eventually, Dad found a series of cracks in the foundation. Even though it was pretty far from the house, the weeping willow's roots had tangled beneath the surface, pushing against our concrete for years—until it won.

That's how caring got to you. While it pressed against your walls, it made you think it was beautiful, until it broke you, flooding your insides with destruction and hurt.

"Samuel," Winnie said, breaking into my thoughts. "Tell your sister to go to the dance Saturday night."

"Lila, go to the dance Saturday night," Sammy said. He picked up my napkin and used it to scrape off the cream cheese. "Hey, Winnie. Are you religious?"

I frowned. "Sammy! You can't ask people if they're religious."

"Half Jewish and half Catholic," Winnie said. "My dad used to call me his little 'cashew.' "

He took a bite of the bagel and cocked his head. "Well, you're the answer to my prayers," Sammy said.

And then I got it. He thought he was *flirting* with her. And I knew where I'd heard those awful jokes before. "Did you seriously bring Dad's joke book to camp?" I asked. "Did you?"

Sammy winked at me. "Do you like raisins?" he asked my bunkmate.

"Hate them."

"How would you feel about a *date*?"

Winnie had a gleam in her eye. "Ohh," she said. "Sam. You are one *cunning ham*." She looked pleased with herself. "Get it?"

I groaned. "You deserve each other," I said, balling up my napkin and throwing it at my brother. "Too bad you'll have to wait another million years till you're legal, Sam-O. At that point, Winnie will be approaching twenty-six."

"No interest in throwing *cradle robber* on my résumé," Winnie said. "What does the O stand for?"

"What O?" I asked.

"The one in *Sam-O.*"

"Just a nickname," Sammy muttered.

I grinned. "The O is random. Because his middle name—"

"Is on a need-to-know basis." Sammy leveled me with a look.

"Easy with the interruptions, Samuel Tennyson Cunningham."

Sammy tossed his hands in the air. "Why are you trying to ruin my game, Lila?"

Winnie laughed. "Even for someone whose given name is Wainwright Flores, that's a strong name . . ." She trailed off. She scanned Mess Hall, and her face lit up. She turned back to me. "I'm sorry."

I frowned. "For . . . ?"

She leaned out of the booth and waved her fingers. "Noah, come here!"

My stomach hardened. *"Winnie."* Out of the corner of my eye, I saw Noah striding across the floor. I sucked in a breath. "What did I ever do to you?"

Noah put down a plate piled high with pancakes, then seated himself across from me. "Ladies," he said in greeting before nodding at my brother. "Sam."

"Tell Lila she should go to the dance," Winnie said.

"You should go to the dance, Lila," Noah said. He leaned forward and pulled a grape off my tray. "With me."

I held my fork in midair. My first thought: *What?* Second: *Why is everyone eating my food today?* Third: *What?*

Winnie leaned toward Noah. "Do I know you from somewhere?" She cocked her head, narrowing her eyes. "Why do you look so familiar?"

"Guess I just have one of those faces," Noah said. "Or maybe you caught *People* magazine's 'Twenty Grieving Hunks Under Twenty' issue?"

I clapped my hand over my mouth to hide my snort. A grin broke over Winnie's face.

"Hey, I'm the man of the family now," Sammy said. "You gotta ask me for permission."

I flicked my hand dismissively. "What am I, your old spinster sister? I don't need your patriarchal permission." I turned to Noah. "Thanks, but no. I'm not going to the dance. Alone, or with anyone."

Noah picked up a pancake and folded it in half before dragging it through a puddle of syrup. "Then who am I supposed to go with?"

I cleared my throat. "Not my problem."

Winnie clapped her hands. "This is turning out to be an amazing breakfast, but none of you are really helping my cause. Lila. Just come."

"You have my"—Sammy eyed me—"*blessing*, Noah," he finished.

"Thanks, dude."

I poked my fingers into Sammy's side. "Go away. Tell Mom we had breakfast."

"Well, we did. I ate your bagel. You did the thing where you rolled your eyes and complained a lot. Just like at home," Sammy said. "This place has a sweet breakfast menu. Hey, Winnie. How do you spell *menu*?"

"*M-E-N-U.*"

"Close. I prefer *Me . . . N-U.*"

Noah groaned. "Where'd you get that from? A listicle of pickup lines?"

Sammy winked. "My dad used to have a joke book. But he lost it." He tapped his head. "Good thing my memory is a sieve."

"No, if you remember stuff, it's not a sieve," I said. "It's—ugh, forget it."

"Just did," Sammy laughed. "At least it's better than yours. Yours is so pen-*sieve*."

I swatted at Sammy again, but he scampered off. When he got back to his table, he gave each of the kids there a high five.

On Friday, I skipped breakfast at Mess Hall in favor of a pair of truly disgusting all-natural granola bars so I could get to art early. The morning's dewy grass left razor-thin strips of condensation on my ankles. No one was in the art room, so once I was inside, I wiped off my ankles with a clean paint rag and set up for the day's task.

During the last session, Madame D. had said that today we'd sketch out ideas for our summer projects. Last summer, I'd stayed up late texting my friends and crafting all kinds of crap. I cut worn T-shirts into beach cover-ups and tote bags (thank you, Pinterest), drew people from the yearbook, used Mom's old watercolors to paint the sunsets we'd watch from my aunt's house down the Cape whenever we went there for dinner. Then I'd sleep until noon.

Life then had held the blessed absence of trauma. It was so hard to imagine doing anything like that anymore. There was such privilege in staying up late and painting without raw, uncontrolled emotion threatening every brushstroke. I stared at the cabinet of supplies in the corner, a gush of hope twisting my hands in my lap. Art had always been such a safe space, and I wondered if safety could still be found there.

I brought a tray of colored pencils, a gray putty eraser, and a stack of creamy linen paper back to my desk. I fingered the edge of one sheet, as thick as five pieces of computer paper. How expensive was this place, anyway? I imagined Jeff fundraising for the Nice Stuff for Half-Orphans Charity. They probably had black-tie pity parties for children of parents like ours.

I doodled on one of the thick pages, drawing cartoonish renditions of animals. Nothing felt right. I gave a giraffe Ariana Grande's ponytail.

How could I recreate this project at home? Dad had some wood scraps in the basement, and we had a bin of clay and paint, old coffee cans, and scraps of yarn down there too.

*Good idea, Little Lyon,* I imagined him saying, and of course that's when it came to me.

The pencils flew across the page: reds, auburns, oranges, and browns. I laid a pencil's point flat, shading in contours. When I had the shape roughed in, I grabbed a packet of oil pastels and smeared the sister colors across the page. Muted tangerine. Rich, peanut-butter brown. I used my thumb to smudge the colors together, blurring the lines.

When I was done, I sat back. I wasn't the world's best sketcher, but I had a decent handle on color and depth. Good, even.

The lion's fur took up the majority of the page, a whorled-together palette of Madame D.'s cocoa-to-mahogany rainbows: taut muscles, regal shoulders, the ghost of a tail.

"Hey, that's pretty good."

At the sound of his voice, I whipped around. My hand grazed

the tip of a pencil, flipping it off the desk. It hit the hardwood floor with a small *tink* and rolled away, picking up speed like a small thundercloud. "Is there some reason why you enjoy sneaking up on me, Noah?"

"I didn't sneak up on you."

"Sure did. First that day with the leotard. And now when I'm alone at art."

"You think it's on purpose? It's not my fault you prance around in weird Nineties Workout Barbie gear and break into the art room before class." Noah dropped into the seat beside me and tapped my paper. "Whoa. I didn't take you for an artist." His body radiated heat. Goose bumps pricked my bare legs.

I shrugged. "I'm not. Not really. I just like doing stuff with my hands."

The eyebrows again. "Noted." He winked. "In all seriousness, my mom draws and paints and stuff. You're good."

*Draws. Paints.* Present tense. "Thanks."

"She has an Etsy shop." He picked up the paper and studied it. "Have you ever done pressed flowers?"

It was my turn to shake my head. "No." *You mean to tell me this boy can talk about pressing flowers?*

This was getting complicated.

While I wiped off my fingers, he launched into his explanation. He spoke with his hands. They were expressive but practiced, like those of a pianist or a masseuse. He used them to shape his mom's artwork: Make a sandwich out of flowers, waxed paper, and paper towels, and cook it with an iron. The more delicate the flower, the better. "Basically, you know in kindergarten, when you bring a fall oak leaf to school and seal it in wax paper? That's what my mom does, but with flowers. Well, for her side gig. She's a doctor."

I could hear the sounds of campers arriving outside. "So you're from New England too?"

"Really? That's your takeaway?" He shifted on the seat, moving a fraction of an inch toward me. I resisted the urge to lean closer to him.

"The autumn-leaves-and-wax-paper thing." I paused. "And, while less so, the doctor mom whose idea of free time is running an online business." Especially while grieving.

His jaw relaxed. "That's my mom. And, bingo—Connecticut."

"Me too." At the look of confusion on his face, I clarified. "I'm from New England, I mean. Not too far from Connecticut. Massachusetts."

"Ah. Yeah. Not far at all." He stood up abruptly and ran his hand through his hair. "Anyway, it looks like your class is starting, and I have a meeting with Jeff. One-on-one." He made a face.

"Oh," I said. My fingers jumped to my throat, feeling for my missing necklace. "So why'd you come in?"

"Saw you through the window."

Heat. It's a funny thing. It flashes through you when you least expect it—bad news, good news, embarrassment, attention from a boy.

His eyebrows knit together. Behind Noah, other campers streamed in. Winnie wove through the desks toward us. She pointed to Noah and did this weirdly suggestive shimmy with her shoulders.

"Right, then," I said. I felt color flood into my cheeks. "Uh, later."

He took a step backward. "Hey, Lila." My name in his mouth was soft and sweet. To counteract the effect it had on me, I pressed my thumb into my thigh as hard as I could and focused on the bruising pressure. He raised his eyebrows. "One season for the rest of your life. Summer or fall?"

Impossible to choose. The warmth of the sun, the buzz of lawn mowers, and the relief of ice cream? Or sweaters, cider, comfortable temperatures, art festivals, and craft markets?

"Fall," I said. "Something about the fresh start of it. What about you?"

"Oh, summer. Every time. No school sounds good to me." He backed up. "Even if you don't come to the dance with me, I still hope I see you there."

I jerked my head down and up. Up and down. My thigh throbbed. "Um. Thanks. Have fun at it, anyway."

"Hello, Noah," Winnie said, practically trilling his name.

He lifted his chin in cool-boy greeting. "Later, Winnie."

Winnie dumped a tote bag on the seat next to me, beaming. "Does this mean you're going? Oh God, did you draw that? How did you do that? What are you wearing to the dance tomorrow?" She pulled out a sheaf of papers with honeycomb diagrams and capital letters. "I brought research on the molecular makeup of a hair follicle—more specifically, on the human growth hormone. My art project will be an actual molecular structure! Madame D. said the project had to be alive. She can't argue that our basic human hormone molecules are dead. Long live Ariana Grande's luscious locks. Pass me that paper. I want to look at the lion."

"Still not going," I said. I crumpled up my lioness likeness in my hand and shoved it into the corner of the desk. "And, no. It's nothing."

# Chapter Eleven

A thunderstorm rolled in Saturday afternoon, rushing over the lake and leaving little lake-baby puddles in its wake. We'd had a morning of free time, which I'd spent walking with Sammy to the Lodge so he could mail his friend Freddy who knew what before I came back to the bungalow to pack for home. My bunkmates buzzed around, pulling out makeup and clothes and sharing one electrical outlet for dozens of pieces of hair-managing equipment.

Outside, droplets chased themselves over the windows and hammered on the roof. It was the perfect background music for me to ignore the getting-ready madness. Instead I was engrossed in the new Angie Thomas, which I'd found tucked into the side pocket of my bag. My mom, ever the reader, had loaded my duffel bag with enough books to last the average teenager an entire year. No wonder it was so heavy.

A sheaf of cloth hit me mid-blink.

"Hey," I said, hooking my index finger into the fabric and pulling it off my face. It took on the vague shape of a cropped doily. "Do you mind?"

"You'd look great in that shirt," Winnie said. "It's one of the twins'."

"Mine," Heather-Emilia said, slipping her feet into her Birkenstocks. "It's made from hemp. Sustainably sourced."

"Oh," I said. "Thanks for the offer. But I'm not going." I tossed it back to Winnie.

"When my cousin hates something but doesn't want to

offend anyone, he says 'I like it, but I don't want it right now,' "
Madison said.

My cheeks reddened. "I don't hate it."

"You shouldn't. Growing hemp on a massive scale might help prevent climate catastrophe before it's too late for all of us." Heather-Emilia held the door to the bungalow open for her sister. "We'll see you at the soiree."

"Besides, we didn't offer it to you, anyway." Emilia-Heather sailed out the door. "Winnie did."

The door slammed behind them. Winnie laughed. "Geez. Double-mint doom, much?"

"Textbook example proving mom deaths are worse," Madison said, peering at her reflection in a tiny square of cloudy mirror tacked to the wall. She plucked at one perfect yellow lock and let it drop back into place, where it bounced and nestled into the rest of her mane like a happy puppy. "Rain ruins my hair."

"Your hair looks exactly the same today as it has all week," I said.

The bungalow door opened. Mari stepped inside. Her long, dark hair was plastered to her face, her baby-blue T-shirt now the color of darkened sky. "Ugh, so gross out. You guys ready? The Healing Center's all decorated." She peeled off her shirt, tossed it in the hamper, and rested her eyes on me, my thumb stuck into the book to mark my page. "Why aren't you getting ready, Lila?"

"I'm skipping," I said.

Mari pressed a towel to her skin. "What? Is everything okay?"

The truth was that the Ghost of Lila Cunningham Past was a person who loved to go to dances. But now, I leaned against the pillows, eager for them to finish up and leave so I could keep reading. "I'd just rather . . ." *Do anything but go to an all-camp dance?* "Read."

Mari bit her lip. "We could go to the Quiet Area, I guess. It won't be that quiet, because of the dance and everything. Or we could maybe go to the Lodge."

*We? Quiet Area? Lodge?*

"Uh . . ." I glanced around. My bunkmates were watching us. "No, I think I'll hang here. I have to pack, too, since my mom picks me up tomorrow."

"Campers aren't really supposed to hang out here alone during all-camp events. You can skip it if it's a grief emergency, but if it is, then I'd need to chaperone you."

My stomach dipped. "So if I don't go, then you can't go either?"

"Right."

Winnie danced around. "You're going to make Mari miss out on a night of dancing with Jeff?"

Mari's cheeks reddened. "Wainwright, I—"

"Oh, *please*. You're like a great American love story for grown-ups finding a second chance."

Mari rolled her eyes, but didn't bother to correct Winnie.

Neither option was favorable. I either:

1. spent the night being babysat by Mari and ruining her chance at happiness, or
2. feigned interest in hanging around with a bunch of people I'd never see again.

I traced the cover of the book. My shoulders stiffened in protest against my camp-issued pillow. The worst part of all of this was that my choices were, once again, not really my own. If I could do anything in the world right now, I would teleport to my bed at home.

Strike that. If I could do anything, I'd find a time machine and go back and tell the Home Depot employee not to sell the rope to my dad.

"Look, Mari. I appreciate all you're saying here, but, really. Can't we break the rule just this once?"

Mari tossed the towel into the hamper. "The *rule* was designed for the campers' benefit. So, no." Her easy, honeyed voice was harder than usual, which hit me like the aural version of taking a bite of a brownie only to find a trail of unmixed butter or flour in your mouth.

"I just don't see the point."

Mari's eyes narrowed. "The point is that you're at a camp meant for healing, not one where you burrow in your bed like a groundhog. Healing is hard. It's uncomfortable."

"Yeah. I'm aware," I said, trying to match the octave of steeliness in her tone. "But no offense, or whatever—why do you get to decide whether or not I lie in my bed and read?"

"I get to decide because I've *done* the healing." Mari's jaw jutted out. "Except that when my sister Amara died, I had no fancy camp like this one. I had pamphlets from her hospital written for siblings of children with incurable cancer. And after I watched Amara spend eight months in a hospital bed set up in what should have been our dining room, so she could have a view of the street outside, you best believe I fought and clawed my *way* to heal."

I imagined Sammy in a tiny bed in our dining room. Resolve slithered from my body, sank into the cracks in the wooden floor. "I'm so sorry, Mari."

She put a hand on her hip. "And? I've watched others *not* do the healing. Like one particular former camper who died way, way too soon. And without her, you wouldn't have the privilege of being here."

The other camper. I'd been so stuck in my own head, I'd never considered what Mari's story could be, and I'd nearly forgotten the camper I'd never meet. Across the room, Madison slammed a makeup lid closed. I cleared my throat. "Winnie, do you still have that shirt?"

"Good choice," Mari said. "I don't care if you're leaving in a minute or an hour or in August. You make the time worth it, you hear?"

I nodded. "I hear."

As soon as Mari left, Madison's shoulders slumped. "Now we have to wait for you to get ready?" She toed the side of my duffel bag with her foot. The rustle of the cookies' cellophane crackled through the room, and my father's Moleskine notebook slid out onto the wide plank floor. My handbook. My fingers clenched.

"Sorry," Madison said, the word coming out somehow innocuous but not quite innocent.

My breath caught in my throat. I jumped down from the bed, but Madison was cheetah quick. She snatched up my handbook and dangled it from her forefinger and her thumb.

My brainwaves turned to static. If she opened it and read my rules, I'd curl up on top of the patterned pot-holder rug and go comatose with sheer embarrassment. "Thanks." I held out my hand, feeling my heart pound in my chest.

She looked at the blank black cover. "What is it?"

"It's private," I said, fighting to keep the waver out of my voice.

Madison ran her finger along the book's spine, and I shivered like she'd done the same to my own. "Is this your diary or something?"

I said nothing, stretching out my palm further.

"Just give it back to her," Winnie said. When Madison didn't move, Winnie made a sound of exasperation. "*Madison*. It's not her fault Cat's not here."

*Cat.* Was she the other camper? I frowned.

Her name seemed to break Madison's spell. She held my handbook out to me without actually handing it over. I had to reach for it, and I did, shaking. "That was my dad's," I said.

Her face colored. "I wasn't going to read it," she muttered.

By the time we got to the Healing Center, which had been transformed for the WELLcome dance, most of the other campers had already arrived.

Mari and the blue-tee team had done a good job. They'd propped open all the giant glass windows, and the resulting breeze floated through the sheer hanging curtains. Strings of Christmas lights soared over the makeshift dance floor and lined tables of snacks.

"Ah, the age-old tradition of jamming a bunch of hormonal teens into a small space ripe with sexpectation, putting on loud music, providing grocery-store snack sustenance, and then turning out the lights and seeing what happens," Winnie said. She shook raindrops out of her hair. "Whatever shall go wrong?"

I smiled. "Sexpectation?"

"Sexpectation: the expectation of sex, or the JV version, which involves applying sexually charged feelings to routine social interactions," Madison said. "Am I close, Winnie?"

Winnie waved her hand like a British aristocrat. "Spot on, darling."

"One of my neighbors went to some theater school in New York a few years ago, and the first week ended with a coming-out dance," I said.

"A coming-out dance?" Madison asked.

"Yeah. Where a bunch of people who'd been closeted their whole lives finally come out. Be themselves."

Madison put one hand on her hip. "And what's wrong with that, exactly?"

"What? Nothing. I think it's great."

Madison relaxed. She nudged Winnie. "Into any particular person these days, my friend?"

Winnie rolled her eyes. "All the people. As always." She glanced at me. Though she tried to appear casual, I could tell something was up, almost as if she was checking to see if I had a reaction to what she was saying. A twist of surprise pinged my stomach, bringing with it a reminder: Even though my parents had always taught me love was love was love, even though we had plenty of family and friends on the queer spectrum, my heterosexuality was steeped in privilege in too many places in this world.

"Trust me," I assured her. "Not that you need my blessing, but I support you."

Winnie's face softened. "You just never know," she said. "People are weird. Last year, one girl accused me of watching her change."

"Who's watching who change?" Deese's voice came from behind me.

"That is some entrance," Winnie said. I reached over and squeezed her hand, and she threw me a grateful look.

"Hey," Noah said to me. "You came."

"It was this or be babysat by Mari all night." I turned to Deese. "Deese, do you know everyone?"

He shook his head. "We should have name tags. They could say our names and why we're here. Like: Deese. Drunk driving, adulterous dad."

Well, that was one way to get in front of it.

Winnie laughed. "Winnie, real name Wainwright. Dad. Car accident."

"Madison, real name Madison. Mom. Overdose."

"Lila. The father, in the woods, with a rope."

For a moment, I thought I imagined the beat of silence. Finally, Winnie brushed my shoulder.

Noah's jaw tightened, then relaxed. "That's really difficult," he said softly.

I nodded. "What about you?" I asked him.

He lifted one shoulder, let it fall. "Asthma's a bitch."

The evening was divided into a before and an after. Before: Girls stayed to the east of the bathrooms while the boys planted themselves at the snack table. There was a punch bowl at the teen table that, true to form, may or may not have been spiked by the middle of the dance—which, in my estimation, led to the after: Everyone started to dance. The little kids, Sammy and his crew of sweaty boys included, took over most of the dance floor until later on, when the teenagers edged them out.

I hung back, munching on a plate of fruit salad and those butterfly-shaped crackers and little slices of cheese while Winnie pulled a reluctant Madison out on the floor for some line dance. The other campers circled them, clapping and calling. Deese jumped in and did the coffee grinder, his bulky arms easily holding his weight. Noah stood beside him with another couple of kids I recognized from their bungalow, laughing. When our eyes met, he made a face as if to say, *Can you believe this guy?* I made one back that tried to convey *I know, right?*

I must have failed with my facial choreography, because a look of confusion crossed his face. He said something to one of his friends and then headed in my direction.

Right when a slow song came on.

"Perfect timing," Noah said, taking my hand and tugging me toward the dance floor.

A smile curved my lips, but my heart plummeted. *Handbook rule number one.* I felt pulled in so many directions, like one of the bendy, sticky, lizard-shaped prizes in the retro gumball machine at the Mug. You could hold its tail in your hand while it stuck to the ceiling.

Some part of me was very, very drawn to some part of him. The ruddy cheeks, the questions, the delight when I found the non-Google-search-engine loophole. The way he *moved.* Graceful but quick, like a tap dancer who doubled as a magician.

And that part of me was petrified. I could barely string two thoughts together when my feelings steered even close to the idea of desire. Because desire led to cloudy judgment, which led to the potential of getting close to someone, which led to the potential of losing someone, which led to an extreme violation of the handbook.

"Impressed by Deese's moves?"

I relaxed. "Incredibly so."

"C'mon. Let's see yours."

"I was good as a kid, but my dance career ended there," I said. He spun a confident arm around me, and I somehow found the armhole he created and ducked my head in.

"Nonsense. You're a natural."

I wrinkled my nose. "I wish. Are you a dancer?"

"Nope, but my lacrosse coach made us take ballet." He blew an exaggerated breath out. "I could not *believe* how difficult it was."

I'd quit ballet before I got ahead, but I was all too familiar with the sensation of my heart pumping, my hair flying, and my calves bathing in lactic acid. I was also mildly out of breath now, at this grief-camp dance, which meant that it was a damn good thing that I was no longer running the Falmouth with my dad.

Noah adjusted his arms, and I was suddenly . . . closer. Much closer. Too close. I pulled back a little, resisting. "So. Friends?" I asked, studying him.

"You're going home tomorrow," he said, zipping around me in some kind of male-dancer twirl. "What do you care?"

"Friends," I said again. I heard the stubbornness in my voice.

Noah grinned. "Don't you think it's a bit presumptuous to assume otherwise?"

Oh. God. I swallowed. "I—"

"Nah, I'm kidding. Friends it is."

In the center of the dance floor, surrounded by pairs of campers swaying to the music, I circled my arms around Noah's neck. "I'm sorry about your dad."

"My dad?"

"You've talked about your mom, so I assumed . . ."

Dappled light passed over his face. He flicked his gaze over my shoulder. "It's my brother."

I closed my eyes. "Oh, Noah." My voice was thick. "I'm sorry."

"I know, I know, I'm the life of the party." Without warning, he spun me around and dipped me. He bent over my body till we were both almost parallel to the floor. "You move well."

Silence slipped between us while I cast frantic lines into my brain to figure out what to say. "Um. You're tall."

Beneath my arms, his muscles tensed. "You're observant. I am tall."

"I'm not, obviously. But I'm not short, either. The last guy I danced with wasn't this tall."

Gently, he eased us both upright. "Do you always babble when you're nervous?"

I tried to relax my shoulders. "Sorry. It's been a while." I paused. Ran my tongue over my teeth. "Well, not that long." Pause. "And I'm not nervous."

"Hmm?"

I didn't answer. My hips found their rhythm, and after a minute or so, my body loosened. I inhaled, breathing in his scent. Something clean, strong, and vaguely piny filled my nose. Below my belly button, my muscles tensed, drawing almost impercep- tibly toward him.

*Down, girl.*

"There we go." Noah reached up, took my hand, and spun me gently before giving me another dip worthy of a reality TV dance show.

Which I very promptly stumbled out of, to my utter embar- rassment. "Whoa," I said. "Fancy."

He shrugged. "It's nothing, really. My parents—" He stopped. "I . . ."

I poked his arm, teasing. "Do *you* always babble when you're nervous?"

He laughed. His eyes were bright and warm, his voice a mur- mur. "Are you flirting with me?"

I opened my mouth to object, but what came out surprised me. "Maybe."

Noah pulled away, catching my elbows in his palms. He stared at me. "I wish things were different."

"What do you mean?"

"I mean, I wish this was your run-of-the-mill summer camp, and I was a guy here for some recreational summer fun, who happened to find the most amazing girl here on the first day."

I swallowed. I didn't know what to say. Any possible response I could have formulated was halted by his reference to *the most amazing girl*. We swayed together for a moment.

"I just didn't expect . . . this."

"We're friends, Noah. Besides, we're all in the same boat." I gestured at the other campers around us.

"Are we?"

"Sure," I said.

Noah tore his gaze away from me. "I don't think so. Some life rafts are meant for one."

He was right. We weren't sailing on the same sea. How could we be? There's a world of difference between your dad killing himself on purpose and your brother dying of an asthma attack. My situation was different. Set apart.

A tap on my shoulder pulled me from my thoughts. I broke away from Noah and saw Mari. "Lila, I'm so sorry to interrupt," she said. "Jeff asked me to walk some of the younger girls back, because it's getting late. Do you mind grabbing some refills? Crackers, cups, and punch. They're in the Quiet Area."

"No problem," I said. "Thanks for the dance, Noah."

"I'll come help."

As the song ended, we threaded our way through the other campers on the dance floor, the long, gauzy curtains fluttering beside us.

At the doorway to the Quiet Area, I stopped. Feeling a bit

silly, I knocked, just in case someone inside was in the middle of some kind of life crisis or something. When I heard no answer, I opened the door and fumbled for the light switch.

The tiny room was lined with neatly organized cartons of finger-busying, mind-numbing crafts. A well-intentioned, perfect kind of inane. *So your dad killed himself, Lila? Here! Knit a key fob.*

Tomorrow I'd be far away from this place.

Inside, I handed Noah a box of crackers, and hefted up a gallon of juice. "To answer your question from before: No. I wasn't flirting with you."

"Okay."

"Okay?"

"Sure." Noah bent down and picked up a plastic bag of cups set beside the door. "These too, right?"

I nodded. "I just . . . I'm not looking for anything right now."

"Right."

"I'm an island."

He laughed. "Got it. Tough to reach, total seclusion, and hot. Perfect description."

*Man.* He really knew how to flirt. "Not that kind of island. I'm the kind that bans people who I'm at risk of . . . really liking," I said, amending my number one handbook rule so he didn't think he was a candidate for *love*, "because people hurt the ones they're close to. *That* kind of island."

Noah stepped closer. "That doesn't sound like an island," he said. "That sounds like more like a castle. With a drawbridge over a moat. And a little troll guarding it with a password." He swung the plastic bag of cups toward me, grazing my leg.

"A castle. Sure." I shifted the gallon of juice to my other hand, reached up, and turned off the switch. The light winked out, highlighting the dance floor down the hallway.

"Lila," Noah whispered.

"Yeah?"

"What's the password?"

The hard pebble of stubbornness I clung to, my life raft in the middle of Noah's moat, dissolved. His face was open and honest. Curious, maybe. Curious in a way I could only describe as *uncomplicated*.

And uncomplicated was compelling. Attractive enough to maybe even break a rule.

A smile lit his face, and he raised his eyebrows.

In response, my brain forgot to tell my body to breathe. So instead I did something I would classify as illogical. I dropped the juice on the floor and stepped forward, closed the space between us in that little Quiet Area, raised my weight up to my toes, and kissed him.

My face went numb, my lips lit on fire, and adrenaline shot into the darkest recesses of my body and out my fingertips, out my hair follicles, out the heels of my feet. His mouth was warm and sweet. He dropped something—the crackers?—and cupped my face with the palm of his hand. One finger laced around my neck. My eyes were closed, but little sparks of light flashed in front of them like bullets. One after the other.

I broke away. "I'm sorry." I stepped back once, then twice, dizzy as I'd ever been, my breath coming in rapid hitches. "I shouldn't have done that."

"Lila, don't—"

But before he could finish, I took off.

# Chapter Twelve

I crashed out of the Quiet Area, knocking my hip against the doorjamb. My brain felt wild and hot, and I started moving too fast. I darted my way through the darkened dance floor, needing, more than anything, to get out of there. Put some distance between me and Noah.

What I wanted to do was go home. Not the home where Mom likely sat right now, overstretched and just left of Zen from her yoga retreat with Aunt Shelly. I wanted to go back to the home I'd grown up in, the one that was full of laughter and a plural number of parents.

What I didn't want to do was give in to the small part of me whispering to hightail it back into the dark of the Quiet Area. With Noah.

Try as I might, I couldn't stop thinking about it. The moment our lips met, the moment I took a proverbial lighter to my handbook, the sloshy, splashing sound the juice made when the jug hit the floor.

The fact that now I'd let Mari down too, and not refilled the juice.

*Stop it*, I told myself. *You'll only get hurt again.*

Outside, the light was too dim. I had to slow down to avoid tripping, which dialed my frustration higher. My legs begged for the release that came from exercise; my heart pounded, and my lungs contracted. I melted right into my old hurdling rhythm: *Right, left, right, inhale. Left, right, left, exhale.*

This, at least, was familiar. It was like coming home.

Before long, my body protested the distance. I slowed to a jog, gasping for breath. The dirt path beside Mess Hall was spongy and puddle-strewn from the afternoon rain, but the clouds in the dark sky had cleared. The moon was a tiny scrap of lemon zest.

*How could I have kissed him?*

In February, Mr. Balboni had taught a unit on the science of love. It was kind of weird: The big excitement of Valentine's Day coincided with permission slips sent home for the "sex and health" portion of the curriculum. Like science was trying too hard.

Josie and Rose sold secret-admirer carnations, delivered to classrooms throughout the day, which felt archaic and horrifying until Mr. Balboni's husband bought him a dozen. We watched *The Notebook* in class. My parents got into it too, I remembered now, jogging along the path. They had a contest for the sappiest love card, and my dad sang old fifties songs and the soundtrack from *Grease* to my mom the entire day.

*Right, left, right, inhale. Left, right, left, exhale.* I leaped over a rock.

As I approached the Lodge to turn down the fork that led to the girls' bungalows, I heard voices. On the Lodge's grassy lawn, where Mom's car had been parked just six days ago, a handful of younger boys circled around two figures, calling out to one another. In the shadows, I could only make out their excited movement, and flashes of light hair.

Blood thumped in my veins. *Sammy.*

My feet moved toward the pack of boys faster than I thought possible. And when I saw a kid about my height push my brother in the chest, something in my body snapped.

I aimed for his nose, but I connected somewhere between his cheek and his mouth. My aim sucked even more than I thought it possibly would.

I blinked, stunned by the swath of pain that zinged through my knuckles and down, arcing toward my wrist. I stared at it, wholly unfamiliar with having a sensation of that magnitude on the top of my hand. It turned out that punching hurt. A lot.

The kid grabbed his cheek and doubled over. "What the hell?"

An icy calm settled over me. I tried to shake out the thrumming in my hand. "Don't touch him."

"Lila!" Sammy's hand, on my arm. "Stop!"

I recoiled. "Stop?"

My brother wasn't a crier, but his eyes were bright with tears. "What'd you do that for?"

With one exception—the moment he'd found out Dad was dead—I'd never seen Sammy so upset. I stepped back. "I'm not going to see my little brother get pushed around."

"He was just teaching me how to block a roundhouse kick. Like *karate*. And *self-defense*."

My body slumped. Another rule for the handbook: *Assess the entire situation before throwing a punch.*

The kid who I'd punched straightened up. It was too dark to see if I'd done any damage, but not too dark for me to determine that even though he was my height, he was closer to Sammy's age. "I'm a brown belt."

I crossed my arms. "If you're a brown belt, then how did I take you by surprise?"

The kid's eyes narrowed.

"Just ignore her, Mike," Sammy said.

"Sammy." I touched his shoulder.

He shook me away and swiped a hand across his eyes. "Stop trying to protect me. I can take care of myself."

I threw my hands in the air. "I made a mistake, okay? I've been dealing with a lot."

*"Don't."* He kicked at the ground. "Dad left me, too, remember?"

My heart crumpled in my chest. "I'm just trying to—"

"Go away, Lila."

And then a heavy hand clamped down on my shoulder. Not hard enough to hurt—just firm enough so I wouldn't try to run away from it. Before I even turned around to meet his eyes, I knew how disappointed he would look.

"Come with me, Lila," Jeff said, his voice such a dead ringer for my father's *you're in trouble* tone that I immediately burst into tears.

# Chapter Thirteen

Jeff's office was much smaller than I'd expected. "Wait here," he said. He deposited a laptop, which he'd presumably carried back from the dance, on his desk. "I'm going to go check on Mike."

I sank into a leather chair. The office had the expected knick-knacks. His diploma, a trophy, and a signed baseball stood on a shelf. In the corner, a paper-thin television was mounted over a tall silver file cabinet. The walls were painted a dark, dark brown, the color of Noah's eyelashes when he'd leaned in to kiss me back. I flushed.

My right hand pulsed, swollen where I'd made contact with poor Mike's face. The skin was red and promised to bruise, but I could wiggle my fingers and bend it okay. I peered at it, remembering my father's knuckles: forever cracked and bleeding. He carried tubes of ointment with him, slathering it on where his skin had dried out and broken.

After a while, Jeff came back in, holding a package of frozen blueberries. He tossed it to me, and I automatically caught it with my right hand. I sucked in air through my teeth.

"Well," Jeff said, raising his eyebrows. "First time hitting someone?"

"Yeah." I covered my sore knuckles with the blueberries, grateful for their cool relief.

"You tuck your thumb?"

I stared at him. "Huh?"

"Like this." He held up his hand, gripping his thumb inside his fist. "You never want to punch like this. You can break your thumb. You didn't, so I imagine it wasn't that hard."

I was silent. He was right. I'd tucked my thumb.

"I better never see you using this again, but . . ." He cleared his throat and rearranged his hand similar to the American Sign Language letter *S*: the thumb wrapped on top of the fingers.

"Why are you showing me this?"

He perched on the corner of his desk. The moment he sat down, the top drawer of the file cabinet rolled open. Grumbling, he leaned over and pushed it back in. "Uneven floors. Such a bear. Anyway, I showed you this because it's my belief that everyone should know how to defend themselves."

Guilt, heavy and liquid, flowed through me. "I'm sorry."

"You'll have to say sorry to Mike."

"I will."

"We don't condone violence here, Lila." His tone was gentle but firm.

"I know. I'm sorry." I pressed my tongue against my bottom teeth. "I thought he was hurting Sammy. I've never done anything like that in my life."

Jeff's face softened. "I realize you were trying to protect your brother." He tapped his desk with his knuckles. "But he wasn't in danger. That's a good group of kids he's running around with."

I nodded, miserable. Tears blurred my vision.

Jeff crossed his arms. "Now, the ugly part. Let's talk consequences."

The guilt turned to stone in my veins. Was he going to call the police?

"Basically, you have two options. Number one, Camp Bonaventure could send you home. There's no refund for the remaining seven weeks of summer, though." He waited a moment for that to settle in. "It's in the contract: no refunds for behavior problems. The second option—the one I'd think would be preferable to all parties—is to stay and complete the last seven weeks of camp."

"You seriously want me to stay? After I . . ." I swallowed. "After I hit someone?"

Jeff leaned back in his seat. "You know the kids in high school who are straight-up smart-asses?"

Following this man's train of thought was like being a spectator at a foreign sporting event. Observer only, with no knowledge of the rules. "Sure?"

"When I was in high school, this kid—one of those smart-asses—got in a fight." Jeff rocked a little bit in his chair. "As a punishment for the fight, the principal made him switch his academics schedule to all honors courses."

"Doesn't sound like much of a punishment."

"Sure it was. Extra homework, harder stuff."

I examined my hand. "Haven't you read any viral social media articles? The kid was probably bored in class, which is why he was a jerk in the first place. He should've been in the AP courses from the start."

"Probably."

"So . . ."

"So that's the genesis of this. Yes, you can choose to stay on to fulfill your punishment for punching a kid four years younger than you. Full eight weeks of camp. Or you can forfeit the money and go home."

*Ouch.*

I wavered. When I'd agreed to stay a week, I'd assumed Mom would be refunded for the last seven weeks. I would give it a good old one-week try, earning me dutiful-child points. She'd be out way less money, earning her less stress. A win-win.

Before I could decide which was the least-evil option, Jeff

spoke again, his tone a bit more kind. "First step, though. No matter what you choose, it's time to call your mom and tell her what happened." He checked his watch. "It's almost eleven. Maybe we should call in the morning?"

The only thing worse than calling her tonight would be waiting up all night with the crickets and my snoring bunkmates, worrying about calling her tomorrow. "No, she'll be up."

I dialed with my good hand, my fingertips damp on the keys. When she answered, a lump formed in my throat.

"Mom?"

"Lila? Is everything okay? I'm just getting some stuff together to come get you tomorrow," Mom said. "What's going on, sweetie?"

I'd never been in real trouble before. So I burst out: "Mom, I'm really, really sorry. I messed up."

"Honey? What? Are you okay? Is Sammy?"

"We're both fine. I sort of . . . punched someone."

"*Lila*. What on earth has gotten into you?" She launched into a lecture about how violence was never okay in our house, and how Aunt Shelly had stepped in to pay for camp as a gift, and how would I explain my irresponsible, out-of-character teenage behavior to my aunt, and what was she going to do with me. She was a writer, she said, and I was the daughter of a writer, so I should know better. Writers used words as fists.

As she spoke, tension unraveled in my shoulders the same way caffeine lifted my fatigue. *Aunt Shelly*. Things were tight for us and probably always would be, but at least Mom wasn't remortgaging our home so Sammy and I could come here.

I suppressed a smile. I hadn't realized how much I missed my mom. As much as she was piling on, every word she spoke somehow gave me solace, made me comfortable with the berating lecture. "I didn't know Aunt Shelly was paying. I feel bad."

"She wasn't, at first. I was. But while we were away this week, she wouldn't take no for an answer. Said it was the only way she knew how to help." Mom sighed. "You really are worried about money, aren't you?"

"I guess so."

"Honey . . . I'm working on it. The life insurance will be enough to get us by until I can figure something out for good. I really don't want you worrying about that, but I understand why you would. But that does *not* excuse your behavior tonight."

"I thought Sammy was in trouble."

She paused. "Was he?"

"Um. No. I made a mistake."

"So Sammy's okay."

"Yes."

Jeff held up his palm, and mimed hanging up the phone.

"I'm sorry, Mom," I said.

I could hear the exasperation in her groan. "You are not supposed to punch people."

"I know," I said. "I'll call you back." I hung up and sat down, resisting the strange urge to slide under Jeff's desk, close my eyes, and go to sleep.

"That was some scolding," he said.

I wrinkled my nose. "She has a handle on guilt vocabulary."

Jeff nodded. "What did you want from camp, Lila? I mean before you got here."

"I didn't want to come to camp."

"Then what did you want?"

Wasn't it clear? I wanted the impossible.

It was easy to miss Dad at the obvious moments. The pocket-square occasions. A color or two for every important day, like the wall of paint swatches at the hardware store. What I hadn't expected was missing him in the daily routine that was life on Whittier Lane. For three straight months after he died, I kept tripping on the stairs, where we left our shoes when we came home, because Dad had always been the one to cart them up to the closets.

His absence left a gaping hole in the calendar of my regular day. He no longer started the game of stepping on the backs of our shoes, giving us a flat tire in the cereal aisle at the grocery store or on our way out the door for school. Mom preset the coffee at night now, so there were no quiet early-morning creaks of wood floor beneath his socked feet.

I wanted the impossible. I wanted to turn back time and save him. Since I couldn't do that, though, I simply wanted to know *why* he did what he did—why I wasn't enough, or why we weren't enough, to keep him around.

I pressed the back of my hand into my eyes. When I pulled my hand away, wet mascara was smeared across my skin. Excellent.

"Nothing," I mumbled.

"Nothing?" He tapped a pen on the desk. "You can't want *nothing*."

"Why not?"

"Because what's the point?"

"There isn't one."

"There isn't one," he repeated. He sat back in his chair and stared at me, waiting.

Finally, I shrugged. "What's that old Nietzsche saying? 'Life sucks, and then you die.' "

His freckled lips grinned. "Nietzsche, huh? 'Cause I'm pretty sure I saw that on an episode of *Daria*. You know, that show from the nineties?"

I hadn't seen it, but I was pretty sure it was on one of the streaming sites. "I was joking."

"I mean," he said, drawing out his words, "would it be so bad to leave here and be a little happier, Lila?"

I tilted my head, considering.

"You a Winnie fan?"

*What?* "Um. Yes? She's a lot nicer than Madison."

He shook his head and pointed at a poster of a honey-eating bear above his desk.

"Oh—Winnie-the-Pooh. Christopher Robin. Piglet. That Winnie. I've read the stories, seen the movies, yeah." *Not since I was what, five?*

"Great." He tapped the pen on his desk again. "See, Lila, the way I look at it is that you have two choices. One is to plod through life like Eeyore, moping through your days and weeks and months. You can be pissed when it's raining, because you'll get wet; you can be pissed when it's sunny, because the light is too bright." He shook his head. "That was almost me."

I was silent. I pictured all the days after my dad died, when I didn't get out of bed until the afternoon. When my mom brought me a little biscotti cookie, because everyone dumped all kinds of food in our house that we didn't know what to do with, and the salted chocolate melted in my mouth and zipped into my blood sugar and I remembered what it was like to enjoy something. When I got out of bed and watched a movie with Sammy, who'd taken to sucking his thumb, cuddled deeply into my side on the couch. When Josie and Rose came over and sat with me on my bed. They didn't say the right things, but at least they came.

I thought of what it felt like to actually laugh for a second with Winnie, or, even briefly, get lost in that kiss with Noah.

He plucked a small red book from his desk and held it up. *The Tao of Pooh*. "This book identifies Pooh's uncomplicated, simple approach to life as being exemplary, but I'm of the mindset that you could carry pieces of the whole ensemble with you. Be young and adventurous like Christopher Robin. Analyze your baggage like Piglet. Be a good friend and do the right thing, like our pal Pooh." He spread his arms wide. "Heck, you can even bounce off the walls here and there, like Tigger."

It sounded good. Great, even. But impossible. I shifted in the chair. "How?" I asked. My voice was so low I practically had to lean in to myself to hear it.

"Well, the first thing you have to do is probably take the second option and stay. Then make use of your time here. Hang out with friends. Take risks. You can even—*gasp!*—use some of the stuff we talk about at group or individual therapy to heal, or discover something hidden about yourself you never knew."

I folded my arms across my chest, cradling my swollen knuckles in the crook of my elbow.

What choice did I really have? The last thing Mom needed was a screw-up of a daughter who couldn't even stay at a summer camp for sad kids, let alone one who'd take all the money her sister had spent on the place and put it through an imaginary shredder.

*Plus, Noah.* The kiss had been such a brilliant departure from my ordinary life. Finally I shook my head and sat back. "Yeah. I'll give it a shot. Not much to lose at this point, is there?"

"Splendid," Jeff said. "Operation Give Camp a Chance is now in session. You head on over to the bungalow and I'll call your mom back." He pulled the bag of blueberries off the desk and tore it open. "Ever have a frozen blueberry?"

"Nope."

He dumped out a palmful for me. I popped one in my mouth. It was cool and tangy, bitter with its own sweetness. "Hey, these are pretty good."

He held up his palm. "Stains," he said, grinning. I couldn't help but grin back. His teeth were spotted blue. Jeff was like someone's gangly, dorky older brother.

By the time I got back to the bungalow, everyone else was asleep. I undressed and slipped under the covers, suddenly weighted down by physical exhaustion flavored with emotional under-tones. I slid my hand beneath my pillow, only to find a crinkled scrap of paper, about the size of a bookmark.

Imprinted with a pressed wax-paper flower.

It looked like something a grandmother would decorate her home with, but even so, I fell asleep quickly, for the first time in what felt like forever, staring at the delicate petals. Smiling.

# Chapter Fourteen

Everyone else seemed to have settled into camp by the beginning of the second week, but it took me a little while longer. On the Fourth of July, I gamely threw myself into activities like archery (I was better than I thought I'd be) and crab soccer (embarrassment central).

When I told everyone I'd be staying for the summer after all, Winnie was one kind of cool, Madison was the other; Emilia-Heather shrugged, and Heather-Emilia blinked and said, "You weren't staying this whole time?" I barely saw Sammy, even when I went by his bungalow to apologize to Mike for punching him. Classic avoidance.

On Monday, Madison knocked over my shower caddy with an accidentally-on-purpose "Oops!" And on the way to archery Tuesday morning, she "let" the bungalow door slam in my face. I recoiled just in time.

"*Madison,*" Winnie warned.

Madison cast a glance my way. "Didn't see you there."

I lifted my chin. "Like my shower caddy yesterday?"

"Right."

"You need to stop, Madison," Winnie said. Her forehead wrinkled in frustration. "This isn't going to make things better."

"You know what?" I said. "You two go ahead. I'm not hungry."

Without another word, Madison walked out. Winnie paused at the entrance. "I know she's awful right now," Winnie said. "She's been through a lot this year."

"More than whatever happened with her mom?"

Winnie nodded. "Oh yeah. I'm worried about her. This isn't like her at all."

"If you say so."

On Tuesday afternoon, I left art feeling both stuck in my own head and hungry. Now that I was here for the summer, I needed to commit to a creative way to sculpt my lion. A couple of the animal projects were already coming together. Someone had painted a bunch of tin cans in black-and-white stripes, stringing them together in what I bet would someday look like a zebra.

I wiggled my fingers. I was limited by my bruised knuckles, though the pain was fading faster than my humiliation. Every time I thought about that night, I walked backward to kissing Noah. And when I thought about *that*, I chewed the inside of my cheek until I tasted blood. What was I *thinking*? I'd spent the entire dance telling Noah I only wanted to be friends, and then I'd all but flipped both middle fingers at that thought.

At the entrance to Mess Hall, I paused. I couldn't tell if the fluttery feeling in my stomach was nerves or hunger. For the last few days, I had successfully managed to avoid Noah. I'd swapped a session of group therapy for a one-on-one with Jeff. I darted in and out of Mess Hall, grabbing what Dad called "hurricane food," because it wouldn't spoil when the power went out: bagels, apples, and sunflower-butter sandwiches.

Now, I entered, breathing in an aroma that was a cross between grilled pizza and maple syrup. Without my permission, my eyes quickly scanned the space, landing almost instantly on Noah. He sat at one of the round tables with Deese, perched on a turned-around chair, his head tipped back with laughter.

Our eyes met. He rose from his chair. My heartbeat rushing through my ears, I collected whatever I could find in front of me (an untoasted baguette, cream cheese, and strawberry jelly—very Parisian) and slipped away before he could weave through the crowd.

In bed that night, tucked beneath a thin flannel sheet, I woke to something tickling my cheek. I clapped my hand over my face and opened my eyes to find Winnie, dressed head to toe in black. Given my supreme insomnia, my first thought was surprise to find that I'd actually been asleep. My second was annoyance. "What is it?"

Winnie opened her mouth, but then she tensed. Behind her, Mari—sleeping in the bungalow for a change—rolled over in her bunk.

"What time is it?" I asked, squinting. Behind Winnie, Madison stood with her arms crossed over her own all-black ensemble.

"Two," Winnie whispered.

"Why did you wake me up?"

"Get dressed."

"Why?"

Winnie checked on Mari, then turned back to me. "Lila, it's Silent Scream."

"What the hell is Silent Scream?"

"Just get dressed. And wear dark colors."

Was this what Jeff meant about giving camp a chance? The corners of my mouth twitched. My stomach roiled with either worry or excitement.

Madison took a step back. "Or don't come. No one's forcing you."

Well, that settled that. I swung my legs over the side of the bunk, sweeping the sheet off my bare thighs. "Have you seen my sandals?"

Outside, Winnie and Madison led the way around the lake. The water lapped gently at the shore. Moonlight licked its glossy surface.

I couldn't help it. "Are we going to get in trouble?"

"You are way too loud. You need to shut up." Madison's exhale was heavy. "Winnie. Why did you insist on bringing her, exactly?"

I stiffened. "I didn't ask to be woken up."

Madison turned to me, her eyes gleaming like the lake's surface. "So go back to sleep."

"Madison. Cut the shit. And Lila, we won't get in trouble if we don't get caught." Winnie put a finger to her lips. "You'll see," she whispered.

We arrived at the gymnastics building, which was tucked neatly into a bank of trees at the far end of the grounds. Below a papered-over window stood a stack of gleaming plastic milk crates. Winnie looked at me. "Ready?"

I froze. *For what?*

Madison stepped in front of us and climbed on top of the crates, and Winnie reached up and rapped on the pane twice quickly, then a third time after a passing beat.

"You have a secret *knock?*"

Winnie raised a brow. "Of course."

Someone inside pushed the window up. A pang of anticipation pulsed in my chest.

"Let's go," Madison whispered.

One by one, we hefted ourselves through the window. I went last, nearly tumbling to the floor, but Winnie steadied me just in time. Inside, the only light came from the moon, which filtered in through windows too high to be covered. Before long, my eyes adjusted to my surroundings. We stood in what looked to have been an elementary school gym, covered in all kinds of equipment. On one side of us was a trampoline, and on the other was a large, slightly elevated fabric floor, blue in the moonlight. Lining the back wall, a series of cones formed a long hallway that ended in . . . was that a gymnastics vault? I watched as a shadowy figure ran down the marked path, launched himself onto—yep—a vault, and disappeared into some kind of splashless swimming pool.

"Foam pit," Winnie said under her breath.

A few dozen kids tore around the place. The scene reminded me of the birthday parties I'd gone to as a kid at the local gymnastics center, except for one thing: It was quiet. Silent, even, the kind of silence that left electricity in the air—the feeling of doing something against the rules. I shifted my weight back and forth, an excited tingle blooming in my core.

"Silent Scream," Madison breathed. "I'm going to the trampolines."

"Can someone please tell me what Silent Scream is?" I whispered.

Winnie spread her hands wide. "It's an oxymoron that has become a tradition to shake out the heavy existential psychology of going to a camp for a bunch of grieving kids." She paused. "Really, it's a name for the occasion for us to stay quiet so we don't get caught breaking in to the gymnastics building, even when we feel like screaming with delight."

The hush lent the room a dual undercurrent of something both eerie and exciting. I took in every part of it: The blur of other campers running by, doing cartwheels and round-offs. The kids bouncing up, up, up on the trampolines, landing on their butts, and flipping over, somehow squealing without making a sound.

"Here," Winnie said, breaking my reverie. She produced a water bottle. In the dim light, I couldn't tell what was in it, but the liquid was not clear.

I went to parties at home, but after one unfortunate incident involving a pack of cards, Josie's citrus-flavored rum, and the entire next day spent with my head dangling in the toilet, I wasn't the world's biggest drinker.

I wavered. The difference between then and now was that now, I had knowledge that there might be some sort of ancestral link that predisposed me to have addictive tendencies. But before, I'd never felt that burning need or compulsion to imbibe time and time again.

I took a sip and gagged on the white-hot burn of alcohol in my esophagus. "Are you trying to kill me with this?"

"Gatorade and vodka." Winnie held out her hand. "Share."

My eyes watered. I shook my head to clear my vision and handed it back to her, relieved.

"Too strong?" She took a sip and exhaled through her teeth. "Oh, wow. Yes. Let's go slow with this one." She took my hand. "Ready?"

It was impossible not to be caught up in the excitement of it all. Running through the dark. Feeling the power in my legs as I jumped on the trampoline, high, higher, highest; racing to the vault to launch myself into the foam pit. We patted our hands with crumbling white chalk and shared a handful of controlled sips from the adulterated water bottle. When I'd had enough, I did cartwheels until I fell over, dizzy with quiet, gasping laughter. After a while, although everyone was drinking, things got even quieter.

And darker.

It was the first time I'd felt anything akin to freedom since my dad died. Sweating, I took another running dive off the vault. I sailed through the air, a warm glow spiraling in my throat and the wind whisking through my hair, and landed with a light, fluffy bounce in the soft belly of the foam pit.

Who needed swimming pools? Not me.

"Nice one, Lila." From Winnie. She'd taken a turn lifeguarding, making sure no one jumped on anyone else.

I closed my eyes. Luckily, the dozen or so sips of alcohol I'd had didn't make the room spin. My face ached, though. I moved my cheeks around to figure out why, and then it occurred to me.

Like the legs of a sorely out-of-practice runner, the muscles that supported my cheeks hurt from smiling.

And then something soft hit my face. My eyes flew open just in time to see another piece of foam ping off my forehead.

"Hey!" I whisper-called, craning my neck to find out who it was, though a small part of me had already guessed.

"Good form," Noah said softly. "I'd give it an eight out of ten."

"I'd like to see you do better."

In the foam pit, we had no solid ground to stand on. Movement became lurching and awkward. Yet Noah somehow rolled over to where I reclined, staring at the ceiling.

"Hi," he said. Above us, a camper launched himself off the vault, soaring over our heads. When I squinted, I could just make out

Deese's outline, arms splayed like an Olympic diver. He whooped at an impressively low decibel.

"*That's* an eight," I said.

"Deese? Pure seven. Too big of a splash."

I laughed under my breath, but shut up the moment Noah's leg brushed my own. The gesture was tentative. Questioning. My breath caught in my chest. When I made no move to back away, his leg settled—no, sidled—alongside my own.

He tipped his foot to mine. "Rumor has it you have a spectacular right hook," he murmured.

I shrugged. "I'm just a protective big sister."

"Sammy's lucky to have you."

The warmth in my throat dipped lower then. I mimicked his earlier movement and clinked his foot with my own. "Thanks."

"So you're staying?"

"It appears that way. I'm piloting a new program of Jeff's called Operation Give Camp a Chance."

"Good thing you have some new friends to keep you company."

My breath hitched. "Right. Friends."

Noah shifted to face me, and the foam that supported my weight betrayed me. My body tumbled toward his. We were nose to nose, and I was hyperaware of all of it. All of him. His body, his breathing. My Gatorade breath, my staticky hair, and his muscular leg sandwiched between my own.

Thankfully, Noah moved his mouth. Unthankfully, he moved it to my ear. "You have a funny way of showing your friendship, Lila," he said. His breath skated over my cheek. The vee between my legs hovered over his shorts-clad thigh. My brain fuzzed, my heart clattered, and my breath joined Team Traitor.

"Noah," I began. But at that moment, a shriek pierced the silence of Silent Scream.

# Chapter Fifteen

At the sound, everyone in the gym took a collective breath. The only movement was Deese, who had been mid-jump off the vault. His body continued its trajectory, even though his limbs flailed in panic at the interruption of the scream. For one horrible, horrible moment, my mind went to his father's car accident—the helpless feeling of becoming an out-of-control projectile. The feeling tasted sour and tangy in my throat.

I lifted my gaze and locked in on the halo of Winnie's hair, backlit in the dimness. "Shit," she said, the second loudest sound I'd heard all night. She heaved herself up and ran toward the trampoline.

"We'd better—" Noah started, but I clambered over him and followed Winnie. Another, steadier interruption filled the room: sobs.

When I got to the trampoline, I winced. A slice of moonlight illuminated Madison, who was clutching her ankle. With each heave of tears, the trampoline quivered.

Winnie took charge. "Out," she said, pointing at the crowd of gawking campers. "All of you."

Deese shook his head. "We'll go get help."

Winnie held up her hand. "Nope," she said. "Not worth the risk." Her eyes flickered around, settling on me. "Especially you, Lila. You're already in trouble."

Madison's face was pale. "My dad's gonna kill me."

Noah walked to the edge of the trampoline. "I broke my ankle last year," he said. "Lacrosse."

"You think it's broken?" Her eyes welled up again.

He squinted at it and leaned close to her, without touching, before stepping back. "No idea."

Winnie swore. "What the hell should we do?"

Noah tapped his hands against his thigh. "Deese and I could carry her?"

"Jeff can bring her to the Lodge on the golf cart. We'll go get him," volunteered the typically surly Emilia-Heather. She grabbed her sister's hand, and they slipped away toward the windows.

Winnie put her hand on my shoulder. "Lila, *go*."

I owed Madison nothing. She'd been varying shades of icy and unwelcoming to me my entire time here, but . . . Winnie was a good judge of character, and Madison was Winnie's friend. There had to be something redeeming about Madison. "No," I said. "I'm not leaving."

Winnie threw her hands up in the air. "Fine. If you'd like to get kicked out of camp, then by all means, be my guest. But first make sure there are no bottles or cups lying around."

She pulled something out of her pocket and tossed it to me. Automatically, I palmed it. Gum. I pulled out a piece and folded it into my mouth before passing it to Noah. The gum's minted fruitiness exploded in my mouth, seeped into my taste buds.

Outside Jeff's office, a fireplace, a group of leather chairs, and a mahogany bench sat beneath a large painting of pine trees. Madison slumped on the bench, and Winnie and I had taken the chairs.

"Madison, your dad is not happy. And I am so wildly disappointed," Jeff said, wringing his hands. He'd tried to get Madison to stay in the gym, but she'd insisted on waiting for the paramedics in the Lodge. Jeff's hair was ruffled from the open-air golf cart ride back to it.

"You were a camper here," Winnie muttered. "Didn't you go to Silent Scream?"

"It doesn't matter what I did, and I don't care that it's a tradition. Everyone does stuff they regret." Jeff exhaled, staring up at the ceiling. "Clearly, it's not safe. And now an injury. *Harrumph.*"

Okay, so he didn't actually say *harrumph*, but it was the sound he made. I sat quietly, mostly thinking this would have been unequivocally worse had he known we had been drinking.

"Your families trust me to keep you safe," he muttered. "How can I do that if you're someplace you're not supposed to be?"

The air solidified in my chest. Sometimes people weren't safe where they *were* supposed to be. Like Dakota Frothingham, the murdered girl with the state-park name, from the news story back when my family was still a couch party of four, braving a winter storm together. Like my neighbor, whose grandson was paralyzed after his mom reversed her car over him in the driveway. Or Noah's brother, suddenly breathless during some everyday activity—soccer practice? A run after school? Sometimes, being exactly where you were supposed to be, doing exactly what you were supposed to do, still brought people to this camp. "Disasters can happen anywhere," I blurted.

Jeff set his jaw. "Sure they can. But using all that equipment in the dark, unsupervised, is inviting tragedy." He gestured at Madison's ankle. "Case in point." Cue another round of pacing. He raked a hand through his hair. "You know what? I'm going to write up this incident report. After that, Winnie and Lila, you two will call your moms. Right now, the three of you stay here in the lobby until the paramedics get here." He slammed the door to his office.

For one long moment, no one spoke, but then Winnie cracked up, Madison snorted, and laughter bubbled from my chest.

It felt weirdly good, actually, to have someone yell at me. I hadn't realized what a lack of parenting I'd gone through since I'd been half orphaned, and even more since I'd arrived at Camp Bonaventure. After a while, I leaned back and closed my eyes.

"You didn't have to do that, you know," Madison said, breaking the silence. "Wait for me like that."

My eyes snapped open. I shrugged.

"Why did you?"

"Because it was the right thing to do."

She shifted in her seat and clenched her jaw in pain. "Yeah, but still. I've been horrible to you." When I opened my mouth to respond, nothing came out, so she continued. "I owe you an apology. It has nothing to do with you, actually. It was really unfair of me."

"What?"

Madison grimaced and steeled herself. "Before you came here, someone else was in your place. Cathriona, but we called her Cat. We were new the same year, and we clicked right away. Her mom had died too. A suicide. Which, well, you know how bad that can mess you up." She paused, checking for Jeff.

My rolling gut agreed. I nodded.

"After her first summer here, we were really close. Like, miss-your-friend-all-year, pen-pal close. We texted all the time and even met up over the winter." She peeked at her ankle and winced. Tears spilled out of her eyes, trickling down her porcelain cheeks and skimming the edges of her mouth. "She was the first person I met who knew what it was like to not have a mom. I don't know about anywhere else, but in our tight Georgia suburb . . . the other moms in my neighborhood planned playdates, came on field trips, and made supper every night." She drew in a shaky breath. "After Mom died, my dad decided to pay our elderly neighbor to do my hair in the mornings before school, instead of, you know, learning how to do it himself."

I thought of Mom—making us breakfast in the mornings with her hair falling out of its sloppy ponytail, spraying my own unruly hair with conditioning spray and combing out the tangles, shepherding my class to the obstacle course on Field Day. I'd been able to depend on her without even thinking about it for my entire life. "I know what you mean," I said.

Madison nodded. "So Cat . . . it sounds silly, but she made me feel so much less alone. This camp in general does, but she *really* did." Madison paused. "But then last summer, Cat was different. She'd become the scary kind of skinny?" Her voice ended in the uptick people get when they turn statements into questions. "And she had all these scars and scabs on her legs from cutting."

I'd read Call-Me-Connie's warning-signs pamphlets. I was surprised to find tears pooling in the corners of my eyes. Winnie reached over and rubbed Madison's shoulder, and I nodded again.

"Cat had binge/purge anorexia. Which we didn't figure out until halfway through the summer, when we caught her puking up s'mores in the Com after a campfire. I told Jeff, and he got her help for a while, but then she went home. Jeff fought and fought to help her there, too, conferencing with her dad and telling him she needed more. More resources, more therapy. I guess they were treating her for bulimia, but not anorexia, which is more deadly." Madison held up her hand. "She was so impulsive and reckless and so, so sick. If it gets bad enough, goes on long enough, it leads to a bad heart."

"A heart attack?" I guessed.

Madison opened her mouth to answer, but her face crumpled.

Winnie sighed. "It just happened this spring. They know it was a heart attack, but they don't know if it was caused by the eating disorder or—surprise plot twist!—the drugs she'd started doing. She overdosed, and during it, she had a heart attack. Which is pretty striking, right? Two for one."

I pictured her. The girl who'd once had my bunk. Wasting away, needing help and maybe getting it but maybe rejecting it, or perhaps not getting the right kind. "That's awful," I whispered.

Madison nodded and swiped the back of her hand across her eyes. "Yeah. And the last time I talked to her, I basically . . . I . . ." She squeezed her eyes shut. Her face was puffy and splotchy from crying. When she spoke, it was in a rush. "I told her I was tired of being her therapist. I mean, she'd changed so much—she went from someone I could talk to about my period and boys or mindless reality TV or whatever to someone who was stormy all the time. She whined about how awful her life was and how it would never get better. All. The. Time." She straightened up in the chair, defensive. "So I kind of snapped on her. My mom was dead too, and you didn't see me puking my guts out or doing drugs or anything. I just got fed up and told her I couldn't help her, and now I feel so guilty . . ." Here her voice wavered. She covered her face with her hands.

After letting her have a few moments to herself, I reached over and tentatively rubbed her back. "It's okay," I said. "Now, you really need to stop crying. Your perfect face looks weird with red eyes. It would be like if the Mona Lisa was frowning or something. Or if some movie star had a giant zit on his forehead."

She gave me a watery smile. "Thanks."

I sucked my top lip into my mouth and released it. "You're grieving all over again."

"Exactly."

Another person with more than one bad thing that had happened to them. It seemed like that grief lightning handbook rule was right after all. I stared at my fingernails, trying to work up the courage to ask my bunkmates how to fix me. "How do you get over it?" I whispered.

Winnie and Madison exchanged a glance. "Even though it feels mountain-shaped, I don't know that it's something you can get over, exactly," Winnie said. "Sometimes you're going up. Sometimes you're going down. Eventually you figure out that there are tunnels and that maybe you're on one mountain of many, but no matter what kind of hiking boots or backpack you get, you're still climbing a fucking mountain."

Madison nodded. "It's not something you get over; it's something you wade through. It just becomes one of your memories."

"Which bubbles at a pretty low burn for me," Winnie added. "A daily simmer. Like, while I feel like every day is pretty much the same without my dad . . ."

"I get really upset on anniversaries. My mom's birthday, death day, holidays," Madison finished.

"I can't concentrate." I traced the edge of my shorts. "I think about my dad constantly. I can't sleep. My whole life took this massive turn without me asking for it. I didn't get to say goodbye. To use your metaphor"—here I gestured to Winnie—"one second I had a mountain guide, and the next he'd just . . . evaporated. And I don't even know *why*."

"You don't know why he did it?" Madison asked, her voice gentler than I'd ever heard it.

"No. And I'm positive it would help."

Winnie leaned forward. "Your mom won't tell you? Or does she not know either?"

"She knows. She said she's waiting to tell me when the time is right."

"She's snooze-buttoning you," Winnie said.

I sat up. "Wow. She *is* snooze-buttoning me." And by agreeing to give her grace, I'd subscribed to respecting the snooze.

Winnie squinted, thinking. She waved us closer. We both leaned toward her, Madison yelping in pain when she shifted.

"Who filled out your application?" Winnie's voice was as quiet as it had been earlier that night, in the darkened gym.

"My application?"

"To get into camp."

"My mom." I remembered her waving it around in our yellow kitchen the day Call-Me-Connie's information train left the station.

"He's got to have the files in his office," Madison said to Winnie, catching on.

Winnie's eyes gleamed. "On it, there's a 'reason for attending' section. What if your mom . . ."

"Wrote down why," I whispered back. That was it.

Jeff poked his head in. "Paramedics are here."

Two uniformed guys wheeled a stretcher inside the office. Winnie and I stood up. "Madison? Thanks for telling me about Cat."

As the paramedics loaded her onto the stretcher, Madison's face went pale with pain. "Sorry I've been so awful, Lila."

"It's okay," I said. "If you want to talk about boys or reality TV when you come back, I'm here."

Winnie tipped her head onto my shoulder. "Time to call our moms," she said.

I patted her hair. "And after that, I think I have a plan."

Back in the bungalow, my ego was thoroughly bruised from another one of Mom's scoldings. I lifted the cookies as carefully as possible to avoid crunching the wrapper while I pulled out Dad's Moleskine notebook. I snagged a pen from the clipboard on Mari's bed, opened up the thick pages of my handbook, and wrote:

6. Sometimes, people can surprise you in a good way.

# Chapter Sixteen

Swimming. So far, I'd managed to avoid it, along with its wealthy stepsister sailing, with the following list of excuses provided to Mari:

Mind if I sit out today? I have a headache.

Sorry, I have a one-on-one with Jeff.

I have my period. What? Yeah . . . still. No, I get really
long ones.

I get seasick.

I didn't bring a bathing suit.

When I was four, my parents left baby Sammy with a sitter and took me out on Aunt Shelly's old boyfriend's boat. I remembered the day so clearly—we'd left out of Marina Bay in Quincy, the city next to our little town. It had all these shops and restaurants and stuff, and people sat out on their boats and grilled burgers, drank beer, and played music. Aunt Shelly's boyfriend had a little girl about my age. She had the cool Barbie car my parents wouldn't buy me.

When it was time to go, we had to take a wide step from the boat to the dock. My mom went first, and then my dad picked me up. I buried my face in his shirt, smelling sunscreen, sweat, and the charcoal smoke from the grill. "I got you, Little Lyon," he said. He stepped toward the dock just as the boat rocked away from it, leaving a gap we promptly fell into.

That fall—which by the laws of physics or what have you should have been a second long—seemed like twenty minutes. Since losing my dad, I've learned life keeps going on—it's part of my third rule, after all. But sometimes it feels like time really does slow down at pivotal moments, almost to the point of reversing, and then speeds up to catch up to everyone else's timeline. It's the only explanation I have for the few times I've had that feeling in my life, like when the police came to the door and said, *Is this the home of David Cunningham?*

The cold water ate every kernel of heat from my body. Dad and I just kept . . . sinking. I thrashed in his arms, but he clung to me. Water—salty and bilious—climbed inside my sinuses and trickled into my throat.

But then, before I knew it, we surfaced. In between hitching sobs, I heaved gushes of cold water, bits of half-digested hot dog rolls.

"You pulled me down, Daddy," I'd said.

He'd explained something like: *No, Lyon, we just continued our fall. Together we weighed more than apart.* He'd needed to wait for our plummet's trajectory to slow before swimming upward.

Ironic that all these years later, his absence was like that clinging weight, pulling me down without any clear timeline for me to come back up and break the surface.

After that, no matter how many times my parents tried to get me into swimming lessons, I refused. Mom tried pizza, ice cream, sleepovers, toy bribes. Nothing worked. (Last year, she wrote an article about bribing that went viral—the bad kind of viral. She got slammed for her "parenting style" by a bunch of ballsy internet sanctimommies and was mopey afterward for weeks.)

By the beginning of my third week at Camp Bonaventure, though, I'd run out of excuses. And, consequently, an appetite, evidenced by the full plate of scrambled eggs, bacon, and toast cooling in front of me at Mess Hall. "I don't get it," I said to Madison. "Won't you sink, with the boot brace?"

At the hospital, the doctors had confirmed Noah's diagnosis: Madison's ankle had a small fracture. But Madison, using some powerful combination of acting skills, likely some pestering, and probably a pity card or two—they knew she was from grief camp, after all—had coaxed the ER doctor into only giving her a boot instead of a cast.

Our days-old truce was still a bit awkward. I understood Madison's standoffishness more now, but it didn't erase the belittling she'd done before our talk. "It's an Aircast boot," she said, drawing out the name. "It weighs almost nothing, but I can't submerge it fully, anyway. I'm supposed to wear it to walk for six to eight weeks, but I should be able to dunk without it by the end of camp."

Winnie volleyed her eyes between us. She'd been skeptical of our newfound friendship, as if waiting for one of us to turn on the other. "I don't get you two," she said, shaking her head. "But I like it." She tapped her shoulder to indicate my bathing-suit straps. "So you're finally in for swimming, huh?"

*Not at all.* "Finally in."

"Aren't you glad I found that bathing suit in your cubby?"

Madison sniffed. "I thought you said you didn't have a bathing suit."

I sighed. "Thought I didn't. My mom must've thrown this monokini in my bag, though." *Traitor.*

"Oh, nice. I like those. They stay on when you do flips off the dock, too."

"Can't wait," I muttered.

With that, Madison leaned over and pulled a strip of bacon off my plate. "Lila . . . any chance you feel like updating us on this plan of yours?"

With all the commotion, I'd kept my idea to myself. I plucked it from her hands and took a bite. "I do." I swallowed. "I'm going to break in to Jeff's office and read my application on the night of the bonfire."

They stared at me, waiting. I forked a bite-sized portion of eggs onto my toast and lifted it to my mouth, but Winnie reached over and lowered my arm. "Um. Come again?"

"You heard me. I'm going to break in and read my app," I said, trying to sound breezier than I felt. In reality, the concept made my internal organs wither. "I don't see how else I can get this information. I scoured Dad's office at home, and my mom is still silent." I mimed zipping my mouth shut.

Madison squeezed the bridge of her nose. "We're really doing this?"

I blinked. "This is not a *we*. It's a *me*."

"Oh, girl," Winnie said, her tone dripping with sadness. "When are you gonna learn?"

"Never?" I smiled. Out of the corner of my eye, I caught sight of Sammy's familiar towhead. "Hey, I'll be right back."

I carried my plate up to the bin. Across from it stood Sammy, holding a bowl with a few stray remnants of soggy cereal. Lucky Charms.

"Aunt Shelly would have a heart attack if she saw you eating that," I said.

He glanced up, startled. Sammy was tanned all over, like a

little golden-retriever-puppy summer child. He frowned. "What's it to you?"

He was still upset about the Mike incident. I placed my plate inside the plastic bin and held up my palms. "Nothing. You're free to eat whatever you'd like."

He furrowed his brow. "Don't tell Mom."

I smiled and poked his side, a weak spot in our lifetime of tickle wars. "Your secret's safe with me."

His mouth curved into a smile, and the clouds left his eyes. "Hey," he protested, but stopped. "Lila?" He stared at the strap peeking from under the collar of my T-shirt. "That's not . . . is that your . . . *bathing suit*?"

I nodded, my mouth grim.

"You don't swim."

"No, I don't."

Sammy wavered back and forth, as if he didn't want to miss me drowning but was still angry with me for punching his friend. "Good luck," he said. He stuck his hand out between us for me to shake. "It's been real."

I gripped it, gave him one hard shake, and then ruffled his hair. Feeling a little bit lighter, I wound my way back to Winnie and the hobbling Madison. If I was going to drown, at least I'd die with Sammy's forgiveness.

The day was cool and cloudy, one of those New England July days that would either break into glorious sunshine or result in a torrential downpour later this afternoon. I prayed for the latter the entire way to the lake, but even with Madison's slow pace on crutches, we arrived in what felt like record time.

"Mind if I leave my towel here with your stuff?" Madison asked. She tilted her head toward the dock. "I'm going to go lounge and wait for a passing boater to sweep me off my feet."

"Foot," Winnie corrected.

I squinted toward the dock. A handful of campers were busy with the sailboats tied to it, and others sat on its edge, dangling their feet in the water. And there was Noah, leaning against a pole and laughing at something Deese was saying.

*Great.* I plucked at the strap of my bathing suit.

Winnie stripped off her T-shirt and shorts and threw them on top of our towels. "Lila? You going in clothed?"

"Just a little cold. When does the lesson start?"

"The lesson?" Winnie frowned. "What lesson?"

"The swimming lesson," I said, the volume of my words trailing away. Around us, pairs and trios of campers arrived, dumping their stuff in small piles on the sand.

"Today isn't *lessons*, Lila. It's just free swim."

I tried to say *Oh*, but the noise that came out of my throat was more like a garbled "Ungh."

Winnie cocked her head, studying me. "What's the matter?"

An invisible vacuum suctioned my insides, and beads of sweat dampened my hairline and my upper lip. "I don't feel good."

"Why not? You barely ate breakfast. Are you sick?"

"No," I said. *Crap.* "Yes?"

To distract myself, I watched Madison make her way down the dock toward Deese and Noah. In response to something she said, Deese grinned, handed Noah her crutches, picked Madison up, and stepped onto one of the docked boats as if he did that sort of thing every day. She circled her arms around his neck and tilted her head back in laughter.

*Hmm.*

Frowning, Winnie put one hand on her hip. She rocked a great bathing suit, one of those high-waisted retro ones with thick halter straps and polka dots. "No breakfast," she said, holding up her other hand to count off her rationale with accusatory fingers, "and I've never seen you in your bathing suit. Do you have something going on?" She wiggled a third finger, then dropped her hand, her face taking on a look of alarm. "Wait, you don't have one of those disorders like Cathriona, do you? Anorexia? Bulimia? That exercise one I can never remember the name of? Do we need to get you help?" She smiled encouragingly at me, then gestured to herself. "Bodies can be healthy in every size, you know."

"No!" I said. I wiped the sweat off my face. "It's. Uh." *Now or never, Lila.* "I can't swim."

"You can't swim." Threaded into her voice was the sort of incredulity that accompanies questions like *You've never had chocolate?* or *You don't own a cell phone?*

"Nope."

"I don't get it. How can you live on the coast and not know how to swim?"

I raised my shoulders. "Bad experience. I fell in when I was a kid." *Down, down.* "Plus, it's not like everyone knows how to swim."

Winnie chewed her lower lip and then brightened. "I'll teach you!"

"You?"

"Relax. I learned when I was like six months old or something, at my parents' country club."

Country club. "Is everyone here mega-rich, except for me?"

139

"Mega-rich, no. Rule number one about the mega-rich: You don't know they're rich when you meet them. This is equally true for old-money people. It's the nouveau riche and the people who don't have enough money who flaunt it."

"Where do you learn this stuff?"

"Finishing school." Winnie winked. "So, what do you say?"

I groaned. *Operation Give Camp a Chance.* "Okay. On one condition."

"What is it?"

"We start tomorrow."

For the next few days, Winnie made my lack of swimming skills her pet project. Jeff gave us permission to skip art (to my dismay) and use all our free time toward this useless endeavor. (He more than gave permission, in fact—he winked and said, "You're a give-camp-a-chance champ, Lila!" Groan.) Our lessons went like this:

Winnie: Let's start by getting our feet wet, shall we?

Me: Did you say "shell we"? Is that some beach pun?

Winnie: No. It's a bitch pun. At least dip your toe in, Lila.
    Nothing in here will kill you.

Me: Are you serious? Are there snakes or something? Is
    some kind of eel or reptile going to bite me?

Winnie: Didn't you lose a parent? There's always something that can bite you. At least put your palm in the water. You take showers, don't you?

Me: *[incoherent grumble]* LEOTARD.

Winnie: Splash, Lila!

Winnie: Okay, today you're going to try blowing bubbles.

Me: Is it better than blowing—

Winnie: LILA! Focus.

Me: Kidding. Wouldn't know, anyway.

Winnie: Think you're ready to go underwater?

Me: No. I don't want to get water up my nose.

Winnie: Don't be the dipshit who pinches her nose.

Me: I don't get it. How do you not get water up your nose if you go underwater?

Winnie: *[demonstrating]*

Me: Hey, are Deese and Madison sitting together again?

Winnie: Lila. Focus. But yes.

# Chapter Seventeen

On the night of the bonfire, Jeff picked the three of us up in the golf cart, a perk of being friends with the girl with a broken ankle. The breeze was crisp and thin, the kind of air you couldn't help but inhale. The golf cart clattered over the rocks by the lake, making talking difficult.

"Your mom coming up for Visiting Day next weekend, Lila?" Jeff shouted. Halfway through the season, Camp Bonaventure hosted a parent (usually, singular) visit day. I'd tried putting it out of my mind, but I was really looking forward to it. I missed Mom.

"Yeah," I said, pulling a sweatshirt over my head. She'd sent Sammy a long, effusive letter last week with a one-liner for me at the end. *Tell Lila I'll see her on Visiting Day.* I guess that's what you get when all of your communication with your living parent is in the form of chastising phone calls.

"Winnie, yours?"

"Yup."

"Madison? Your dad?"

"Wouldn't miss it." Like me, Madison had anticipated the cooler evening, except she had on what looked like a men's button-down shirt with linen shorts. Very summer chic, like something out of a Madewell catalog. "Hey, Jeff, the whole camp goes to the bonfire, right?"

"Whole camp!" he shouted. "Why?"

"Just trying to estimate how many s'mores will be consumed," Madison called. She angled her body to mine and widened her eyes.

Winnie tugged the strings on my sweatshirt. "Whole camp," she breathed. "You know that means—"

Anticipation curled in my rib cage. "I know what it means," I whispered back.

It meant no one would be in the Lodge.

It meant Jeff's office would be empty.

Before long, Jeff pulled up on the lawn in front of the fateful gymnastics building from Silent Scream. Five or six small fire pits dotted the grass, circled by wooden benches and flat rocks. Someone had hooked up a radio, and all the songs of summer I hadn't known I was missing became the soundtrack to our evening.

I spotted Sammy sitting with a group of kids his age, including Mike (whose face had healed entirely since I'd punched him). Sammy caught sight of me and, instead of waving, lifted his chin in that cool-boy nod the boys my age gave each other in the hallway at school. My throat tightened. I'd never seen him make that gesture before. I smiled and raised my hand in a wave as we made our way to the fire pit closest to the lake.

"Are you guys sure about this?" I asked, my eyes downcast on the sand.

Madison sat down, lowering her crutches beside her. "We're sure."

"Are you?" Winnie asked.

"No," I confessed. "But also yes." I placed a blanket down on top of a rock and helped prop Madison's leg up on it, then I sank down on the bench.

"We're in it together, no matter what you decide," Winnie said, and my chest filled with the good kind of warmth at her words. I was officially part of a group of people who knew how to take ownership of something.

The sun dipped low on the horizon, the sky darkening in slow fractions. The counselors passed out supplies for s'mores, and campers trickled around the lawn, visiting the neighboring fires. Madison tossed me a wrapped chocolate bar.

"Godiva?" I asked, unable to keep the incredulity out of my voice. I touched the heavy gold foil with my fingertip. "This camp uses Godiva for *s'mores* chocolate?"

"Huh?" Winnie said. "It's chocolate."

"What's wrong with Godiva?" Madison asked, frowning. "My dad invests with them."

"Nothing is wrong with Godiva. It just seems like a waste." I shifted on the wooden bench. I was imagining the rest of my night: my mouth, still sticky with graham crackers and bougie chocolate, while I rotted away in a jail cell, booked for felony breaking and entering. Was it still a felony if you didn't steal anything physical? "I mean, whatever happened to good old Hershey's?"

Just when I wanted to melt into the cracks between the boards and disappear, I was saved by a visitor. "Rich widowed parents must have confidence that their half-orphaned children are developing fine epicurean palates," Deese said. He sprawled next to Madison, who straightened her shoulders and got very blushy and adorable. "It's the American way."

Tremendous sense of timing. "Apparently so."

Deese twisted around on the rock. "Yo, Noah! There's a seat over here. And bountiful piles of expensive chocolate, along with discount brands of marshmallows and graham crackers."

*Noah.* The familiar butterflies stirred in my chest, and I squinted into the darkness. The fires were moons in the night air, highlighting the groups of campers and leaving everyone else in inky darkness.

"Speaking of chocolate, I was obsessed with *Charlie and the Chocolate Factory* when I was a kid," I said. *Speaking of chocolate? Smooth, Lila.* "The Roald Dahl book, the movies . . . I made my dad buy dozens of those candy bars to try and get a golden ticket. You'd win a trip or free chocolate or something, but in my mind, I'd find one and go to Willy Wonka's factory itself, just like in the story."

"I remember that," Noah said, settling next to me. He smiled. Bright white, perfectly spaced teeth, those ruddy cheeks a deeper hue than usual, perhaps from the cool air, the hot fire, or both.

To cover my nerves, I picked up one of the wooden skewers and willed all my concentration onto the art of spearing a marshmallow.

"It's all about strategy," Noah said.

"Strategy?"

"The perfect roast."

"Easy, mansplainer. I've roasted a marshmallow before, you know." My dad used to plunge the marshmallow into the fire, flash-crisping the marshmallow's puffy exterior. My mom preferred the slow burn, and Sammy and I did too: circling the marshmallow on its sharpened stick until the outside was a toasted light caramel, the inside perfectly, evenly melted. I tilted the marshmallow into the fire, hovering it about a foot away from the flames.

I wanted to snap a picture of it: the fire, our feet in front of it, even the empty Godiva wrappers. Without my phone, some of these moments didn't feel quite real. This feeling—that unless

145

I recorded it, it would not be my memory to keep—was its own special brand of sadness.

"Anyone up for a game?" Madison asked.

Winnie sandwiched graham crackers over her marshmallow, pulling it off the skewer. "What, like Truth or Dare?"

Madison shook her head. "Two Truths and a Lie."

"I've heard of it, but I've never played." Deese handed her a magazine-worthy s'more.

"It's easy. We all go around and say three things," Madison said. "Two of them have to be true, and one has to be a lie. Mix up the order, and we guess which one's the lie."

*Lie.* Even the word dropped a heavy pit into my stomach, falling like a stone next to my worry about turning into a criminal. "I'll watch."

"Me too," Noah said. He flipped his baseball hat, a black one with some kind of Classic Teenager sports logo embroidered on the side, from backward to forward.

Madison crossed her arms. "C'mon!"

"I'm in," Winnie said. "Don't be boring."

Noah glanced sideways at me. "I will if Lila does."

"Fine," I said, relenting. "So, what—favorite food, song, or whatever?"

Madison wrinkled her nose. "No, make it more fun than that."

"You go first, then," Winnie said. "And no cheating. Don't say things we already know."

Madison tilted her head to the side. Something about her was rehearsed, though—I could tell she was pausing for effect, instead of for the purposes of combing her brain's memory files. "Okay. One: When I was nine, I wrote a letter to a talk show host with a show idea, and they wrote back to me. Two: My great-great-great-grandparents drank some of the first Coca-Cola ever invented. And three: I have two uvulas."

Deese stared at her. "Two uvulas," he repeated, an expression of awe coming over his face.

Winnie threw up her hands in mock disgust. "It's not like two vaginas," she said. "Calm down. It's the dangly thing in the back of your throat."

"And you're telling me it's not sexual?"

Madison laughed. "Two uvulas is not sexual. Is that your guess?"

"Definitely."

"Anybody else?"

"Two is the lie," Winnie said.

The double-uvula thing was too weirdly specific. "Agreed."

Noah shrugged. "I suck at this, so I'll go with them."

"Correct. They drank some of the second batch, though, not the first. Deese, you lost, so why don't you go?"

"Not until you show me your two uvulas. Uvuli?"

"Uvulas," I confirmed. "And what's this about a talk show letter?"

"I suggested they have a kids' talent show. I'm mortified when I think about it." She turned to Deese and opened her mouth.

Deese peered in and shivered. "Okay, that's just weird. Here goes. One: I'm a sucker for horror movies. Two: I wore cowboy boots every day for three years. And last: I've never had beer before."

A mystified silence hung like a curtain around our campfire.

"One?"

"One. No, three."

"Two," I said.

"Final answer?" Deese asked.

I nodded.

"Bingo," he said.

Madison laughed. "Seriously? You've never had beer before? I thought that one was a fake-out. I know you're gluten-free, but they make GF beer. My uncle drinks it."

He nodded. "Yeah, but it's expensive. And most people at parties aren't drinking it."

"So what do you drink?" I asked.

He tipped his hat. "Wine, vodka. Pick your poison."

"You must be the life of the party," Winnie said.

"Not particularly," he said, shrugging. He nodded in my direction. "Your turn."

My stomach filled with dread. "I thought I could do this, but I don't know if I can," I said. "I really, really, really hate lying. I never do it. Not under any circumstance."

"*Never?*" Noah teased, nudging my shoulder. "Not even to tell your friends at home that you're too tired to go out? Not to tell your teacher that you left your homework at home?"

I frowned. *Gross.* "No. I tell them I don't want to go out. And I do all my homework."

"It's just a game," Madison said. "We know you're lying, which makes the lie not really a lie. It's a purposeful fib. A fake-out."

"Plus, the follow-up is immediate," Winnie said.

They had a point.

"Okay. I give in," I said. "First, my front teeth are fake." Got the lie over with. Mine weren't, but a kid in my elementary school had had fake teeth. He'd run into a goalpost on the first day of fourth grade. Then came my truths. "Second, I had surgery on my ankle in fifth grade, and part of it is plastic. And for my third, a couple months after my dad died, I quit hurdling."

"Odd but common, medically specific, emotionally specific," Madison said. "I vote one being your lie."

Winnie nodded. "Good logic. I agree." The boys did too.

I scowled. "I'm that basic?"

"An open book," Winnie said. "I'll go. One, I still sleep with my baby blanket. Two, I believe sexuality is a choice. And three, I was supposed to be a twin, but I sort of absorbed them into myself. I had a stomachache when I was eight, and they did an X-ray and found teeth in my abdomen."

Silence.

"Well," I said.

Noah laughed. "What the hell?"

Deese's jaw hung open. He closed it. "You ate your twin?"

Madison said, "Two's the lie. You're bisexual and you've been spouting the opposite of that statement for years. Too easy."

I held up my hand. "I mean, two's obviously the lie. But, more importantly, you had a vanishing twin?"

Noah turned to me. "That's a real *thing*?"

"Sure," I said. Biology class, just this past year. "It's when someone's pregnant with twins, and pretty early on, one of them stops developing. It's usually a chromosomal issue. Anyway, the mom can miscarry one and keep the other, or sometimes the tissue is absorbed—usually by the mom." I glanced at Winnie. "Or by the remaining twin."

"Gross," Madison said.

I shrugged. "There was this case where a mom had three sons. She needed a kidney transplant, so all her sons volunteered to be donors. But when they were tested?" I leaned forward.

"Two of them weren't even her biological sons. Even though she conceived them herself. Her eggs were made up of her unknown vanished twin sister's DNA." I looked around. "Pretty wild, right?"

Winnie beamed. "Exactly! Noah, your turn."

Noah twisted his mouth. "I'm boring."

"No skipping," Madison said.

"All right, fine. I've never done drugs. My favorite food in the world is my mom's spritz cookies. She makes them at Christmas, and they're buttery and sugary and I once ate two dozen of them. And . . ." He perked up. "I skipped a grade!"

Deese popped a graham-cracker-less s'more in his mouth. "Too perky on the last one, bro," he said around a mouthful of marshmallow and chocolate.

"And too detailed on the second one," Madison said, frowning. "You do drugs?"

Noah shook his head. "Wait! No. I messed up. I forgot to lie."

I laughed. "Seriously? You completely failed the game."

"Oh," Noah said. He wore a mildly surprised expression.

I studied his face. "What?"

"You have a great laugh."

Pleasure thrummed in my body, flooding from my core outward. I reached upward and lifted the baseball hat from his head, then fit it over my own.

Noah's lips parted. His eyes softened at their edges. "Hey," he murmured.

"Hi," I said back, but I shifted my gaze to Winnie and Madison. Because here was the thing. My handbook had a set of rules that I'd committed to living by, but there was a huge hurdle—the biggest one I'd ever try to jump, I imagined—blocking me from knowing how to commit to the rules. I was in an emotional tug-of-war that pulled outward like a spiderweb: Grief. Friendship.

Desire. Trying to move on without leaving my dad behind. Everything spun together in the question-mark-shaped center.

No matter what the answer was, it wouldn't change what
had happened, but it could maybe give me the drive to move on.
That information was *mine*, or at least my mom's, and who was
she to decide when I was ready to know it or not?

I was ready.

"Girls?" I said. "Anyone want to go to the bathroom with me?"

"Why do you always go as a group?" Deese moaned. "I'll
never solve this."

# Chapter Eighteen

Though the Lodge was technically an open hangout spot, everyone at camp was at the bonfire, so it was dark. Inside the lobby, the leather chairs cast tall shadows against the wall; the mahogany bench where Madison had sprawled just last week glinted in the low light.

"Last chance," I said. My mouth was as dry as it had ever been. "Are you sure you want to do this?"

"I age out at the end of this summer," Winnie said. "College-bound. Jeff's not going to kick me out."

"And I've only been in trouble this one time," Madison said, tapping her Aircast with her crutch. "Besides, I won't even be inside. I will be on watch, so long as I don't succumb to drowning by sweat from hauling over here with these." She glared at her crutches. "My armpits are on fire."

"Getaway drivers still get in trouble," I muttered.

"Do you want to?" Winnie twirled her purple streak around her finger.

I gazed at the darkened room. "Want to? No. But I need answers, and I'm tired of not getting them." I tugged Noah's baseball cap more firmly onto my head. "Remember, Madison. If you see *anyone* coming—"

"I drop Winnie's water bottle, and if it's Jeff or Mari, I tell them my brace is irritating my skin and I need some ointment," Madison said. Her words had more conviction than I felt.

I turned to Winnie. "And you?"

Winnie's nod was solemn. "Flores reporting for duty." She

crossed the rest of the lobby area in three strides, just barely skirting the round glass entryway table. "Let's get this done."

Jeff's office door was unlocked. "Open-door policy," Winnie whispered, leaning against the heavy wooden door. The creak was impossibly loud in the darkness, and we both flinched. I reached over and laced my hand in hers. Inside, the computer's screen saver lit the space with a dull, brackish light. Together we edged in, sliding on the pine floor to avoid making more noise, before we stopped. The dryness had spread from my mouth to my throat.

"What next?" Winnie whispered.

"I don't know."

"You don't *know*?"

"I'm not exactly a professional burglar, Winnie!"

She gripped my hand with a truly stunning level of strength. "Okay. Fine. Let's think." Her breathing was quick. "His computer is clearly password-protected—"

And a massive personal violation. "I don't want to even think about that. That's private," I said.

"All this information is private."

"My application can't be private. It's *my* info. I'm not looking for case notes or anything like that. Nothing . . . patient-y." I didn't need Jeff's professional observations about the handbook-sized suit of armor I'd constructed around myself to avoid stumbling on potential trauma trip wires.

"Well, no duh. Plus, that stuff has to be locked up by law." Winnie pointed to the file cabinet. "But that has to be where all the paperwork is kept."

I let go of Winnie's hand and made my way over to the cabinet. It was four drawers tall. I crouched, my knees cracking in protest, and squinted at the labels in the dim light.

NOTES

My eyes climbed to the drawer above it.

SESSION NOTES

Too sensitive. I rose, my thighs straining in tired protest. Next drawer.

GROUP THEMES/ACTIVITIES

My eyes flicked upward to the final drawer.

APPLICATIONS

"Hurry," Winnie urged.

I cleared my throat. "Here," I said.

"There are keyholes on each drawer. They must be locked."

A roaring sound rushed in my ears. I unstuck my tongue from the roof of my mouth and tugged on the top drawer, marked *Applications*. It opened about two inches before it halted with an audible hitch. "Shit," I breathed. I pulled again, and it stopped with a bang. "It's broken."

"We need to get back," Winnie urged. "We don't have much— Lila, what are you doing?"

"Go ahead, if you want," I said. I remembered sitting in one of the chairs in front of Jeff's desk, catching a bag of frozen blueberries after my reckless right hook, while he placed his weight on the corner of his desk. *Uneven floors*, he'd said, his weight knocking the top drawer of this very same file cabinet flying open, just so.

I sat.

The floorboards groaned.

And sure enough, as I was positive it would: The top drawer flew open.

"What the goddamn hellfire kind of magic did you just *do*?" Winnie's words were a jumbled hiss.

"The powers of observation," I said, triumphant. I heaved myself off the desk and rose to my tiptoes.

The applications were filed in manila envelopes, organized in alphabetical order. I flipped through the *A* and *B* files quickly, navigating to CUNNINGHAM. In the folder were two applications— mine and Sammy's. I plucked mine from the file and turned toward Jeff's desk to read it in the glow of the computer light. My heart hurtled up into my esophagus.

I inhaled, held my breath, and exhaled slowly while I scanned the basic details. They were what you'd see at a pediatrician's office or on a job application. Name, birth date, address, email, allergies, the answers all penned in my mother's neat, careful script.

My heartbeat blipped. Seeing it made me miss her.

I flipped the paper over, pinching the staple at the top.

# Reason for Enrollment

And below that, in Mom's beautiful hand:

*My kids lost their dad to suicide in*

*March. It was very unexpected for them,*

*and our whole family is in a state of*

*grief. They could really use the time*

*this summer to heal, and learn that his*

*hurt and pain was very separate from*

*how much he loved them. Because his*

*struggle was invisible, it's really hard for*

*me to convey to them that he was in a*

*place where his judgment was clouded.*

My fingers clenched the paper, the pressure wrinkling it. This was it? This wasn't the reason. It didn't tell me why. It didn't tell me anything, other than a reminder of what a tunnel of sadness my father must have been in. A crushing wave of emotion—disappointment, I knew immediately, perhaps peppered with rage and a sense of unfairness—coursed through me. My heart rate returned to normal; my breathing deepened; sweat flooded my face.

"Looks like we're not stealing anything after all," I said.

Winnie put her hand on my shoulder. "Nothing?" she asked, her voice soft.

"Nothing." I turned back to the file cabinet, ignoring the tears that leaked out the edges of my eyes. I slipped my application back into the CUNNINGHAM folder, and paused. "You interested in yours, Winnie?"

Winnie snorted. "My world is an open book, Cunningham."

I gave the folder one last push into the stack before I went to close the drawer, but as the files shifted, I paused, because one particular name leaped out at me.

KITTERIDGE

Noah's file gaped open, much thicker and heavier than the other ones here. Even more strange: His last name, in Jeff's blocky letters, was affixed to a label, unlike mine, which was written right on the folder. A cursory glance at the rest of the files had told me that the other names were also written right on the folder.

I frowned. KITTERIDGE was filed incorrectly—out of alphabetical order, behind the Lagharis' folder. I reached for the folder, tracing the manila edge, and stopped myself from opening it. It was a massive violation, one I wouldn't be able to take back. Too private. I drummed my fingertips against my thumb. *But*, a small, ugly urge wheedled, *how much could one simple look hurt?*

My hand shook as I reached for it. My fingers made contact with the thick manila edges. I pinched it between my thumb and forefinger, and—

*Thud.*

The sound made both Winnie and me jump.

"Lila." Fear rang in Winnie's whisper. "The water bottle."

I whirled around, shutting the file cabinet and swearing in the same millisecond. We froze, listening.

"Mari, over here," Madison said.

"You scared me!" Mari's voice. "What are you doing?"

"My brace is itchy. I was hoping you guys had some kind of cream or something?"

"Oh, yuck. That sucks. I remember using a pencil to scratch under a cast when I broke my wrist. And, sure, it's in Jeff's office."

We heard the sound of Madison's crutches clink against the floor. "In the office?" she said, her voice climbing several octaves.

Winnie and I stared at each other. Her face tensed. "What do we do?"

"Under the desk," I managed. We piled beneath it as the footsteps and crutches drew closer. This time, Winnie grabbed my hands. Both of hers were sweaty, but so were mine. I ducked my head against my knees and we waited, barely breathing, for the sound of the metal doorknob turning.

It came. The light turned on. Pinpricks tingled in my hands. Winnie trembled next to me, and I squeezed harder.

"Can I get it for you?" Madison asked.

"Don't be silly. There's a kit right here," Mari said. I wasn't sure where *right here* was, but the sound of rummaging filled the room. My fingers slid in Winnie's.

"Got it!" Mari said, cheerfully.

"Awesome. Would you mind, um, walking me back to the bungalow? I'd rather put it on there," Madison said.

"Cool beans," Mari said.

I lifted my head and met Winnie's eyes. *Cool beans?* I mouthed.

The sound of the door closing was like a pressure release valve. A gush of dissipating tension rolled through me, and my body gave an involuntary shiver of relief.

We waited until it was dark; we waited until it was quiet. We waited one more minute, and then I let go of Winnie's hands. "Ready to go back?" I whispered.

"Cool beans," she said.

# Chapter Nineteen

"I one hundred percent do not believe you," Madison said the next day. "Spit."

We each flipped down cards. I pushed the two of hearts toward the middle of the pile. "Are you saying you think I'm . . ." I lowered my voice. "You think I'm lying about being a virgin?"

Another afternoon, another New England thunderstorm. My hair wings stuck out from my head like spiral pasta, the humidity staking its claim on my scalp. We concentrated on the three-way piles in front of us for a moment, landing cards where we could with a soft flick.

Due to the rain, campers had been granted a reprieve from swimming (hallelujah) in favor of watching *To All the Boys I've Loved Before* in the gym—until the power went out. Under a giant umbrella, we made our way back to the bungalow with a pack of cards and the promise of takeout pizza for dinner. We'd been sprawled on the rug for the last forty-five minutes, trying to remember how to play card games from when we were little. I lay on my stomach, snacking on pretzels and hummus (because apparently luxury grief camps don't toss bags of chips to their campers to placate them), but Madison's comment made me sit up.

Madison shook her head. She had her foot elevated on a stack of thin pillows embroidered with the Camp Bonaventure logo. "You have that whole confidence thing going on. Like you don't care what people think of you. I bet guys are into it."

Winnie collected a pair of cards from her piles and tossed them to the side. "Definitely. Guys are definitely into it. One guy in particular."

*Noah.* I thought of his large file yesterday, the last name carefully spelled on the white label. I still couldn't believe we hadn't gotten caught. I'd been skating carefully on an icy mix of guilt and rationale ever since we'd gotten back to the bungalow the night before.

Breaking in to Jeff's office? Wrong.

But all that angst, and it hadn't even given me what I wanted. I reclined sideways onto my elbow and propped my head on my palm. "Well, I don't know about guys being into me, but I do know that no guys have been *in* me," I said, thrilled when Winnie gave me an appreciative snort. "And I don't lie, so you should one hundred and fifty percent believe me." I checked my cards. "I can't go. You guys?"

"I'm teasing you," Madison said. She tossed a card down. "Relax."

"I am relaxed. I am the picture of relaxation." I rearranged my piles of cards on the rug in front of me and yawned. "I'm not against sex. As long as it's, you know, consensual and protected and what have you—babies and STDs aren't exactly something I want to lasso myself to right about now. It just hasn't worked itself out yet." I told them about my last-summer boyfriend, and how I'd almost had sex with him—*thisclose, really*—but at the last second backed out. But when I got back in the house, buzzing from the high of our date, I'd been mortified to see that what I'd thought was the sexy kind of vaginal wetness was, actually, my period. I'd dodged the bullet of mortification with that one.

"That happened to a girl in my high school," Madison said. "Everyone called her Red Sue after that."

Winnie frowned. "That's awful."

"It is," Madison agreed.

"What about you two, then?" I bit into a pretzel.

160

"Pure, unadulterated virgin," Madison drawled, pointing to her chest. "My doctor said the pill was one of the options to help prevent my ovaries from going rogue and growing more cysts, and my dad completely overreacted. He's so strict I practically have to court gents in our parlor."

I coughed on the pretzel. "You have a parlor?"

Madison nodded, tucking a strand of hair behind her hair. She reached over, grabbed a pretzel, and dipped it in hummus. "Anyone new with you, Win?"

Winnie flushed. "Let me guess. You want to know what sex is like with girls."

Madison threw her cards at Winnie, making a noise on the same decibel level as a squeal. "*Girls*, plural? Wainwright! We tell each other everything!"

"I had sex with precisely one girl," Winnie said. "Who I'm still sort of seeing, by the way. We're pen pals." She grinned. "I almost hooked up with another, but I backed out. Wasn't into it."

"Better or worse than with a guy?"

Winnie tilted her head, considering. "Hmm. Same." She tossed her cards to the side.

"A woman of many words," I said, at the same time Madison shouted, "How can it be the same?"

"Well, it's not like it's the same feeling. I mean, for one, boobs. Different body parts and different feelings and sensations."

Madison raised her eyebrows and picked up more cards.

"But," Winnie continued, after a pointed look at Madison, "it's just sort of the same, you know? Girl wants to be sexually satisfied. Girl is sexually satisfied by the sexual experience of the person, not by Sir Penis or Lady Vagina."

An oddly distinct image of genitalia dressed up as high royalty flitted across my mind. I laughed. "I can get behind that."

"Fair point," Madison said. "Why'd you back out with the second girl?"

Winnie shrugged. "We were in her room, and she was all 'Don't tell anyone at school,' and I was all 'That's a turnoff.' Which it was. Because why would I go around telling people about it? So I pulled away, and she started babbling about how her parents couldn't ever know she was into girls."

"How did you react?" I asked.

"I told her she was lucky to have two parents, and then I left."

Madison's eyes danced. "You did not."

"You've got to look out for yourself," I said.

"After a football game last fall, I made out with one of the seniors at a party," Madison said. "He told me not to tell anyone, so I told him he was an asshole. And he was—he had a girlfriend, which I learned on Monday when I saw them making out by their lockers."

I leaned forward. "No way."

"Way."

"So what'd you do?"

Madison pretended to check her nails. "I sent her an anonymous email that her boyfriend's tendency to bite his kissing partner's lower lip was dangerous."

Winnie rolled onto her back and laughed. "You. Are. Awful."

"What? She deserved to know that her boyfriend was an asshole."

"She dump him?" I asked.

"Nope."

"Ugh," Winnie said. "My biggest problem? The second I get with a guy, he's like, 'You like girls—let's have a threesome.' But if I'm with a girl, she's either talking about becoming a Pride activist or buying a metaphorical padlock for her proverbial closet." She mimed turning a key in a lock, then tossing it behind her. "Plight of a conservative-state resident. I'm over here, just one bisexual girl with dad issues and no political agenda, coming right up."

We laughed. It felt so good, like an echo of the life I used to know, to sit and talk about something that wasn't a loss. I hefted a sigh, remembering my promise to Jeff. *Take risks.*

"Okay, real talk," I said. "Remember the WELLcome dance? The reason I left the dance so abruptly was because I kissed Noah."

"You *what*?" Madison threw her cards down and cupped her hands around her mouth. "Game over. Speak."

"Slow clap," Winnie said, miming from her perch on the floor. "Details. Now."

I told them everything, down to the gallon of juice in my hands. Winnie only interrupted once: "So *that's* why you keep avoiding Noah." And Madison, twice: "How much tongue, exactly?" and "Oh, his brother? That's awful."

"So then, what are you waiting for?" Winnie asked when I finished. "I mean, you're into each other, right?"

What was I waiting for? A time machine. A preventative salve for pain of the heart. "I—I don't know," I said. "It's too soon."

"Too soon?" Madison asked. "Did you have a bad breakup or something?"

"No. It's just that everything with my dad was just a few months ago, okay?"

They were quiet then, because they knew what I knew.

The card games, the banter, the snacks, and the sex talk. That evening, after the storm quieted but its heaviness still clung to the air, I couldn't help but compare my afternoon to every one I'd spent with Josie and Rose, dissecting sex stuff. Positions. People. It was different with them, though, because we knew all the same people, and we also knew what the others had worn to eighth-grade graduation. Ever since my father's death, there had been this Great Divide, an impenetrable wall between us.

But not here. Not with Winnie and Madison. With them, I could just *be*. Every conversation didn't come with a pallbearer. Instead we were just three teenage girls, talking about sex and love over snacks, brought together by something—death—that by definition had happened to someone else, the aftereffects of which we were left to learn how to live with.

I rolled off my bunk, thinking there was maybe some kind of rule I could draft about relating to others in the same stage of life. When I pulled out the notebook, its edge caught on the zipper of my duffel bag. It flipped open, landing with the back cover exposed, revealing something I'd never noticed before.

A pocket.

With the curled edge of a piece of paper protruding from it.

My heart drummed in my chest. The paper took some prying to remove. The pocket was incredibly tight, almost flush to the back cover. Easy to miss. Apparently.

Finally, the paper slid loose. I unfolded it, working hard to steady my trembling hand so I could make out what was on the page. Phrases were scrawled in my father's slanted, microscopic writing, so different from my mother's and yet equally as recognizable.

*Bot. line = what public picks, not nec. winner.*

The word *underdog* written in all caps and circled.

The explanation wasn't exactly paint-by-number clear.

Frowning, I scanned the paper for the full-color truth. Row after row of shorthand detailing deceit that pinned my heart to the floor.

*Date. Bookmaker. Sport. Team/Player. Type of Bet.*

*Game. Result.*

Slowly, the words and phrases materialized into what I'd been looking for: the reason. His addiction. My dad was betting money on games. Day after day. Bet after bet. Dollar after dollar. Loss after loss.

I bit my tongue, thinking. Over the last few years, Dad had become more and more attentive—perhaps the word was *invested*—in sports. He'd always been a basketball fan, but at some point it became routine for him to have one earbud in, listening to podcasts or "catching one more play," as he'd explain to Mom when she gave him a Significant Look.

I traced the ink divots of his neat penmanship, his precarious notes. His truths. His immoral code. Large sums of money—larger than I'd imagined us having—promised to others based on the trajectory of a ball to a net.

*9/25. Online. Football. Patriots. Exact score. $7500—Loss*

*9/26. Online. Baseball. NY Yankees. O/U. $4490—Loss*

Before I knew what was happening, I was out the door, storming through another torrential downpour to the Lodge. I jogged up the steps, my fingers clutching the black notebook so tightly they'd grown numb. Inside, I was momentarily relieved to find Jeff still in his office, instead of in the apartment he stayed in upstairs.

"I need to call my mom," I said.

Jeff looked up from his computer, his agreeable face dropping when he saw mine. I worked to keep my eyes directly on his, determinedly ignoring the file cabinet towering in the corner.

My expression must've rung with what Grandma Gladys referred to as a *snake in the grass with a whole lot of sass.*

"I'll give you my office," Jeff said, his eyes flickering from me to the paper I clutched in my hand.

I dialed, the notebook with my rules splayed before me, my father's careful log spread atop it. When I heard the call connect, I didn't wait for her to say hello. "I wish you had told me," I said.

"Lila?" Mom said. "Told you what?"

I fought to steady my shaking voice. "I found it."

"Found what?"

"Everything." A strangled laugh hiccupped from my throat. "A detailed record of his addiction. His *gambling* addiction." The words felt like bullets leaving my mouth. "Days, times, teams, amounts. Basically everything except what color underwear the players wore. But maybe that's on another page." Jeff's AC was on, and goose bumps raced one another over my damp skin. My body did a giant involuntary shudder.

Other things made sense now, too: Our mother had been shielding us from this knowledge. She'd known he couldn't be trusted to manage something like a bank account. If Sammy or I needed field trip money or school-activity fees, we knew to go to Mom, since she was the only one with a checkbook. I remembered the summer before freshman year, Mom railing on him for bringing home this massive, expensive crate of lobsters, complete with etched-metal shell crackers, ramekins for melted butter, and plastic bibs. At the time, I'd thought she was upset he'd overspent, but Dad had been gleeful about it—maybe after some kind of big win? Mom had relaxed, and it had become one of my favorite memories, but now all I could think of were her tight-lipped smiles and reluctant indulgence.

"Oh, Lila," she said, exhaling. "I wondered where he'd kept this kind of thing."

"In his desk."

"I looked there."

I shrugged, then remembered she couldn't see me. "Not closely enough. It was in the back of one of his notebooks. The notebook itself was empty, so I took it to . . ." I trailed off. Over the line, I heard the sound of her computer starting up. *I took it to make a list of rules to live by, the way any self-respecting grieving teenager careening into adulthood might.* "I took it to write in."

"I was going to tell you when I came up next week for Visiting Day." She swore. "I'm so sorry you found out like this."

"I don't understand," I said, my hand scrabbling over my daffodil necklace's old resting place. "We don't have . . . I mean, where did he get this kind of money?"

Her voice was so quiet I had to press the phone to my ear. "You remember how he helped take care of Uncle Frank."

It wasn't a question. It was a statement. Because Uncle Frank had had money socked away. Which could only mean one thing. "Dad took money from him?"

"A chunk of it, at least," she said. "I told you, I don't know the whole story. And it's despicable, but a good sign of how desperate he was to satisfy his addiction."

My mom's uncle had had a body that curved like one of Josie's mom's sliced bell peppers. He'd amassed a small fortune running a barber shop for sixty years, and he'd given free haircuts to war vets and kids with autism. A flare of anger coursed through me when I considered my father taking money from this man who'd so carefully saved every penny.

"How could he do that to Uncle Frank?" I whispered.

She exhaled. "It's another symptom of his brain making choices outside the man we knew. People who are addicted to something . . . sometimes it's like they have someone else inhabiting their control centers, making decisions beyond the logic of people without addictions."

My eyes skated over the paper in front of me. The teams, the bets. The money. "Do you want me to tell you what's here?"

She sniffed. "Let me open a spreadsheet."

I shoved the phone in the crook of my shoulder, trying to read off the list the way I would a book report, but hearing the wobble in my voice anyway. My eyes traced the shape of the letters, deliberately disassociating from the minute details. I wasn't even a quarter of the way through when she interrupted me. "You know what, honey?"

I held my knuckle on the page, marking my spot. "What?"

"Forget it. Jeff has a fax machine, doesn't he? Just send it to me."

*Addiction, noun: chronic disease of brain reward, motivation, memory, and related circuitry.*

Thief of people.

Destroyer of families.

Murderer.

# Chapter Twenty

The next morning, I leaned against the doorjamb of the Tsunami Room, arms crossed. I'd been unable to get warm since yesterday, and even the muggy, stifling air of the Healing Center's annex didn't help. It was as Jeff had promised that first day: padded, and full of Nerf balls and bongos.

At my feet sat CP, the youngest, smallest camper, who now—getting in to the fourth week of camp—desperately needed a haircut. To our left, Noah and Deese sparred with a hanging punching bag. Noah held it firm for Deese, who balanced precariously on one foot and snapped his other toward the bag. Noah flinched.

"Hold it still, bro," Deese said, gritting his teeth. Sweat plastered his hair to the back of his neck.

Across the room, Alicia—trendy glasses, sour attitude—beat the absolute hell out of the padded wall. She let out a war cry, ran at it, and even partially scaled it before collapsing backward.

"She's wild," whispered CP.

"Definitely," I agreed. "But can you blame her?"

He shook his head. "Nana says it takes one to know one."

I smiled. "Does that mean you're wild?"

"Maybe," he whispered. I grinned.

"Lila, CP," Jeff called. "Join us!"

CP hiccupped. "I c-c-can't," he said. "Asthma."

My heart melted at the hopeless look on his face. I glanced at Noah to see if he'd heard, thinking of his brother, who'd probably also lived a life where he sat on the sidelines, until . . .

I sighed. "I'm keeping CP company," I called back.

Jeff frowned. "C'mon, Lila. Not up for a challenge?"

I nearly snorted. My whole *life* was a challenge. And the worst part was that as much as I'd thought learning the truth would let the tension out of some of my grief, my sadness had simply moved over. Shifted gears. Flipped a couch cushion to hide a stain. It was still there. Knowing this truth had been my whole focus for almost five months, and the answer had turned out to be sad and trivial and unbelievable.

*A challenge.* Unlike my mind, my body craved the physical activity. But a small worm of fear wriggled in my stomach when I considered jumping in. What if I made the effort, gave this therapy thing everything I had, and it didn't work?

I uncrossed my arms, but they dangled at my sides, lifeless. I recrossed them. "Snooze button."

"Acknowledged," Jeff said.

CP tilted his chin upward. "You don't have to stay with me."

"I know." We watched the scene in front of us: a weird Stephen King novel full of traumatized children preparing for some kind of battle.

"C'mon over, guys. Let's roundtable here," Jeff called after a while.

We joined the others in a circle on the mat. Deese and Noah had taken turns with the punching bags, and I could smell their body odor. Not altogether unpleasant, especially in this emotional boxing gym. Alicia, though, was an entirely different story. She dripped sweat. Her glasses were completely fogged over. She pushed them up into her hair and wiped her forehead, grinning.

"So, how'd that feel?" Jeff asked.

"Good workout," Deese said.

Noah didn't meet Jeff's eyes. "Fine."

Jeff cocked his head to the side. "Care to elaborate?"

I wanted Noah to go on, but he just shook his head.

Jeff sighed. "Anyone else?"

"Fucking killer," Alicia said, leaning backward onto propped-up elbows.

Jeff put on the bland expression someone wears when they pretend swearing doesn't bother them. "Language," he said. "But, good. The theme of the week is catharsis."

Catharsis. *Cathriona*, I thought.

"Catharsis?" CP asked, pushing his glasses up on the bridge of his nose. "What's that?"

"It's a process or action where you work on making a really strong emotion a little lighter."

"Like through physical exertion?" Deese asked.

Jeff nodded. "That's one way. Studies show that when you put your body to work, the mind benefits."

I frowned. "Isn't this entire camp supposed to be about catharsis?"

It was the first time I'd spoken voluntarily in group therapy. To Jeff's credit: If he was surprised, he didn't show it. "You might think of it that way, but it's supposed to be a respite. A place where you find common ground with others who have lost someone." He paused and leaned back. "It helps if you put in the work."

His words crept right under my skin. He'd spoken lightly, but the way he said the last sentence made me think he had no hope I'd talk about anything—no hope that I'd progress here at all. I stared at the door to the Tsunami Room, imagining the billowing white curtains beyond it.

"Anyway, guys," Jeff said, turning to face the group. "The point of this room is not to promote the idea that punching something is the solution to anger." Amazingly enough, he managed to not look at me when he said that. He pointed at the wall above him. Painted on it was an acrostic sign:

ACKNOWLEDGE
NOTICE
GRAPPLE
ECLIPSE
RISE ABOVE

"Once you *acknowledge* the feeling, and *notice* how it makes you feel, working it out is more on the *G-E* spectrum—you *grapple* with it, and *eclipse* it so you can get past it, or *rise above*."

"Easier said than done," Alicia muttered. She pushed up her glasses and swiped a sleeve over her sweaty forehead.

"True," Jeff said, nodding. "Too true. So, today I'd like you to share an experience in your recent past where something made you angry."

I pulled my knees to my chest, the backs of my thighs peeling away painfully from the plastic mat. Everyone else moved too: crossing or uncrossing legs, leaning back on palms. The question seemed to unlock something in the room. Jeff went around the circle, and everyone offered something: Alicia was angry with her father for getting engaged to a woman so soon after her mother's death. Deese was angry with himself for not saying anything after his longtime best friend's mother asked him to go home and give her son "a break," since it "wasn't in his best interest to be friends right now." CP was angry with his grandmother for taking down pictures of his parents.

Listening to the group made me wonder if we felt the deepest fury when something threatened what we cared about the most. I'd never before considered how what we got angry with, or at, demonstrated what made us vulnerable.

I'd have to write that one down when I got back to the bungalow. *If* I could stomach looking at that notebook.

"Noah?" Jeff prompted.

Noah's eyebrows were furrowed. "I'm angry with my brother," he said. His fingers curled up, and he didn't meet anyone's gaze.

My heart rippled in sympathy. I knew what it was like to be angry with someone who'd left you. And at least . . . at least parents were supposed to go first. The circle of life and all that. Losing a sibling must be impossible. And I couldn't even fathom what it must feel like to lose a child the way Jeff had.

I was usually of the opinion that no one person's tragedy was worse than another, but maybe some were.

"Are you angry with him, or at the events that transpired to get you here?" Jeff asked.

Noah's body went rigid. "I'd think everyone here would be angry with whatever it was that made them a candidate for grief camp."

Jeff's expression was earnest. "Of course that would be fair to say, Noah." He seemed like he had more to add, but instead he relaxed against the wall behind him, waiting for Noah to speak. A wordless silence filled the room, exacerbated by the sounds of a clock ticking and everyone breathing.

I believed this was what was called a pregnant pause. Swollen with meaning, and untenable for too long. I couldn't bear it any longer. "I learned some new information about my dad," I said, the words blurting into the silence. *I volunteer as emotional tribute,* I thought wryly. "Since his death, the details . . . they've been sparse. And every time I learn a new one, I'm angry all over again."

Everyone in the room turned their attention to me. Me, who had been mostly silent for every session so far. Relief spilled over Noah's features. I dropped my gaze to my hands.

Yesterday, after I'd hung up with Mom, Jeff had asked me if I wanted to talk, but everything had been too raw. "Go on," he said now, his tone supportive.

"Right before I came here, my mom told me my dad had some kind of addiction. But I didn't know much other than that. I didn't know if he was doing drugs, or drinking, or something." I licked my lips. "I keep wondering if I'm going to inherit whatever gene it is that's connected to addiction."

"You know," Jeff said, "addiction, as a disease, is incredibly complicated. Some people disagree, but I tend to think of it as something that's a perfect storm of sorts. Genetic and environmental. Many diseases are like that." He glanced at Noah, who was watching me. "And when these people who are predisposed to it, by birth or by chance, find the right substance—it's almost like finding a piece to complete a terribly unsatisfying puzzle."

I swallowed. "My dad's wasn't a substance, though. It was gambling."

"Gambling is a behavioral addiction, according to the *DSM*, the continuously evolving manual that defines these kinds of things," Jeff said. "It's similar in both experience and biology to substance addiction. People who are addicted to gambling report they feel the same urges and cravings that other substances provide, and neurocircuitry studies illustrate the same."

I absorbed that information for a moment. "Really?"

"Really. So what someone might experience with problem gambling isn't at all dissimilar to, say, what a person who abuses cocaine might feel."

His words were like a series of small gifts of understanding.

"I wish I'd known all this before, but my mom didn't have all the pieces either." I glanced at Noah. Unlike all the guys back home who didn't know how to act around me anymore, his expression wasn't a put-on mask of sorrow, pity, or confusion. It was empathetic, instead of sympathetic.

I thought back to right before the funeral, when Mom had said she was too angry to do the eulogy. Sammy was too young, so—even though I wasn't the writer in the family—the task fell to me.

My laptop had thrummed in front of me, but I was afraid that if I opened it, I'd purge every thought I'd ever had into it. Instead, I'd sat at my desk and prepared the old-fashioned way: with a pen and paper.

Once the pen was in my hand, though, I had no idea what to say. Should I write about the time Dad carried me to the bathroom after I had my ankle surgery? The time he taught me how to do a cartwheel? The time he came running outside because I'd fallen off of my bike, and since I was wearing face paint from a carnival, he thought I'd skinned my face off?

Here, on the floor of the Tsunami Room, a feeling surged inside me. Hot, raw anger.

"Lila?" Jeff's voice was encouraging.

"I wrote my dad's eulogy. There were ten thousand Disney-perfect memories in my head. But"—I snapped a string from the frayed edge of my shorts—"that wasn't my life anymore, so I wrote about our sink." I lifted my head and saw a circle of puzzled, expectant faces. I tried to laugh, but I didn't recognize the sound that came out. "The kitchen sink at my house was broken. Dripping all day long. And in my head, it became kind of a symbol of everything *Dad*. He fixed everything. He rebuilt the deck, put down the hardwood floor, and rewired the electricity."

I stopped. Looked at Noah. One corner of his mouth turned up, and he nodded his head as if to say: *Keep going.*

So I did.

"He was the parent I called in the middle of the night when I woke up from a bad dream." I knocked my knuckles into the padded floor, pressing down with all my might. "He was the one who brought us to the emergency room for broken bones and stitches. The doer. The fixer. And after . . . after he was gone, all I wanted to know was who was going to fix that damn sink."

The rhythmic push and pull of expectant breath filled the room. Color rose in my cheeks. Deese cleared his throat. "So?"

"So?"

"So, who fixed it?"

This time, when I did laugh, I sounded like me. "The three of us. My mom, Sammy, and I did. With the help of YouTube how-to videos and two trips to the hardware store."

Once it was done, we were giddy with the sense of accomplishment. A celebration of epic magnitude commenced: Mom, her face smeared with grease, doing this little jig, Sammy attempting the worm on the tile floor. Who knew fixing a sink could carry so much power?

But along with that pride came agonizing heartache. It should've been my dad. The Cunningham quartet had lost its fixer, and solving the sink problem was a nice debut for our new trio. In some ways, though, it felt like all my emotions now dripped from me without my permission, waiting for someone else to fix them.

Small bites of pain pricked my hand. I glanced down, wondering if a bee or an array of stinging ants had somehow gotten into the room. Instead, I found my fingers curled into tight fists, my nails digging into my palms. *Unravel,* I told them. *Relax.* I unfurled my fingers. Elbow-macaroni imprints dotted my skin. I rubbed them with the pad of my thumb, trying to physically erase the evidence of my thought train, thinking of the drip, drip, drip of water, when suddenly it occurred to me.

Dad was gone, an irrefutable fact. And so we'd taken fixing the sink into our own hands. A problem of my own: I was scared to swim. And no one was going to fix that for me but me.

"Would you rather, special rewriting-history edition," I heard. I glanced upward. At some point, Jeff must have moved to wrap up the session, because now Noah towered over me on the mat. I blinked, clearing my head. Off to the side, Deese and Jeff were deep in conversation. "Someone who could've come over and fixed the sink for you guys, or the way it played out with You-Tube guidance?"

"Definitely the latter," I said. "Tutorials for the win. The whole give-a-person-a-fish versus teach-them-to-fish thing."

He smiled. "Deese and I are going to Mess Hall for a coffee," he said. "You want in?"

I shook my head, savoring the mild disappointment that brushed his features. "Thanks," I said, extracting myself from my seat. "But there's something I have to do."

# Chapter Twenty-One

On my way back to my bunk, I stopped at the Com. I yanked my bathing suit from the hook where it had been drying since yesterday, slung it over my shoulder, and marched to our blue bungalow. Inside, I stripped off my shorts and tank and tossed them in the general direction of my stuff, but the armhole of my tank hooked onto one of Madison's crutches, leaning against a wall.

Winnie and Madison sat on Winnie's bed, surrounded by spools of embroidery floss. Friendship bracelets. Winnie had the end of hers looped around her toe, while Madison had hers safety-pinned to Winnie's quilt. Colorful strings splayed out on their laps, tied and knotted together.

Madison glanced up. Clenched between her teeth was a single purple strand. "Want to make one?"

"No." The word came out in a snarl (residual anger from the Tsunami Room?), so I relaxed my tone. I turned to face my bunk and reached behind myself to unhook my bra, then I shimmied out of my underwear. The bathing suit was musty and stiff from drying, but I shook it out and stepped into it anyway. "Thanks."

"Lila, what are you doing?" Winnie's voice was wary.

"Going swimming." *Me. Going swimming.* The words prickled my stomach. Why was there only one flip-flop? I frowned.

"You hate swimming." From Madison.

I kneeled down, rummaging under the bed. "Yes." Aha! There it was. In the farthest corner beneath the bed, kicked off and forgotten. I strained to reach it, hooking my finger onto the vee of the rubber thong. When I pulled back, my elbow hit my tote bag, crunching against the bag of my dad's cookies.

*Hi, Dad.*

"God, I still love that monokini. But why—"

Winnie interrupted Madison. "You haven't even gone underwater yet, and you're going swimming?"

"Yup." When I stood up and faced them, Winnie had discarded her bracelet in favor of folding her arms across her chest, and Madison was adjusting the Velcro on her boot.

I frowned. "What are you doing?"

"You think we're missing this?" Winnie shoved her feet into sandals.

I shrugged. "It's your afternoon."

Madison squinted at me. "Something has your back up."

Winnie whistled in agreement. "Girl. You are Katniss Everdeen, featuring Alicia Keys."

"Huh?"

"'This girl is on fire!'" Madison sang unhelpfully.

I rolled my eyes. *"Please."*

"Lila, you are a walking anthem right now," Madison said.

Winnie was right. I *was* on fire.

But when I got to the dock, with my audience of exactly two, I couldn't justify wading into my big moment. I knew I'd chicken out when the lake water hit somewhere between my knees and my shoulders. So my resolve carried me to the edge of the dock, beneath which the water lapped like a thirsting dog. Hungry for me.

I gazed out at the horizon: deep, pine-green Christmas trees, pillow-dough clouds, and the lake water beneath, reflecting it all. The sky was a flat, listless blue, and the wind whipped against me, gently pressing me back and away from the water's edge. I drew in a long, deliberate breath through my nose and commanded my body to jump.

But nothing happened, except for maybe a knee jerk. My feet stayed rooted to the grainy dock.

I shaded my eyes to focus on the shore, where Winnie and Madison stood, holding hands.

Slowly, Winnie raised her arm in the air, her fingers making a V.

I thought of my mom. Of Noah, and how confusing he was. Of Dad.

And I jumped.

The impact made the sound of a thousand pieces of paper being ripped in half; the water spanked my chest, lassoed my breath. And then the cold enveloped me, shocking my skin and making my heart tremble with the memory of being clenched by my father: down, down, down. Panic slithered through my veins, quelling only when my feet touched the sandy bottom. Gravity continued to propel me downward, but once I squatted on the ground, I engaged my leg muscles the way I always did before a hurdle, reminding them how to move. I pushed with everything I had and rocketed upward.

I broke the surface and inhaled the clean, lovely oxygen. Before I'd even opened my eyes, I heard them: Winnie and Madison, celebrating as if I'd won the Super Bowl, shouting my name and screaming. Winnie raced in to join me, shrieking when she hit the water ("Jeez, this is cold!"), while Madison did an awkward little one-footed jig on the shore.

I performed a lurching dog-paddle maneuver in Winnie's general direction to heave myself back toward a manageable depth. (Gold-medal swimmer I was not.) When I reached her, she threw her arms around me. We jumped up and down like little kids.

"You did it! Maybe I should be a swim instructor."

"You should! You so should!" I took a deep breath and dunked underwater, rolled over to face the surface, and opened my eyes. The filtered rays of sunlight broke through the water. I opened my mouth and screamed in delight, bubbles racing from my mouth and arcing upward, popping once they reached the surface. I'd never pictured what it would look like to scream underwater.

When I resurfaced, I saw we had company. A handful of people, Noah and Deese included, were tying a sailboat to the edge of the dock, which was farther away than I'd thought. A ripple of pleasure fluttered in my veins. In the distance, a group of kids Sammy's age approached the shore, flicking one another with towels.

"Open swim?" I asked Winnie.

"Open swim," she confirmed.

Campers hurled themselves into the water around us. "Thank you," I said, facing Winnie. "I don't know how to repay you."

"You don't repay me, silly." Her eyes flicked up and over my shoulder: a split-second giveaway that someone was behind me.

The more obvious giveaway was the faceful of water I caught when I spun around.

"Hey!" I spluttered.

Noah grinned. His body was achingly perfect: lean and muscular, tan and shadowy. His hips came together in an athlete's vee, which I very determinedly avoided with my eyes. He

181

pushed his hair off his face, and it stuck up in wet tufts. "You went swimming."

"I did. And you went sailing." I realized then that my face was beaming, and I worked to make my expression into something more cool and casual.

"We did. Your lips are blue."

I touched them. "Are not."

"It's okay. I like blue."

"Stop looking at my lips." I glanced over my shoulder to check for Winnie, who'd rejoined Madison on the beach. She shook water from her curly hair.

"I like looking at your lips."

"Stop saying you like looking at my lips."

"You're very bossy."

I switched tactics. "Your cheeks are pink."

"My cheeks are always pink. I have rosacea."

"Oh." My turn to flush. "Sorry."

"Now your cheeks are pink."

I took in a deep breath, let it out, breathed in again. My blood pounded so hard in my chest I could feel it in my ears.

Noah made me forget about the handbook, which was dangerous and risky for all things related to my heart. But I craved falling into him, laughing with him. I didn't want to want him, but . . . I did.

So I took a step toward him.

Another.

I closed my eyes and angled my face up to his.

And . . . nothing.

I opened my eyes, confused. Small crinkly lines appeared in the corners of his. His bottom lip twitched.

My lungs froze, emotions jabbing them like icicles

falling down on the first warm spring day. Confusion. Lust. Embarrassment.

I waited for him to make the next move. Would he step back, palms up? All *You must have made a mistake, Lila*? Would he lace his fingers though my hair and clutch me to him? Would he laugh at me?

One breath, two breaths, three.

"I can't," he said.

A nervous laugh burped out of me. "I didn't mean—"

"You think I wouldn't like to kiss a beautiful girl?" His eyes studied my face. "There's possibly nothing else in the world I want more at this moment than to kiss you."

"But—"

"When I said I liked staring at your lips, I meant it," he said. "But I like other things about you, too."

"Other things," I croaked.

"I like your laugh. And I like the way you straighten your shoulders when you're angry." He ran his finger along the slope of my shoulders to emphasize his point. My nerves danced beneath his touch. He moved a fraction of an inch closer to me, and my heart started its wild percussion again. "I like you, Lila. But you burned me before."

"I burned you?"

"At the dance."

The dance. The Quiet Area. My hand clenched, remembering the gallon of punch. "I didn't mean—"

"I don't blame you," he interrupted. "I get it. I do. But I—I know what it's like to be rejected."

*He* was afraid of *me* hurting him? "I like you, Noah," I said quietly, my insides churning like the water.

He stepped as close as he could to me without touching any

part of my body. His lips trailed along my ear, and the warmth from his skin radiated into my own. "Prove it," he whispered.

Dual flares of fire ran through me. One melted my insides to goo. Yet the second woke up something else: pride.

I stepped back. "*Prove* it to you? I'm not some desperate girl who's going to cater to your whims, Noah Kitteridge. I have no idea what the hell you think this is." I crossed my arms, shaking. What was he like in his high school, anyway? I had no doubt he had his pick of people who'd fling themselves into his pants, but I was not one of them.

"That's fine."

"That's fine?"

He threw his hands up in the air. "I'm not sure what you want from me, Lila, but I need some kind of assurance that you're not going to chew me up and spit me out."

"Me?"

"Let's see." He rubbed his chin mockingly. "We meet. I'm into you. I think you're into me, but you refuse to come to the dance with me, so then I think you're not. You kiss me in what's basically a dark closet. You run away from me—by the way, the juice you dropped broke open, and that stuff stains. Then you avoid me for days, and the next time we have any sort of real interaction, we're sidled up against each other in the foam pit during Silent Scream. I'm seeing a theme here. You're only nice to me in the dark, and I've had enough of that to last me a lifetime."

I swallowed, feeling both giddy and stung. On one hand, I was full of elation—still high from facing my swimming fear, and even though he was listing all the ways I'd treated him badly, that meant he was *thinking* of how I treated him, which meant he was thinking of me, and I very much liked thinking of him thinking of me.

But on the other hand, *womp*. Buzzkill. I imagined my lips puckering in front of his, and considered how unscientifically possible it would be to simply melt into the water and dissolve into nothing right now.

"So what I'm saying, Lila, is that I want you to prove to me that you're not going to burn me again. Damaged kid here, remember?"

I plucked at the strap of my bathing suit. "How?"

He took a step back. "How am I damaged? I won't—I don't want to talk about it."

I shook my head. "No. How do you want me to prove it to you?"

"Oh." Relief washed his features. "Surprise me."

# Chapter Twenty-Two

One afternoon a few days later, I stood in the center of one of the intramural fields, watching arrows fly in front of me. Camp Bonaventure had a pretty smart setup for archery. We took turns going into a partitioned-off space, where, under the supervision of Mari, we could use real arrows. While we waited, we practiced with rubber-tipped ones. They bounced off the red-and-white targets with satisfying *thunks*.

I hefted the bow up, settling into the stance Mari had taught us. Squinting, I arranged my fingers around the arrow nock, pulled back, and released. The arrow nicked the bottom of my target.

"Relax your bow grip," a voice said behind me. A familiar voice.

Excitement teased low in my belly. I resisted the urge to whirl around. "I don't need the advice, Noah."

"Okay, but I'm telling you, I can see your knuckles turning white."

I strung another arrow. This time, when I lifted the bow, I loosened my grip. "Since when are you an expert archer?"

"I'm a natural talent."

I turned my head a fraction, just enough so I could see him. "Prove it," I said, smirking.

And then I was hyperaware of his presence directly behind me. He curved his hand over my right one, where the arrow quivered between my index and middle fingers. "That's it," he murmured. I pulled back and let go. Together, we watched the arrow nail the center of the target before it fell away.

"Lucky shot," I said.

On the night before Visiting Day, I lounged in bed finishing an assigned summer reading book: *100 Years of Solitude* by Gabriel García Márquez. Across the room, Madison read a magazine, her ankle elevated on a stack of pillows. On the other side of the bungalow, the twins played a game of chess, and Winnie flipped through a catalog of classes for college in the fall. Tomorrow was the halfway point into my sentence at Camp Bonaventure. Almost four weeks down, four to go. I stretched my body, my muscles oddly tight from swimming. I was full of the restless boredom I occasionally experienced when I had the urge to do something new. Make something. Create something I'd never created before, or travel somewhere I'd never been. "I am full of ennui," I said, flopping my arm over my face dramatically. "I wish there was someplace different for us to go, or something new to do."

"There is," Winnie said, sitting up. She laughed that deep, contagious laugh of hers, and Madison and I both smiled, because it was really hard not to smile when Winnie laughed her laugh.

"What?" Madison said. She shoved a pencil under her brace, poking at what I presumed to be an itch.

"Madison, do you still have that wine?"

Madison leaned over and tapped the side of her suitcase, then winked. "What wine?"

Winnie pumped her fist in the air. "The Shed?"

"The Shed."

I sat up, intrigued. "The what, now?"

We collected Noah and Deese (who promptly offered Madison a piggyback ride), then made our way to the Shed, a run-down wooden overhang built into a rock wall in the woods behind the gymnastics building.

There, we sat on an old, tattered quilt that looked as if it had been left there for centuries. We leaned against the rock wall, wooden posts, one another. Winnie unscrewed the cap from a bottle of Orient Point and sloshed some wine into a row of cups she'd swiped from Mess Hall. I passed the cups around.

"Cheers," we said in unison, our plastic cups making a hollow clink. I took a sip, steadfastly ignoring the fact that Noah sat beside me, our legs close but not quite touching. As if he sensed my thoughts, he nudged my foot with his own.

I eyed him. "Our feet can touch, even though I haven't *proved* myself?"

He pursed his lips. "Hurry up, won't ya?"

We drank for a while, killing off one bottle and then another. The evening was warm and pleasant, the air balmy but not too hot. Late July in Maine.

Deese put down his cup and turned to me. "Remind me how good you are at running?"

"I'm not good at running. Just hurdling."

"She's super fast." Winnie's cheeks were rosy in the moonlight.

"Who says?" I asked.

"Sammy told me." *That kid and his mouth.*

"That true?" Deese asked. "Wait. What's your last name?"

I tipped my hand back and forth, as if to say *Yeah, it's sorta true,* but kept a smile on my face. "Cunningham."

"Lila *Cunningham,*" Deese said, mock whistling. "I thought you looked familiar. I recognize your name now. What's your hundred-meter hurdling time?"

"It's pretty good."

Deese crossed his arms. "What is it?"

"Thirteen-oh-five?" It sounded like I was asking him a question, so I cleared my throat and tried again. "Thirteen-oh-five."

Winnie looked at Deese. "Is that fast?"

He mimed closing an open jaw. "Impressively. Only four high school girls have broken thirteen seconds. Like, in the country."

She sat back. "Thought so," she said. "My hundred-meter time is probably twenty minutes."

Deese shifted himself toward me. "I've slowed down a ton here. The camp curse. I could use a training partner. You interested?"

I took a sip of wine to purchase enough time for my slightly buzzing brain to formulate an appropriate response. "I'm not hurdling anymore, and like I said, I suck at running. I'm an athletic oxymoron," I joked, even though swimming had reminded me how good it felt to use my muscles. I pointed and flexed my feet. Maybe I *would* start running again.

Running. Track meets. League All Star hurdler the last two years. Dad, cheering on the sidelines. Our plans to run in the Falmouth Road Race.

Maybe it was the night itself: dark, but cuddled and cozy around us. Maybe it was sitting on these blankets in this old wooden structure that felt like it had been built and left just for us and our sticky plastic cups of Orient Point.

Or maybe it was because I'd done something I never thought I would do: *I swam.* If I could do that . . .

Something rose up inside me then: a quiet flame of confidence. I'd never notified the road-race organizers about withdrawing. *What if . . .* The idea was in my head, and I spoke before I could chicken out. "Sure," I said. "If you can help me run for distance, I'll coach you on sprints."

Winnie clapped her hands together. "Excellent."

"How far are you looking to go?" Deese asked.

I closed my eyes and pictured the course. Seven miles of hilly hell, about four miles of which were right beside the ocean. The race took place smack in the middle of August, the week before camp ended. I opened my eyes. "Seven miles."

Deese grinned. "Good. I was afraid you were going to say a half marathon or something."

"It'll be a challenge," I warned. "I currently can't run a mile without feeling like death."

He reached out and clasped my hand. "Right on," he said. "My co-captain is going to smoke me when I get back if I don't watch out."

"Are we done talking about activities I can't participate in?" Madison asked, wiggling her boot.

Deese slung his arm over her shoulder. "It'll be off in a month. Just in time for school. You can run then."

She reached up and squeezed his hand. "Oh, I'm not good at running, and I don't do things I'm not good at."

Winnie moaned. "I can't believe school is a few weeks away. College. Real life."

College seemed to me like an eternity away, which was probably why I'd told my mom on the way here that I didn't care about it. But for the first time since February, I let myself poke into the idea. Campus visits. Going someplace new. "It might be a lot like this," I said.

Noah shook his head. "Nothing is like this."

"Too true, man," Deese said. He turned to Winnie. "What are you studying?"

She shrugged. "Liberal arts. Women's studies. I don't know. I'm a cliché."

"You are far from a cliché," Madison said.

"Oh, I am. So are you. You're going to be an elementary-school teacher, right?"

Madison sighed. "Fair enough. And, no. I want to be a journalist."

"I miss knowing what's going on in the world," I said. I rested my chin on my knees. "Well. I miss Twitter telling me what's going on in the world, at least."

Deese threw his head back and drained his cup. "Doctor for me. If I'm going to take care of my ma and grandma, I'll need lots of money."

"Lawyer for me, I think," Noah said.

"A lawyer?" I was surprised.

"Sure. I like debating. Either that or I'm heading out to Bali or Hawaii or Thailand and opening a beach bar."

"You're not the beach-bar type," Winnie said. "Corporate goobers who retire only to open island bars always have to change their identities. They grow a beard, go from Preston Briggs Hubert the Fourth to 'Just Hugh,' wax on about the pain in the souls of all the visiting women, then mysteriously vanish into the night."

"Easy for you to say, Wainwright-Winnie," I teased.

"You've got a good made-for-TV movie lined up for you right there," Noah said. He nudged my hip. "What's something you want to be when you grow up?"

My entire life, I'd vacillated among the standards: teacher, firefighter, doctor, lawyer. The dress-up professions, because how would a kid wear a costume as a data analyst or a nonprofit founder? But ever since I took psychology last year and we visited the local prison, where we learned about behaviors and impulses and the impact of trauma on the psyche, I'd been hovering around a new career idea, though I'd never spoken about it to anyone except for Call-Me-Connie. "I'm thinking about being a psychotherapist."

"A *therapist*," Winnie said, her voice full of glee. "You're a cliché too! Every damaged kid wants to be a therapist."

"I just think brains are cool," I said, choosing my words carefully because my tongue felt warm, slippery from the wine. "There was this study that watched two different brains. One of a speaker telling a story or explaining some kind of concept or whatever, and one of a listener. To find out what parts lit up."

"What parts lit up?" Madison repeated.

I bobbed my head up and down. I loved this kind of thing— talking about science and research and medicine. "When the listener understood what the speaker was saying, their scans matched. If you mapped out what portions of their brains lit up, they'd be twinning—with a lag of about one second. Just long enough for the listener to comprehend what the speaker was saying. Almost as if their brains were telling the same story, or playing the same song. As the story progressed, different parts lit up.

"But if the listener didn't get it, everything fell apart. Their brains would ping off in different directions. Maybe the speaker grasped that the listener didn't get it and was frustrated, or maybe they literally were on two different wavelengths." I gestured to the wine, and Winnie topped off my cup of Orient Point. "So when there's communication between two people, when there's true understanding, their brains are mirrored. They're one. And I guess . . ." I trailed off, looking around the Shed, which was full of people who'd been there. Who'd lost someone really important to them. Who probably got me better than anyone else in the whole world. "I guess I want to try and help people get on the same wavelength."

Our conversations soon diverged, Deese talking about med school, Madison wondering how people started careers as social-media influencers. ("That's the worst," Winnie said.) Noah put his hand on my leg. "Okay, Cunningham," he said. "Tell me a story. Let's see if our brains light up."

I play-swatted his hand. "You tell me a story. Tell me about something fun from when you were a kid."

"Snooze."

"You're snoozing a childhood story?"

"Rule says you can snooze whenever, doesn't it?" He turned his head then, as though he'd heard a noise.

"What is it?"

"Just a squirrel or something."

I frowned. "Should we be quiet? Is it someone?"

"Nah, I'm probably imagining it. Hey, you'd be a good one, you know," he said. "Therapist."

"You think so?" I asked, smiling.

"Yeah. Cool study."

"It is," I said. "In some cases, when a listener was really in tune with a speaker and could maybe guess where the story was going, the listener's brain would actually change *first*. Like the listener knew what the speaker was going to say before he said it, and their brains commingled and kept singing along together."

"To the tune of the same drummer," Noah said.

I was only half listening to him. It could have been the warm, sweet wine, or maybe it was the experience of being around people like me in the dark. For whatever reason, though, I'd known he was going to say that.

# Chapter Twenty-Three

The next morning, Sammy and I stood on the grassy lawn in front of the Lodge, watching Mom park in the same spot she'd left us in just shy of a month ago. I scanned the grass for Noah, searching among the campers greeting their families while trying as hard as I could not to look as viciously hungover as I felt.

"What happened to your tan?" Sammy asked. "Your freckles are really dark, but you look pale."

I felt pale. "It's been cloudy."

"No, it hasn't."

Mom saved me by getting out of the car. Sammy threw himself into her arms, and then I wrapped my arms around them both.

"I missed you, little birds," Mom murmured. She squeezed us hard. I pressed my forehead against her collarbone and breathed her in, smelling the good parts of home: laundry detergent and our favorite hand lotion.

She kissed the crown of my head. "How have you grown so much in just a few short weeks?"

In honor of the dirge of widows, widowers, and mourning parents descending upon our pristine camp, Mari and the staff had packed picnic lunches for everyone, and Jeff put a bin of blankets out in front of Mess Hall. We were free to take the property bikes around and eat with our families. Sammy and I biked with Mom to the sand in front of the lake, where we spread out lunch: perfectly proportioned turkey sandwiches, shiny apples—crisp on the outside, cold and juicy on the inside— and thick slices of soft chocolate cake with white glazed icing.

My stomach turned over at the sight of the food, but once I took the first bite, it settled a bit.

Sammy jabbered about his friends, basketball, and his art project (a cow) and mine (the lion). When he moved into his exploits with water sports—sailing and paddleboarding—Mom interrupted.

"Show me," she said.

Sammy jumped up. "'Kay. And while I'm gone, Lila can tell you about her *boyfriend*."

My cheeks flooded with heat. "Shut up," I said, sounding like a ten-year-old. "I don't have a boyfriend."

As we watched Sammy on his paddleboard, Mom and I sat in the good kind of silence—the watch-movies-on-the-couch, hang-around-reading-books kind of silence. Companionable.

Mom looked better than she had since forever, really. She had a light tan, which brought out the freckles on her nose. By the end of the summer, they would come out on her lips, too. She'd tied her hair back in a neat ponytail, and she wore little sparkly earrings. Her arms were toned with muscles I'd never seen on her before. A feeling I didn't recognize spread through me, and my fingertips tingled.

I frowned. "Mom? Are you . . . dating someone?"

She shook her head, looking surprised. "No," she said, after what seemed like a full minute of watching Sammy on the paddleboard. "No."

"Then why do you look so *good?*" She wrinkled her nose in offense, so I went on. "No dark eye circles. No tired-lady lines." I poked her arm. "She-woman muscles. A calm vibe."

Mom leaned backward on the blanket, groaning. "It's Aunt Shelly. Her yoga-and-yogurt regimen has taken over the house."

"Well whatever it is, it's working." I kicked off my sandals and wiggled my toes in the sand. "Knowing Aunt Shelly, I'm surprised she doesn't have you on Match or eHarmony."

"Nope. Just Tinder."

"Mom!"

She smiled, pleased with herself. "No, Lila. I don't know when or if I'll date again."

It was weird, thinking of Mom dating someone else. She and Dad had been—well, just her and Dad.

And yet so finite was their infinity.

"My therapist says that being single for a year after something like this is recommended," Mom said, breaking into my thoughts.

I nodded, wondering how someone came up with that arbitrary timetable. Was that a lesson you learned in therapy school? I pictured some old professor, stroking his beard and adjusting his glasses.

"But how could you?" I asked. "I mean, why would you? What if you got hurt again?"

Mom looked surprised. "Oh, honey," she said. "Life's not about that."

"What do you mean?"

"Life's about taking risks and chances with yourself. If you cut yourself off from everything—if you close off all those beautiful parts of yourself, then why bother?"

"You sound like Jeff."

Mom laughed again. "I sound like my therapist," she said. "So it's probably good the guy running things here sounds like that." She squinted at Sammy, who had begun showing off on the paddleboard after spotting a couple of girls his age. Mom shook her head ruefully. "What am I going do to with him?"

"Sammy's okay. You don't have to worry about him."

"No." Mom smiled. "But you, I do."

Her face changed then: her mouth melting into a line, her eyes glossing over. It was her *I have to tell you something* face. Before she spoke, I knew she was going to say something I did not want her to say. "Look, Lyon."

"Don't call me that." My words bit into hers. "Mom, what changed? How did everything spiral out of control so fast? Were you guys in some kind of trouble? I could have picked up more shifts at the Mug, you know. To help out."

Mom pressed her shoulders down and tilted her head, a look I knew all too well. "Lila. My therapist told me to be honest with you. Open."

My stomach rolled, and my head pounded so forcefully my vision blurred. "Honest?"

She sighed. "I don't know if it's the right thing to do, telling you. But then I keep asking myself: What if I wait too long? What if you find out from someone else?" Her mouth turned up into what was technically defined as a smile, but it was more of a resigned grimace. "You have enough fodder to resent one parent forever. I don't want you to resent me, too. Your dad . . . It wasn't the first time."

"What wasn't the first time?"

"It—the suicide. He'd tried before."

"He what?"

"It was the third time."

The pounding in my ears became African drums, my stomach an ocean of bile and old wine. I swallowed forcefully, willing myself not to throw up.

"How?" I managed.

She seemed surprised. "How?"

"Yes. Tell me how."

"I don't think—"

"I need to know."

So she told me. The first time, I was almost four. Right before Sammy, I calculated. She'd found him in the garage.

The second time, I was eight. He waited for us to have a sleepover at Aunt Shelly's, and overdosed in their bed after taking leftover pills from Mom's root canal.

Every few years, life became too much for him. When I was three. Eight. Sixteen.

I searched my memory, holding a microscope to moments I thought I knew. Sleepovers at Aunt Shelly's weren't rare. Sammy and I loved them because they meant staying up late, telling stories, hearing what Mom was like as a kid, watching movies, and baking treats so healthy they were generally inedible.

But . . . as I studied the lake in front of us, an unfamiliar image surged to mind. A tennis net flapping in the wind. A green lawn. A memory I didn't know I had pieced itself together, solidifying into something so weighted and heavy it nearly stole my breath. There, by a lake in Maine, I remembered clutching a doll I was too old for already, one I didn't want, while I sat beside Dad in a hard plastic chair in a café that smelled like an elementary school cafeteria. Eau de chicken patty. Mom standing, her back stiff and straight as a telephone pole, with Sammy, no longer a toddler and too old to be carried like one, astride her hip regardless.

"There was a place," I said, the words falling out of my mouth the way popcorn cooks: slow, fast, then burned. "With tennis courts. And some kind of brick building. With a basement café."

Mom's red-rimmed eyes widened. "You remember that?"

"I remember a doll."

"I bought it for your dad to give to you." Her voice was thick with the raw, clogging salt of tears. She shook her head. "I'm floored, Lila. I can't believe you remember that."

"What was that place?"

"A treatment center for mental health."

"How long was he gone?"

"He was inpatient for a month. Thirty days, before the insurance ran out. We were lucky enough to get that much. His therapist said that seeing his kids—his family—would be good for him. Give him perspective. We'd told you he was at a work retreat." Emotion rained over her face. "They recommended another thirty or sixty days, even, but he declined more treatment. Said he was fine. Insisted."

The shadowy image of her stiffened back, so regal in the cafeteria, swam into my vision. "How could you stay with him, Mom? I mean . . . why?"

She pressed her fingers to her eyes. "He took so much from me, Lila," she whispered. "But I loved him, and he loved you both, and I wanted it all to work out. He took my trust. He took my money. He took my grandma's gold jewelry and hocked it at pawn shops, like . . . like . . ." She struggled to find the words. "Like what I valued—whether it was abstract or sentimental— was secondary to his own selfish requirements. And I'm struggling with that. I flip back and forth from heartache for myself to heartbreak for the man who must've suffered so much that he'd take away everything in the world from those who he loved the most. And he did love us, Lila."

Pain raked my heart. Pricked my brain. I knew. Knew with an icy, iron certainty what she meant about the ache of it all. The longer Dad was gone, the more I came around to what she meant about the heartbreak: the agony he'd suffered. I tensed my muscles, only releasing them when they screamed in protest and

I couldn't hold them any longer. I wanted to lie down. One single tear traveled a sharp path, racing down my cheek and over my chin, curving along my jaw and climbing my neck until it settled in the gentle dip of my throat, hitting me with a gutting, final truth, a grinding alarm clock of loss.

*Why, Dad?* "Mom," I said. "My daffodil necklace."

Her shoulders shrank. "I know," she said, her voice glum. "I mean, I don't *know*. That necklace was worth a hell of a lot more in sentimentality than it was in money. But I certainly suspect."

The rest of the afternoon passed in a blur. I sat silently beside Mom while she told Sammy a gentler version of what she'd told me—third time was the unlucky charm—but he took the information better than I did.

"Are you okay?" Mom asked him.

I could read it on his face. He wasn't, but he was trying to be. "Dad's still dead, isn't he?"

The next morning, I was in such a shitty mood that I skipped breakfast and let myself into the art room. Over the last week or so, the studio had morphed into a macabre zoo of half-sculpted animals. It was like the Island of Misfit Toys from *Rudolph*: a hedgehog made of knitting needles, an elephant made from bent wire. An owl without eyes, fashioned from metal scraps, perched in the corner next to the unpainted ceramic turtle and lumpy clay dinosaur Noah and Deese had told us about. Winnie's Ariana Grande ponytail was a true work of art: long, golden-brown thread sculpted with some kind of glue mixture into the hair's unrecognizable molecular structure. A colorful orangutan made from pipe cleaners leaned against the back wall. It was my favorite piece there. I was certain it would be chosen for the Guggenheim. Sammy's cow—surprisingly recognizable, coming from his previously inartistic soul—was made of crumpled-up paper stuffed into Hefty trash bags, and black cutouts of construction paper.

My lioness was a mash-up. Papier-mâché, golden paint, and rich ruby, mahogany, and golden yarn for its tail. I'd finished my attempt at the body last week, and now in the early morning light I worked to define the lion's flank, mixing chocolate brown into my palette and shading in taut muscles.

The paint had dried unevenly, making blending impossible; the body wasn't smooth, but instead full of air bubbles. Not at all how I'd envisioned it. If this was supposed to be my animal representative, then my fight song was pretty weak.

"Ugh," I muttered, stirring black paint into the mix. But when I went to smudge it onto the lion's hind legs, I poked a bit harder than I'd intended, and my paintbrush broke right through the sculpture, leaving behind a gaping crater.

Tears pooled in my eyes. A growl of frustration spilled from my throat. Before I could stop myself, I lifted my fist into the air and brought it down on the lion's back.

Again.

And again.

It finally cracked on the third try, along with my resolve. My anger lifted up and away, the way nausea does after a stomach bug or a hangover. In its wake, I felt just like I would have after one of those, too. Weak. Tired. Achy.

Empty.

It was about the lion, but it wasn't about the lion. *Three times?* For pretty much my whole life, my dad had tricked everyone. Through all my hurdling meets, all my brother's soccer games, through Christmases and business trips and Easters and those treasured weeks down the Cape. Every time we watched a movie, he'd rather have been dead. Every breakfast we ate, every laugh we shared—he'd have picked whatever else was or was not out there over it.

Over us.

Over *me*.

I folded my arms on the table, put my forehead on them, and sobbed.

# Chapter Twenty-Four

After a night spent tossing and turning, I was up with the birds for my first training session with Deese. I almost chickened out, until I thought of how impressed Coach would be if he heard I'd trained with someone from Deese's school. State champs, year after year. When I got to our meeting spot—the Lodge—he was bent in half, doing light calf stretches. His corkscrew curls had grown out a bit over the last couple weeks, and were pushed off of his face and held back by a headband.

"How far do you want to go?" he asked, rolling out his shoulders.

"Confession time," I said. "Remember when I said running a mile was hard? Running even a tenth of one is tough for me."

His eyebrows rose. "Guess you weren't kidding about the short-distance thing."

I rose up on the balls of my feet, then rocked backward. "Nope."

He thought for a minute, and then a smile broke out over his face. "Ever do intervals?"


Deese's version of intervals involved running for a minute and then "taking a break" to jog for thirty seconds. During the slower moments, sweat pooled on my lower back and flowed over my face, cooling when we sped up.

Just as I was about to beg for mercy, Deese slowed to a walk. He pressed a button on his watch. "Two miles," he announced.

I heaved air into my lungs and let it out, unable to suppress the flip of pride in my belly. "Seriously?"

He nodded. "Yeah. But . . . ."

"But what?" I asked. I put my hands on my hips and shook out my legs, trying to cool off.

"I don't want to be rude."

"Say it."

"I've never met someone with a heaven-sent talent for hurdling who can't easily run two miles."

"Believe me, I don't get it either. My dad and I used to race each other down our street, but other than that?" I kicked a pebble. "Quick sprints, big leaps. That's all I'm good for. How long did those two miles take?"

He winced. "Twenty minutes."

If they weren't competing, most of my teammates would've done two miles in twelve or thirteen minutes. "You know what? I don't care," I said. "That's more than I've done since my dad died."

Deese held out his fist for a bump. "Right on."

I managed to lift my fist high enough to meet his, then dragged my forearm over my sweaty forehead. I couldn't keep the smile off my face. I felt lighter than I had since Mom had broken the news yesterday.

Two miles wasn't seven. Not even close. But it was a hell of a lot closer than zero.

When I got back to the bungalow, I found Noah sitting at the entrance. He tossed me a towel. "How was it?"

Blood pulsed through my body. I wasn't sure if my cheeks were red or purple. "How does it look like it was?" I wiped my face with the towel.

He handed me an icy bottle of water. "It looks like . . . you survived."

"Barely." I drank from it, grateful for the cool rush down my throat, into my core. "Want to get breakfast? I just need to shower first to rinse off."

He grinned. "Better yet, how about a swim?"

That was how I learned there was something very exhilarating about jumping into a body of water after a workout.

"How much butter?" Winnie asked.

I checked the piece of glossy paper in my hand: an old Betty Crocker recipe, torn directly out of the cookbook and sent by Aunt Shelly. The very act of her mailing it to me, along with the ingredients, demonstrated two things: (1) that Aunt Shelly would never make anything as unhealthy as spritz cookies, and thus would never need the recipe, and (2) that despite her commitment to avoiding sugar and gluten, she loved me, a lot. "One cup."

"You're putting a whole stick in here?" Winnie asked.

"Two sticks," Madison said. "Two sticks makes one cup."

Winnie mock gagged. "That's even worse." But when I wrinkled my nose, she dismissed me. "Oh, what do you care? You have the metabolism of a nuclear power plant."

"It's from hurdling." I used a blue spatula to scoop the butter into a large metal bowl. "And you have the curvaceous, confident badassery of a naked-woman painting."

"*Rubenesque* or something?" Madison asked.

"Only if you want women through the lens of the white male patriarchy," Winnie said. "How about a Monica Kim Garza painting? She's a dynamo."

I smiled. Just last week Madame had told us about the woman who'd left teaching to paint works depicting curvy women of color inspired by girl-power icons. "Perfect comparison, Win."

The heady fragrance of the flour coated my throat, hardening like Play-Doh that's been left out too long. It was the Sunday scent of my father, yeasty but sweet with the tang of sugar in the air.

I closed my eyes, unsure if I wanted to shut out or savor the memory of Dad baking the only recipe he knew how to bake from scratch: blueberry muffins. Maybe my pain of being left behind paled in comparison with the white-hot shadows of my dad's internal agony, but this version of him—whistling, his hair damp from a post-run shower, decked in Mom's floral apron, idly combining the ingredients for our breakfast—was probably the one I missed most of all.

"Lila?" Winnie said my name like a question. "Are you okay?"

"Sure." I paused. "No. Why?"

"You look tired," Madison said.

I put down a metal measuring cup. "My mom told me . . ." I swallowed hard to fight the lump of spiky emotion that had settled in my throat. "My dad tried more than once." I paused. "He'd attempted several times over the years. So it wasn't some sudden thing that escalated; it was in him for a long time. My whole life."

Madison bowed her head. "Ugh, Lila. That flat-out sucks."

Winnie slid the sack of flour closer to her. "Have I shared with you my cake theory?"

I blinked. "You have a theory about cake?"

Her nod was firm. "The cake theory of mental health."

I shook my head. Madison leaned against the counter, listening.

"Well, it's all about ingredients and variables and trauma." She grimaced and pointed at herself. "Take a recipe for a cake. You've got your standard ingredients—sugar, vanilla, flour, baking powder." She gestured with her hands. "They have specific recipes and steps, like the chemical makeup of people. My abuela's tres leches cake uses three milks—condensed, evaporated, and whole—and when you put them together, it's as light as a cloud." She leaned forward. "But sometimes our ingredients don't act like they're supposed to. Like, maybe a baker keeps being handed one ingredient and being told, 'This is sugar, this is sugar.' It comes in a box that says *S-U-G-A-R*. The baker reasons, rightly so, that they're using sugar. They combine everything in the right order and put it in the oven, and it looks like a cake and cuts like a cake, but it tastes like a salt lick. Or maybe the sugar really *is* sugar, but one outside factor is off. The oven temp is out of whack—the environment. Or the pan was overfilled, or the power goes out, and just like that the metaphorical cake-person suffers due to biology, or trauma, or abuse, or some combination of all of those. Sometimes your ingredients or genetics are right and your environment changes them anyway. Not the cake's fault."

A sense of peace flowed into me. I picked up the recipe, reading the ingredients, mulling over how the cookies would turn out if condensed sugar were labeled *flour* or if baking powder and baking soda were switched. It wouldn't be the cookies' fault. "The cake theory of mental health," I said.

"Trademarked," Winnie said, confident. "Well, not really. But. Pretend it is."

"Decent theory, Win." Madison peered at the recipe in my hand. "Did your aunt send a cookie press?"

"A what?"

"It's like the appliance baby of a gun and a hair dryer," Madison said. "You load it up, and then punch the cookies down onto the sheet."

"Violently domestic," Winnie said.

I bit my lip. "Can we still make them?"

"We can try," Madison said. "Maybe kind of shape the dough? Like this." She pinched some between her fingers, demonstrating.

Winnie took a small glob of the butter-sugar-flour mixture and rolled it in her hands. "How do you even know what a cookie press is?"

"I'm from the South," Madison said, an excuse we both oddly accepted. At least I did, until she added, "Now can we talk about why we're baking cookies for a boy?"

Madison and Winnie exchanged a look. Winnie cleared her throat. "The idea of having to prove yourself to a man via homemade cookies is just . . . a little much?"

My stomach leaped into my throat, then settled back down. I pinched some batter into a leaf design. "I know. I told him that too, but he makes a good point. I have been a little . . ." I paused, searching for the word. "Inconsistent."

"Well, we support you." Winnie bent closer to one of the little mounds of dough. "So long as you're not asleep on your feet."

"Wide awake," I said. "The last time I was excited about baking was with an Easy-Bake Oven."

"You know, horses really do sleep on their feet," Madison said. She hefted the oven open and slid our tray of dubiously designed cookies inside. "Or doze, at least. They have this thing called stay apparatus, where they lock their kneecaps using some kind of system of ligaments and tendons so they're standing, while asleep."

"I wish I had that ability during gym class," Winnie muttered.

Madison snorted. "Yeah. But it's not enough. They need to lie down for real REM sleep, which they only do if they feel safe."

The kitchen door banged open. Deese walked in, holding a plastic bag of what looked like gummy candy. "Ladies," he greeted us. "Are you"—he sniffed—"baking Christmas cookies?"

"Holiday cookies," Madison corrected.

"Patriarchy cookies," Winnie clarified.

"Awesome." Deese hiked himself up on the kitchen counter.

"Deese?" A smile curved Madison's lips. "What are you doing here?"

"Me? Drugs." He lifted the bag with a serious expression.

"Drugs?" Winnie raised her eyebrows.

Deese nodded. "My mom sent me these. Her naturopath put her on 'em for joint pain or something."

Winnie stacked dirty dishes into a pile. "Your mom sent you drugs?"

I held up my hands. "Let me see?"

He tossed me the bag. I checked the label and fought to suppress a laugh. "Deese."

"What's up?"

"This is CBD."

"And?"

"Deese," Madison hissed. "If my dad finds out that you're into drugs, he'll go all Brutal Protector Dad and ban me from seeing you."

I shook my head. "No. People. CBD is cannabidiol. There's no THC in this, which is what makes you high. Having one of these things will give you none of the euphoria. No sedation or feeling any different, unless you're one of the super-small fraction of people who get affected by something like acetaminophen." I tossed the bag to Deese. "Not sure what you're looking for here, buddy, but getting high isn't gonna happen."

Deese looked crushed. "I thought my mom was being so cool for my off-season."

The timer went off. I slid the cookies from the oven—they were perfectly done, if a bit misshapen. Winnie and Madison set to work on the dishes, Winnie washing and Madison drying, while I pried the cookies from the sheet with a spatula and sent them tumbling onto a cooling rack.

"You know, you and I have something in common," Deese said a few moments later.

I handed him a cookie. "Dead dads?"

"Well, yeah, but besides that," he said around a mouthful. "Preventable deaths."

I bit the inside of my cheek. "You're right," I said. "Winnie's dad was an accident. Madison's mom was an accidental overdose upon relapse. Noah's brother. The twins' mother died of cancer."

"Adds an extra layer to the whole thing, doesn't it? A zesty suck factor of the highest order."

It did. I nodded.

Deese swallowed the cookie. "At first I kinda felt like I wasn't allowed to grieve. If it had been a sober car accident, I would have felt so different."

"Angry at the world, instead of at him?"

"Exactly."

"I totally get it. If my dad had gotten hit by a car, or had a heart attack or a brain aneurysm or whatever, and sudden loss was the only thing I was dealing with?" I shrugged. "I'd be traumatized and sad, but with this, I also have to carry around his—"

"Shame," Deese finished.

"Shame. Agreed."

"I mean, you're still *you*. After everything with my dad, know what happened? I ate cereal for dinner, 'cause no one felt like cooking, not even my ma. I played *Madden*. I went to school. I went to bed and woke up. Just because my dad made a tragically heinous decision to drive while intoxicated doesn't mean I'm not me. A person who makes his own choices."

He was right. I was changing, but I was still me: a girl who ran, loved reading and science, wanted to draw or paint or sculpt, yet was still so totally lost in her father's decisions. When I spoke, my voice was quiet. "You're right. I'm still me. I'm just different now. A different me."

We watched Winnie and Madison load the cookies into a giant plastic bag and then a tote bag. "You know, my ma loves this saying that her grandma used to say," Deese said. "I think it might help you."

"What is it?"

"'The moment you realize you don't have control over what anyone else does is the moment you find yourself comfortable with your world.'"

I wanted to cry, and write it down, both at the same time. "Hope I get there."

# Chapter Twenty-Five

After yet another night with little sleep, I left the bungalow early the next morning. I made my way to Mess Hall with the tote bag of cookies slung over my shoulder. When I got there, it wasn't open yet. Outside, I settled down on the cement stairs, put the cookies at my feet, and rested my head on my knees. The sun-baked steps warmed my butt, and before long, I developed a serious case of swass.

"Great," I muttered. A sweaty butt was just what I needed to get me through the day.

That, and the healthy dose of self-pity lounging in my veins.

"Lila? Is that you?"

I lifted my head to see Mari and the camp's youngest member, CP. "Hey."

"You're up early this morning."

"Couldn't sleep."

Mari jingled a ring of keys. As she unlocked the door, she rolled her neck, which emitted audible cracks and pops. Beside her, CP scuffed his foot on the ground. "What's in the bag?"

"Cookies." I glanced at Mari and tapped the back of my neck. "Doesn't that hurt?"

She shook her head, smiling that big open emoji smile of hers. "Nope. Just warming up. Gets a little cool out at night now."

She was so weird.

"Wanna eat with me?" CP asked.

"Sure."

"Why do you have a bag of cookies?"

"It's a long story."

Inside Mess Hall, the rattling of silverware and ceramic pinged from the kitchen, along with the sizzle of breakfast foods: bacon, eggs, potatoes. I hadn't realized how quiet camp was in the morning until it came alive. More and more voices joined us, until they blended into a humming background noise.

I watched, mesmerized, as CP put away a lumberjack's breakfast, as my dad used to call it: two of everything. Eggs, bacon, sausage, pancakes. French toast, covered in butter and drizzled with syrup. One glass of milk, one of juice. He spilled half the breakfast on his shirt and slurped at the orange juice, staining his upper lip a deep sunset hue.

I loved him.

"I guess you were hungry," I said, spooning one more bite of cereal into my mouth before pushing it away.

He swallowed. "Why?"

I pointed to his plate. "Do you always eat that much?"

"My grandma makes half-Korean, half-American breakfasts. Soup, spicy seafood salad, kimchi, but also eggs and sometimes beans." He drained his juice. "This stuff is like what my parents used to make." He nudged his glasses up his nose. "Hey, you excited for dodgeball?"

"Dodgeball?"

"Yeah. We all gotta play at the end of the week." CP dragged a napkin over his face, wiping away sticky crumbs. "I played in gym class last year."

"What grade are you in, anyway?"

"I'm not in a grade."

"Huh?"

"Well, I will be in September. I finished second grade, but

213

I haven't started third yet. So right now I'm in between two things."

That was pretty much how I felt all the time now. Between two things. Waiting for something else to start. I reached over to him and squeezed his hand. "I like your logic."

After breakfast, we walked to our session of group therapy. I sent CP inside the Healing Center gazebo and waited beneath the shade of an oak tree for Deese and Noah.

To my surprise, Noah walked up by himself. He wore a green shirt, gray shorts, and Sperry sneakers. "Hey," he said. "What are you doing out here?"

I traced my thumb along the strap of the tote bag, then up to the empty hollow of my throat, wishing for my daffodil. "I'm, uh. Waiting for you."

Noah's face tightened. "I wanted to talk to you," he said. "I need to take back the proving thing."

He what? "You what?"

He shook his head. "I think it came out wrong. I told my mom about you."

My fingertips tingled. "You told your mom about me?"

"Well, yeah."

"When? At Visiting Day?"

Noah rubbed his jaw. "Why?"

*Only because I was looking for you the entire day.* "Just curious."

"I told her what I asked you to do. You know. Um. Prove how much you liked me."

"And?"

"And she called me an ass."

I grinned. "Your mom called you an ass?"

"Yes. She did. Very warm and cuddly, that mother of mine."

"So no more playing games?"

"Well." He cupped my elbow, drawing me closer to him, then brushed his palm down the length of my arm, lingering at my hand. "In any game I play, I'm more of a pawn than a king."

"Clever." Relief and desire laced my blood, warming my veins. I drew in a breath, let it out, and slipped the tote bag off my shoulder. "Well, now that the pressure's off, here's my proof."

He opened the bag and pulled out the container. When he saw the spritz cookies, he gasped. "You remembered?"

"I did," I said, ducking my head.

"It's like Christmas in July." A hot breeze stirred the leaves above us, dappling shadows over Noah's face.

"Today's August first," I said, realizing it had been five months since I'd last seen my dad. For a heartbeat, I wondered if I'd ever lose track of how long it had been. I shook my head, watching Noah bite into the cookie.

He wiggled those eyebrows at me. "This is perfect," he said, popping the rest of it into his mouth. "You remembering how much I like these is very sexy."

My breath caught in my throat. "Really?"

"Really," he said, nearly breathing the word.

When I'd started my handbook, I'd had a single goal: protecting my heart. After all, life with my dad had taught me that only those who you love can really hurt you. The number-one rule.

What I hadn't counted on was that someone else might be able to swim in a mire of grief and see me for who I was. Not just a daughter of suicide. Not just weighted sadness. Not defined by a raw, newly fatherless trajectory.

The handbook was my way of trying to make sense of my world. But the part of me that had penned that first rule hadn't considered that someone else might make me feel . . . happy. Safe.

Wait. That wasn't quite right.

I hadn't considered that I could make *myself* happy and safe while allowing someone else into my heart.

Even though I didn't want to risk it, I had a growing, nudging sensation that what I was feeling for Noah might be something that could turn into more. I wasn't in love, not yet, but this was maybe like a low-volume version of it. He was on my mind all the time. And yet what if we kept going here, fell in love, and then had to deal with the physical separation of miles between us? What if I had to deal with the fallout of that pain—the pain of missing someone very much alive?

I took in the sight of his honest, open, ruddy-cheeked face, the slope of his shoulders, and the wave of his hair. I thought of the what-ifs in books I'd read and movies I'd watched and artists I'd admired and poetry I'd learned, and on the off chance that Sammy's middle-namesake, Tennyson, was right when he wrote *'Tis better to have loved and lost, / Than never to have loved at all,* I decided that maybe what was in the future wasn't what my heart needed to worry about right now. Maybe it was the shade of the oak tree, or the poetic struggle of my endocrine system, or the very setting of where I was: a bucolic camp designed for people who knew loss at its most intimate. I grasped whatever that feeling was that I was having, rose up on the balls of my feet, hyperaware of the tight contraction of my calf muscles, and my lips found those of the boy who might just understand exactly the kinds of emotions swirling through me.

His mouth was warm and soft, and I leaned into it as if he could swallow me whole. In the moment, there was nothing I could imagine better: Noah consuming me. My fingertips learned his cheeks were warm from the sun.

The barest tip of his tongue met mine, retreated, returned to torch my body. I wanted nothing more from this day than to do just this. The memory of the first time I saw him floated into my brain, and desire crackled through my chest. I nudged his nose with mine, as if to prod him into agreeing to do this every day for the rest of ever.

When he finally broke away, I was hit with two things:

1. the reminder that oxygen was necessary for survival, and
2. a billowing, all-encompassing wave of disappointment that the kissing was over.

I stopped. My handbook was screwed.

"Now I'm angry with myself," Noah said.

I blinked, a little dazed. "Huh? Why?"

He tugged one of my curls. "I missed out on doing this for weeks."

I caught his hand in mine. "Checkmate."

# Chapter Twenty-Six

Over the next few days, I discovered a beautiful secret:

Camp with Noah > Camp without Noah.

Seemingly overnight, we went from two people orbiting the same planet to two people on the same rocket ship. We hiked the property, talked about our friends from home, and ate meals together. Daylight grew shorter, our kisses grew longer, and for the first time in a long time, I felt time speed forward, flying with crows instead of crawling with ants.

One afternoon, we went pedal-boating on the lake, our legs churning in sync while we made plans for next week's "field trip" to downtown Kennebunkport.

"My aunt loves it there," I said. "There's a whole shop devoted to mini-doughnuts."

"And equally delicious to the average-sized doughnut, mini-doughnuts are even better because you can consume multiples. I'm down."

"Exactly." We stopped pedaling. I leaned back and lifted my face to the sun. "A bunch of cafés, too."

Noah trailed his hand in the lake water. "Would you rather drink only hot coffee or only cold coffee for the rest of your life?"

"Mine's easy. You go first."

He tapped his fingers on his thighs. "Iced, I guess."

"Hot for me. Especially if it's from the place where I work, the Mug." I thought about what it might be like to share my life at home with Noah, imagining bringing him to our hometown theater or hiking with him through Frothingham Park. "What's your town like?"

"My town?"

"Yeah. You know. At home, what do you do with your friends for fun?"

"The stuff everyone does, I guess." He shifted on the hard seat.

"Like . . ."

"Like this." He raised one of his trademarked eyebrows, ran his hand along the front of my required life jacket, and tightened the straps. Without warning, he pressed his lips against mine, stood up, and cannonballed off the side of the pedal boat, whooping and yelling.

A heat wave crested that first week of August, bringing with it a heavy dose of humidity. One night, my bunkmates shifted in their half sleep, kicking sheets to the ends of beds, sighing, and taking great, prolonged sips of water. At breakfast, all Winnie, Madison, and I could stomach was yogurt, fruit, and enough iced tea to turn a profit for any local coffee shop.

"I feel like the air is hammering on my skin," Winnie complained.

Madison put her head on the table. "I'm sweating even when I sit still. This is aggressive." She heaved herself upright. "Jeff is having me organize the dodgeball tournament, since I can't play. Will you guys help me sort out the balls and split everyone into teams this afternoon?" She put her hands together in a very Jeff-like pose. "He thinks it'll teach me *great responsibility* and *effective communication*."

"Oh, joy," Winnie said. "You forgot *leadership skills*." She paused. "But why not? Nothing better to do."

"Noah and I are going to hang during free time," I said. "I'll meet you there this afternoon?"

Madison threw me a grateful smile. "Done."

Three hours later, zero wind stirred the trees. Even a swim wasn't refreshing, the lake sun-warmed and teeming with campers, the air difficult to distinguish from the water. You could sit absolutely motionless outside, and still be covered in a muggy mist.

"I wish we could go to the movies," I said. "It's always cold there. I want to sit in an icebox."

"I could use a roller coaster's amount of breeze." Noah tilted his head back. My eyes trailed the angle of his jawline, the hard lump of his Adam's apple. "Okay. Would you rather, day-date style. Bike ride, or lie on the grass and bemoan our uncomfortable existence?"

"I'll choose door number one."

At the bike rack by the art room, I picked out a cool, mint-green retro number, while Noah chose a zippy red one. We sailed around the property, pumping our legs up the gentle incline toward the camp's entrance, then coasting back toward the main buildings to win some breeze.

"You've got some strong legs, Lady Lila," Noah called on one of our trips up to the camp's entrance. Instead of turning around and flying back down the hill, he steered the bike in a graceful loop, curving around the mouth of the entrance.

*He noticed your legs. Be cool, Lila.* "Been training with Deese." I adjusted my helmet and joined his wide arc, the tires of my bike trusting his path.

He slowed to a stop, and I pulled up beside him. I slid forward on the seat, the balls of my feet tapping the ground in a rocking motion. "This air is thicker than a sauna. It's like trying to breathe in hot biscuit batter." I tucked an escaped strand of hair back into my braid.

"What an image," Noah said, wrinkling his nose. "Okay. Would you rather, weather edition. One full year of this muggy mess, or blizzards?"

Blizzards are nice for about two hours. No question. "This."

He shifted his foot so his leg met mine. The wiry tufts of his leg hair brushed against the smooth expanse of my skin. Not altogether unpleasant. "I think I'd go blizzard," he said. "I love skiing."

"Not me. My mom tore her ACL the only time she went, so we've never gone."

His face lit up. "Maybe . . . this winter, I can introduce you to it."

I swallowed. Real life, coming to a theater near you in just a few short weeks. He pressed his leg against my own, this time more insistently. A pleasant glow spread through the area of my body perched on the bike seat. I gripped the handles of my bike. "I'd like that. Do you ski a lot?"

He nodded. "My parents love to travel. We go to the White Mountains in New Hampshire every year. And my grandparents have a house on Cape Cod, so we used to go there for two weeks in August."

"I was going to run a race there this summer with my dad. The Falmouth." I debated telling him that part of me still hoped to this year, the week before camp ended, if my mom would entertain the thought of getting me there. Just the thought of running it made me feel closer to my dad than anything else had so far. But for now, I held that to myself, something to keep between my dad and me.

He covered my hand with his own. "I heard that one's hard."

"Brutal," I said, wrinkling my nose. "Is your grandparents' house anywhere near Falmouth?"

He let go of my hand, reaching down to adjust his bike chain. "Nah. The Cape is huge."

"I know. We usually stay in Harwich." I curved my arm up as if I were flexing my bicep, replicating the tail on Massachusetts. I touched the skin on my triceps, near my elbow. "Right here. Where do your grandparents live?"

"I always forget the name of it." He straightened up. "Race you back to camp?"

I frowned. There were tons of towns on the Cape, but he'd been going there since he was a kid. "How can you forget the name of it?"

He let out a breath. "It's one of these little ones. Like a village. I don't know," he said. "To be honest, I don't like thinking about it. It reminds me of hanging out with my brother. Is that okay?"

A wave of empathy cut through the humidity in the afternoon air. I ducked my head. "Of course," I said. I hadn't even begun to think about what our family vacations would look like, now that Dad was gone.

Noah pushed off the pavement. "Let's see what you're made of, All-Star Hurdler," he called over his shoulder.

I'd let him lead before, but I'd kept up easily. Now he tore away from me, blazing back to camp. Even with me standing, pedaling my legs with all I had, he beat me. I found him sitting on the step of the art room, leaning against a deck pillar, a smug smile on his face.

Later, I showered the sweat from my body and twisted my hair into a wet knot on top of my head. Singing under my breath, I toweled off, threw on a cotton romper, and walked carefully back to the bungalow, making sure my thighs didn't touch and my armpits were exposed to reduce the odds of immediate humidity sweat.

Inside, fans whirred. Madison and Winnie were sprawled on their bunks, weaving more bracelets.

Winnie glanced at me, then fiddled with the strings. "You're in a good mood."

"I am, actually." I flushed. "I had fun today."

"Where have you been?" Madison's voice was even.

I furrowed my eyebrows, trying to figure it out. "We went for a bike ride."

Madison threw her half-woven bracelet down. "Thanks for your help today."

"My help?" Heat crept up my neck, spidering into my cheeks. The dodgeballs. "Oh. Shit. Oh no. I completely forgot, you guys."

"Cool. Thanks for the help."

"I mean . . ." I crossed my arms. "Did you really need me? You knew I was hanging out with Noah." I fought to keep my voice steady. "I had a *good day*. He made me feel *better*. Why am I being punished for that?"

"Look. Your grief is new. I get it. I get it twice over—first my mom, and now, even more recently, my friend." Madison's eyes hardened as Cat's unsaid name slithered into the room. "But right from the start, you've been so stubborn, Lila. Remember the leotard? Your insistence you were only here for a week?" She paused. "This whole camp isn't about you."

I opened my mouth, closed it. Truth had a funny way of prying itself to the surface. I didn't want to admit it, but she had a point. I glanced at Winnie. "I don't know what to say."

Winnie looked at me sadly. "It was organizing dodgeballs. We're two capable people. It's not that we needed the help; it's that you said you'd be there, and you weren't."

Tears stung my eyes. I said nothing. I'd been so caught up in the day—in the click of the bicycle spokes, the rush of thick air, the heady feeling of falling for someone—that I'd neglected to do what I said I'd do.

There in the bungalow, the last several weeks of fun with Madison and Winnie evaporated into the humid air. From its stashed place in my duffel bag, the first rule in my handbook taunted me. Reminded me not to love anyone, because all love and trust did was lead to pain.

"It won't happen again," I muttered. I shoved my feet into my running sneakers, pushed the wooden door of the bungalow open, and ran.

# Chapter Twenty-Seven

Word about Noah and me being a "thing" had traveled to Sammy, and at his insistence, we met him for lunch at Mess Hall after my run the next day. After a morning spent training—I'd left extra early to avoid a still-sleeping Winnie and Madison—Noah and I arrived to find Sammy in a booth, his hair slicked back, and Dad's cobalt-blue-and-beige pocket square, now faded, pinned to the front of his shirt.

A wave of nostalgia swept through me, the familiar feeling of homesickness for a person and not a place. I blinked tears from my eyes at the sweetness of that patterned fabric.

"Sit down, Noah," Sammy said. He inclined his head toward me in greeting. "Lila."

"I like your outfit choice," I whispered.

Sammy fought to keep his face straight. "Thank you."

Noah sat, snaking his arm around the back of the booth. His fingers played a light tune on my shoulder. "What's up, Sammy?"

"Mom says I'm the man of this house now," Sammy said, pointing at the space between him and me. When I raised my eyebrows at him, he hissed, "Mom *said*."

"Mom said that to make you feel better."

Sammy frowned. "What's gotten into you?"

*My friends are angry with me for letting them down.* I twisted in the booth to make sure they weren't coming in to Mess Hall. The coast was clear. I let out a breath. "Nothing."

"Move on, Lila." Sammy recovered. "So, Noah. When I was playing basketball the other day, Mike told me you're dating my big sister."

"You heard correctly, little man."

Sammy reached his hand across the table and shook Noah's. "Excellent. Welcome to the family."

"That's it?" Noah asked, bemused.

For the record, I wanted to kiss him when he looked bemused. Mostly because I wanted to kiss him all the time. But I held off, because Sammy furrowed his brow and crinkled his nose. It was the face he'd worn since he was a toddler when he was trying to figure something out. "Should I ask you something else?"

"Maybe if my intentions are good."

"Are they?"

"Yep."

"Okay. Good." Sammy raised his hand then and waved.

I turned around and saw CP approaching the table, balancing a tray piled with slices of pizza. "Sammy. You did not ask CP to bring us our food."

"I'm providing our meal," Sammy said, grinning a sly little grin.

"*Samuel.* You need to be nice to CP. Don't make him bring you things."

"I *am* nice to CP. I asked him to come so I can take him to dodgeball later."

*Dodgeball.* My stomach flipped. "Then why are you forcing him to serve us pizza?"

"I invited him to eat with us. He's a cool little dude."

"He's what—three years younger than you?"

Sammy ignored me, turning his attention to Noah. "Noah. Brother to brother, I need your advice."

Brother to brother? I put my head in my hands and groaned.

"On what?" Noah asked.

CP set the tray down in between us and whispered hello to

me. I ruffled his hair, and he pushed his glasses up on his nose. "Hey, CP," I said. "Make sure Sammy's being nice to you."

"Sammy's the best." CP slid a plate of pepperoni pizza toward me.

Sammy took a slice. "Noah, man. You gotta help me out with Alicia."

"Alicia?" Noah asked.

"Yeah. Heather and Emilia's sister."

"Wait a second," I said. "They have a sister?" And she was the angriest kid here—Alicia, of the very cool trendy purple glasses, from group therapy? That kind of fit, actually. "Since when do you need advice on girls? Plus, don't you have a girlfriend at home?" Three, actually. I couldn't keep it straight. The last time I'd picked him up from school, he'd been off kissing a girl "on a dare" behind the swing set on the playground.

"You really have your head in the land." Sammy shook his own.

"The *sand*," I clarified.

"What?"

"Forget it."

"See?" Sammy pointed at me. "Girls. So confusing."

"I have no advice on confusing girls," Noah said, poking my shoulder.

"Alicia's *scary*," CP said. His eyes were round behind his glasses. "She draws bad words all over her pants."

Sammy sighed. "She certainly *swears* the pants in our relationship."

I caught sight of those curse-laden jeans later that afternoon, when I stood in a state of complete bewilderment in the field behind the Lodge, surveying my fellow red-faced, damp-haired campers as we partook in the oddest game of all time.

Maybe if I had remembered to help Madison and Winnie, I'd have learned that it was not your standard-issue gym-class dodgeball, where opposing teams attempt to eliminate players by hitting them with regulation balls. Instead it was Jeff's therapeutically questionable version: Three-Legged Ditch-It Dodgeball. We were split into pairs and had to tie ourselves to our partner at the leg with a set of knotted bandannas, hence the "three-legged" moniker.

"Deese, you're with her," Madison said. She moved on without a glance in my direction.

I squinted at Madison. "She won't even say my name?"

Deese raised his eyebrows. "What'd you do, Cunningham?"

I ignored him, bending over to tie my right leg to his left. A barking Madison paired Noah with Alicia. It was probably a good thing; I would just have been distracted by Noah's leg on mine again.

"Here's the catch: Every time someone throws a ball"—here Jeff held one aloft—"you shout something. Let it out. Purge the strongest feelings you've been feeling by screaming them into the safe air of the camp." He tossed the ball to Winnie. "So long as it isn't a personal attack on someone else," he added hurriedly.

What commenced was like the child-safety-lock version of a Roman bloodbath. Campers screamed obscenities, darted around the field like cheetahs, and chucked rubber balls at one another. At one point Mike, the kid I'd clobbered in the nose that first week of camp, beat at his chest with his fists after getting Winnie and Sammy out. They waddled off the field and untied themselves. Winnie collapsed cross-legged beside Madison, who checked names off on the clipboard.

I shook my head. "This is intense."

Deese wobbled his leg, and mine automatically followed. "Imagine doing this for a track meet," he said.

I laughed. "That would be a sight."

". . . your mama!" someone called.

"Did you seriously make a 'your mama' joke? What are you, a hundred years old?"

"My mom is *dead*, you asshole!"

All while slinging dodgeballs at one another.

It was a remarkable scene, set in the heat from the late-summer afternoon. The only relief came from a hose hooked up to the back of the Lodge, where campers took turns spraying themselves and drinking from the spout.

"Lila, move!" In front of me, CP and his partner, one of the Lagharis—both surprisingly spry—rolled to the ground.

"Duck and lunge," I directed Deese. Moving as one, we lunged forward. I palmed the ball, threw it in the air, and spiked it toward the other team.

But there was a reason I didn't play sports involving balls, as evidenced by the direct hit to Madison's head.

"Ow!" she cried. She clutched her head and whipped around, trying to figure out who'd thrown the offending ball. When her eyes landed on me, her perfect face went overcast. She narrowed her eyes. I held up my hands and shrugged.

By the time Alicia nailed me with a ball, I was laughing. It didn't quite hurt—it was almost like a less-intense version of getting your eyebrows waxed.

"Sorry," Noah called. His grin was supposed to be apologetic, but it still spread warmth through my belly.

Deese gave him a peace sign. "Good game."

"So?" Jeff said, at the end. He'd corralled everyone back onto the field, sweating and tired. "Anyone feel better?"

The anger and vehemence from the earlier shouts were gone, replaced by joking and the weird sense of camaraderie shared by a group of people with one harsh reality in common. The truth was, I did feel better—almost. The murky sadness had been lifted, scrubbed, with one glaring exception: the sticky hurt on Madison's and Winnie's faces whenever they looked my way.

# Chapter Twenty-Eight

The next morning, Deese and I partially circled the border of the camp, running maybe four miles. Deese was able to chat throughout his run, waxing on about Madison in one breath and his grandma and ma in the next. I huffed alongside him, sucking air into my crampy rib cage and grunting half-intelligible replies.

"Drive those knees forward," Deese directed. "Pretend something you want is in front of you. It's magnetic. Pull your knees to it."

*Something I want?* I concentrated, thinking of Noah. "Am I doing it?"

"Right on. And make sure your hands aren't crossing your midline."

I relaxed my arms down through my fingertips, keeping them parallel. "Like this?"

"Great form."

We fell silent, our steps sounding *patpatpat* on the dirt trail. I willed my knees forward, picturing Noah the way he was on our bike ride, the image evaporating when I remembered what that day had cost me. My reliance. My dependability. My newfound friends' trust.

Kicked-up dust clouds poofed at our feet. Emotion swelled in my throat, and I moved faster. I mean, sure. I'd lost track of time and hadn't shown up when I'd said I would, but did that mean our friendship was over? I could own my mistake, but why did everyone I wound up caring for just up and peace out on me? I sucked in a breath, clinging to one thought.

*Noah.*

I wouldn't let him ditch me too.

"Pick it up," Deese said, starling me from my reverie. He checked his watch. "We're about to hit mile five."

"Faster?"

"Yup." Deese increased our pace, and I struggled to match his steps.

He glanced at me. "Are you going to run for school this fall?"

"This fall?" I breathed out a laugh. "I don't do cross-country."

"Yeah, but you could sprint."

"I could, but—" Out of nowhere, a knifing pain gripped my right calf muscle in a boa constrictor-worthy vise. I inhaled and then forgot to exhale. White dots danced across my vision.

"Lila?"

I'd come to a halt right near the gymnastics building. "My calf," I managed. "Spasming."

"Probably a charley horse," Deese said. "Sit down." He pulled a flask from his running belt. "Here, have some water."

I tumbled to the ground and gripped my calf, pressing into the contracted muscle with the pads of my thumbs. "Ow."

"Have you ever had one before?"

I set my lips and shook my head.

He sat down beside me. "They hurt."

"Thank you, Captain Obvious."

"There's that winning sense of humor," Deese said.

After a minute or so, the pain edged away, leaving a throbbing tightness in its wake. I stood up and tested my leg.

"How is it?"

I gritted my teeth. "Better. Let's keep going."

"Uh-uh," Deese said, shaking his head. "You're limping. Let's walk back."

"But—"

"Trust me. You don't want to run on it if it doesn't feel right. You could really injure it, then be out of running for weeks."

I was surprised to find myself blinking back tears. "When can I run again?"

His face was sympathetic. "I'm no doctor, but I'm always told not until it feels a hundred percent."

My confidence flagged. How was I ever going to run those seven miles in Falmouth if I couldn't even get through five? And how was I supposed to do that in just a week? "This sucks."

Deese shrugged. "All part of training, Cunningham."

That night, I got ready to meet up with Noah at the Shed. One glance in the Com's mirror told me my hair could win the camp superlative for Most Catastrophic. "Great," I muttered, scraping it up into a topknot. I bent over to swipe my bare legs with a bug-spray wipe. My right calf muscle was tense to the touch.

At the Shed, I ducked into the little alcove where we'd met up to drink Orient Point wine the night before Visiting Day. I was the first to arrive. As I lowered myself to the ground, I winced at the small twinge of pain in my calf.

"Not a good sign," I said aloud, mulling over the merits of suffering through a long walk to the Lodge to ask for some ibuprofen. Just then, Noah arrived.

He crawled in next to me, and I'm pretty sure we said hi. But then we were kissing for a while—a long while—and that ate my short-term memory, so I couldn't be sure.

What I could be sure of was that when his hand traveled

down to my sore calf, I yelped. With vampiric speed, Noah backed away from me.

"I'm sorry," he said, panting. "I didn't mean to—"

"You didn't," I said. "I'm just really sore from my run this morning."

The relief in his breathed *oh* was so palpable I smiled.

"Come back," I said.

He did. But we took a break from kissing, instead lying back on the quilt. Noah put his head on my shoulder, and I curled my arm around him, tickling his hair, his ear, his neck.

"Feels good," he said.

"Yeah." I smiled with swollen lips. "My first day here, I would have bet the odds were one to a million I'd be doing whatever it is we're doing with a cute guy at camp."

"You think I'm cute?"

I poked his side and said nothing.

"One in a million, huh?"

"Yup."

"Like the odds of finding those golden tickets in the Roald Dahl candy bars you like."

I laughed. "Willy Wonka, but sure."

"Nearly impossible."

"I must've eaten a hundred of those things, so I'd say it certainly felt that way."

"What about now?" He nudged something rectangular into my hand. In the moonlight, the purple wrapper shone nearly silver.

"You didn't," I said, utterly delighted because he had.

"Open it."

"Where did you find this?"

"My mom did. On eBay."

"You get your mom to romance girls for you?"

"Only when they like weird things. Plus, I owed you something tasty after those cookies."

As I peeled back the paper and foil, my hand shook. I broke it open all the way, hoping the silver would melt to gold . . . but nothing.

"Come on," Noah said. He pulled the chocolate from me, lifted it up, and inspected the packaging. "I knew she should've paid extra for a guaranteed golden ticket."

"That would be cheating."

He broke the bar in half and handed me squares of chocolate laced with toffee and nuts. "At least we have the chocolate."

"To the chocolate," I agreed, clinking mine with his. We ate, and I savored the sweet, creamy sugar melting the moment it touched my tongue. I swallowed. "Are you excited for tomorrow?"

Noah leaned back. His eyebrows knotted. "Tomorrow?"

"Yeah, the field trip. Kennebunkport."

"The field trip!" A smile broke out over his face. "Yeah, I am. You?"

I nodded. "I'm just starting to feel cooped up here."

"It's a date, then."

"Is it?" I pictured us walking the streets of the seaside town, strolling hand in hand. I covered my mouth, still full of chocolate, and smiled.

"It is. But the day after tomorrow . . ." He faltered.

"The day after tomorrow what?"

"You know what? Snooze button. I'd like tomorrow to be a perfect day."

I frowned. "So whatever you were going to say would spoil it?"

"You're really reading into this, huh? You *did* say you want

235

a career in therapy." He brushed his knuckles across my jaw and gave me a crooked grin. "Respect the snooze."

I remembered our first night in the Shed, soaked in Orient Point wine, Madison declaring herself the journalist, Deese the doctor. Noah, the beach-bar-owning lawyer. "I suppose I did."

"Did you have to go to one? After your dad."

I imagined Call-Me-Connie's pointy index finger. "Just the school adjustment counselor, so far. Did you?"

I felt his head move against my shoulder. "Yeah, I've seen one."

"Did it help?"

"Not in the way you might be thinking." Before I could ask what he meant, he changed the subject. "You can tell me about your dad, you know. If you want."

Maybe it was easier because I couldn't really see him. Nighttime in Maine is made of the sort of inky, black-on-black darkness that floats across your eyes after you've been in a bright room. It folded in on itself, giving me a thin layer of bravado to hide behind.

"My dad, he . . ." I took a deep breath, remembering. God, I missed him. "Maybe most teenage girls without strict dads might say this, but he wasn't like most dads. I really, really liked him. I mean, outside of him being my parent. I used to think all adults were super smart because of him. He knew all these facts."

"Facts?"

I nodded. "Right. Like, what's a word in the English language that presents all the vowels in alphabetical order?"

Noah thought for a moment. "I give up."

"*Facetious.* Or *facetiously*, if you want to include the 'sometimes *y*' rule. Do you know a word that has three double letters in a row?"

"Nope."

"My dad did. It's *bookkeeper*. He knew something about everything, and I just admired that so much." I fell silent. My father could rattle off the periodic table of elements. He built a wooden deck for our elderly neighbors, just because he could. He did flawless imitations of Kermit the Frog, Mickey Mouse, and JFK. Whenever I fought with one of my friends or was moody about a guy, he took me out for ice cream and a movie, without asking about anything. Part of him just knew.

Noah took my hand in his. Running the pad of his thumb over my palm, he said, "I bet you miss him."

My mouth twisted. "So much."

"I bet he misses you."

Would he? Even though my parents had a pretty story about how much they'd wanted me, their little Lyon, how would I ever know whether it had all been bullshit? They might've liked their life together fine without us. Maybe Mom would've had the chance to write a book like she'd always wanted. And Dad? Dad might have become a doctor, the way he'd planned to before his life changed tracks and he wound up at the university. He might not have grown into the kind of person who believed his family would have a better life without him.

Those were his words, the ones in the note he'd left us the night he died. *A better life without me.* This germy idea—that by leaving us, he'd provide this so-called better life—latched onto his brain and stayed there, festering like an infection, marinating like someone else's overseasoned steak. *A better life.*

Which was all very confusing, of course, because I'd liked my life just fine, and it was heartbreaking that he thought the world would be unburdened without him. I swallowed, trying to dissolve the lump in my throat that formed at the exact spot my daffodil necklace used to rest. It was the spot where my empathy sat, the spot that hardened when I thought of the sort of pain my father had experienced.

How could he have possibly thought that a better life for us was a world without him in it? My own emotions felt torn in half, stuck between my growing understanding that he must have been using gambling to try to fill some kind of void, feeling guilty about what that meant for our family, ping-ponging to the murkier, more selfish, shameful part of me that asked, *Why didn't he love me enough to stick around?*

"Who knows what he thinks, or where he is," I said. "I don't know what I believe anymore." I brushed my thumb along my clavicle, tracing my missing chain, wishing I knew what to believe. How to feel. But I was with Noah, who'd gone through something tragic too. The space between us was one I could fill, with someone who could actually understand. I steeled myself. "When he died, everything in my life that I knew to be true just changed so fast. My mom's uncle Frank died on a Saturday. On Sunday night we sat around, all four of us, watching *Bridesmaids*. I had my feet on his lap." The last time I ever touched my dad. Our bellies full of a rare winter cookout dinner. I told Noah what I'd learned: how Dad had lied to Mom about his addiction, completely hiding it from us, and taking money from Uncle Frank.

In the moonlight, Noah tilted his head back and listened, waiting for me to finish. "And once your uncle died, your dad knew you were about to find out that money was missing."

I wrapped my arms around myself and nodded. "That's my guess, too."

"That's heavy," he said, echoing a word I recognized from Jeff.

"Yeah."

"What did he gamble on?"

The image of the Moleskine notebook rose like a flame, sputtered out. "Sports. He kept track of everything, a careful record of games he'd bet on. Basketball. Football. Tennis. College sports. Plus the type of bet, like head-to-head—I don't even know what that means, but the words are still engraved in my brain. All the numbers kept getting higher: how often he bet, the amounts of money he put down. It got to the point where he bet on, like, curling and Ping-Pong." Mom had said it had all started with lottery tickets, and that when she'd found a whole stack of them, he'd turned to doing everything online. No paper trail, unless you counted my little find. "I guess you could say it became anything and everything, until it was nothing."

Silence fell between us again, but not for long: A symphony of croaking frogs, rustling trees, and the gentle lap of lake water became our music.

"The day he died . . . He'd left before any of us got up, which was weird, but things were already weird because Mom's uncle had died, you know? No one was home when Sammy and I walked in after school. That was a little out of the ordinary for us, since Mom was usually there writing. But she was with her cousins, planning her uncle's funeral. When she came home, she asked if I knew if Dad had picked up the dry cleaning. I said he wasn't home. She started firing all these questions at me—when he'd left, if he'd called. When I answered, she got this look on her face I'd never seen before, which I now recognize as panic." I paused. "She kept repeating, 'Have you seen him, Lila? Have you? Oh God, have you seen him?' I obviously thought this was a huge overreaction, and I told her so. She called him. On repeat. Over and over. Honestly? I thought there was something wrong with her. Then she found a folded note on the corner of the counter, in with the mail and the spare car keys. It was folded into quarters. Computer paper."

At some point in my story, Noah had closed his eyes. He opened them then, and when I met his gaze, his smile was sad. "I'm so sorry, Lila."

I sighed. "The note was the worst part. It was like, 'I'm so sorry, my life-insurance money should take care of you—oh, by the way, I love you guys.' Which: (a) the life-insurance money will not be enough to do much with at all, according to a conversation I wasn't supposed to hear between my mom and my aunt Shelly, and (b) there was a grammatical error in the note, which was super unlike him."

"He wasn't in his right mind," Noah said.

"I know he wasn't. I can't . . . Before all this? I was so confident in how much he loved me." I picked at the Wonka Bar wrapper and peeled pieces of the shining silver paper away, letting the curling tendrils pile into spirals in my lap. "I've started to think that him resorting to taking his own life tells me he was in depths of pain I'm lucky to be unable to fathom. Weirdly enough, that grammatical error—he used the wrong *your*, adding apostrophe-R-E where there wasn't supposed to be one—confirmed that for me. If he had been thinking clearly, then it wouldn't have happened. Mom's the writer, but he knew that stuff too—he'd often check over all our essays."

Noah gripped my hand tighter. The night swam around us.

"At the bottom of the typed note were two handwritten additions. You'd think they'd be all 'I'm sorry' or 'I'll love you all forever,' right? But, nope. One was that he'd gotten the mail and it was on the counter. The other was that he'd won a video-game system at work and it was in the closet."

It's funny, the way our brains process things. Not ha-ha funny, but finding-the-meaning-in-literature funny. Ironic. Those two boring details seared themselves into my brain that day, somehow making it more real and more painful than I sometimes thought I could bear. "So," I said, rushing to get the words out, to get everything out, "the details: He walked into the town forest, which is at the end of our street, and . . . he used a rope he'd bought that day at the hardware store. The police found him at three in the morning."

I'd been sitting, wide awake, in a dark corner of the living room, my brain scrolling and analyzing the contents of Dad's note. Sammy, who as far as I knew had still never read it, was asleep on the couch. Mom was in the bedroom. The police came up the walkway slowly, but with purpose, their feet shuffling on the concrete steps.

Two hollow sounds.

*Knock.*

*Knock.*

Noah leaned back. "I can imagine it, but I also can't." His words were careful, cradled the way one might hold something delicate or dangerous. "I don't know what to say."

"You don't have to say anything."

"No, I do. I . . ." His eyes were half-lidded, the whites just barely visible in the dark. "I hate that you went through that. I wish I could do something to make it better."

I tapped his hand with my fingertip. "Thanks."

"Before all this, I thought I was the only one in the world who felt the way I did."

"All this?"

"Camp." He squeezed my hand. "You."

My heartbeat hiccupped in my chest, unraveling like the

ends of a frayed ribbon. "It's so much different than I thought it would be," I said. "I didn't even want to come."

"I did. Camp was my idea."

"You said that in therapy that first day. But how did you even know about this place? My school's adjustment counselor told me and then my mom about it. Otherwise I never would've known it existed."

"My mom and Jeff go way back."

The wind picked up then, electrifying my hair. I pulled my hand away to tuck in a stray escaped lock, using the distance between us to study his profile. The bold eyebrows, the ruddy cheeks, blue eyes pale in the dusky moonlight. I wanted to know more about him. Everything about him. I touched the bare skin of his leg. "Do you want to tell me about your brother?"

He shifted his eyes toward me. Away. Said nothing.

"You don't have to," I said when the silence billowed between us.

Noah tilted his head back again, fixing his gaze on something up and to the left of us. When I followed it, all I could see were the tops of the trees. "No, I should. You did." He fumbled for my hand again, and a relieved energy crackled through me.

"Well. I'm here. If you want to tell me, that is."

"It's not like your story. It's just—I lost my brother in a way that's nearly impossible to believe."

I chewed the inside of my cheek. Hadn't he said it was asthma? Asthma wasn't usually a killer, but it's not as if it was impossible to believe.

"So. Like I said. Not the same." His words were clipped.

"Still, though."

Noah tilted his head to the side, popping the joints in his

neck with an audible crack. When he moved, his hand squeezed mine. His palm was so much larger than my own.

"That's terrible," I continued. "But—didn't you—before, at the dance. Didn't you say something about asthma?"

His hand twitched. "Yeah, he had asthma."

"You said, 'Asthma's a bitch.' I took that to mean he'd died of an asthma attack."

Noah exhaled. "How many times can one person press the snooze button before they're irrevocably late?"

I ducked my head to hide my frustration. We were quiet for a very long time, tension building between us. I fought with myself—I didn't want to push him into talking about something he wasn't ready to talk about, yet I was frustrated by enormous amounts of curious. "What are you thinking?" I asked finally.

"Right now?"

"Right now."

He sighed, crooked his elbow under my chin, and ran his palm over my jawline. "Right now, I'm thinking we are two people living profoundly terrible situations."

"It's nice to take a break from it all," I whispered.

His answer was wordless, but my body heard it.

When it came to having sex, I had always pictured it going a certain way. The reality was both how and not how I'd pictured it. It began with a question, my nod and yes of consent, and a dawning sense that this was really happening.

Time was compressed here at camp. We were staring down a tunnel of two weeks left in this place—this oasis, really—away from reality. Every day had taken on a new, fleeting meaning, an unspoken agreement between everyone to not acknowledge how quickly it passed.

My first time was somehow warmer, clunkier, and more natural that I had imagined it would be. Gentle, but without a steady rhythm, my hair tangled from wind and night and the darkest of our spoken truths.

I thought I'd care a lot more about how I looked. Care about what underwear I had on (faded blue) and whether my hair formed a halo of its own accord. But I didn't. Because together we were warm, despite the quiet, cool night. I sent a thought of gratitude out to the wide expanse of sky beyond the Shed's wooden overhang that instead of what I'd nearly experienced with last summer's guy, crammed in the back seat of his Jeep, I was able to have this rite-of-passage moment this way. Because even in the middle of it, especially in the middle of it, I knew it was precisely that—a rite of passage, with this person, in this place.

He pressed his lips to places I did not know begged to be kissed: the plane below my ear, my collarbone, the tip of my chin, the peak of my hip bone. My nerve endings were on fire, my body so alive.

I settled my knees on either side of him, one nudging the empty foil of a condom wrapper, the other in damp grass. I hovered over his mumbled "Is this okay?" and "Are you okay?" and "Does this feel good?" and answered him with a trio of yeses.

# Chapter Twenty-Nine

At nine the following morning, a yellow school bus idled on the dirt road adjacent to the Lodge. The taillights of a second bus already driving out of camp glowed bright red as they passed into the shade of the wooded road. I joined a crowd of campers waiting to board, checking around for Noah's dark hair.

*Noah.* A warm glow spread through me, and I hid a smile. I'd always pictured feeling so different after having Done It. Like I'd be marked as being older, wiser, more confident somehow, or as if I'd come home and my parents would just *know*. When I'd brushed my teeth in the Com this morning, I couldn't believe I didn't look more mature. I'd run my hands over my lips, trying to trace them as if I were someone else. I'd read so many articles about how sore I'd be the next day, but so far my body felt pretty much like it always did. Anxiety billowed in my stomach, and I rubbed my arms to try to calm myself down. Where *was* he? And then, with horror: *What if I was awful last night?*

I bit my lip, clenching my teeth until my jaw ached. Pushing the thought from my mind, I scooted over until I was behind Sammy's white-blond mop. I picked up my foot and gently nipped it at the back of his sneaker, giving him a flat tire—the old game of Dad's that had annoyed him since the dawn of Sammy time. Sure enough, he whipped around with a look of disgust on his face, which relaxed when he saw me.

"Lilaaaaaah," he said. He bent to fix his shoe.

"Good morning to you, too."

"CP's saving me and Mike seats. Wanna sit with us?"

I shook my head. "Thanks. Hey, did you see Noah? He didn't board the other bus, did he?"

"Didn't see him. I did see your smokin'-hot friend Winnie, though."

Winnie. Something inside me broke, but I tried to ignore it. "What happened to Alicia?" I asked, shifting my weight from side to side.

Sammy frowned. "She's my long game, but time's running out."

"A man with a plan. What is the plan, anyway?"

"That's for people on a need-to-know basis."

"Who's in that club, exactly?"

"MYOB. Hey, what does a nosy pepper do?"

"What?"

"Gets jal-a-peño business!"

"Sammy. That is an *actual* Popsicle-stick joke." I groaned.

After a while, the bus doors hissed open. The crowd of campers filed into a haphazard line, jostling to be the first to board.

"Hey, what time is it?" I asked the kid in front of me. He seemed to be a few years younger than me.

He checked his watch. "Twenty after nine." Five minutes after the bus was supposed to leave.

I wavered, glancing over my shoulder. "Do you know Noah? Have you seen him? I was supposed to sit with him."

"Earlier this morning, yeah. Walking with Jeff."

Noah *must* have been on the other bus. A tiny worm of worry ate away at the sweetness of last night. My brain spiraled into dozens of questions about why he wouldn't wait for me. With a pang, I realized that after weeks of being without a phone, I hadn't even brought mine. It had completely slipped my mind that the center of a quaint tourist town probably had cell service. Not that I even had his number.

Fifteen minutes later, I stood in a large parking lot off Kennebunkport's Dock Square. I shaded my eyes with my hand, scanning the horizon for bold eyebrows and blue eyes. If Noah had boarded the first bus, I figured he'd be waiting right in this parking lot for me to show up.

He wasn't. As I tried to figure out what to do next, I told my furrowed brow to relax, remembering what Grandma Gladys had said to Mom after Dad's funeral. *Christ almighty, Jenny. Smooth that brow. You can't help getting older, but you don't have to sign your own ticket to looking it.*

Oh well.

I left the parking lot, flipping a mental coin and turning right. I walked over a long bridge, passing a wooden sign welcoming me to town. Feeling sorry for myself, I kicked a broken piece of concrete off the edge and watched it plunk into the water below.

Like our bungalows back at camp, the storefronts lining the sidewalk were bright and well tended, with flower boxes, little wares set up outside the doors, and pinging wind chimes. I scanned the interior of each store, peering through the reflections of the drifting overhead clouds, hoping to spot Noah doing something necessary. Something required, like buying his mom a birthday present or sending some little-kid cousin a toy. Salt from the ocean below scented the air, somehow both pleasant and marshy.

I turned the corner and spotted a ramshackle coffee shop wedged between a children's clothing boutique and a stand selling discount T-shirts. The sign read NIRVANA COFFEE. My stomach growled. I decided to feed my feelings with sugar and a barista-brewed cup of good coffee.

Inside, I ordered a black coffee and pointed to an icing-slathered cinnamon bun. I chose a corner seat with a fairly good view of the street outside, where I saw my fellow campers trailing around in pairs or groups of three. The chair wobbled beneath me. I let my head tip back, hot tears edging into the corners of my eyes.

Yup. I'd been ditched.

I straightened up and pulled the pastry from the waxy brown bag. When I bit into the cinnamon bun, the sugar melted onto my tongue. My fingers itched for my phone. Just as I was about to reach for a castaway newspaper, the little bell over the door jingled. In walked Alicia. She stamped her feet as if she were shaking off snow.

I sipped my coffee and watched her. When she caught sight of me, she nodded. I nodded back. She collected a bagged pastry from the barista and joined me.

She pulled out a scone and bit into it. "Why are you alone?"

I almost smiled. She was just enough Eeyore for my mood. "Why are you?"

"I like being alone."

"So do I. Hey, I didn't know that your sisters are Heather and Emilia."

"My sisters suck."

I winced. Sammy got on my nerves, but as my right fist recalled, I'd defend him until I turned blue. "They're . . . nice," I offered.

She snorted, shoving another piece of scone in her mouth. Said nothing. And then, after a tense silence: "Your friend is looking for you."

I sat up. "Who? Noah? Where is he?"

Alicia turned to the window and checked her reflection, raking her hand through her hair and sort of flattening it across her forehead in a seeming attempt to hide beneath it. "No," she said finally. "The curly-haired one."

*Winnie.* I put down the cinnamon bun, no longer hungry. "Oh."

"Gross."

"What?"

"You're a lovesick puppy. It's repulsive."

I drained the rest of my coffee to buy time, but all I could come up with was a pretty unfortunate "Am not." And then inspiration struck. "Hey, which bus were you on?"

"The first one."

"Was Noah on it?"

"Nope."

The cinnamon bun became a brick in my stomach. Where *was* he? I drummed my fingers on the table, unable to shake the cloud of dread that nagged my brain.

Alicia's tone softened. "If he ditches you, then he's not worth it."

"Thanks for the tip." I managed a smile. "I can see what Sammy likes about you."

She scowled. "You do your brother's homework, too?"

That was enough for me, so I got up. "Any chance you know the bus schedule?"

"I think unless you have to stay with a counselor, they're going back when they fill up."

"Cool. Thanks. See you at camp." I balled up my trash, stuffed it in my coffee cup, and tossed it into a bin.

Her eyebrows shot up. "You're going back already?"

"Yup." The bells jingled when I opened the door.

"If I see Winnie again, I'll tell her you're looking for her," Alicia called.

I tugged the hem of my shirt, thinking about how much I'd let Winnie down. How guilty I felt. "Don't bother," I said.

"Back so soon, dearie?" The bus driver squinted at me. He was an elderly man, with grizzled stubble, a gray ponytail, and a gold hoop earring in one ear.

I gave him a tight smile and nodded.

"I'm not supposed to bring anyone back until at least five of youse are on board."

My heart plummeted. I'd never find Noah.

He tapped a knob on the dashboard. "But if you let me listen to my station, instead of the tinny junk on your stations, I can take my foot off the brake and send us rollin'."

I laughed. "Roll away."

I chose a seat halfway down the aisle. Leaning into the warm, cracked vinyl, I drew my knees up and braced them on the seat back in front of me. The bus driver turned up his music. One of my dad's favorites: Van Morrison.

What was I doing here? Rumbling over long, open stretches of some random Maine road instead of tracking sand through my family's beach rental? Instead of slicing tomatoes with Dad, or getting ice cream with Sammy, or gently waking Mom when her nose pinked up on the beach. I was alone, minus a friendly neighborhood bus driver.

My face warmed, my throat thickened, and hot tears once again filled the corners of my eyes. And there, halfway between the quaint little village of Kennebunkport and camp, speeding past the rolling green fields that had greeted me almost two months ago, I fell apart.

I missed my dad. I missed Mom, too. I missed my bed. And after last night, I didn't want to leave camp at the end of the summer and miss Noah.

Losing your virginity was supposed to result in you basking in a romance cocoon for days thereafter, not aggressively hiccupping your way through weepy sobs and listening to an elderly bus driver croon about sailing into the mystic. I remembered my dad belting out these same lyrics with his car windows rolled down. I'd have traded almost anything to be with him now, heading out for the healing power of ice cream after a boy had crushed my heart.

The music swelled, and the wind whipped across my face. It pushed my tears into the edges of my hairline, leaving grainy trails on my skin. I rubbed at them.

Finally, it came: the numbed-face feeling that accompanies the end of a crying session. Just in time, too, as the bus driver steered into camp.

"Thanks for a pleasant ride, dearie," he said as I picked my way down the aisle. "Nice to listen to my own stuff. Betcha didn't know a single song."

I shook my head. "I did. My dad liked Van Morrison. And the song that was just on is from an old show I like. *Parenthood.*"

"'Forever Young'?" He pulled a lever, opening the door.

"That's the one."

He whistled. "Color me impressed. You know Dylan?"

With everyone gallivanting around Kennebunkport, Camp Bonaventure was like an eerie ghost town—still except for the late-summer breeze rippling across the lake and whispering between the leaves. No one swimming, no one out by the art room.

I should have grabbed a bike. Instead I ran, my feet clad in unsupportive sandals, my calf complaining each step around the border of the property. I checked the gym, the sports fields, the art room. Mess Hall. Each empty building plucked my anxiety up another octave.

This really didn't seem like Noah.

*Especially* after last night.

By the time I got to the boys' bungalows, my legs ached in protest. I raised my fist and knocked on the blue one, the twin to my own.

Silence. I turned the knob and poked my head in, just as I heard someone call out "Just a min—"

From the entrance, I saw two people tangled together on one of the bunks. One of them could only be Madison—confirmed by the cast-aside crutches on the floor. Her petite form and blonde hair were immediately blurred by the deft pull of a sheet over her face.

For the briefest of moments, I had a new worst fear: I'd see Noah lift his head from behind the blanket, dark hair and dark lashes and dark eyebrows in perfect contrast to the flushed skin and blue eyes I'd lost myself in last night. But I'd barely had the time to consider that thought before Deese's sheepish face materialized.

"Oh God." I took a step backward. "I'm—I didn't mean—"

"A little busy here, Lila," Deese said.

"I was just looking for Noah," I said, speaking in rapid bursts. "Kennebunkport, uh, couldn't find him. Didn't know anyone was in here. I'm—have you seen him?"

"I have not." Deese adjusted his position on the bed. "But if you'll just excuse us?"

"Oh. Of course. I'm so sorry." I said, backing away. "Weren't you in town?"

"We came home early."

"Oh my God," Madison said. "Lila. I'll forgive you for skipping out on me. But I will *not* forgive you for this if you don't leave. Right. Now."

"Got it," I said. My voice was high and chirpy, a cartoon bird's. "Er, enjoy!"

"Lila?"

Deese's voice halted me. I turned, hopeful he'd remembered something.

"Mind closing the door?"

"Right." My face burning with the fire of a thousand charred s'mores, I put some distance between myself and the boys' bungalows. Despite the raging sense of embarrassment swirling through me, I grinned.

They really did like each other.

But since Deese had no knowledge of Noah's whereabouts either, I had only one option, other than the boys' Com (because gross). I'd have to go talk to Jeff.

A few minutes later, nearly breathless from exertion, I opened the Lodge door. I crossed the lobby in three long steps and burst into Jeff's well-kept office. He stood in its center, facing away from the door. I stepped inside and followed his gaze, where this time, up against the deep mahogany of those walls, that razor-thin TV was on, glowing from its perch above that frigging file cabinet.

And on it was Noah's face.

Noah's. Face.

I froze.

He wore a suit. The camera zoomed in on his downcast profile. He held one hand protectively on the back of a woman next to him. Based on their matching height and hair color, I guessed she was his mom. Beside them was a lanky bald man. They were all being escorted by a team of serious-faced men and one no-nonsense woman.

FAMILY OF COLIN LAWTON ARRIVES AT COURT, the caption at the bottom of the muted screen read.

And below that:

*Developing story: Alleged killer of Maine philan-*
*thropist Richard Frothingham's daughter Dakota*
*expected in federal court this afternoon.*
*STAY TUNED FOR DETAILS!*

# Chapter Thirty

A strangled sound escaped my throat. Jeff tore his gaze away from the screen and looked at me. "Oh, Lila," he said, his voice full of so many things—grief, reproach, anxiety, kindness—that I wanted to pummel it like one of the hanging bags in the Tsunami Room. Beat it back in.

Everything from my hair to my stomach hurt. The stream of tears that threatened to escape my eyelids—so cathartic on the bus—slid down the back of my throat, and my guts roiled. "I don't understand." My voice, high-pitched. Unrecognizable.

"I don't blame you." Jeff's eyes shifted. Me. The screen. Back again.

"Why is Noah on there?"

He moved across the room to the two chairs set up in front of his desk. He cleared some papers off one and sat in the other. "Why don't you sit down?"

*"Why is he on TV?"* I'd read the caption, but none of it made sense. My brain raced and stopped, its own version of the tortoise and the hare. Even as I asked the question, I didn't want to know the answer. Dakota Frothingham. The murdered girl with the state-park name. I blinked, and tears rolled down my cheeks.

"Here," Jeff said, handing me a tissue. "Take your time."

I stared at my lap, watching the tears dot the bare skin of my thighs. Thighs that Noah had stroked with what seemed like such great affection last night. Thighs that burned from my runs with Deese, thighs that had never jumped in the water when Dad was alive.

I remembered Call-Me-Connie's deep-breathing exercises, inhaled, and exhaled, and with just two hiccups my breakdown ended. I was grateful when the tingling numbness washed over me, and a deep, nearly peaceful wave of exhaustion settled into my muscles.

I wiped my eyes. "Okay."

"Noah wanted me to tell you he was sorry," Jeff said. "He was really looking forward to the field trip. The lawyers came a day earlier than he'd thought."

I shook my head. "Lawyers?"

Jeff rubbed the back of his neck, that nervous gesture I remembered from the beginning of camp. "I'm sorry. He said he hadn't talked to you about this stuff yet."

When I spoke, my voice was flat. "Yeah. I still don't understand."

"It's complicated."

"Try me."

"Well." He tilted his head toward the screen. The TV was still muted. On it, a woman with a penchant for hairspray spoke gravely toward the camera, staring right at her audience. At us. "How much did you see?"

Not enough. Too much. I dug my nails into my palms. "I saw Noah. Standing with his mom? And a bald guy, who I'll assume was his dad. The caption read something about Colin Lawton's *family*"—the word tasted like rocks in my mouth—"arriving at court." This was something I would have followed closely on Twitter, but, alas: no internet.

"They're Noah's parents, yes." A grimace touched Jeff's lips. "And Colin is his brother."

"*What?*"

Jeff tried to repeat himself, but I cut him off.

"Noah's brother is *alive*? And he's *Colin Lawton*?" Liar. Liar. Liar. "They have different last names."

Jeff nodded. "Noah used to be Noah Lawton. He's in the process of changing his last name to Kitteridge, his mother's maiden name."

A thought came into my mind then: his file, sorted out of alphabetical order, the name rewritten, the file bulkier than the rest. "Why didn't he tell me?" I asked, my body crumpling inward on itself.

"It's not a simple answer." Jeff's voice was low, gentle, and something else. Thoughtful.

"Obviously," I muttered. "But he lied to me."

Jeff rubbed his mouth. "Sometimes the truth is harder than a lie."

"No. *Usually* the truth is harder than a lie." My words were firm, and I folded my arms over my chest. "That doesn't make it right."

"No, it doesn't." He leaned an elbow on the chair. "Would it change your mind about me to know that I used to lie all the time?"

I tilted my head. "What do you mean?"

"You might have heard about my son," Jeff said. "Aiden." When he spoke the name, his eyes brightened for a moment. "I used to open up the camp season with this story, but this year I didn't."

"Why?" I asked.

"Up until the moment I didn't tell it, I planned to. But then I looked out at everyone's faces. Everyone looked tired. I *was* tired. And then I saw Noah, who, as you might've noticed, looks a lot like his mom. Sara's a friend of mine. After 9/11, she taught me how to rise again after tragedy, and Noah just looked so sad . . ." He trailed off. "It's not exactly logical, but I didn't want to pile it on him."

My nod was slow.

"My son had leukemia. I used to lie to him all the time." Jeff exhaled. "A lot at the beginning, things like 'You'll definitely get better, buddy,' or 'You won't feel this bad for long.' And then especially toward the end. Like when he asked me if it would hurt when he died." Jeff's voice lowered. "Or if I thought it was okay with Mommy if he went to sleep and never woke up."

"I'm so sorry," I said automatically, hating the phrase even as the words left my lips. That was what everyone said to me, too. I shook my head to clear it. "No. That's not the kind of lying I mean."

"I lied to my wife, too, Lila. First it was that Aiden would get better. Then, after, that I was okay. That we'd be okay. That we'd make it." He paused. "I wasn't. We weren't. We didn't."

Jeff wore a T-shirt with a little logo on the pocket, and I fixed my stare directly on it. "That isn't fair."

"No, it isn't."

"But . . ." I deflated, thinking of the ugliest, most unfair rule in my handbook. *Remember that grief lightning can strike twice.* "You'd already had your bad thing happen to you," I said.

Jeff was quiet. Up on the TV, the camera panned to the outside of a courthouse. U.S. DISTRICT COURT, BARNSTABLE, the caption read. The building looked like an office building or an elementary school, not a place that determined the fate of murderers.

"It's not fair that you lost your dad on 9/11 and then lost your son to cancer and then your wife to . . . the fallout of all of that."

Jeff nodded. "Right."

"Why is one person allowed to have that many bad things happen to them?"

"I'm the sort of person who believes we're given what we can handle."

"But you said you didn't handle it with your wife," I said. "The lying?"

"You're right," Jeff said. "But that's why I'm in therapy." A faint smile. "My point is that sometimes it's easier to lie than it is to tell the truth. Sometimes—like with Aiden, I believe—it's even kinder. And I imagine that it is much easier to lie than it is to tell the truth when your brother is accused of committing a heinous act of violence."

My resolve wilted. "But why would he lie to *me*?"

Jeff steepled his fingers. "If I had to make a guess, it's because he was scared you'd associate him with his brother's actions," he said. "Everyone who comes here has lost a lot. You'll all carry *something* with you for the rest of your lives, but Noah's burden is especially weighty."

I frowned. "How did he qualify for camp, if no one is dead?" Oh, wait. I tapped my temple. "His mom is your friend."

He nodded, a small smile touching his lips, but not his eyes. "Sara was my counselor when I was a camper. We met here."

It was stunning, when you thought about it: No one had asked for any of this. That was the heart of the whole thing. The state of my father's mind had been incomparably worse than what I'd ever feel, and yet his loss had put more gravitational force on my soul than I'd have ever thought possible. Jeff's son hadn't deserved his disease any more than my father had his.

I realized then, sitting in Jeff's office, across from the file cabinet where I'd made my debut as a juvenile delinquent: No matter what I did, life kept violating my rules. In my *Half-Orphan's*

*Handbook*, rule number one was very much influenced by rule number two.

1. The only people who can truly hurt you are the ones you love. Therefore, love no one.
2. Stay away from liars. Liars are the worst.

I wished I'd known that to go near Noah would be to go near a liar. And that to go near a liar would be to love one.

# Chapter Thirty-One

I tried to get Jeff to turn the TV's volume on, but he shook his head and ushered me from the office. On my way out of the Lodge, I heard a massive clattering on the steps outside, followed by the sound of Winnie's voice. "Jeff! Jeff! Have you seen Lila?"

She burst into the lobby, then halted when she saw me. Her face was nearly purple, her shirt damp with sweat. "Lila—"

"Right here," I said. I must have been a swollen, cried-out picture of imperfection, but I didn't care. "What is it?"

Winnie's shoulders slumped. She leaned over and braced her hands on her knees, like an athlete trying to recover from a grueling race. "I'm too late, aren't I?"

Ice water clogged my veins. "You knew?"

"Found out this morning," she said between gasps. "There was a TV in the coffee shop I was in. I tried to find you." She straightened up, and a pained expression came over her face. "Oh, Lila. I'm so sorry."

I held up my hand. "Don't," I said. "I know."

Winnie winced. "You're right. I hate the *I'm sorry*s more than anything." She took a deep breath, let it out, and squared her shoulders. "Let's go back to the bungalow."

On the way, Winnie told me what she'd been able to get from a loop of what was probably the same broadcast I'd seen in Jeff's office. She'd stood, openmouthed, watching Noah on the screen, long enough to confirm what her eyes were seeing: Our Noah was that Colin's brother.

"Noah's family released a statement, read by one of the lawyers," Winnie said as we crossed the sandy shore of the lake. "They opened by offering their condolences. Standard legalese, seemed genuine. Profound sorrow for Dakota. I'd heard they were really close to her too—she and Colin had been together for a couple of years. And then, when the lawyer read the next part, all of them sort of bowed their heads. They said they were good people. Involved in their son-slash-brother's life." Winnie opened the door to the bungalow. "I honestly believed them, you know? Noah's mom started crying, and the tips of his ears went red. The lawyer kept repeating it: Nothing in Colin's behavior had changed. He was twenty years old, hadn't closed himself off, wasn't into violent video games. He'd had a history of drug abuse in his teens, but they'd gotten him help. He hasn't spoken a word to his family since everything happened."

As Winnie droned on, I stripped out of my sweat-dampened clothes and changed into an old Tigers T-shirt, stretched with age. I'd slept in it practically every night my freshman year of high school. *Go, team.*

"Lila," she said. "I'm sorry about the whole dodgeball thing. I don't want to fight. I really tried to find you today, the second I was sure. I ran all over town, asking everyone if they'd seen you."

"I know. I ran into Alicia."

"I really am sorry—besides about Noah," she added, when she saw my *do not dare pity me* look. "*I* am sorry. Me. Winnie. For our fight."

"I'm sorry too. You were right, though. I forgot to meet up with you because I was caught up with him." I paused. "Plus, you were right all along. You said he looked familiar, and there was even that thing you said about a corporate guy opening a beach bar? Someone with something to hide. He *was* hiding something."

Winnie bit her lip. "It doesn't feel very good to be right."

I smiled. "Ha. I know the feeling."

"Are we okay?" Hope lit her eyes.

Of course we were. Our fight seemed so trivial now, and I missed them. With a pang I thought of Josie and Rose back home. I'd judged the hell out of them for not knowing how to act around me. *Shit.* I nodded. "We're okay."

She sprawled backward on her bunk. "Thank God. We have so much to talk about later. Madison and Deese much?"

Despite my overwhelming sense of despair, I managed another smile. "I have a story for you involving that. And me. Accidental spectator."

"No," Winnie said. Then, after a pause: "What'd they look like?"

Winnie was a true friend.

We kept the lights out and talked for a while, the only two people in the bungalow on a beautiful day. The other campers were probably having the best day of their entire summer— swimming in the ocean, eating ice cream, buying little trinkets for the remaining member or members of their family.

"I mean, can you imagine?" Winnie was saying. "You have a kid. Two kids. Both seem great. You do the parenting thing. Equal parts nagging and hugging." A light shake of her head. "One turns out like Noah. The other kills his girlfriend. How do you get past such a senseless tragedy?"

"She makes pressed wax flowers," I said.

"Huh?"

"Noah's mom. She does this craft thing where she makes pressed wax flowers."

"And does what with them?"

"Bookmarks. Framed things. I don't know."

"A woman who DIYs Pinterest-worthy crafts has a son who . . ." Winnie trailed off. "Unbelievable. She'll *never* get past that."

"Who says we get past anything?" Then, in my head: *Who says we want to?* Noah's poor mom probably punished herself every time she opened her eyes in the morning.

Even with just the two of us in the room, a desperate desire for privacy threatened to overwhelm me. I pulled the covers over my head. Winnie must have gotten the message, because she stopped talking. My tears spilled over again, soaking my cheeks, salting my lips, staining my pillow with sorrow. I ran through my options and settled on the one I should have started with in the first place.

The only choice I had was the same one I'd had since March. To guard my emotions, to make sure no one else could leave me or betray me or hurt me, I had to silence my heart. I closed my eyes, pleaded with my body: *Stop feeling. Go numb. If you must function, then do so only to keep me alive. Turn colorless and see-through, a functional piece of flesh to propel me through this world, instead of the punching bag you've become.*

# Chapter Thirty-Two

I stayed in bed the rest of the day, pretending to sleep when my bunkmates returned back from town or the boys' bungalow. I sank back into the vortex I'd whipped up right after Dad's death. The second I'd found out, I'd known his death would be my *thing*. The policemen stood in the doorway, sweating and somber. Mom had to ask them to repeat the words twice, but the truth hit me right away. I slid to the floor, the room sucking air from my lungs and the carpet burning my knees.

Later, all I could think was: *From now on, I will be the Girl Whose Father Killed Himself with a Rope from Home Depot.*

It was awful and terrible and every other negative superlative, but now I knew what crappy card I'd been dealt. A father who made imaginary plans for the future, coaxing his daughter to join him in running a race he had no intention of finishing.

At orientation, Winnie had mentioned that Jeff had tragically gone from have to have-not with his family, but I hadn't known the extent of the damage. I'd been so convinced that *his* thing was Child Affected by 9/11 that I'd forgotten that his story had had an epilogue, and that it was a nasty one.

How was any of this fair? Noah's ruddy cheeks and floppy hair flashed across my closed eyelids. I pushed the image away, a black cloud swirling into my gut.

I ached for my father. I wanted to go back to before I knew we were on borrowed time, to watching movies on laptops, to analyzing meet-cutes and bantering over Shakespeare and science and the state of my unclean room.

My misery train was interrupted when someone shut off the bungalow lights. I breathed a sigh both relieved and bitter—the former because I wouldn't have to deal with anyone else that night, and the latter because it suited my wallowing.

I breathed in, out, in, listening to the rhythm of my heart.

Ignoring how silly I felt, I sent a message out to my dad, wherever he was. *I know you were messed up. But you also really messed up, Dad. And it sucks.*

I stared at the wooden planks that made up the ceiling of the bungalow. *There's always someone who has it worse than you do,* I thought. *Aren't we all trying to find meaning where it hides? Aren't we all just trying to feel good and be happy?*

*Screw the handbook.* With that thought, I fell into the deepest sleep I'd had since my dad died.

I woke sometime in the middle of the night, my mouth full of the sourness that accompanies not having brushed your teeth. Hot tears cut their way through my cool sweat, and my body shook. Shivered. I rolled over to press my face against the pillow.

My mom had once told me that our dreams were influenced by the second-to-last thing we thought about before we went to sleep. I tracked my thoughts back: *Noah. Dad. Handbook.*

*Check. Bingo. Check.*

The night after my dad died—and all that next week, really—I couldn't stop imagining what he'd been like, inside, the last day before he died. What was he feeling while we watched *Bridesmaids*? He'd had to have known it would be his last night.

There in the bungalow, my heart contracted in my chest. I'd never doubted how much he loved us, but in the state he was in, he really must have believed we'd be better off without him.

And we weren't. We never would be.

How did you decide this was it, the last time you'd go downstairs? The last time you'd carefully unlock the door—when you unlocked our door, you had to press hard into the lock so it wouldn't make the *scree* sound it normally made.

He'd had to *think* about that. He'd had to unlock the door with a deliberate quietness, to make sure that he wouldn't wake me up and I wouldn't ask him where he was going and he wouldn't have to be all, *Oh, Little Lyon, I'm going to go kill myself. Want to lock up behind me? Good luck in that race!*

Beneath me now, the bed shook. I tried my Call-Me-Connie breathing exercises, but my pillow was soaked through with my sweat and tears and, instead, I coughed.

And then a lamp snapped on.

*No.* I drew my knees up to my chest, trying to make myself as small as possible.

Madison squinted in the light. Winnie, two steps ahead of her, climbed into my bed. Madison joined us, wrapping her arms around the two of us and squeezing with such surprising force, my breath caught.

At that moment, I didn't care what might happen to the three of us in the future, or that I'd known them for the amount of time I'd spent here.

Neither one of them spoke. I didn't either. They knew what I needed, maybe even more than I did.

# Chapter Thirty-Three

Despite my best efforts, the next few days were a complete blur. It was as if my body puppeteered my mind, which obediently followed its every command.

**Body to mind**: Shower in Com. Clothing not optional. Skip art for the millionth time.

**Body to mind**: Meet Winnie and Madison at Mess Hall for Smiley Fry-Day.

**Body to mind**: Accept fries (say thank you). Get ketchup. Also fruit. No need for overkill.

**Body to mind**: Smile, nod, eat grinning potatoes.

The motions my body did were familiar; my mind was a pleasant blank. When Winnie and Madison got up to refill their plates, I congratulated myself for acting reasonably like myself.

"Earth to Lila!"

Sammy snapped his fingers in my face. I blinked, bringing him into focus.

"Hey." I swatted his hand away. "Stop."

"Are you okay?"

"Tired." I held up a smiley fry. "Here. Happy *Fry*-day."

He accepted the fry and popped it in his mouth. "Are you sure you're okay? CP heard Noah's brother is some killer cannibal. He had nightmares all night."

"He's not a cannibal. The other thing, maybe."

Sammy sighed. "That sucks. I like Noah."

"Me too." I rubbed leftover traces of salt and oil between my fingers.

"Does Mom know?"

"No." I thought about her at home, hopefully writing and eating enough and doing yoga with Aunt Shelly. Blissfully ignorant of the fact that her daughter was consorting with the brother of Public Enemy Number One. "Not yet."

He nodded. "Sucks," he said again.

"Tell me about it."

He leaned closer, lowering his voice. "Hey, you're going to the art show tomorrow, right?"

Where had that come from? I shook my head and ignored the flip of my stomach. "The art show is already tomorrow?"

He nodded. "Madame D. will give us a take-home project next week, and then we do an end-of-summer clean-up."

*Home.* Something in my chest constricted at the thought of going home. Returning to my new-old life. I wondered if Mom had kept the garden going this year—in summers past, Dad had been on water duty, spraying the tomato cages and cucumber vines. Each night, Mom would serve sliced veggies, sometimes with green basil, and dress them with salt and cracked pepper and the sharp cut of vinegar. Was she eating that this summer, the flavors a burst of the familiar in her new unfamiliar? "Besides, I don't have anything to show."

"I know, but come see mine." His face was pleading, insistent—very un-Sammy.

I folded my arms across my chest and leaned back. "Since when do you care about art?"

"Since now."

"Why?" The image of Sammy's cow project came to mind, and I felt a pang of guilt. "Do you want me to come support you or something?"

His face changed then, a picture of relief. "Support me. Yes," he said, nodding. "Exactly. So you'll come?"

I'd have to avoid Madame D. Years of being a golden student had trained me to never skip class, and I couldn't believe I'd made it this far doing so. "I'll come."

The next morning, Deese and I bent the rules for our run, electing to leave the camp boundaries in favor of pavement and new scenery. We figured that if anyone caught us, at least summer was nearly over. Jeff wouldn't send us home now.

The camp's property was set off from town by a series of endless, open country roads, complete with quaint barns, fields of cornstalks, and stretches of postcard-worthy marsh. As we crested the last hill before returning to camp, Deese spoke. "You're running like shit."

"Am . . . not." But I was. My ribs crackled with cramps; my legs protested every time Deese upped the clip.

"You are. You need to get out of your head."

Sweat stung the corners of my eyes. I pulled up my tank top and swiped it across my face. "Believe me. I'd love to." We coasted right, onto the long dirt driveway back to camp. "I invite you to pull me directly out of this head of mine."

"So do it."

"How?"

"Run as hard and as fast as you can," Deese said. He tapped my arm with his fingers. "Get it, girl."

I took off. The ground thumped beneath my sneakered feet, my legs pumping, my knees driving forward. I held my arms low, using them to propel me.

I wasn't breathing properly. This wasn't a sustainable speed, and my form was crap. If I'd been back home, Coach would have been screaming at me.

But I didn't care.

I *flew*.

The wind dried my sweat, cooling my overheated cheeks and snaking through my soaked hair. Every time I felt myself flagging, I pushed harder. Blood pumped through me, feeding into my muscles, reminding me I was alive.

It was great.

No. It was *amazing*.

I tumbled to a stop on the field behind the Lodge. Little black dots paraded in my peripheral vision, and by the time Deese jogged up a few minutes later, I was flat on my back, gasping for oxygen. Above me, a few tree branches were tinged with red and orange, the way the edges of old paperbacks yellow: from the outside in. The sun was setting on this summer.

"That," he said, "is how it's done."

"This . . . is," I panted, "short notice. But . . . any chance you want to run a race with me?"

Deese knelt beside me. "Sure," he said. "I knew you had some kind of hidden agenda. When is it?"

"Uh . . ."

Deese raised his eyebrows and waited.

I smiled. "Sunday?"

"Sunday, like Sunday next week?"

"No, Sunday like tomorrow."

He laughed and then looked at my face. "Wait. You're serious?"

"Sure am. Seven miles serious."

"Let me make sure I heard you right. The most we've done

271

is four, maybe five miles. You want to run a seven-mile race *tomorrow?*"

"I do. The Falmouth."

"Falmouth's one hill after another."

"Yep. My dad was supposed to run with me, so I have an extra bib."

Deese collapsed beside me. "Sure. Why not?"

"Good. And. I've decided." I drew in oxygen, let it out. "I'm going to run this fall."

I expected him to say something like *Right on, Lila,* or *I knew you had it in you.* Instead, he groaned.

I lifted my head and frowned. "What?"

"You're on par with the girls' team at my school," he said. "You'll kill us at State."

Later that morning, I walked over to the art show with Winnie. When I saw Madame D. standing at the door, passing out the Guggenheim contest brochure, my stomach bubbled. I wasn't used to being outside any teacher's best graces. "Madame D.," I said. "I'm really sorry I haven't been here in a while."

She wore a long, gauzy skirt, and feather earrings fluttered beneath her frizzy hair. "All is forgiven," she said. *All ees forgeeven.* "I am glad to see the canary drag in the cat."

Winnie wrinkled her nose. "I think you have a cliché malfunction, Madame D."

Madame D. smiled. "Alas, Wainwright, you are incorrect."

"What do you mean?"

"The first day, you claimed you would make a ponytail for an art project—an animal art project. I figured you were being difficult, but the end result is most beautiful. Like a canary."

Winnie beamed.

I bumped her with my hip. "Go, Win."

Madame D. inclined her head toward me then, like a queen considering her royal subjects. "And you, my dear Lila, are the cat."

*The cat?* "I beg your pardon?" I asked, feeling like a class-A dipshit.

She bent low, her faux accent all but disappearing in her whisper. "The cat is feline. Much like a lioness."

*Lyon.*

I entered the art room. The tables had been cleared away for the exhibit, save for one in the back that held trays of sweets and bottles of water. I passed the final versions of the sculptures I'd seen throughout the summer: the owl with its oversized eyes, the hedgehog made of knitting needles. My favorite pipe-cleaner orangutan hung from the ceiling with one monkey hand, its mouth agape in a giant grin. Noah's turtle had been painted, but not in the murky turtle colors you'd expect—it raged with reds, purples, and blues. Winnie's molecular ponytail was now capped with a lifelike Ariana Grande ponytail—abstract, yet recognizable and fun.

I found Sammy standing in front of his cow, which had grown into a massive sculpture. Much taller than him. "You came," he said, his mouth cracked open wide.

The Guggenheim paper was damp in my clenched hands. "I came."

He stepped to the side, waving his arm with a flourish in his imitation of Madame D. "Your lion awaits, *Madame Seester.*"

There was my lion, in all her glory. Where I'd cracked her back, someone had glued little tufts of autumnal fur, brilliantly delivering exactly what I'd been going for.

I sensed someone standing beside me then, and turned my head to see Madame D. "Your lion," she said.

"How . . ." I tried to recover. "Who did this?"

Sammy shrugged. "It wasn't a big deal. I was already done with my cow. Madame D. said I could fix yours."

"You did this?" Sammy, Mr. Too Cool for School?

Sammy raked a hand through his hair. He smiled his goofy smile. "Yeah."

I threw my arms around him. "I can't believe you," I whispered. "I don't know what to say."

He squirmed in my grasp, and then relented. "Man of the house," he whispered back.

"I'm so *moo*ved."

"It was a rare—er, *roar* opportunity."

I pulled away. "Hey, Sammy? Remember, no one needs a 'man of the house.' So if you ever want to, you know, just be a kid . . ." I let the words linger for a moment. "That's cool too."

He shrugged. "Just wanted to do things the way Dad would've."

I met his eyes. "Do things the way *you* want to, dude."

"Really?"

"Really. Besides, you're a lot funnier than Dad."

"Aw, Lila."

"You are. You make me laugh all the time."

"Go on."

My art counselor cleared her throat. I released my brother and wiped my eyes. "Thank you, Madame D."

She smiled. "My pleasure. I love this little lion. And, as it stands, the folks at the Guggenheim agree."

I held my breath, hardly able to believe what she was saying. "But I didn't do it all."

"Nonsense," said Madame D. "You did all the hard work. Your brother was the caretaker who picked up the pieces." She reached over and patted the flank of Sammy's cow. "Besides, the cow and the lion will keep each other company there," she said. "Along with that hanging orangutan and Wainwright's clever project."

Sammy and I high-fived. A small part of me found comfort in the fact that no matter where Winnie and I went in the next year, our projects would be tucked into some back corner of a famous museum, with little plaques next to our names.

I had to admit, in that moment—and for the second time that day—I was pretty proud.

# Chapter Thirty-Four

"To Winnie and Lila," Madison said, raising a glass of seltzer in our direction. "Artists in residence." We raised our plastic cups and clinked.

We'd grabbed our favorite corner booth in Mess Hall straight from swimming (which, shockingly, was another thing I was startled to realize I'd miss).

"I've been trying to get in that damn museum for years," Winnie said, twisting her damp curls into a bun on top of her head. "We should do something. Celebrate."

I hesitated. *Celebrate* meant Orient Point wine. The Shed. A shaky next morning, which would interfere with my training—not to mention my plans for tomorrow. "I better not," I said.

Madison narrowed her eyes. "Why not?"

"Because my team's running double sessions next week. I can't be there, but I can pretend. And hungover Lila and double sessions do not friends make."

"Your English is severely hurting while sober," Winnie said. I elbowed her. "Seriously, though—no one's forcing a funnel into your mouth. Do what you want." Her eyes widened. "Wait. Does this mean . . . ?"

I smiled. "It means."

Madison caught my grin. "You're going to run?"

I nodded. "Jeff let me email Coach this morning."

"Even more cause to celebrate," Madison said.

"Good for you," Winnie said. "*A Girl with Agency: The Lila Cunningham Story.*"

Madison clasped her hands. "This is like when I went back to dance."

"Karate, for me," Winnie said. "And, you know, studying." She tightened the bun on her head.

"Our lives carry on."

I bit my lip. They were right. I *was* moving on. An ugly thought trickled its way into my belly. Was I leaving my dad behind? I remembered what Madison had said, way back when we were baking the cookies, about horses catching some sleep by locking their knees with ligaments and tendons. Autopilot. Ever since the first of March, I'd been unable to rest in my grief, always slightly on guard that something was coming for me. But even horses needed to lie down sometimes, secure in their safety.

*Traitor,* my inner voice sniffed.

But was it so bad to want to move on?

"Hey," Winnie said, her voice gentle. "It's a good thing."

*Beat that, inner voice.*

Before I could respond, a white envelope sailed across the table, plopping right on top of Winnie's turkey sandwich. "Mail," Mari said.

Winnie sighed. "Gross, Mari. You got mustard on it." She checked it. "Oh, Lila. It's for you."

Other than a few stray letters from Mom and Aunt Shelly, I hadn't gotten much mail over the summer, so this was something of a surprise. Until I recognized the handwriting. After all, I'd written prank letters with her, sketched our old Pop Warner choreography, and passed notes in class with her until we got our phones and could secretly text. The sight of Josie's writing filled my throat with a lump so lumpy I fought to swallow it. It was made of all our history: hundreds of sleepovers, our legs covered in mosquito bites and our stomachs full of popcorn and candy. Josie was a huge part of who I had always been, even though things were strained between us after my dad died. Something swelled in my chest, and it took me a long blink to choke the lump down and recognize it. *Homesick.*

For something no longer there.

"Lila?" Madison asked, frowning.

Instead of answering, I splayed the letter across the table.

*Lila,*

*I hope you don't mind me writing to you. I got this address from your mom. And I googled it, and saw what the camp is really all about. I talked to my mom about it, and I need to tell you that I feel awful about how I left things with you.*

"About time," I muttered. I angled the paper more to my friends, and bent over to keep reading.

*I can't stop thinking about how bad I feel for how I treated you after your dad died. It scared me, Lila. I loved your dad like a second dad. He was so funny and smart. I'd never had anything like that happen to me. It was really hard for me to even believe he'd done what he did. It's not an excuse. Actually, it is. It's just a crappy one. So I want to say that I'm so, so, so sorry for saying I needed a break after your dad died. I didn't need the break. You did.*

*Anyway, I asked your mom if I could drive with her to pick you up at the end of the summer. She said yes. I'll*

*come unless I hear from you. (Mwa-ha-ha! I know how*
*much you hate to call people!)*

*I really miss you,*

*Jos*

Winnie and Madison sat back. "What do you think?" Madison asked.

Lost in thought, I stacked my lunch plates. What did I think? I was still angry at her, but this was *Josie*. I'd been told my whole life that as you grew up, friendships changed. Mom only talked to people from college, and Dad had lost touch with most of his friends from high school too. All of Aunt Shelly's friends were from her gym and the natural-foods store.

But . . . Josie? It was hard to picture my future. I had no idea what was in store for me with the easy stuff, such as what I would eat for breakfast tomorrow. I was doing my best to block out the darker things, like winter sweaters and applying to colleges.

But I knew one thing about my future: I wanted Josie in it.

"We'll work it out," I said, standing up to drop off our dirty dishes.

Winnie wiped her hands, staring at me. "That's it?"

"That's all you're going to say?" Madison echoed.

I shook my head. "No. I don't know what to think. But what I do know is that I want both of you to come on a little road trip with me tomorrow."

Madison's eyes gleamed. "Ooh. I'm in. Where to?"

"The Cape." I stood up. "More specifically, Falmouth."

Winnie looked confused. "Cape Cod?"

I pushed the lever on the exit door to Mess Hall and held it open for Winnie and Madison. "I'm running the Falmouth Road Race, and I want my friends there to cheer me on."

"You're *what?*" Winnie asked.

Outside, the late afternoon sun warmed my shoulders. My skin felt sun-tightened, my legs confident in their newfound (refound?) strength. "Running the Falmouth." We headed toward the bungalow to banish our wet bathing suits. "Deese and I decided this morning. Seven miles. You in?"

While we changed, I told them about my plan. Three-plus-hour road trip, seven-mile run, one excellent celebratory lunch.

Winnie crossed her arms. "Just how are we getting to Cape Cod, exactly?"

"I called my mom earlier when I e-mailed Coach." She had whooped so loudly I'd had to pull the phone away from my ear. "She's driving up with my aunt Shelly tonight. They're doing a girls' night on the town, and then they'll pick us up early tomorrow morning."

"How early are we talking?" Madison asked.

I wrinkled my nose. "Um. Three-thirty in the morning or so?"

"Excuse me?" Winnie groaned. I opened my mouth to respond, but the words died on my lips.

Because atop my pillow were pressed wax wildflowers, spelling out one word. My heart picked up speed, beating almost painfully as I read:

*S-O-R-R-Y.*

It was as if a bucket of ice water had been rigged over my bunk, tipping the knowledge over my head with a shocking, insulting whoosh.

Noah was back.

# Chapter Thirty-Five

One uncomfortably early morning (really, it was still so dark that it was only morning by definition) and a four-hour drive south (Mom and Aunt Shelly co-piloting) later, Deese and I stood in a mass of fellow runners. The day was muggy and overcast, the air so thick with ocean salt you could cup it in your hand. My hair lifted off like a helicopter, in stark contrast to the sleek, slicked-back ponytails of most of the women around me. They wore neon-bright spandex strewn with logos, their phones snapped into armbands and cordless headphones nestled in their ears. The non-runners were easy to spot because their sneakers were brand-new.

Though physically I was present in Cape Cod, I was mentally still orbiting the boys' bungalow in Maine, where a boy who had spelled a word on my pillow in flowers was probably still sleeping. Instead of trying to face Noah before the race, I'd stayed in the bungalow the night before (Sammy had brought me a bagel to "carbo-load," vowing to cheer the loudest from the sidelines).

The race was moments away from beginning, but I felt the weight of a series of endings, and I wasn't sure if metaphorically I was running away from everything or running toward something new. The last time I'd crossed the bridge to the Cape, I'd been a completely different person. I'd had a living father. I'd never met Noah. Last summer, Dakota Frothingham was still alive. Last week, Noah was a boy I did not know was a liar.

I glanced down. My black tank top was faded, my running shorts had a small tear over my right thigh, and my sneakers were dusty with what I could only call *Maine*. "I don't think I can do this," I said in a tiny voice, longing for the confidence I'd felt in the car.

Deese pulled out one of his earbuds. "Okay."

I frowned. "Okay?"

He shrugged. "Your choice, Cunningham. I'm still running. What's the worst that could happen?"

*Hmm.* I ran through the list of possibilities. Getting injured. Fainting. Dehydrating. The memory of the charley horse gripped my legs.

Failing.

But what if Deese was right? It wasn't like Mom or Sammy would love me any less if I couldn't finish. Even I'd get over it if I never crossed that finish line.

Dad was supposed to be the one standing beside me. Dad, with his freckly forearms, nerdy visor, high socks, and scuffed white sneakers. Picturing him here hurt less than I'd thought it would, the ache in my chest dulled with nostalgia. He'd coaxed me into this mess in the first place, then left me to do it by myself. This wasn't about letting him down.

It wasn't about letting Deese down either. It was about letting myself down. And I wasn't going to do that.

"You know," Deese said, "Noah didn't tell me the truth either. It sucks. But neither you nor I can change that."

"Did you talk to him?"

Deese's glance was sidelong. "I did."

"And?"

Around us, runners settled into starting position. A few race officials stood by the sidelines, ready to cue us to begin.

"And," Deese said carefully, "he is what my dad would have called a 'hurtin' pup.'"

I shook out my hands. Wiggled my legs. "Okay. You're right.

I can't change any of this." It was time. I squared my shoulders, tossed a wave to Mom, Aunt Shelly, Sammy, Winnie, and Madison, and tensed my legs. "Ready?"

"Ready."

*Crack.* Go.

Hills are hard.

On a flat run, the goal is to keep an even pace. Not on hills. On hills you aim for even *effort*. Which becomes doubly difficult when there's a breeze, and triply so when the breeze is a strong sea one.

By the time we reached the first mile marker, the sun had started poking holes in the clouds. Within a minute, the road opened up to the ocean and the haze burned off, inviting the sun and blue sky to reign overhead. The road was lined with cheering onlookers holding out small plastic cups of water.

"Holy heat," Deese said, accepting one of the cups. He drank it in one gulp, crumpled the cup, and tossed it to the road with all the other ones. "Want some?"

"Not yet," I said. "Hills. Hard."

We crested the hill, coming to a familiar grand white lighthouse. At home was a photo of all of us on the lawn in front of Nobska Light, taken during one of our last family vacations. In it, Mom is hugging Dad, her face upturned to his, and Sammy and I are holding hands. As I inhaled, a small stitch settled into my side.

"Cramping," I said.

Deese glanced at me. "Uncross your hands."

I concentrated on dropping them and keeping them parallel. As I breathed, the stitch dissipated. "Thanks."

We continued down the hill in silence, coasting into a tree-lined, blessedly shady section of the street. The ocean was not in sight, but the air was thick and heavy with its salted humidity. Just before the two-mile mark, we passed under a bridge filled with cheering onlookers, waving signs and shouting.

*Right, left, right, inhale. Left, right, left, exhale.*

I glanced up at the cheering squad, meeting the eyes of an elderly man. A toddler waving one American flag and one rainbow one sat astride his hip. "You can do it!" the man hollered.

Asinine, but it seemed almost as if he were speaking directly to me. A swell of pride filled me, making my steps feel lighter. I didn't need him to tell me I could do it.

I *was* doing it.

The open road was long and hilly. I matched my stride to Deese's easy one. Soon my legs burned, and my clothes were soaked completely through with sweat. When we reached Surf Drive—long, flat, and lined with people cheering and drinking out of red Solo cups—I accepted a small cup of water held out by a little girl. The ocean was so impossibly big after a summer spent by a lake in Maine. The sun beat down, with no trees to offer shade. I yearned for the clouds from . . . I looked at my watch. Thirty minutes ago.

Wow.

After the fifth mile marker, the course veered sharply to the left. Sweat pooled in my eyes, blurring my vision. *Right, left, right, inhale. Left, right, left, exhale.* "Coming up on six miles," I said. "I've never run this far in my life. Wait'll Coach hears this."

"You're doing great." Deese's voice was strained.

I glanced to my right and saw him working to keep up with me, for a change. "You okay?"

"My leg's tight."

"Does it hurt?"

He grimaced. "Not yet."

As we ran, the decibel level of the crowd's roar increased. With less than a mile to go, the view opened up, the sun glinting off a long band of ocean. Thousands of people waved flags, signs, or just their hands, pausing only to take pictures with their phones. Across the bay, the hazy shape of Martha's Vineyard took form.

Half a mile to go. One more hill. I angled my body forward, and Deese vanished from my peripheral vision.

I whirled around as best as I could while still propelling myself along. "Deese!"

He held up a hand. "I'll be okay." He half limped, half ran toward the spectators lining the shoulder of the road, his gait lopsided. "You go on."

"Yeah, right." I jogged to where he stood.

He doubled over, panting. "Keep going!"

I raised my face to the beating sun. Runners streamed by us, putting on speed as they mounted the last hill. "No way. What's wrong?"

He shifted his weight onto his right leg, guarding his left. "It's my hamstring. Totally seized up."

"Like a charley horse?"

He shook his head. "Think it's pulled. Lila, *go*."

I turned toward the course. The crowd screamed encouragement to the runners. In the distance, as the runners made it to the top of the hill, they waved their arms and pumped their fists in the air. Home stretch.

I'd intended to run this race beside my dad. Then I wasn't going to run it at all. Now I was running it for myself. But there was one thing I wouldn't do: leave anyone behind.

I bit my lip and faced Deese. "Let me see."

He pivoted. Right above the back of his knee, a vertical bruise had bloomed. I swiped my sweat-soaked forehead. "Um. Ow."

A girl in the crowd leaned over the barrier and tapped my shoulder. "Excuse me," she said. "Is something wrong? Do you need any help?"

"No," I said, at the same time Deese said, "Yes."

"I'm not leaving you," I told him.

"You're guaranteed to finish in under fifty," he said, tapping his watch. "Less than a half mile to go, and we're at forty-one minutes. Don't waste that on me."

*Under fifty minutes*, I marveled. *Take that, Dad.*

"There's a medical tent back that way," the girl interrupted, pointing. "I could walk you?"

I squinted and saw a red tent two or three tenths of a mile behind us. I inhaled the sunny, salty air. Something light hit the side of my leg and fell to the ground. A crumpled water cup.

And then something else hit me—an idea.

I turned to the girl in the crowd. A folded T-shirt was slung over her shoulder, like a baby's burp cloth. "Actually, you can help," I said. "Can we borrow that shirt?"

"Her shirt?" Deese asked.

The girl shrugged. "Sure. It was a free handout." She tossed it to me.

"Thanks," I told her. "Do you want to give me your phone number, so I can get it back to you?"

She shaded her eyes. "It's yours. Good luck."

Deese crossed his arms. "Why do we need her shirt, exactly?"

I stretched the shirt between my hands. It smelled of the

girl's sunscreen. "I believe you're well acquainted with a little game I know. Do you recall Three-Legged Ditch-It Dodgeball?"

Our legs looped together with the girl's shirt, we made steady progress up the incline. Deese hooked his arm around my shoulder, and I braced mine around his waist.

"Your leg is sweaty," Deese said.

I grunted, straining with the effort of half carrying his muscular body up the hill. "Shut. Up."

"Lean forward," he advised.

"Eat less," I muttered.

I'd thought my legs were burning before, but now they were on fire. I sucked air into my lungs, my tongue drying out in my mouth. A woman, maybe Aunt Shelly's age, skirted by us, wearing a shirt that read WILL RUN 4 WINE. "You kids need help?" she called.

I loved the utter camaraderie that was in the atmosphere—the crowd holding out water, the girl giving us her shirt, and this woman offering to help us. Noah's face flitted into my mind.

I smiled at the woman and shook my head. "Thanks. We got it."

After another minute or so of body-breaking haul, Deese spoke. "Lila, look."

I lifted my head, gasping. We'd reached the top of the hill, both our bodies flushed and drenched with sunlight and effort. I gazed at the finish line below us, pride slamming into my chest. The road, gray and wavy with heat, beckoned us.

"Almost there," Deese said.

"Almost," I echoed.

The breeze at our backs, we trotted down the slope. Deese's limp grew more pronounced as we neared the blazing red banner arcing over the finish line. Ten more steps.

*Right, left, right, inhale. Left, right, left, exhale.*

And then that was it.

We'd done it. *I'd* done it.

Accomplishment surged through my body. All that training, down to *this moment*.

I'd finished.

I hadn't had a prayer of winning, of course, but knowing I'd faced the challenge made me feel like I did when I won a hurdling event. Actually, this felt better than winning.

Maybe that lesson belonged in my handbook. *The more difficult the challenge, the better the return.*

We slowed to a stop, and three medics jogged over to us. "Right on," Deese said as one of them untied us. "Look."

Above us, the official timer read 49:56. My cheeks tingled. "I can't believe it."

"Lila!" Mom shouted, engulfing me in a hug. "Deese, are you okay? Should I call your mom?"

"I'm fine," he said, waving off a stretcher. "It's a grade-one pull," he told the medic.

The medic frowned. "Are you studying medicine?" he asked.

Deese shook his head.

"Then you're coming with me," the medic said.

"In a minute," Deese said, because then everyone else had caught up to us. Aunt Shelly and Sammy danced in a circle, and Winnie and Madison rushed to hug us.

"You did it," Sammy said.

Excitement surged through me. "I did."

Behind Mom, I caught sight of a familiar Afro. "Mom? Is that . . ."

"Surprise," she said.

"Josie? Josie!"

Josie stepped back, her face uncertain. "I hope you don't mind . . ."

"Mind?" I rose up on my toes to hug her. "I miss you."

She buried her face in my shoulder. "Oh my God. You stink."

"That's what happens when you run seven miles," I said, unable to keep the pride out of my voice.

The rest of the day passed in the most incredible blur. Josie came with us to lunch, where she melted right into conversation with Winnie and Madison. We gorged ourselves on lobster rolls and fries, then split ice cream sandwiches for dessert. Deese was right about the grade-one pull; he'd be okay by the time the season got underway. Sammy told everyone stories about our dad—the time he sprained his shoulder playing flag football at a department picnic, the time he'd been left behind on a field trip with Sammy's class—and somehow the familiar sting that filled my chest every time I thought of him had lessened.

I relaxed into my chair at lunch, surveying the people I loved—even the new ones—despite the rules in my desperate handbook. The day was pretty close to perfect. Even so, I couldn't stop looking for Noah. It didn't matter that I knew he was back at camp, and that I hadn't even wanted him to come. I searched everywhere. In the face of our waiter, in the patrons of the restaurant, and even in the guy who sold me Tylenol after the race.

I never found him.

# Chapter Thirty-Six

The next day, the late-afternoon sun rays ricocheted off the lake, refracting into a million pieces in the white-and-glass room where we sat for our last group-therapy session. I had yet to see Noah, who'd been excused from group. Deese, Alicia, CP, and I arranged our beanbags in a square and snacked on popcorn while Jeff made this big show of passing out all kinds of pamphlets and business cards and contact phone numbers for if we ever felt alone. "If you guys need anything between now and next summer, then start here," he said. "Okay. Last group is now in session. Our leading question today is: If you could change one thing about yourself, then what would it be?"

"Can it be anything?" CP asked. "Like, I could change that my parents are dead?"

I glanced at Jeff. His freckles had exploded, interconnecting until his face was darkly tanned. In the past few days, he'd grown a rough beard, the stubble carroty compared to the hair on his head. His smile was sympathetic. "No, buddy. The thing can't be about your life's circumstances. This is a harder task, because it asks you to look at the things about *yourself* that you don't like or that you'd like to improve."

"So you want us to say that we'd like to be smarter or stronger or something," Alicia said. "Yawn. What's next, asking us what we'll be when we grow up?"

Jeff spread his hands wide. "Alicia, I don't think you're destined to be one thing when you grow up. I'm pretty sure you'll take this world by storm." He paused. "And if you want to pick one of those, you can. But I'm hoping you'll dig deeper than that."

"Fine," she said, shrugging. "I wish I felt compelled to be nicer. But I don't. Next."

I laughed. "That answer was perfect, Alicia."

A smile twitched on her lips, threatening her curated expression of boredom.

"I wish I was older," CP said. "Does that count?"

Jeff wrinkled his brow. "I'll consider it. Why do you wish you were older?"

"'Cause then I'd have more memories of my parents. Sometimes I think I'm already forgetting them."

I knew what he meant. As many memories as I had of my dad, some of them had started to fade around the edges. On the ride back from the race, I'd spent a few minutes trying to remember the exact shade of green of his eyes—neither grass nor emerald, but something more like hazel pine—and whether or not he'd had a beard when he died. He'd had a habit of letting it grow out for a week or two, sporting a five-o'clock shadow that thickened into a beard, then shaving it clean every day for the next few weeks.

I shifted myself on the beanbag so I faced CP. "When you go home, you should find all the pictures you can of your parents, and paste them into a notebook," I suggested. "Next to the pictures, why don't you write down what you can remember about them, or any memories you want to make sure not to forget."

Jeff pumped his fist in the air. "What an excellent idea," he said. "Any of you could give that a try."

"I'll pass," Deese said. "Maybe my dad's other woman will make a baby book, though."

I grimaced. *So complicated.* "What's yours, Deese?"

"Other than the obvious?" Deese leaned back on his beanbag, propping his head on his arms. "I wish I didn't have the tendency to feel *less than* around people I've known my whole life. It's like my dad's choice is a shadow I'll walk in forever. Even though I had nothing to do with the decision, I'll forever live with its side effects."

I recalled what Deese had said that first day about stigma— that even though he'd done nothing wrong, and it should have been impossible to blame him for his father's actions, they still followed Deese, his ma, and his grandma like a rabid fox. Deese would even have a half sibling as a reminder of his father's betrayal. My own experience with stigma involved the shadow suicide had cast on my own family. Perhaps Noah had understood more than he'd let on.

*Noah.* His absence was a gaping, open hole in my chest, spiraling out of control since his return to this zip code. I was one of those trees that fell over after a storm, seemingly healthy and growing on the outside, but missing its vital organs on the inside. A desperate, urgent need to see him coursed through me. I did not recognize this part of myself: protective of my heart, but also ferociously defensive of him. A bit like a lioness.

"How about you, Lila?" Jeff asked.

I thought back to my first therapy session here, where I'd sat, clenched up, unwilling to share my story with the group. To sitting on the bed with Mom, refusing to believe that any of this—camp, therapy, running—would help me. It all seemed like ages ago.

I wondered what Noah would transform about himself. I shook my head.

"I think I'd like to be more open to change," I said, the words leaving my mouth slowly. "My whole life, things were pretty much perfect. Dad, Mom, brother. I liked my friends and my school. I was really good at hurdling." I glanced outside, toward the perimeter of the camp, where Deese and I had trained for half the summer. "The day before my dad died—hell, even the morning he died—if someone had sat me down and told me what he was about to do, I wouldn't have believed a syllable they said. The idea that my father might kill himself was just a non-issue in my life." I pursed my lips. "And obviously, I miss him every day. I want to call him and tell him things." *Noah. Winnie.* "But now, what's changed . . ." I heaved a sigh. "Well, I guess I'm working on accepting that some things are out of my control. And learning how to adapt to that." *Camp. Running. Falmouth.*

After a few more minutes of chatting and reminiscing, Jeff ended the session. CP, Alicia, and Deese got up to file out, but I remained seated on my beanbag.

I'd never been good with lasts. The last day of school, the last hurdling meet of the season—every time I knew I was experiencing a last, everything about it would feel that much more poignant and significant.

Over these past almost-eight weeks, I'd fallen into the groove of feeling safe in this sunny, glass-walled space. Raw stories and experiences had poured from my new friends here. Sure, we were bound to have had a certain camaraderie, and there was something poetic about all the glass and all the light, but one person had been responsible for steering our healing. One person who, as I'd said out loud one night over those bottles of Orient Point, I might want to emulate one day.

Deese turned around. "You coming?"

"I'll catch up with you at movie night," I said.

"'Kay. Later."

I waited until the door closed behind him. "Hey, Jeff?"

He straightened up, holding the empty popcorn containers. "You rang?"

"Is it hard to listen to us every day?"

"What do you mean?"

"Everyone here has a sad story or two to tell. I imagine it can be like . . ." I searched for a comparison. "When you drop your phone in a toilet, and you have to shove it in a bag of rice to try and dry it out. Like, maybe, you do what you can to soak up our sadness . . . until it gets to be too much. Is it like that?"

He thought for a moment. "People in my line of work call it being a sponge. I think if you're in any position where you deal with people's feelings and experiences, there's a risk of that, sure." He crossed his arms. "The way I see it, I'm more of a rock. A buoy. Something to hold on to. Instead of soaking up your sadness, my goal is for *you* to process the emotions you have from your own lived experiences."

I stared at my feet, thinking. After a moment, I met his eyes. "I wanted to thank you, Jeff. Everything you did for me this summer means a lot."

"I'm proud of you, kid," he said. "You put in a lot more work than you realize."

I sent a brief, silent *if only* wish to the universe: if only my dad had put in this kind of work. Because it *was* work. "I guess so?"

"I get it. After all, I understand what you feel. I just work hard to not absorb it." He gave me a wry, sad smile. "I carry more than one sad story in my own pockets, remember? That probably helps." Jeff scratched his beard. "I've been meaning to catch you, Lila. I wanted to let you know that we have anonymous donors who put together scholarship packages. Full summer's worth. Just in case you were thinking about coming back next year."

I pressed the tips of my fingers to my lips. "Really?"

"Really."

I smiled. "Thanks. Maybe I'll apply for one." I turned to go.

"Oh, and by the way," he called. "That photo journal was a great idea for CP, you know. Maybe you'd be a good writer."

Maybe I would.

# Chapter Thirty-Seven

Back in front of the gymnastics building for movie night, I felt like an undercover cop staking out a prime suspect. Mari and her crew had set up a bunch of blankets and pillows, with boxes of pizza and paper cups of lemonade balanced on a table behind the campers. A large screen had been set up right next to the window where we'd snuck in the night that Madison broke her ankle. Seated between Winnie and Madison, I was jumpy and anxious, and my fire flamed high when a certain boy wearing low-cut sneakers arrived halfway through the movie. I pressed my tongue to the back of my teeth while he searched the crowd. When his eyes settled on me, he strode purposefully in our direction.

"Shit," I said. "Shit shit shit—"

"Can I talk to you?" Noah's voice was quiet.

Madison crossed her arms. "Go ahead."

Winnie reached across me and tapped Madison's wrist. *"Madison."*

"What?"

I stared at my feet. "Fine."

Noah reached out a hand to help me up. I ignored it, hauling myself to my feet and trailing behind him to the lake. He climbed the lifeguard tower, turned around, and again offered me his hand. Waving it aside, I gripped the ladder and hoisted myself onto the wooden platform. I settled beside him, leaving a few inches of space between us. It might as well have been ten feet.

Neither of us spoke. I waited for whatever apology he would offer, staring at the spot in the lake where I'd moved to kiss him the first time I swam. Where I'd promised to *prove* myself to him. I breathed a huff of air through my nostrils.

I couldn't stand the silence. The more I worked myself up, the more certain I became that I'd cry. "You lied to me," I said, even angrier when my tears fell. I swiped at them, scrubbing them from my skin, furious I couldn't get through one moment of this without keeping my composure. "And you *know* I have a problem with liars, that I can't tolerate them. They *gut* me, Noah. I said that in therapy; I said that when we played the truth-and-lies game with the s'mores."

"Wow," he said softly. "Not even a second to explain?"

"Not even one second to tell me *you were leaving the day after we had sex?*"

"You know, sitting in that courtroom, I felt awful about missing Kennebunkport. It's why I left you the flowers." He kicked the wooden chair. "I thought you were different, but I guess I should just accept that nothing good happens to me anymore."

I had to work to not let my jaw hang open. He was angry with *me*?

"All that talk to Deese about someone else's actions not reflecting who you are? You're full of it." In the moonlight, his face was like a mask. "You think I'm poisonous because of my brother. I get it. You're just like everyone else."

Cold shards of ice stabbed at my spine. "You think I'm angry with you because of your *brother*?" I shook my head. "Don't you know me at all?"

Noah clenched his jaw. The pain on his face bored into my brain, adding another memory to my collection. Noah holding me in the dark. Drinking beside me at the Shed. Squinting down at me when I wore that purple leotard.

Guiding his mother into a courtroom, his hand mild and gentle on her back.

All different parts of me—every molecule—went to war. I wanted to pummel his jaw, squeeze it between my palms, and kiss it until I couldn't breathe anymore.

When Noah spoke, his voice was bitter. "I thought I did."

"You *lied* to me," I repeated. I didn't know what to do with my hands. I didn't trust them not to wind into his T-shirt and pull him to me, or push his chest as hard as I could. "And you completely ditched me. I had no idea . . . one moment you were there; the next you were just *gone*. Don't you get it? You thought *I* was different? Well, congratulations on being the same as everyone else. You're just like my dad. And all the other liars in this world."

His body seemed to droop then, as if all his Noah atoms had taken on water. "I didn't lie," he said. "I just couldn't tell you the truth." I had to lean forward to hear him. "I didn't want you to blame me. Or hate me."

"Oh, please. You didn't lie?"

He shook his head, vehement.

"You said asthma was a bitch."

"It is."

"You said you lost your brother in a way that's nearly impossible to believe."

"Is it not nearly impossible that my brother is a murderer? A lifetime of Legos and pancakes and laughs pushed aside for life in prison. Besides, not every loss is a death." He cleared his throat. "I also jumped in the lake when we were pedal-boating so I didn't have to tell you that I have basically no more friends, and I dipped you at the dance when you asked about my family. I was trying *not* to lie to you."

The wind whipped off the lake, blowing my hair across my face. I brushed it away. "But you didn't correct my assumptions," I said, stunned, rifling through each and every interaction. Me cutting in and telling the kitchen-sink story when he was uncomfortable in therapy. The time I asked him about his childhood and he acted like he'd heard a squirrel. "And like I said that time to Deese, I'd never judge you for what someone else did. I'm devastated over what your brother did to his girlfriend."

"To Dakota."

The sadness in his voice when he said her name made the whole thing more real. I nodded. "To Dakota. I'm not angry at you because of your brother, Noah. I feel betrayed by *you*."

Noah closed his eyes. "It feels like the entire world is against my family," he said, his words husky. "I couldn't bear to have you be against me too."

"You never gave me a chance. And for the record? I'm not."

He drummed his fingers on his knee. "When it happened, we were *reviled*. It was as if the media discovered vampires were real, and my brother was their leader." He scuffed the wooden deck of the guard chair with his toe. "What makes it even worse is that the pain, the public shaming, *everything*, it's a fraction of what Dakota's parents are going through. Dakota and Colin were together for two years, and we loved her too, you know? It took me a whole month to stop throwing up every morning. And it wasn't my fault. It wasn't any of our faults, except Colin's."

He whispered that they'd all asked the same question, over and over again. *How could the parents not know?* A metallic memory filled my mouth, because so much of it felt so familiar. *How could we not know about you, Dad?* "Who is 'they'?"

Noah stretched backward. "My 'fans,'" he said, giving the bitter words air quotes. "When the story broke, the news had Colin's name right, but the first report mistakenly used a picture of me, and the rest followed. They pulled the wrong picture from one of my parents' Facebook accounts. Thousands of people followed me on Twitter, where I didn't have my full name listed, in the span of half an hour. People sent me these messages . . ." He collected himself. "Even after they stopped running those pics, the messages didn't stop. Neither did the comment sections on anything."

My mind walked backward, to Winnie saying that Noah looked familiar.

"We all stopped sleeping," Noah continued. "It would be three a.m. and my entire family would be up reading or watching television. One time, my mom got it in her head that I must be hungry, so she made me this big Italian dinner. Spaghetti and meatballs. It was six in the morning."

I nodded. "My mom and I finished about two dozen gifted biscotti cookies in the middle of the night after my dad's funeral."

"It's weird how that goes." Noah gripped the material of his shorts in his hands, then smoothed it out. "I didn't know how to tell you the truth."

I stared at the rippling lake. "Why?"

He bit his lip. "I've done hours of googling. My brother had none of the signs of a killer-to-be. He wasn't obsessed with weapons or the Devil. He did mess around with drugs, and my parents remortgaged the house to send him to this expensive rehab with the best success rate. But we have no idea if that has anything to do with what he did to Dakota. We don't know why he snapped.

We don't know if they broke up, or if someone cheated, or what, not that any of that is even a valid reason as to why something like this happens. We don't know if he was using. We do know the police found a diary and kept it as evidence, but that's about it." With every new detail, he tapped his fingers on the wooden bench between us. "And now I'm just trying to live with the idea that I used to watch Saturday morning cartoons with someone who grew up and did something so reprehensible, and so unforgivable. And that Dakota's gone."

I cleared my throat. "I don't know exactly how you feel, but I know what it's like to be in a space where you're grieving something that—" I swallowed. "That didn't have to happen." Noah's family was grieving, sure, but Dakota's family? I couldn't imagine.

"Yeah, you do." Noah cracked his knuckles. In the distance behind us, the campers broke out in laughter. "You feel like walking around the lake?"

"Sure."

Without another word, he launched himself onto the sand with his trademark athletic grace.

I climbed down and put my hand on Noah's shoulder. It was tense beneath my touch. "I'm so sorry," I whispered.

"I feel so awful inside, Lila." Noah tapped his chest. "Like I have this constant raw ache right here. Cancer-filled or something. Before, I was busy. Sports. Friends. Right after . . ." He let out a breath. "Remember that day in the lake, and I said something about you only being nice to me in the dark?"

His hand brushed mine. I took it. "You said you'd had enough of that to last you a lifetime."

"Right after it happened, this girl who'd been my best friend for years ghosted me. My attendance at school became spotty at best, but when I was there, she completely ignored me. I'd eaten lunch, studied, and chilled out with her since middle school. I finally confronted her about it, and she offered to still be my 'friend'"—the air quotes again—"but only if I told no one. Turned off my phone when I was with her. Didn't talk to her in the halls, or sit with her at school things. After one month of spilling my guts while driving around with her after most people's curfews, I'd had enough. She was only nice to me when she felt like it, when—"

"Basically, when it was dark," I repeated, finishing his sentence. "I get it."

He cast me a grateful look. "Yeah. Now, at least, my family is invisible by choice. My parents sold our house. We moved to a rental house in a rural town. No one around for miles. They paid tons of money for Colin's legal fees, but he just changed his plea to guilty. He'll go away forever." He dragged his sneaker in the sand. "I might do my senior year online. It's either that, or be the new kid with a shitty past."

I pressed my tongue against the roof of my mouth, trying not to put words to what I was thinking: that he will always have this past. Just like me. No matter what we did from here on out, no matter what school we went to or who we met, our past was what it was. Part of us, though it didn't have to define us.

I wanted to gather up his pain and cast it away, into the dark air above the blackened lake. But I couldn't.

Circling below this urge, heavy and unforgettable, was a selfish one. I desperately wished he had trusted me enough to be honest.

Noah flexed his fingers. "And you know what?"

"What?"

"I'm *glad* he'll be gone forever." He sat on the sand and

tilted his head down for me to join him. "I hate him." His words were jagged and fierce, shattering the night air like splintered wood. "My mom is so sad. I mean, it's her kid, and she can't forgive him for what he did. We had dinner with the Frothinghams a couple of times—before, I mean. They were nice people. Dakota was one of those people who seemed to do no wrong, you know?" He paused. "Colin's my brother. He's supposed to be my best friend." He shook his head, derisive. "I will never forgive him."

*I will never forgive him.* The words reverberated in my head, a chorus of recognition thudding through me. Not too far from where we sat, the glow of the movie dimmed. It was over. "I think I understand how you feel," I said. "But if it was as out of character as you say . . ."

"It was. It seemed to be, at least."

I shifted on the damp sand, uncomfortable with my own truth, my own hardheadedness, my own reluctance to forgive. "I wonder what it was that made him snap."

"I wish I knew," Noah said, his voice thick and low, like he'd swallowed a tablespoon of something rotten. "Right after, he showed up to my aunt's holiday party. Tried to attack my mom. I was upstairs with my cousins, playing video games, so I didn't see him at first. After, everyone said he was spouting off all kinds of nonsense. But whatever was inside him that allowed him to do what he did? I want to cut out that part of his brain and light it on fire. Then put the ashes into a box. Bury it."

*Cut out that part of his brain.* "Like the doctor who invented lobotomies."

Noah's tense shoulders relaxed. "Um, right. That."

"He had a traveling van he drove around America, giving

everyone from farmers to financiers lobotomies to cure their mental illnesses. He'd use an ice pick to scrape out the 'bad stuff,' until he'd created the cast of *The Walking Dead*." Josie and I had learned all about it in an anatomy and physiology unit. A light ripple of shame coursed through me. *Josie.* I was way out of my comfort zone when it came to Noah's story, the way she and Rose were with mine.

Noah laughed. "Guess I missed my calling."

I closed my eyes, flipping through my memory like an old library catalog. I pictured my psych teacher at home using her trusty blue Expo marker to write on the whiteboard, and finally the word came to me. "Or . . . trepanation!"

Noah's eyebrows furrowed. "Trepa-what?"

"Trepanation. Neolithic people used to drill holes in people's heads so demons could escape. A bunch of archaeologists have the skulls as proof."

"Ahh," Noah said, nodding. His smile was sad. "If only I was a trepanatologist." His fingers danced a rhythm on his thighs.

"If only," I said. I leaned over and bumped my shoulder against his. "Do you know you tap your fingers a lot?"

He looked at his hand, startled. "I do?"

"You do."

"Oh. Wow. I guess it makes sense. After everything happened, I started playing around on this old drum set my dad had in our basement. Ordered some lesson books online." He chuckled under his breath. "Who knew?"

The night settled around us, the trees sighing and the lake relaxing into itself. Something—a bat or a bird—flew above us, cutting across the starry sky. The laughter died on Noah's lips. "I am really sorry I left without telling you," he said.

I inhaled. Exhaled. "Yeah. That sucked. You shouldn't have done that."

"I know. I should have at least left you a note. But, I just . . . What happened the night before meant something to me." He took in a ragged breath. "I was so surprised when the lawyers came, and I didn't want anyone asking me questions. I just wanted to get out of there."

"I understand," I murmured, even though a part of me did not. I knew with absolute clarity that if our roles had been reversed, I would not have left the same way. I would not have abandoned this boy the morning after we'd changed our lives together. I would not have stood him up for what was supposed to be our first real date. I would have probably been able to anticipate his worry, and I wouldn't have wanted him to suffer through the anxiety of not knowing.

But he was not me.

Here on the starlit lakeshore, I was struck by two waves of knowledge:

1. I think I might love him. And even though
   he made a different choice about leaving,
   that doesn't mean he doesn't love me back.
   See prior thought: *He was not me.*
2. When I told him I understood, I halfway
   lied. *Lied. Me.* Lila Cunningham, a sort-of,
   maybe, medium-level liar.

He swallowed and shifted so his leg touched mine. "Thanks for understanding. I'm really, really sorry."

The night breeze moved over us, lifting the wings of my

hair and glossing over my skin with the insight of what I should have known all along: *Some lies exist to save and repair relationships, instead of making them implode.*

My dad had lied for a quilt of reasons: shame, addiction, self-preservation, and to spare himself the pain of disappointing his family. Noah had lied because he was ashamed of his brother's actions, and because he wanted to hide from who his brother was.

I still didn't like lies, but perhaps this was what people meant when they referred to shades of gray. There were different degrees of rightness and wrongness. By saying *I understand*, I became a liar. The kind whose untruth was a gift of sorts, meant to take away the pain of someone I cared about.

Maybe, on the moral scale, the evilness of lies lived in their intent, or their level of malice. There was a difference between hiding actions that were wrong, like what my dad had done, and offering understanding as a form of forgiveness to someone I might just love. I could see how Dad's life had become a vortex of pain, a twisted game: He'd stacked lies on top of lies like Jenga pieces, when he was really trying to play Monopoly the entire time.

"I accept your apology," I murmured now. But I shot to my feet, brushing the sand from the backs of my thighs. "There's something I have to do, though. Find me tomorrow?"

"Want some company?"

I backed up a few steps. "Thanks, but no. I need to do this by myself."

He picked up something—a small rock, or a stick—and tossed it into the lake. "Cool. Catch you then."

I threw him a grateful smile, and then took off toward my destination. I'd only gotten a few yards when I heard him.

"Hey, Lila. Are we friends?"

His words were an echo of the night of our first kiss. "Friends," I called, my second lie of the evening. It pinched my rib cage, swollen and heavy.

His eyebrows lifted. "Friends . . . and maybe?"

The pinch in my ribs eased. I cracked a smile. "And maybe."

# Chapter Thirty-Eight

Here is why suicide complicates grief.

Grief is showering in the old shower stall in the basement bathroom so no one will hear you cry.

It is wearing your dad's winter pajamas to bed so you can use the flannel to soak up your tears.

Grief is ferocious and hot. It is burned-out lung husks; it is your heart resting on glowing ashes and embers.

It is watching the rest of the world Pass You By. Everyone else eats dinner with their families and hands in homework and bemoans final exams and rubs sunscreen on the bridges of their noses but forgets their cheeks.

Grief is a beanstalk-descending giant who takes hold of your house and shakes it while you sleep, scrambling the layout of life you've come to expect. You wake up the next day in the bathtub, try to cook pancakes on the garage floor, and park your car in the dining room. Suicide is a bucket of what-ifs, a stack of if-onlys.

You are left confused, mired in your own sadness.

Wild-card bonus round: Suicide is the action of someone in such desperate pain that they are difficult to blame.

# Chapter Thirty-Nine

Inside the Healing Center, the white curtains caught the beams of moonlight, letting in enough light to navigate. I sidestepped the beanbags and crossed the floor where we'd had group dances and group therapy, the ghosts of the summer's conversations guiding me forward. I sailed past the entrance to the Quiet Area, letting it stay empty, preserving the space for a memory made of spilled juice, the jolt of desire, the first in a story of kisses.

Energy thrummed through my veins, propelling me into the one room I'd left for others all summer. I recalled standing with CP at my feet, my fingertips twitching at my sides, craving the chance to let loose.

I stared at the *ANGER* acrostic. *Acknowledge. Notice. Grapple. Eclipse. Rise above.* I flexed my fingers, picked up a stray Nerf ball. Squeezed it.

I whipped it at the padded wall, zeroing in on the way the release felt in my arm. Good, but not enough. I needed more, so my body gave me more. Gave in to the storm of rage and grief. Fed the giant living in my house.

I tackled the hanging punching bag, hitting it with my fists, elbows, shins, knees, ankles. I gathered all the sadness I'd carried since March, all the boulders and stones and pebbles and dust and molecules, all the atoms that made me Lila Cunningham, and channeled it at the padded wall beneath Jeff's sign. I plucked the images of my summer: the purple leotard, Tennyson's elegy, a Wonka Bar from eBay, the way s'mores taste with sips of crisp night air, the shadow of the Shed's overhang, the rhythm and reverberation on the soles of my feet after a long run, my hair a mess and my head full of feeling and new truths.

I'd been so focused on the absence of my father that I hadn't given him the posthumous grace of forgiveness. I'd been so torn apart by the upending of my world—the proverbial pancakes in the garage, car in the dining room—and wrapped in the flannel of sadness, I hadn't let myself absorb something so profound and yet so simple.

Spent, I collapsed on the soft, spongy floor, panting. Noah's pain was visceral and real. I had worn those shoes. It was impossible to comprehend the magnitude of such acts of violence, whether they were as grotesque and beyond redemption as what Colin did, or self-inflicted like my dad's.

The hard and terrible truth I didn't want to consider was that mental illness had been a part of my father he could no more scrape from his soul than I could the freckles from my face. It was a great fact—the big kind of *great*, not the good kind—that my father's beautiful/awful double life was just a single one.

I rolled over, and my hip bumped into something hard. The bongos. I dragged my exhausted body into a sitting position, leaning against them. I tapped one finger on the smooth top of a drum. A hollow sound seeped into the corners of the room, filling the dark.

I didn't know Noah's brother. I didn't want to know Noah's brother. There was not a world in which I wanted to sit at the dinner table with him. He was, by all accounts, a murderer. I did not like thinking of him, because doing so forced me to consider the fear Dakota must have faced. My heart broke for her family, and the broken pieces of it burned when I thought of Noah and his parents, left behind in the aftermath.

I thought back to my dad buying that rope at Home Depot.

To the cashier who unknowingly sold a man with a fractured mindset something that could tie a boat to a dock, secure a bundle of wood, or kill a man. A low, mournful melody chased my thoughts as I tapped the softest of rhythms on the bongos, tears mixing with the sweat on my cheekbones.

I wished with a desperate, unrealistic urge for a way to fold myself backward through time so I could beg my dad to face the side of himself that was sick. So I could leave Noah's brother's problems in a place where his parents could find them. Because if there was one thing I could count on, it was the strength of my own mind. And as skeptical as I'd been of all this—therapy, Jeff, camp itself—I was grateful for it. Thanks to the reluctant effort I'd put into this place, I was about to emerge confident and comfortable in my own headspace.

If only my dad had sought help, had hurled himself into it with the gusto with which he'd appeared to live his life. If only he'd had the direction, or strength, or wherewithal to extract himself from his addiction, from shrouding his life with lies. I folded my arms on the drums, bowed my head, and wept.

# Chapter Forty

Overnight, cooler weather marched into the camp like some omnipresent hall monitor reminding us to get to class. On the last full day of camp, I donned a pair of leggings for my final morning workout with Deese.

Despite the sharpness of the air, I felt my muscles burning, loosening from their overactivity the night before. "You'd think summer never happened," I said. "I can practically see my breath. It's like I can taste school starting."

"When in Maine," Deese said.

"When in Maine," I echoed. Deese's leg wasn't back to 100 percent, so we fell into a nice rhythm: a slow trot with a bunch of breaks for stretching. I pictured all those autumns at home, Dad lacing up his white sneakers for a jog down the damp, leaf-strewn sidewalks. When I got home, I'd probably have an adjustment period all over again. But I could find some ways to keep him with me. A pocket square sewn to my pillowcase, a clear glass mug of coffee for Mom, Dad's recipe for Sunday blueberry muffins for Sammy.

Slowly, Deese and I picked our way farther and farther along the path. Sweat flowed down my temples and stuck my shirt to the small of my back. Running was still not easy—far from it—but every time I did it, it was a little bit less difficult than the time before. I liked the time I could spend in my head, and I liked pushing my body to new limits.

I shifted my stride so I'd be closer to Deese, then reached over and gave him a little shove. "I'll miss our runs."

Deese held up his fist for a pound. "It's been fun training

with you, Cunningham. Even if my coach destroys me for consorting with the enemy." He winked.

He's a good friend, that Deese.

That day, summer-reading books sprouted all over camp like a literary plague. Campers lounged in Mess Hall, out on the lawn in front of the Lodge, and on the sunny dock by the lake, cracking the spines of paperbacks untouched since the first day of camp. At lunch, I saw Alicia with her nose stuck in a copy of *Lean In*. CP needed an emergency session with Jeff after finishing *Bridge to Terabithia*.

Tonight we'd go to the FareWELL Dance. Tomorrow Mom would come—with Josie—and we'd go back. Back to Massachusetts, back to school. Back to a home empty of Dad.

When I took my own emotional temperature, I felt like a human version of a Magic 8 Ball. Shake me up, and I'd feel all the things. *Outlook is good. Signs point to yes. Reply is hazy, try again.*

So now, thinking about going home—because it was still home, even without Dad—I was surprised to find another feeling nudging its way into my kaleidoscope of confetti emotions. *Impatience.* I was impatient to get back to the three Ls found on decorative canvases and notebooks everywhere: *Laughing. Loving. Living without guilt.*

Back in the blue bungalow, Mari insisted we pack our bags before the dance. She left a giant plastic bin marked LAUNDRY by the door. "For your sheets in the morning," she said, stripping the mostly unused ones from her bed.

"You sure you don't want to bunk with your charges for our last night?" Madison asked.

Mari chewed her lip. "I'm sure you guys want one last night of authority-free gal time."

Madison arranged her features in what was meant to convey innocence. "Mm-hmm. And how's Jeff doing these days? I mean, these nights?"

"Pretty cold out there after dark," Winnie said.

"I'll survive," Mari said, flushing to the tips of her braids. Madison winked at us, her knowing expression reflecting ours. It's easy to stay warm when you're cuddling.

Winnie put on the radio, and we lapsed into comfortable silence. I folded my shorts and cotton T-shirts, but wound up crumpling them into a ball to make them fit inside my duffel bag. After a while, the twins got into an argument over which college tours they'd go on first in the fall.

Carrying a stack of books, I bent over to grab my tote bag. It was heavier than I expected. I peered inside. The crinkled cellophane winked back up at me, both comfortingly familiar and emotionally weighty at the same time.

Stashed beneath the cookies was Dad's old Moleskine. My handbook. I flipped it open and, rubbing the bridge of my nose, read the rules meant to bring me some measure of comfort and control at the hardest time of my life. Two I'd written before camp, five I'd added here.

*1. The only people who can truly hurt you*

are the ones you love. Therefore, love no
one.*

2. Stay away from liars. Liars are the worst.**

   *Free passes: Mom, Sammy, Aunt

   Shelly, ~~Dad~~

   **Example: Dad

3. No matter what, life goes on.
4. Remember that grief lightning can strike
   twice.
5. Assess the entire situation before throwing a punch.
6. Sometimes, people can surprise you in a
   good way.
7. You'll only get angry over the things that
   you care about the most.

A lot of these still rang very true—most important, maybe,
rule number three. Life did go on. I traced my thumbnail over
the second part of the first rule—*Therefore, love no one*—thinking
about everything Jeff had said about taking risks. How maybe I'd
uncover something hidden.

Hidden. *My daffodil.* Wild hope raced through me, turning my
heartbeat into a jazz song. Because

Maybe

Maybe

*Maybe maybe maybe*

I flipped to the back of the book, where that fateful pocket lay,
patient and quiet, and was that small bump anything oh please let
it be

I tore the pocket from the back of the notebook—
Empty.

All I'd seen—or had wanted to see, anyway—was a crease in the pocket, the barest of marks to illustrate that someone had used it before, like the names of previous users in the front of a textbook.

I waited for the crushing disappointment. It didn't come. Perhaps someday I would find that necklace, behind the vanity in the bathroom or caught in a curtain, or clasped around a stranger's neck. But just as I'd never fully know the secrets of my father's life, I might never discover the whereabouts of my daffodil necklace, and whether or not Dad had anything to do with its disappearance.

My muscles tensed. Before I could stop myself, I ripped out the page of rules and crumpled it in my fist. I grabbed a pen from my duffel bag, spread the torn-up handbook on my bunk, and wrote

1. You can trust yourself.
2. You're going to love people. They're going to let you down. If they didn't, then maybe you wouldn't know how much you valued them in the first place.

I tapped the pen against my cheek, thinking of what I'd felt at the close of the Falmouth Road Race, my leg tied to Deese's, my effort and energy solely my own. I bent back over the handbook.

3. The more difficult the challenge, the better the return.

I slipped the handbook back into my duffel bag, held the fist-ful of old rules in my hand, cradled the bag of cookies, and stood, throwing both items in my tote bag.

"Hey," I said. "Madison, Winnie. Care to join me out by the lake for a few minutes?"

The sun swung low in the sky, the last few rays warming me just enough on this perfect late-summer night. The divots in the sand cast a pattern of shadows around us, and the trees were silhou-etted against one of the last Maine sunsets I'd see for a while. Briefly, I wondered if Dakota's family was watching the same sunset. If they'd ever find any kind of peace in Colin changing his plea.

Beside me, Madison shivered. "I'm cold," she said. "What are we doing out here, exactly?"

Winnie pulled her hands inside the cuffs of her long-sleeved T-shirt. "Yeah, Lila. Speak now, or forever hold your peace." She paused. "Wait. Is it *peace*, like hippie peace and love, or *piece*, like a piece of pizza? How can you hold the love kind of peace?"

I squeezed my crumpled rules between my fingers and turned to Madison. "At the beginning of camp, you took a note-book out of my bag."

Madison's cheeks burned. "Well, I didn't exactly *take* it."

Winnie gave her a pointed look. "You might as well have."

"It's okay. In that book, I wrote down . . . rules, kind of. Rules to live by. To try and prevent anyone from hurting me the way my dad did." I glanced at my friends. They were quiet. "When I got here, I would have been absolutely mortified if you'd read them. But now . . . now I think I need to leave these rules here." I leaned over the edge of the lake and shredded the rules into it, watching as they dissolved into the depths of the water.

"Whoa," Winnie said, awestruck.

"That was something," Madison agreed.

I leaned over and pulled the blue plastic package of cookies from the depths of the tote bag.

"You had those all summer long?" Winnie moaned. "I miss processed food."

I smiled and traced the letters on the package. "These were my dad's. He hid them behind the healthy stuff so no one would eat them."

Madison put her hand on my back. "You okay?"

I shook the cookies. "At home, after he died, they became this link to my dad—all I had left. I started checking on them every day after school. I was panicked someone would eat them."

Winnie's voice was quiet. "It's funny what we hold on to, isn't it?"

I slid the cookies from their flimsy tray. They were broken, dusted with crumbs. I shook a handful into Winnie's palm, another into Madison's, and scooped the last in my own.

"Make a wish," I said. And then I reared back and flung the crumbs into the lake, listening with satisfaction to the smallest of splashes.

# Chapter Forty-One

I'd thought the last night's FareWELL Dance would be a reflection of the first week's WELLcome dance: all light and floaty, the camp's version of fun (until I stomped all over the handbook and kissed Noah, that is).

It wasn't the first time I was horribly mistaken.

In every corner of the Healing Center, campers hugged. Grasped arms. Sobbed. During one slow song, Sammy and Alicia clung to each other. She was several inches taller than him.

Toward the end of the evening, Winnie, Madison, and I crowded into the single bathroom to wash our hands. Overhead, bugs zipped and pinged against the fluorescent lights. Madison, who'd kept one hand firmly gripped in Deese's for most of the evening, was no better than the rest. "I hate goodbyes," she said, tears threatening to spill out of her eyes again.

"Of course you do," Winnie said. "We're kids who've lost a parent, remember? Our whole life is one long goodbye."

"Hey," I said, turning off the faucet. "It's not goodbye. It's see you later."

"Both of you have to come visit me during winter break." Madison threw her arms around me and nuzzled her face into my shoulder.

"I have eight weeks off or something. You won't be able to get rid of me." Winnie sighed and handed me paper towels. "I can't believe I'm not a camper anymore."

Madison pinched Winnie's side. "Cut the dramatics, Shakespeare," she said. "You get to wear a blue T-shirt here next summer, remember?"

I stared at Winnie. "You're going to be our *counselor*?"

She lifted her chin. "Does this mean you're coming back?"

I smiled. "I guess you could say I'm considering it."

For the last half hour, everyone finally quit crying and hit the dance floor. Jeff cued up fast, fun songs on his laptop, Mari bobbing her head beside him.

We sang; we shook. By the second song, we were damp with sweat; our hair clung to our scalps and licked our necks. By the fourth, we'd given in to it. We squatted on the floor, drumming it with our fists. My throat was raw and scratchy from singing.

I didn't care one bit.

Noah took my hand, and I maneuvered an awkward spin beneath it. Without warning, he pulled me against him and pressed his lips to my ear. "It's our last night," he murmured. "Spend it with me."

My breath whooshed from my chest. "Okay."

Back at the bungalow, I pulled sweatpants and an old college sweatshirt of my dad's from my duffel bag, layering up in case Madison and Winnie were right and it was cold after dark.

Spoiler alert: They were. It was. But not unpleasantly so.

Noah and I arrived at the Shed simultaneously. He carried an armful of sheets and blankets and one pillow.

"It's freezing," I breathed. My chest vibrated under the soft cotton of my sweatshirt.

"Here." Noah wrapped a blanket over my shoulders, then one over his own. We cocooned ourselves in them, and before long, in each other. We tangled together, the sheet tented over our heads.

I breathed him in: soap and camp and laundry, with hints of whatever made up his own smell peeking through. When I glanced up, his head was angled down toward mine. His lips weren't smiling—this confusing, delightful boy—but his eyes were.

"Tell me something good about your dad," he said.

I closed my eyes, traveling through my mind's filed-away boxes. I pictured my father, standing in the tiny bathroom on the first floor of our house, surrounded by the sharp, clean sting of shaving cream. Wearing a white T-shirt with plaid boxers. I imagined him using his hands to explain how to build our deck outside, or gripping a nail gun to install the hardwood floor inside. I could smell Christmas morning, where Mom would stay in bed an extra half hour and he'd get up and bake those famous blueberry muffins and a round metal tray of instant cinnamon rolls, which everyone knows are the best kind.

It's funny. I can't think of a one-word antonym for *liar*. Maybe that's how it's supposed to be, because there's more than one way to tell the truth.

"He used to wear his sunglasses at my track meets," I said. "Even the indoor ones."

Noah brushed his palm against my hip. "Why?"

"I always bugged him about it," I said, smiling. "Until he told me that he didn't want the other parents to see him crying because he was so proud of me."

Noah traced his fingertips over the fabric of my sweatshirt, the pressure both calming and soothing. He grazed them up my neck and over my cheek. "I like that."

"Me too," I said. "They were Ray-Bans. He wore them before they were cool."

"Ray-Bans were never not cool."

His fingers were in my sweat-stiffened hair, unwashed after the dance. I cringed. "Tell me one good thing about your brother."

"Okay." He paused. "I think my fingertips are stuck in your hair."

I laughed, helping free his hands of my tangles. "Watch out," I said. "Old boots, missing jewelry, last week's crossword—you never know what you'll find in there."

He smiled but was quiet. From underneath the sheet, I could almost forget we were huddled beneath an old wooden overhang out in the Maine woods.

Comfortable, quiet, and safe. And, sweatpants. I closed my eyes, drowsy.

I'd tucked my head under his chin and almost fallen asleep by the time he began. "My favorite memory," he said, hugging me to him.

"Is what?" I murmured, pulling back to watch his face.

"We were maybe seven and ten. We'd gone out in the woods, exploring, and found a bunch of old two-by-fours. So we ran back to the house and found my dad's toolbox—pulled out a couple hammers and a bunch of nails."

"A fort?" I guessed.

The corners of his mouth turned up. "A boat."

I raised my eyebrows. "You built a boat?"

"Well, we called it that." He rolled onto his back, but shifted closer to me so I could nestle against his side. "The final product was more raft than boat."

"Did it actually sail?"

"Depends on your definition of *sail*." His chest shook with quiet laughter. "My dad helped us drag it to this little pond, way out back. My mom brought the video camera. Colin came up with the idea of using two-by-fours for the oars, so we pushed it into the water, stepped on it, and sank. There were gaps between the boards. The best part was that we'd named it *When Pigs Fly* after this brand of bread my mom liked."

I laughed. "That's the fittingest name ever."

"No shit. I wound up scraping my foot on a bent nail and needing a tetanus shot. That ironic little raft had no chance."

I smiled and nestled back under his chin, turning my face up to see the winking stars above. We were quiet for a few minutes, easing into that pre-sleep state where your brain empties of its thoughts and your body relaxes into itself.

"Lila?" Noah's voice was thick.

"Mmm?"

"Do you think we do?"

"Do I think we do what?"

"Have a chance."

I didn't answer right away.

His brother, a murderer.

My father, quietly dealing with mental illness and an addiction to gambling.

I could not think of either one of them without feeling an all-encompassing sadness, but we had memories of them that were anything but.

Our memories are fickle. They are being hungry and tucking in to a hearty meal—a favorite stew, perhaps, or a simple, homey dish of roast chicken—only to find something unpleasant: an uncooked carrot or a hard bean shell, or something slimy and unwelcome like gristle, bone, fat.

But they can be the best part of it all too. They can be ice cream full of treats: the nutty cream of peanut butter, the sharp nip of a chocolate chip.

I savor them all, rolling them on my tongue.

"I think we do," I said.

And like that, tangled in blankets and in memories, we fell asleep until dawn.

# Author's Note

On a bitterly cold December night in 2009, my then boyfriend and I were halfway between Boston and Albany, en route to my 102-year-old great-aunt's funeral, when I made him turn the car around at a tollbooth.

There are some things in life that are difficult to explain, and this action is one of them. With every mile we put behind us on that highway, my sense of unease—compounded by unanswered phone calls and unsettled worry—took on a nearly physical form, until I could no longer contain it. I looked at Kevin and said, "Turn around. I think my father is dead."

I was right.

Suicide is an endlessly complex subject. It is the end result of a number of different illnesses, traumas, histories, backgrounds, and/or abuses. The one portrayed in this book is one single experience with few concrete answers and a lot of unknowns.

There are truths in here that are my own. The first, most important truth, is that Lila and I are suicide loss survivors. Both fathers were addicted to gambling (though my father's particular methodology was not tied to sports), both fathers made multiple attempts, and neither father ever once in his life appeared (at least to his daughter) outwardly depressed.

There are differences, too. I didn't have a daffodil necklace, but I did have an iPod and a rose-gold ring. One major difference here is that Lila did not know about her father's history until he died, but I did. This ties to a smaller truth that we share: the *scree* sound the lock made in my childhood home. As a teenager, if I heard the sound after I was in bed, I would sit upright in immediate throes of anxiety, somehow rationalizing that if he went outside after I was in bed, then he wouldn't come home. There are thousands of reasons why someone might go outside after their kid goes to bed—to take out the trash, investigate a noise, look at the stars, get some air—but I zeroed in on the one that would make my worst fear come true. It led to a lifetime of insomnia, which I struggle with to this day. I can only imagine how my father felt when he saw me standing in the doorway, alerted by the lock, those times he did take out the trash or grab his briefcase from his car, my anxious face waiting for him to appear around the corner of our condo walkway. It was that sound I heard in my head, again and again, when I think of answering the door to several policemen holding their hats the night he died.

My dad was the dad who drove friends home with no questions asked. At his wake, all the mourners just kept shaking their heads and repeating how surprised they were. Shocked. They couldn't imagine a guy like my dad—the ultimate joker, the life of the party, intelligent as can be—doing what he did. I couldn't either. Until I could.

I've written about my dad in the past, and I get questions from readers about articles I've published. They ask me if I have forgiven him. They ask if I have moved on. They ask if I am happy.

I can tell you that I cannot stand in his shoes, for many reasons. I am not addicted to anything. I am not depressed, though I do live with functional anxiety largely related to parenting. I have never been suicidal. I forgive him, for all those reasons. How could I not?

That said: I will never move on from the loss of my father. I would have traded a lot of things to be on his arm at my wedding (though my brother did a stand-up job standing in), and so many more for him to be at my dinner table on any night of the week. I know my kids would have benefited from his care, his humor, his on-point Kermit the Frog and dueling Bert/Ernie impersonations. I carry with me many of the "dad jokes" included in this novel, which he sourced from Popsicle sticks and joke books, a habit my now-husband has graciously taken over.

And, finally, I am happy, which is why Lila ends the novel happy. She learns to live with her grief, the way I have learned to live with mine. She learns that people are infinitely complex and complicated, that truth has more than one definition, and that professional help is a really beautiful thing.

It is my hope that Lila's story can help us understand that there should be no shame in whatever point you are on in the mental-health spectrum. It is my hope that we can work to find more empathy for those who are suffering, more understanding of what those left behind are going through, and more awareness that things really can and do get better.

If you have ever been in a place where you're feeling sad and you aren't sure why, or if you're feeling something you can't quite recognize and you aren't sure why, or if your life circumstances seem simply too impossible to handle on your own, or if you carry some sense of shame for something about yourself—then what you should first recognize is that what you are dealing with is treatable. That first step is a big one, but it's a lifesaving one. There are people who will not judge you. There are people who will understand what you are feeling and can give you the words to name those feelings and the tools to make them bearable.

As of 2018, the most recent "official" statistics I can find, the American Foundation for Suicide Prevention estimated that we lose about 132 people each day to suicide. That is 132 too many every day of the year.

   If you or someone you know is hurting, or if you have time or resources you can donate to this cause, here are some resources other people have found helpful:

- **National Suicide Prevention Lifeline** (free, confidential, 24/7)
  - suicidepreventionlifeline.org
  - 1-800-273-TALK (1-800-273-8255)
  - Foreign language interpreters available
  - 1-800-799-4889 for the hearing impaired
  - 1-888-628-9454 for Spanish speakers

- **Crisis Text Line** (free, confidential, 24/7)
  - crisistextline.org
  - United States: Text the word talk to 741741
  - Canada: Text the word home to 686868
  - United Kingdom: Text the word home to 85258

- American Foundation for Suicide Prevention: afsp.org
- To Write Love on Her Arms: twloha.com
- The Trevor Project: thetrevorproject.org
- The It Gets Better Project: itgetsbetter.org
- Suicide Awareness Voices of Education (SAVE): save.org

# Acknowledgments

I've spent my whole life knowing I wanted to be an author, and my gratitude for the village of people who made that come true knows no end. This book was born over several years, from living through my own version of this experience, to sitting down on a flight to go to a work conference and reading an article about the closing of a camp set up for children who lost a parent in 9/11.

Thank you to every single family member who has supported me over the years, from my husband and his family to my mom and brother.

Thank you to my agent Kerry D'Agostino for believing in this book (and in me!). You are a champion. Thank you to my entire team of editors, starting with my acquiring editor, Nicole Otto: Every time I think of that first phone call, I smile. Weslie Turner, I'm grateful for your wisdom, editorial expertise, and eagerness to video call during a pandemic. Thank you Erin Stein and Camille Kellogg for your excitement and enthusiasm, and finally, thank you Kat Brzozowski for flawlessly carrying this book to the finish line. All of you lifted the book up and away from where it started, and your advocacy, ideas, and passion are boundless.

I am grateful to Jean Feiwel and everyone at Feiwel & Friends for welcoming this book home. Enormous thanks to the entire team at Imprint, especially Erin Stein, Hayley Jozwiak, Kathy Wielgosz, and Jie Yang; and for this book's cover art direction and design, Carolyn Bull and Natalie Sousa, along with Dion MBD for the stunning illustration.

Thank you to Karen Sherman, my incredible copyeditor, and Nicole Wayland and Madeline Newquist, my proofreaders.

Thank you Teresa Ferraiolo, Kelsey Marrujo, Melissa Croce, and Julia Gardiner for your support.

Thank you to my think tank: Allison Bitz and Laura Taylor Namey. I would not want to embark on this journey without our daily whirlwind of ideas, workshopping, encouragement, and friendship. Having both of you as writing partners in my corner is an incredible blessing.

Thank you to my mentors, Rebecca Phillips, Katrina Emmel, and Diana Gallagher. It takes a champion to dig into someone else's book and provide advice, and you three deserve medals for it. Thank you, in turn, to my mentees Zoulfa Katouh and Hadley Leggett, for being passionate and enthusiastic, and gifting me with your talent and gifs. I am forever grateful to the Author Mentor Match, Pitch Wars, 21ders, and Inked Voices communities. I send so much gratitude to every reader along the way, beta and otherwise, who provided guidance and feedback on this book as it was shaped.

A small thank-you to a large group of people: everyone fighting to make this world a better place, including mental health professionals and all health care workers.

Storytelling is an art form, and I got my start as a storyteller in another place I call home: the dance studio. I am forever indebted to my Dance Express family, including and especially Ann-Marie Basara, Carol Pickering, and Sandy Maloney, as well as all of my colleagues and students. I treasure all of you.

To the people I'm lucky enough to call my friends: 10143 to Amy, Charlene, Haley, Hannah, Jackie, Jayna, Jen, Jenna, Marissa. To Christine and Jess, my college roommates and my kids' New York aunties. To all my Providence girls: I adore you.

To my Milton friends, for your endless cheer, laughs, strength, and sweat, especially Julie, who FaceTimed me crying after she read an early draft of this book. I am convinced you are a superhero.

To the MFA writing program at Emerson College, and the people I met there; to my professors at Providence College and my high school English teachers. Thank you to my Penmen work team for your confidence in me.

Wherever you are, Dad, thank you for my childhood, for your wisdom, love, and care, and firm disregard for our groaning at your jokes (especially wherever you found the "me-n-u" and nosy pepper jokes).

To the people who make up my incredibly large family, especially Christine and Doug, Matt, Precillia, Maddie, and Emmie, for your eternal support, inside jokes, and long dinners. To all my other aunts, uncles, and cousins, especially Rusty for her unwavering support and loyalty, to Ted and Tina, and Uncle. Thank you to my mom, my brother Christian, and his partner Kelly. To the Paulsons, my found family. All of you make me feel loved, and I love you in return.

To my family by marriage: I could not have done this without you, Barbie and Steve, and Caroline, Adam, and Max. Thank you for being a part of my village. You bring me more joy than I can explain.

To my kids, Lucy and Teddy, and to the two babies who did not make it to this earth—you inspire me every day. Everything I do is for you. I love you infinity plus one.

To my husband. I set this camp in Maine for you (and for us). There are not enough words to thank you for your love and partnership and belief in me, so instead, I dedicated this book to you.

# About the Author

**Joan F. Smith** lives with her family in Massachusetts, where she works as an associate dean, a creative writing professor, and a dance instructor. She received her MFA in creative writing from Emerson College and has written articles for the *Washington Post* and *Thought Catalog* on destigmatizing discussions around mental health and suicide prevention. *The Half-Orphan's Handbook* is her debut novel.